MARKED

VOLUME ONE

CHARISSE SPIERS

Cover Art © Clarise Tan
Cover Image © Darren Birks
Interier Title Image © Deposit Photo
Edited by Jessica Grover
Formatted by Nancy Henderson

LOVE IS TO LOVE SOMEONE FOR WHO THEY ARE, WHO THEY WERE, AND WHO THEY WILL BE.

– Chris Moore

PROLOGUE

Kaylan

I grab my football off of my dresser and start tossing it lightly to keep my hands busy. I'm a little nervous. Registration for the youth team is today and I've been teaching myself, at least the best way I know how. I may not be very good, but I'm trying. I'm starting to get really bored sitting at home alone all the time. It took me giving up my allowance and promising I'd get myself to practice for her to agree to let me play, but it'll be worth it. It has to be. I have to get out of this house. Mom is always gone with some guy and I'm not old enough to do anything for myself away from home. The only reason she is letting me play is because we live within walking distance from my school. I already have to fend for myself when it comes to finding meals from the barely stocked cabinets and doing my schoolwork so Mom can go out, doing whatever it is that she does. The few nights that she comes home I have to help get her to bed because she acts weird and says crazy things.

I'm completely self-sufficient, or at least that's what Mom says that I am. It's kind of a big word for someone of my age; even with me being in excel classes at school. She always says I need to learn to be a man and that no son of hers is going to be a pussy. I think that's a bad word, but she likes bad words. She likes anything that she tells me is bad. Football is my last option. I want to do things that other kids my age get to do.

I look around at my small room, almost bare except for my bed and dresser, and the few toys that I have. Our small townhouse doesn't consist of much furniture, because Mom says she doesn't make much money to buy extra things. My favorite toy is the basketball goal that hangs on the back of my door. When I'm bored and alone it keeps me occupied, because I play an imaginary game, pretending I'm in the NBA. The weird thing is that Mom is constantly buying new clothes and things for herself. I'm not sure where she gets the money, because she always says she's broke. I've been saving up all summer to pay the football registration by sneaking over to Mr. Erwin's next door when Mom leaves to go to work. When he saw me looking at the registration form for about the tenth time, he agreed to let me help him do things for pay since he's old.

Mom starts screaming, but we are the only two here. I throw the ball down on the bed and open my door, now worried that someone else is here. "You've never made an effort to come around before now, Phillip. What do you want with my son now?"

"He's our son, Anna. I do everything you ask of me to take care of him financially, even more so than you need. Neither of you do without. I personally make sure of it when funds are deposited into your account. You know the reason I can't be around. I wouldn't even be here now, but I want to see him, so I'm putting my foot down, what I should have done a long time ago. I need to fucking see him."

At the sound of that word I stop. *Son?* I line my back against the wall of the hallway, trying to stay still so that they won't see me. What does he mean I'm their son? I don't have a father. Mom said he ran off and never wanted anything to do with me before I was even born. She constantly complains about how hard it is to be a single mom.

"No, that's where you're wrong. He's my son. You're just his sperm donor. You made it clear to me that he wasn't yours when you chose your family over us. You told me you fucking loved me and that we were going to be together, but when I got pregnant you ran back to your wife and daughter. We weren't good enough for you. What was the reason, Phillip? Was it because I was your assistant and you saw me as an easy fuck since I was in love with you? How do you think it feels to watch the man you're in love with be a family with someone else while I raise *our* son? Money isn't everything. Sometimes what someone needs is your presence. Do you think I wanted this? I didn't want kids period, so I sure as hell didn't want them alone."

"You knew I was married, Anna. You knew the consequences of what we were doing. My wife and I were going through a hard time and I was attracted to you, I grew to care about you, and in one form I did love you, but you know we were never in love. We both know it now and knew it then. I love my wife. I just made a lot of mistakes back then. I'm paying for it now by not helping raise my son." He sounds angry, his words slithering through his gritted teeth. It's what I do when Mom makes me mad.

I breathe slowly, trying not to be heard in their silence. He has a family? I have a sister? I'm trying to piece everything together. I may only be eight, but I'm not dumb. I've seen movies, a lot of them actually. I know what goes on between grown-ups when they're naked and under the sheets. I may not know all the details, but I know basically what's going on, and I know that's how babies are made. I spend a lot of time alone and the television teaches me a lot.

I peek around the wall to get a glance. He's standing on the inside of the door facing me. He looks up at the exact moment I peek my head around enough to get a good look at him, as if he already knew I was standing here. He looks like an older version of me. He has the same light brown hair and light eyes. Mom is starting to zone out. She's trying not to cry. I've seen that look before, and often. Mostly it's when her latest date stops calling or picking her up. I don't really understand why it makes her sad. She just calls them friends.

He looks back at Mom as she starts talking again. "Does she know about us? Does she know you have a son? Answer that question and I will decide if you can see him."

I hide behind the wall again. My chest starts to rise and fall quickly. Am I going to meet my dad? I place my tiny nails in my mouth and start to bite. I can't see either of them right now. They're behind the wall in the other room. "Yes, Anna. You know the answer to that question. Is this some kind of joke or have you really forgotten? You were in the same damn room. Things could have turned out so much differently. He could have known me, and his sister, but I guess none of that matters now...because she's dead. I am here because I can't stay here. I have to move away. I've never asked you for anything, Anna, but I'm asking you to let me see our son."

She doesn't respond immediately. I'm going to be brave. Mom isn't good at making the right decisions. Even I know that. I step around the wall, showing myself. "Mom..." She turns around at the sound of my voice. "It's okay. I'm a big boy."

I look at the man that looks like me. "So, you're my dad?"

He steps around Mom and walks closer to me with his hands in his pockets. "I am, Kaston." He squats down to bring himself closer to my height, now resting his forearms to his thighs. "Is it okay to talk for a minute? Man to man."

"Okay."

"I'm really sorry you don't know me and have had to grow up without a dad. That's not fair to you, and I'm sorry I've never come to see you, but I have watched you grow from time to time over the years. I even know where you go to school. You never knew I was there, but I was."

I blink, trying not to cry. Boys aren't supposed to cry. Mom told me so. My friends sometimes make fun of me for not having a dad. They said it was weird, and that kids are supposed to have two parents. "Why didn't you ever tell me who you were? Did you not want me? Did I do something wrong?"

The look on his face changes. He briefly looks at Mom and back at me, before rubbing the palm of his hand over his mouth like he's thinking of what to say. "No, Kaston, that wasn't it at all. Sometimes grown-ups do the wrong things even though we know they aren't right. You know how when a kid does something wrong, he has to get punished to make him know that it was wrong, and to teach him right?"

I nod.

"Adults get punished too. We make mistakes just like kids do, and when we make those mistakes we have consequences.

Unfortunately, sometimes those consequences hurt other people too, but I'm here now because I want to make up for the eight years you've lived without me. Kids shouldn't feel like they aren't wanted by their parents. I can't change the decisions I made before, just like you can't take it back after you do something wrong, but now I know what it's like to live without one of my children permanently and not having a choice to change it. I never want to go through that again. I've wanted to be a part of your life for years, but I didn't enforce it harder. I am now. I want to know you, Kaston, if you'll let me."

My stomach feels like it did when Mom took me on that elevator. He's not saying anything, just looking at me. I wonder what he's thinking. Maybe he's waiting on me to say something, but what? "How?"

"There's something I want to ask you and I want you to answer honestly, because it's a big decision, but it's *your* decision. I don't want you to let your mom nor I sway your decision. Can you do that?"

My heart starts beating fast. I feel like I'm about to go over the slope of a roller coaster. He sounds serious. "Yes, Sir. What do you want to ask me?"

"I have to move away...and I wanted to know if you want to come with me. It'll be just the two of us."

"Like hell you are, Phillip! You aren't taking my son anywhere," Mom says.

He puts up his hand behind him, halting her words. He never takes his eyes off of me. "Kaston, if you want to stay with your mom then I will understand, but if you want to come then I want you with me. I know you don't know me very well, but I promise to change that. Who you live with should be your decision."

He turns and looks at Mom. "And neither parent should have a say so in your decision, because it's not your fault that things are this way," he says and then turns back to look at me. "If you choose to come I will make sure you are in a good school, you will always have everything you need, and I will take care of you. Son, understand this is a big decision. You won't live close to your mom, so visitation would only be when you want to come and school isn't in process. You need a good education. You need to be a kid, and from recent information I've received you aren't getting that here."

He is starting to get an angry look about him, his tone changing like Mom's does when I'm aggravating her. I feel funny. I'm scared. I don't want to make Mom mad, but I think she will do better without me. She always tells me I hold her back from doing things she wants to do and that things would be easier if I were grown. I'm tired of being the weird kid without a dad. I'm sick of being lonely while Mom goes out all the time to do fun things. I don't really know him, but as little as Mom is home it can't be any more awkward than living with her.

I look up at Mom. "If you leave me, Kaston, don't think you can just come back. I've raised you for eight years. He's tried to be a father for eight minutes. It's all or nothing."

"Mom, do you love me?"

"What kind of question is that? This isn't the time to change the subject. What's it going to be, Kaston? I could just call the police if you tried to go anywhere. Would you want me to report you as a runaway, or your father for kidnapping you?"

Not once did she stop fussing long enough to actually answer the question. It really makes me wonder if she pays any attention to me at all or if I'm just invisible to her completely. "Do you even remember what today was?"

I've been reminding her all week that I just needed her signature to give consent for me to play football. I can't play without it. I haven't asked her for anything else, but to show up, sign the paper, and then I wouldn't need her to do anything else.

"Stop being silly. There is nothing important about today. Don't try to trick me on your birthday. It's not for a while." She looks at her watch, her eyes still shining from her trying to avoid crying every time she looks at the man in front of me, the one not paying her any attention at all. "You want to be a big boy, Kaston, then now is your chance. You only have one. If you want to go with your father then go, but don't call me when you end up abandoned like I did when I was pregnant with you."

"I've heard enough of your fucking mouth, Anna. What the hell is wrong with you? Kaston, I will never abandon you," he says in response to her snippy comment. "It's been eight years and I haven't once left you. I've been in the shadows through every phase of your life, watching you from the places no one can see."

This isn't fair. I shouldn't have to choose. I'm just a kid. I don't want to hurt Mom, but I know that I'm a boy and boys need to be with their dads. I am tired of raising myself. It's too hard. I just want someone to love me. "I'm sorry, Mom, but I want to go with my dad. Things will be better this way. You'll see. You will finally get your wish and I won't be in your way anymore. You'll finally be happy."

A tear runs down her face, making me feel guilty. "Kaston." I look down at the man that calls himself my dad. "Go pack a bag, Son. I'm going to talk to your mom for a few minutes, okay? You don't need a lot, just enough to get you through a few days and we'll get you everything you need when we get settled."

I nod and back up a few feet. It's probably a good thing, because

I don't really have a lot. "Where will we be going?"

"I'm not sure yet, but we'll decide together. Does that sound good?"

"Okay...Dad. I'll be right back." I look at Mom once more. "Oh, and Mom, today was my football registration. It was the one thing you promised you wouldn't forget or miss because I've begged you all summer, and you can't even remember that one thing. I'm sorry that I get in your way. I try my best not to. I do love you, though. You'll always be my mom."

I turn and walk back toward my room, my heart beating fast in my chest. For the first time in my whole life I feel like someone actually wants me, even though I've only known him for a little while. He may not have been here before, but he came back for me. I finally have a dad like all the other kids. I'll be fine without a mom. I pretty much live without her most of the time anyway...

CHAPTER ONE

TWENTY YEARS LATER . .

I pull into the club and park, ready for a night of release and relaxation. Work was a bitch today. Sometimes I think it was easier to just go to school during the day and party at night with no other obligations. I kill the ignition as my phone starts to ring. I look down at the screen to see that Dad is calling. I instantly answer. "Hey, Dad, what's up?"

"Kaston, how have you been, Son? Everything okay your way?"

"Never been fucking better. You know...grown up job and shit."

"I sense some sarcasm in your tone. You could always come back to Spain and take over the company. I don't really see you taking orders from someone else anyway. I taught you better than that."

"You're the one that was hell bent on me coming back to the states after graduation, old man. An American education is no better than one there. I was fine staying in Spain with you. I do kind of like it here though. What about expanding the PI firm here? Then we could have two locations; the best of both worlds. I could go back and forth."

"Giving up so easily on your dream of becoming part of the FBI?"

"I guess it's kind of like you said. I don't take well to being someone's bitch. It eats at me and just pisses me off. I feel like smoking a blunt a mile long and I hate weed."

He laughs. I have the best damn dad in the world. He gets me and he doesn't act like he has a stick shoved up his ass all the damn time like some parents. He's real. "That could work. I think I might like that. I've been thinking about retiring from my other obligations. I have one last job and then maybe we can do this, just the two of us. I'm getting too old for this shit."

I close my eyes. He's never going to see anything he does as being good enough to avenge her death. "You don't have to fight everyone else's battles, Dad. It's time to give it up. She can lay to rest in peace. You've done more than enough. There's always going to be bad people in the world. You can't get rid of them all. It's time to live. Why don't you let me take the last job..."

"Fuck no. I told you I wouldn't allow you to do this. I want your freedom untouched. I want your conscience clean. I have to do this for her. I would do the same for you. On her death anniversary, I'll retire. I've given it two decades."

"Promise me. One last job and you're done?"

"I promise."

"When is it?"

"Three days."

"What's the hit?"

"Rapist, murderer, and thief. He's a triple threat."

"Be safe?"

"Always. I need to get off the line. Can you fly out next weekend?"

"Yes. I'll fly out Friday."

"See you then."

"Dad."

"Yeah?"

"Be smart. Fucking outsmart him."

"I always do, Son. I love you."

"I love you too, Dad."

The line goes dead. He doesn't tell me about his *side job* very often. It usually doesn't bother me too much, because I know what kind of man he is and this is something he feels he has to do. God knows the rest of the world commits enough sin that I can't judge him, because he's trying to right the world and not make it worse, but this time it's bothering me and I have no idea why. Maybe it's just because I've had a shitty day. I hate my job. Staring at a shit ton of cold case files does things to me I can't explain. When I get like this I need two things: alcohol and pussy. Both, in that order.

I toss my phone in the passenger seat and lay my head against the headrest. I almost don't feel like going in anymore. I close my eyes and breathe deeply. A knock sounds on the window, reminding me that I'm sitting in my truck. I look over and smile. She backs up and I open the door, get out, and shut it behind me. "Makayla, what are you doing here?"

She holds out a beer. "I brought a reward for a hard day's work. Don't waste it. I had to sneak it outside."

She smiles seductively. I take it and turn it up, downing it in a few seconds, before scanning her body very slowly. "You look... different."

"You didn't think the way I look in all those suits is how I always look, did you? That would be boring."

"I kind of like this look. What are those things you call your uniform? Pencil skirts? They form barriers."

"It's not a uniform. I'm not a fucking underpaid officer. I'm a detective, a very good and highly paid one, just like you. Those pencil skirts are designer. Get it right if you're going to call me out, and I'm good at crossing barriers."

She closes in on me and wraps her arms around my waist, pulling me closer to her. Her tits brush against my chest. Her bra must be thin, because I can feel her hardened nipples. She already has her cleavage staring me in the face. That little black dress does wonders for her body. "Isn't it a little cold to be wearing that?"

"I'm pretty hot right now." She grabs my hand and places it firmly on her ass. I squeeze, unable to help myself. I didn't put my hand there; therefore, I don't have to ask. "They don't call us Georgia peaches for nothing, Kaston. Stop pretending you don't want this. You know you do. We visibly undress each other all day at work, before mentally fucking each other. Two grown adults can enjoy a night away from the office. Case files can sit idle for a few hours. What do you say?"

She's causing a lapse in good judgment. Moving my hand to the small of her back, I rotate us and back her against the door of my truck. "There's a no fraternization policy. I can't touch you, Makayla."

"Who's going to tell? I know I won't. Come on, Kaston. You don't look like the type of guy that plays by the rules. Don't think I haven't noticed the tattoos you occasionally forget about and let show underneath your suit."

She grabs my hand again and places it to her thigh this time, inching it up the inside of her leg until she reaches her panties. She slips the tips of my fingers under the edge, leading them to her center. "Come on, touch it. You know you want to." My finger inadvertently dips inside and it's all over. I'm going to fuck her. It's been a long time coming. She's hot as hell and her pussy is warm and wet. I need a release anyway.

I thrust in and out. "You want my cock, Makayla?"

She lays her head flat against the window and licks her lips as she moans out. "Yes. I want to consume it whole."

Her eyes roll to the back of her head each time I thrust inward and hook my fingers. I close in, leaving barely any space between us. I continue, waiting for her to open her eyes. When she opens them there is a hunger present that makes my dick stand at full attention. "You want my dick, I'll give it to you, but I decide when, and right now I need a fucking drink, because when I fuck you, you better be ready. I have stamina, baby. Once I start I don't stop... until I'm done. Twenty minutes isn't worth shedding my fucking clothes for. Follow me."

I withdraw my fingers from her pussy and run the tips along her bottom lip, instructing her to open her mouth. She looks unsure, until she can tell that I'm not leaving until she sucks them clean. I'm not wiping them on my clothes and I don't know where all she's been. Her lips part and I inch the two fingers inside, allowing them to run over her tongue. I stare into her brown eyes. "Suck them clean. Show me what I have to look forward to later."

With that I can see the amusement in her eyes. She grabs my hand in both of her small ones, guiding it as she suctions around my index and middle fingers. She slowly pulls them from her mouth, moaning the entire way, until she releases them with a verbal smack. I knew she was probably kinky as hell. Tonight's going to be fun, but first I need liquor.

I've found over the course of my life that I need whiskey to get off, the opposite of the average man. Whiskey dick doesn't really exist in my world. If I don't numb my mind I can't nut, then I have to listen to the bitching that always follows, usually that they aren't good enough or some other shit about physical appearance. It's the exact reason why I prefer to always fuck drunk, both parties that is, then I can *blame* it on whiskey dick in the case that I can't follow through, even with the alcohol.

Ever heard of a guy faking it? Well, it happens. I always glove it, so it's rarely detectable, especially if she's drunk. All it takes is stilling inside of her and giving her a little moan or groan to confirm it's done. You can always depend on latex to minimize sensitivity.

It's easier for me to get myself off after I'm done than during the act itself. It has nothing to do with any woman, because I've been lucky enough that the women I've been with are always hot as hell. I'm sure my genetic makeup has something to do with that. My mother was a beautiful woman, whether a sorry one or not. I guess my dad is decent in that area as well. I'm not really sure what the problem is to be honest.

I figure it could be one of two things. The first being that once you've had meaningless sex so many times, it just loses its *wow factor.* The second being something to do with how Dad raised me, and that's to shut down all emotions unless you find someone that makes it impossible. Things were very cut and dry between us, emotion slipping in only on rare occasions. It was the only way he knew he'd be able to tell me of his little secret and me not freak the fuck out. There was no way to hide it forever, so he spent years shutting me down, and now there is nothing inside.

I drop my hand and back up, creating a distance between us.

"Come on. I'll buy your drinks. It's been a long day. You're going to need them if you plan on being with me tonight."

I turn and walk away, not looking back to see if she's following behind. She is. They're pretty much all the same. They always want an asshole until the asshole doesn't want them. I'll be wanted tonight and despised tomorrow...when she finds out that unlike some I can fuck and shut it off. If I want more I'll take it, if not I'll send her on her way. Judge me if you want, but it is what it is and I am who I am. A woman can't expect a husband when she throws herself at a man.

The line to the bar comes into view. I skip it. Bruce is at the door. He never makes me wait. I guess that comes with the territory of a detective being friends with the staff. It keeps them out of shit to have a badge on their side. "Kaston, what's going on, man?"

He clicks the counter in his hand twice as he unhooks the rope, letting us enter. The line of people moans in unison as we move to the opposite side. Getting any kind of special treatment in a large city usually has that effect. Bars in Atlanta on Friday night are never quick entry.

I like Bruce. He's been here at least since I was a freshman in college, so I've known him for years. Why in the hell he still works at a bar at his age, I have no idea, but he's a cool enough guy. "Not shit, man. Just pretending to be a grown-up, usually taking one up the ass by the boss. You know how it goes."

"You right." He laughs as I open the door to the bar. "Don't leave without hollering at me first."

I hold up the same two fingers that were just submerged in Makayla's pussy and wave him off as I hold the door open for her to pass. "If you have a hard time finding me don't come looking," I say halfway jokingly.

He nods as he watches her enter the building, knowing exactly what I mean, and that I'm one hundred percent serious. If at all possible I'd prefer to get this over with here instead of having to deal with her wanting to go back to my apartment and me declining. I don't want to go to hers either. This way we can part ways after, instead of her trying to persuade me to stay the night and me feeling like the bastard that I am for not wanting to. I don't have a spare key to the owner's office for nothing.

I walk in behind her. She starts slightly moving her body to the music as we trudge through the heap of people gathered in a large mass. I have one line of vision and that's from here to the bar in the middle. It looks like Danyel is free. I place my hand on the small of Makayla's back to speed her along before the intoxicated bystanders swarm the bar.

A few steps from the bar she spots me and immediately gets a glass ready to fill. I'm a predictable drinker and I tip well. If I come to a bar it's whiskey, always, and this is the only bar I come to ninety percent of the time. Beer is a man's wine. That is for dinner. I stopped getting drunk on beer a few years back. A few too many kegs and frat parties I suppose. I'd have to invest in stock of a brewery to get anything out of it because I get so full I pass out first.

I lay a bill flat on the bar and slide it toward her as we come into arms reach of each other. Danyel is smiling as she thrusts the partially full glass across the bar, letting it glide on the surface of the wood. I open my hand, catching it as the liquid sloshes around on the inside of the clear glass. "I was wondering if I was going to see you tonight. It's about that time."

I clamp my hand around the glass and pick it up as I whirl the amber liquid around the interior. My mouth starts to salivate. I look at Makayla standing next to me and press the glass to my lips, tilting my head back until it's empty. I swallow. The room temperature liquid coursing through my system scratches an itch nothing else can. It's unexplainable, but it calms an urge that I'm still unsure about. That mysterious urge is why I'm in law enforcement. Dad and I both clean up the scum on the streets, just in different ways.

"That it is." I pull out the stool and take a seat. "Get her whatever she wants, okay? Keep them coming. Don't let me run dry."

"Vodka and cranberry, please," Makayla says as she sits down beside me.

Danyel looks Makayla over for the first time as if she just noticed she's here. The look on her face transforms as if she wants to scratch her face and pull her hair out. *Down girl.*

Danyel and I have hooked up on several occasions, none of which I regret each time I remember how she looked riding my cock. Fuck, I've been coming here since I was eighteen and she was the hot bartender only a few years older than me. What better way is there to drink underage than by giving the bartender countless orgasms throughout her shift, in exchange for a wristband and free alcohol? Sounded like a good idea to me at the time. I like her. Have since I met her. She's cool as shit, and never attaches herself to me in an emotional form. Her claws only come out when she's already planned to take me for herself for a few hours and I've made other arrangements...but those arrangements can always be slightly altered.

I smirk as my mind engages in the new thought that is forming; the very one that involves both of them naked and willing to do anything to enjoy the feel of my dick immersed from wall to wall of drenching wet pussy. I look between the two of them, staring each other down, waiting for the other to back down, and making me horny as hell. Two females in heat smells like the perfect meal after a cocktail.

The only way this is going to go my way is to piss off Danyel. She's the instigator of the two. She never says no to anything when she wants something, and I've got what she wants. Women have all the power my ass. Shove a good-looking asshole that knows how to use his dick in their faces and they become putty in my hands, ready to bend and mold into what I want them to be. Makayla will be a little harder to convince. I can tell she's wild, but she lets it build slowly before she explodes.

"Who are you?"

Good girl.

"Makayla. I work with Kaston. Do y'all know each other?"

There's the transformation I'm looking for. Time to relax and watch it play out. I remove a drink straw from the stack and place it in the side of my mouth to chew on until I can get a cigarette. The person that banned indoor smoking is on my shit list. Danyel refills my glass without even looking at it. She has bartending down to an art. People are shoulder to shoulder at the bar, waving cash in the air and waiting to be served, but she never moves from in front of us; the perks of seniority.

"If you want to count orgasmic introductions then I would say so; pretty damn well," she says casually, baiting Makayla.

My dick starts to harden.

Not yet.

Danyel fills the empty plastic cup with ice and slams it on the bar in front of her, before pouring the vodka to her imaginary fill line, and then presses the button on the spout for the cranberry, letting it fill until the cup is full. She then tops it off with a drink straw and slides it toward Makayla. Makayla has said nothing thus far. I shrug it off. Oh well. Would have been fun. I need a woman with a bitch gene, a backbone. I look at Danyel's tits peeking out of the top of her cutoff shirt. She does have a beautiful rack. Maybe I'll just send Makayla home. I already know my way around Danyel's body.

"You want to stay while I *lock up?*" My eyes hesitantly leave their current location and move back to her face. I slam my drink back and take a deep breath, needing the burn.

I open my mouth to agree. "He already has plans, but that's sweet of you to offer. He's done playing in the minor leagues, but at least he got some good practice for the majors."

And now I'm completely hard.

"Before you get all cocky, bitch, why don't we let Kaston decide? Have some class."

"You want to talk about class? You work at a fucking bar. You're no longer entitled to that category."

Danyel starts to reach across the bar and I grab her behind the neck, pulling her to me. I know she could tear Makayla to shreds. I pull her bottom lip between mine and lightly suck, before biting down. She moans. "You want to prove who's better, then do it, but not this way. You need your fucking job. Don't be stupid. I promised her tonight, but there's room for you too."

"You cannot be fucking serious," Makayla says loudly. "You actually think I would do that?"

The side of my mouth starts to pull up as I look into Danyel's brown eyes. Her mouth mirrors mine. That girl will do any-fucking-thing, and that's why I continue to fuck her from time to time, even after all these years. "I'm game," Danyel says with a smile in her tone. "What about you, Blondie? Are you scared of a little competition or are you just going to bow out and let me have him all to myself?"

We both look at Makayla at the same time. She has a disgusted expression all over her face. I shrug. "I never said I was sugar, baby. I like spice. If you can't handle the heat, then maybe you should get out of the kitchen. I'm not looking for a wife. I'm looking for a good time. You in or out?"

She narrows her eyes as she stares into mine. "What the fuck ever. I can't believe I'm going to do this for a hot guy. I'm going to need a stronger drink for this. Fix me a walk me down, and make it a double."

Danyel wastes no time refilling my glass and making Makayla's with a shit-eating grin on her face the entire time. She slides it in front of her. "I guess I'll see you at closing. Make sure you wear that red lipstick. I like it," she says as she winks at Makayla.

Makayla growls out her frustration and picks up her drink. "I'm going to circulate. I suddenly need some air. I'll see you guys in a bit. Oh, and Kaston, you're going to dance with me when I start to feel this alcohol. It's the least you can fucking do."

"I don't dance," I say sarcastically, making her even angrier as I take a sip of my drink.

"You're an asshole away from work. Whatever. I'll find a stand-in."

I turn and watch as she walks away, strutting that fine ass as she does. I'm going to get a better look at it later when I have her bent over this bar. When she disappears I turn back toward the bar and finish my drink. Danyel is still standing there watching me. "There's always one thing I can count on with you, Kaston. You'll never fucking change. That, sexy, is the best quality someone can have."

"I am who I am, and that's the person that I want to be. I don't have a reason to change, because I don't give a shit if people like me or not. Get back to work before you get fired. I'm going to play pool. When the bar is clear I'll be waiting with my cock in hand for you to suck. Think about that while you're serving that fat, ugly bastard in the corner that's drooling over your ass right now."

She immediately turns to verify the creepy motherfucker that probably has a wife at home while he's wishing he were still in his twenties. That's what is wrong with the world. People always want what they don't have instead of just taking what they want in the beginning versus following a crowd. I may be twenty-eight and single, but that's because I choose to be.

I don't have the slightest desire to wear a tux and condemn myself to one woman for the rest of my life. Something happens to couples after they walk down the aisle. They change. At least I'm honest about it. It saves one poor woman from being stuck in bed home alone, wondering where her husband is at night and what he's shoving his dick into. When that happens, you end up with bastards like me walking around. I stand and grab my newly refilled glass, disappearing before she turns back around.

I throw back my fifth shot as I wait for the random college frat boy to take his shot. He's good, but not as good as me. I'm the king of pool. I used to take bets from guys wanting to show off their testosterone levels to the hot girls circulating the bar, as if that was going to confirm their dick sizes. None ever won, and it didn't increase their chances at getting laid. That's the funny thing about women. They can sense a show off a mile away.

22

"You ready to empty your wallet, Wall Street?" He looks at me as he aims his cue stick at the cue ball, pulling the stick back and forth in his finger mount on the felt as he gets ready to try to put the solid into the corner pocket. Both of us have one ball left before the eight ball. *Wall Street my fucking ass.* I'm not changing my clothes just to come to a damn bar. I went to work, I got off, and I came to a bar to numb this twitch I can't seem to get rid of. I'm not even wearing my jacket and tie anymore. I left that shit in my truck. My sleeves are even rolled up to my elbows.

I hold the tip of the pool stick toward him. "You sound confident, frat boy. You sure you got it in the bag?"

He looks up at me with a cocky smile on his face. "I'd be willing to double the pot. What do you say?"

"Aight. Go for it. I'm down." He starts to reposition his aim, readying to take the shot. A drunken giggle sounds beside my ear.

"Wait, waaaait, just one minnnute," she slurs. "Can you beat him with a pretty distraccction in your face?"

I look over at Makayla and she is leaning forward, baiting him with her cleavage. His eyes fall on the center line that disappears into her neckline, his mouth ajar. I shake my head as she traces her fingertip over the full mound toward the center. "I bet you wouldn't be so cocky with a fresh pussy dangling in your face, would you?"

When I look at him he looks like he's about to drool on the pool table. She's hot. I'll give her that, but she's also no different than what I'm used to. For some reason women throw themselves at law enforcement. Maybe it's the suit and badge. In the beginning I used it to my advantage, but after a while it gets boring. "Sweetheart, nothing gets in my way of pool. I'm that good. I've been playing since I was old enough to see over the table."

Makayla turns around and sits her ass on the corner pocket,

before sliding back enough she's completely on the edge, her dress hiked up just below her hips. She plants her hands on each side of her, spinning herself around, and picking her legs up as she does, until she's facing him. She places each heel on the felt, spreading her legs. She seems pretty lit, so I'm not sure how she's not moving any of the balls. He has to make the shot directly below her pussy. His eyes haze over as he takes her in.

The shot girl appears with a new round of shots. I take them and replace it with a bill, shooting one and then the other, not wasting a drop. It's all finally hitting me. I'm fucked up. It's a good thing I live right around the corner, another reason I prefer this bar. The road in between is usually vacant at close.

I lay each palm on the table, letting the alcohol flood my system. I finally feel numb, content. I feel like a fucking junkie on a daily basis, yet I've never done hard drugs. I've been hiding it from Dad for years, but it's starting to consume me. I'm drinking more now than I ever have. Maybe it's time to talk to him.

I look around Makayla's legs, getting a view of what he finds so amazing. Her underwear is thin, showing every outline of what's beneath them. Hell yeah. This is going to be like taking candy from a baby. "Put your money where your mouth is, cutie."

"Alright, I'm game if he is. It has to be fair."

I look at him. "Go for it, frat boy. I won't back down."

His vision veers back to the pink satin between her legs, the place it's been since she spread her legs. He bites his bottom lip and starts to aim again, striking the ball prematurely when she runs her finger under the edging of her panties, bumping the eight ball and sending it into the pocket. "Fuck! Your turn. You miss we both walk away with our money."

I move to the side, taking my position at my ball. To be fair she touches herself again, but this time pulls her panties slightly to the side to give me a peek. A pussy is pretty much the same as every other pussy. Some just grip a dick a little tighter than others. I pull back and take the shot, sending my last ball into the pocket beneath her. She almost looks a little disappointed that I didn't miss.

My mouth spreads into a grin as I stand upright. "Time to pay up, frat boy. Looks like five hundred is mine tonight." He tosses the stick onto the table and reaches into his back pocket, removing his wallet. He grabs a stack of cash and throws it on the table as well.

"Here. Good play. I can't say with that view it was the worst time I've ever lost money." He turns and walks away as they announce last call over the speakers.

"Does that mean I get half? I'd say I earned it."

I look at Makayla as she turns toward me and hangs her legs over the side. "You think so?"

"I didn't see you pulling your dick out as bait. My pussy was the one on display so you could win."

I move in front of her and grab her chin, closing in toward her. She starts to close her eyes until I speak. "Let's get one thing straight, baby. I would have won whether your pussy was present or not, but since you helped by sending him to the bathroom to take care of the hard-on you just created, I'll repay you in orgasms here in a few minutes. How does that sound?"

She grabs a handful of my shirt in her fist, pulling me closer. "Damn, just take me already. I've never been so turned on in my life." She presses her lips to mine and the alcohol takes over, directing all of my muscle movement. I grab her hips and pull her toward me as I roughly kiss her back. She instantly wraps her legs around my waist. I grind her against my now hardening cock. She grabs the waistband of my pants, no longer concerned with where we are.

"Starting without me?"

I release her lips and look at Danyel standing next to the pool table. It's just now that I realize the bar is completely empty. "Where is the rest of the staff?"

"I sent them home and locked the doors. Since I'm the manager I can do that. No one ever complains when being sent home early at closing. No work for them and a good time for me after a long night. It's a win/win situation."

Makayla groans out, clearly frustrated and not wanting to share. I nod for Danyel to come closer and look at Makayla, locking my eyes with hers. "I'm your partner. You trust me in the field, right?" She nods, her eyes flitting from my eyes to my mouth and back again. "Then trust me now. Be open-minded. Just because you try something new doesn't mean you have a label. We're all straight. Danyel probably likes dick more than you do. Got me?"

She breathes deeply, clearly nervous, but nods lightly. "Yeah, okay. I'll try...for you." I'm going to pretend I didn't hear longing in her voice and hope like hell I don't regret this at work Monday.

I reach out and hook my index finger over Danyel's waistband, pulling her closer. I kiss her, starting things slow. She slides her tongue inside my mouth, allowing each of our tastes to mix, creating one of its own. I stop and turn to Makayla, doing the same. She moans into my mouth before I release her lips. "See. You taste her. You taste me. It's no different." I continue to look at her. "Danyel, come show her how gentle you can be. I want to watch."

I step back, allowing Danyel to take my place. I can see the disappointment written all over Makayla's face, but she remains silent. Danyel touches her knee and skims her fingertips up Makayla's thigh, tracing the side of her body until her hand is on the side of Makayla's neck. "Relax, Makayla, and I'll reward you later." Her shoulders immediately drop.

Danyel lowers her face and kisses Makayla, slowly at first, but then you can tell the moment Danyel slides her tongue between Makayla's lips, because she completely lets go and places her hands in Danyel's auburn hair, wanting more. My dick presses against my pants, wanting free as I watch two beautiful women experiencing each other for the first time. The room is hazed from the alcohol, but that's exactly where I need to be.

I walk up to Danyel's backside, pressing my front against her. I press my lips next to her ear as they continue to kiss. "Do to her as I do to you. Are we clear?" They stop and she nods her head, but their breathing is uneven. They're turned on. Good. I grab the bottom hem of her cutoff shirt and pull it over her head, throwing it on the floor. Unhooking the black, lace bra, she lets it slide down her arms. Makayla watches as I grab Danyel's breasts in my hands, large and firm from her implants. She lays her head back against my chest as I rub my thumbs over her hardened nipples.

My hands move lower, down her firm stomach, and over her belly button ring until I reach the button on her denim shorts. I slip the button through the slit and push down the zipper, before working her shorts and lace panties over her ass until they fall to the floor. She steps out of them and quickly reaches down to remove her cowgirl boots, tossing them both to the side, now standing fully nude. I say in her ear, "Strip her."

Makayla slides off the table, giving her access. Danyel grabs the bottom of her dress and inches it up her body slowly, removing it completely, followed by her bra and underwear just as I instructed her. Each body is opposite of each other, but beautiful. I grab Danyel's breasts again. "Touch her."

She reaches out and cups Makayla's breast, mirroring my actions. "Makayla, on the table." She does as I say, returning to her previous position on the pool table. I grab the back of Danyel's other hand in mine, guiding it to Makayla's stomach. Her skin jumps at the initial contact. "Familiarize yourself with her body, like you would mine."

I release her hand and place mine on her hips, waiting to see what she does. Watching two girls that have never experimented with each other is going to be fun. She glides her hand to Makayla's other breast, now covering them both. Makayla lays her hands flat on the felt and leans back slightly, arching her back into Danyel's hands as she begins rubbing her slender fingers over the hard nipples.

Danyel leans in and places her mouth over the small, round, pink nipple, and begins to suck. "Oh, fuck. You have a tongue ring. That feels amazing." She switches from one to the other, massaging the one not in her mouth with her hand.

I snake my hand around Danyel's waist and down her pelvis until my fingers brush over her pussy lips. Touching the tip over her opening, I rub in a circle and slide my now moist finger up her folds connecting with her clit. I press down to get her attention. She bucks her hips backwards, wanting more. I stop, not giving her more until she returns the favor.

She continues flicking her tongue over Makayla's nipples in a rotation to serve them equally, but starts to lower her right hand down Makayla's stomach. My cock hardens some more when she does exactly as I have just done to her, only at a different angle. When she starts to rub in circles over Makayla's clit, I start up again, doing the same to her. They both start moaning simultaneously. I guess they're more alike than they originally thought.

This angle isn't going to work for me. I continue rubbing her clit, and picking up speed, but reach behind me and grab the chair against the wall, pulling it toward me. Pressing Danyel's hips against me, I place the chair sideways between her and the pool table so that the back doesn't get in my way. I push her toward it, signaling I want her on her knees. She gets it, automatically spreading her legs as far as they will go and still be on the chair. Laying my palm flat against the middle of her back I push her forward, in turn, pushing Makayla on her back on the pool table.

Danyel kisses down her stomach, sucking her naval ring into her mouth, before releasing it from her suction, but hasn't stopped rubbing Makayla's clit. Makayla pulls her feet up onto the edge, spreading her legs wider. I want to see more. I change my hand from front entry to back, and then rub my index and middle fingers in a back and forth motion, moistening them, before shoving them into her pussy, slightly pushing her forward. She arches her ass toward me, and I shove them deeper, twisting before I pull out and start the routine over.

Makayla breathes out loudly as Danyel does the same, but she then does something to please me as she starts to finger fuck her. With her free hand she spreads Makayla's lips, revealing her clit, and starts to flick her tongue over it, the ball of her tongue ring coming in contact with the sensitive button as she does. Makayla thrusts forward, off the table. There's my wild girl. That deserves a fucking reward. She thought of pleasing Makayla before herself. That shows character, selflessness.

I reach into my pocket with my spare hand and continue to finger her with the other. Pulling out a condom I place the wrapper between my teeth as I undo my belt and pants. I quickly push them down to my thighs and grab the wrapper with my fingers, tearing the corner with my teeth, before removing it singlehandedly and rolling it on my cock.

I remove my fingers and move them around to the front to begin working on her clit again, as I grab my shaft and align it at her entrance. I rub the head over her pussy, coating it with her wetness. She backs her ass into my dick, but continues with Makayla like a fucking pro. You'd never know it was her first time to go down on a girl. Grabbing Danyel's hip for leverage, I slam my dick into her pussy until it's completely buried. I grind my hips and pull out, before doing it again. "Oh fuck, I'm going to come," Makayla shouts. "Please don't stop now."

I press down on Danyel's clit and rub up and down in a swift motion. She moans against Makayla's clit and it's all over. "Fuck, Danyel! Holy shit." Makayla arches her back, rolling her head against the felt as she grabs onto the back of Danyel's head and holds her against her clit while she rides out her orgasm. Beads of sweat form on my face from the constant high-paced motion of my hips and fingers. I feel Danyel clamp around my dick and she locks her mouth on Makayla's clit, sucking hard. "I can't take anymore." Danyel obviously uses her own orgasm as a motivational tool, because Makayla quickly orgasms again, screaming loudly as she grabs her tits and pinches her nipples to even out the sensations. It's hot as fuck, but I'm still not ready to come.

I halt movement and pull out when she stops contracting her muscles around my dick. Danyel removes her fingers from Makayla's pussy. I look at it, all pink and swollen, covered in milky white cum. It's beautiful. Post orgasmic pussy is the best. I run my wet fingers up Danyel's stomach until it's back on her breast, pulling her upward to meet me. With my free hand I grab her chin and turn it toward me to see her face. "Did you like that, baby? Did you like being the one to make her come like a fucking porn star?"

She licks her lips and I can see the pride in her eyes, whether she wants to admit it or not, but she surprises me. "That was hot as fuck. I could feel her coming on my fingers. Is that the way a guy feels? No wonder you all are so damn cocky and arrogant." Makayla props up on her elbows, watching us, and probably wondering what is next. I could swap, but I'm changing it up.

"Times fucking ten, baby. Go clean up. You've had me to yourself on several occasions, and you will again, but first it's her turn. I'll finish up here, and then I'm out. I swipe my tongue against her lips, getting a taste, and slap her on the ass, causing her to jump. "You just earned yourself a spot in the top three of my call list. Go."

Without hesitation she grabs her clothes and walks away, leaving the two of us alone. Grabbing the edge of the condom, I pull it off and toss it on the floor, reaching in my pocket for a new one to take its place. I may like pussy, but I'm a clean bastard, for myself and for my partners. Using the same condom on two different girls is fucking disgusting.

I look at Makayla heatedly and pull the chair back, giving her room. She's biting her lip. I'm not finished. I've barely even started. I can see the excitement all over her face as I roll the new condom on. "Come to me."

She pushes herself to the edge of the pool table and hops down, before walking closer. She looks up at me. "You aren't too tired?"

"I've only just begun. I could go all night, baby. I guarantee you'll be worn down before I will be. Undress me."

She starts with the top and unbuttons my shirt, one button at a time, until it's completely open, then pushes it off my shoulders and down my arms, letting it fall in a rumpled pile on the floor. "You want me, then show me. Make me hard again."

She licks her lips and places her hands against my firm stomach, before closing her mouth over my nipple like Danyel did to her. She flicks her tongue back and forth, before running her tongue down my torso as she squats to the floor, leaving a wet trail. She drops to her knees and places her hands under the waistband of my pants sitting at my thighs, pushing them down to my ankles. My sheathed, semi-hard cock is staring her in the face. "Suck me, beautiful."

Taking my shaft in her fist and holding down the edge of the condom beneath it, she places her mouth over the head. It doesn't feel as good as it would without the condom, but I never go without, not even for oral. I haven't let a girl suck my dick bare since high school, so I really don't even remember the difference. There is more fucking bacteria in someone's mouth than most places on the body. I take care of my dick. A man's dick is his best friend. Buying a never-ending supply of the thinnest latex condoms on the market is as risky as I get.

She's hesitant at first, undoubtedly because latex probably tastes like shit, but if she wants me hard she'll deal with it. She swirls her tongue in a circle around my head, becoming familiar with the size. Enclosing her mouth around my cock, she relaxes her throat and pushes her lips down my length, running her tongue along the underside as she takes it all. My head falls back when the head of my dick touches the back of her throat and it hardens fully, increasing to full length. She readjusts and continues, creating suction as she pulls back. It's good, but too slow.

I grab the back of her head and push her down my length again, shoving the tip into the back of her throat. She gags a little, but controls herself, grabbing my nuts in her hand as she picks up speed. "Enough," I say as I pull her by the hair until my dick falls from her mouth. I take a seat on the chair behind me and pull her toward me, her crawling on her knees.

She stands as I release her hair. Her cheeks are a flush pink and her eyes are glazed over in a state of euphoria. Closing my legs together I grab her by the waist and pull her to a standing straddle on top of me. "You ready to feel my cock?"

"Hell yes. I thought you'd never ask."

I cup her clean-shaven pussy in my hand, dipping my middle and ring finger inside, checking her wetness. It quickly coats my fingers, running into my palm as she places her hands on my shoulders and lets her head fall back. "Beautiful."

I take hold of my cock in my opposite hand and thrust in and out of her pussy a few times before removing my fingers completely and clamping down on her side, pulling her over me. She squats, aligning herself over my dick, and I move my hand as she sits down, taking my cock greedily until there is no space between us, moaning the entire way. She doesn't immediately start. I can't do this slow savoring shit. I need fast and hard. It's just the way I'm built and the way I like it.

I press the pad of my thumb directly on her clit and start rubbing over it. She immediately plants her feet firmly on the floor and bucks her hips forward, applying more direct contact against my finger. "Ride me if you want to be able to walk out of here."

She starts to move finally, grinding hard as she rocks back and forth on my dick, clenching around me as she does from the stimulation of my finger on her clit. She wraps her arms around my neck and runs her fingers in my short but shaggy hair, pulling it in her fists with each hit against her G-spot. "Damn, this is so much better than I imagined. I'm not going to last, Kaston. I need to come. Fuck. It feels too good. Are you ready to come? Come with me."

I'm not even close to coming. She isn't moving near fast enough for my liking. She wants slow and sweet, and I need a fucking freak in the bed, someone who needs it hard and fast like me, and someone who wants to dominate my cock as much as I her pussy, sending us both into a fucking sexual high, elicited because together we fuck like a couple of mad hatters. The whiskey is now in full effect, but I've already started releasing some through my pores from the sweat occurring from movement. The room is hazy, and my mind and body are numb to everything except her pussy riding my cock and squeezing it. I'll just have to get myself off later. Her pace starts to slow even more as my finger picks up, aiming to get her off clitoral and G-spot simultaneously.

"Yeah." I lie. Her body is hot but not even holding my attention right now. "Come for me."

She rocks forward another time before she starts to come. "Oh, fuck!" She slams her mouth against mine as she rides the wave of her orgasm, barely moving on my dick. When she's done she sits upright, not making any effort to get off my cock, and then looks into my eyes. "I can't wait to do that again. I just came so hard I can barely breathe. I hate condoms. I couldn't feel you come."

What she doesn't know is there won't be a next time. First time is always a trial run. First impressions are everything. She's hot and I like her, but we just don't have the right chemistry in bed to do this again. It's nothing personal. It's nature.

I place my hands on her hips and push her off of me. "Yeah, well, they serve a purpose. Nothing is perfect. I got to get home. I have shit to do tomorrow. You need me to call you a cab?"

She immediately moves back and starts gathering her clothes as I stand and pull my boxer briefs and pants back up, fastening them until I can deal with the condom. I grab my shirt from the floor and pull it on, beginning to button it. "I was hoping I could come home with you, and maybe go for round two," she says seductively as she pulls her dress on.

Fuck. Why can I never avoid this?

"Look, Makayla, we're partners and we have to see each other five days a week, sometimes more. You know this was just sex, or at least that's what you acted like you wanted at my truck. You're not going to make this into something it's not, are you? I really don't need for shit to be awkward at work. Coming back to my place or me to yours would only complicate things. I don't do complicated. I hope you understand."

She looks a little shocked, making me feel like a bigger asshole than I know I am, but she brushes it off. "Of course. I just meant for fun, but you're right. Just forget I said anything. Of course I know what this was. We were just having fun."

She pulls on her heels and walks toward me as I fasten the last button. "I don't need a cab. I have my car. I'm pretty much sober now. I wasn't that drunk to start with," she says with a fake, half smile. "And what I was I've sweated out of my system thanks to tonight." She places her hand on my cheek and kisses me, now almost my height with the addition of the heels. "Tonight was awesome. Just say the word if you want to do it again. I'm ready when you are."

She turns and walks away, clicking her heels against the floor. I grab the other used condom and both wrappers from the floor and shove them into my pocket, before following behind her. "Makayla, wait. I'll walk you to your car. I'm not that big of a dick. The fucking psychos lurk at night, waiting for vulnerable women to be alone, especially in bar parking lots where there isn't much light and people are intoxicated."

She stops, waiting for me to catch up to her. Her smile turns real and she holds up the clutch that she grabbed off the bar. "You know I'm always packing. I'm capable of protecting myself, *partner*."

I internally sigh in relief, as her mood is now playful again. Thank fuck. We start walking toward the door. I push it open for her. "I'd be a shitty partner if I didn't pretend that you were clueless. Humor me."

She walks out the door. Bruce is standing against the brick wall smoking a cigarette. "It's about time, man. I'm ready to go. Shit, you can't get your rocks off in the parking lot? Some of us have to go work a little harder for it at home," he teases. "You good or do you need a cab?"

I let the door go as I walk out into the darkness. The only lights on are the security lights. He holds out his fist and I bump fists with him. "Nah, man, I'm good, and you know I'm too old for that shit. Danyel should be almost done. I heard her messing around in the office on the way out. Hit me up if you're over my way. We'll do lunch. I'll buy. For now I'm out."

We start walking toward the only two vehicles left in the customer parking lot. "Aight, but don't make offers you won't follow up on. I'm a bouncer. You know I don't miss a meal, especially not a free one," he shouts from behind us.

"I keep my word."

It doesn't take long before we're at our vehicles. I'm not sure why I didn't notice Makayla's car beside my truck when I pulled up. I guess I was preoccupied by my call with Dad. She hits the lock and opens the door as I walk around the front of my truck to the driver's side. "See ya at work, Makayla."

"Goodnight, Kaston," she says as she gets in and shuts the door, just before I do. She doesn't waste any time before starting her car and backing out of the space, pulling out in a hurry. I watch her taillights in the rearview mirror as she disappears from my sight. I take a deep breath now that I'm alone.

I reach in my pocket and pull out my keys as well as the used condom and wrappers, reminding me I still have the one on my now soft dick. I start the ignition to empty one hand of my keys and reach into my pants to get the other condom, putting them both in the small garbage bag I keep in my truck. I can't stand shit lying around. I'll just have to empty it when I get home, even though it's not full. Growing up with a dad like mine, the number one thing you're taught is to never leave your DNA anywhere, whether you've done something wrong or not. I cover my tracks always, regardless if I'm law enforcement.

The cloudy haze is starting to clear and slowly the annoying as fuck twitch is starting to resurface. I need my bed and sleep.

CHAPTER TWO

"**W**here are we going, Dad? Do you live close by?" He places his hand on my shoulder, lightly squeezing it.

"Son, where we're going is far, far away. Are you sure you want to do this?" He halts me by pulling me backward as I try to continue walking forward.

I turn to look at him, now squatting in front of me like he was doing back at Mom's. He looks sad. "What about my sister? Didn't you say I had a sister?"

"Kaston, there are people in this world that do very bad things. Do you know what it means to die?" I nod my head. "Your sister died, Kaston. She was in the wrong place at the wrong time. An evil person did bad things to her and now she's in Heaven. It's just you and me now, Buddy. We have to leave the country for a while.

We have to start fresh. Pick anywhere you want to go and we will build a life there."

She died? I'm not sure I understand. "Did the bad guy get in trouble? Why do we have to leave?"

He places his hands on each side of my face and looks at me. "Son, one day I'll explain everything to you when you're old enough to understand the complexity of the situation and the context in which things have to be done. We have a shitty justice system, Kaston. Bad people get away with bad things every day, while the good people disappear like a vapor in the wind. There has to be someone to speak and fight for those that are innocent and good, even if it means doing something bad. They got what they deserved, but we must go. I don't expect you to trust me for being absent in your life, but I'm willing to earn it if you'll let me. Us men have to stand together and create a united front. If you remember nothing else from me, remember this: family must stand together no matter what and always have each other's backs. What do you say, Kiddo? Are you with me?"

I don't really understand, but in some form I do. Be a man. He's telling me to be a man. I grab his wrists and push them off my face. I stand tall, pushing my chest toward him. I make my face as serious as I can, so that he'll believe me. I nod once, mocking a character I saw on television. "I'm with you, Dad, forever. I got your back no matter what."

He smiles at me. "You're a lot like me, Kiddo. I can see it." I bite my tongue until I can taste blood. He's proud of me. No one has ever been proud of me before. I will not be a baby. I will be a man. I don't care how hard I have to try. He turns toward the building in front of us: John F. Kennedy International airport. I know because I can read. "Where do you want to go? Your pick."

I think for a minute. "We studied about this place called Spain last week at school. It seemed cool. What about there? Is that a good pick?"

He squeezes the back of my neck. "That's a great pick. I kind of thought of it myself." He stands and holds out his hand for mine. "You need help with your bag?"

I place the strap of my duffle bag over my shoulder and take his hand; the hand of the man my mother told me didn't want anything to do with me. Girls lie. The only one I've ever known that told me she cared about me did, so I bet they're all the same: liars.

My cell phone buzzes for at least the twentieth time in fifteen minutes. I roll over and feel around on my nightstand until I find it. It's still dark in my room, meaning it's not even 5AM yet. I hold it to my ear after touching the blurry, green answer key. "Cox. This better be fucking good to wake me up this early. What?"

"Kaston?" The Spanish accent immediately has my full attention. I jerk upright in bed, rubbing my fingers over my eyes to try and focus. Pulling the phone away from my ear, I look at the number on the screen: out of the country, but an unsaved number.

Fuck.

"Yeah, it's me. Jose? Is that you?"

"Yes, Sir. I'm sorry to call you so early your time, but I didn't know who else to call."

My heart plummets to my stomach. Bile rises to my throat. Jose is my dad's wingman, his number one trustee. There is only one man that knows everything about my father aside from me: Jose. He's been with my father since we moved to Spain, shortly before Dad started the company. He even helped us gain citizenship. My dad strongly believed in one thing: fucking loyalty. You give it to receive it. It's paid off. He has a crew of men that would give their lives to protect him, because he would do the same for them and their families.

"What is it, Jose?"

"It's your father. There's been a situation."

I jump from the bed and run my fingers through my hair as I pace the floor. That bad feeling I got last night is now back full force and increasing at a rapid speed. A fear ignites throughout my body. There is one person that can shatter me: my dad. No one else fucking matters. "What situation?"

"There was a change in schedule. He got a call. He had to take the job sooner than expected. How fast can you get here?"

My breathing is becoming harder to control. "What do you fucking mean he had to take the job sooner? He never does that. Everything always goes to plan. Where is he?"

"Kaston, you need to come. Now."

My blood runs cold.

My pupils constrict.

A burst of anger consumes me, spreading from my core and moving outward to every limb.

That fear is now controlling my every thought, my every move, and every cell in my body. Only one thing matters: getting to him.

"I'll be on the first flight out. Have someone pick me up at the airport."

"Send me the flight details."

"Will do. Oh...and Jose."

"Yes?"

"Don't let anything fucking happen to him. He is everything to me."

"Don't waste any time."

He disconnects the call and I throw my phone at the wall as hard as I can, watching it shatter on impact. "What the fuck did you do, Dad?" I whisper, my voice cracking. "We have rules for a reason."

I dress quicker than I've ever dressed in my entire life, grabbing the bare essentials before running to the door. I stop at the key ring, pulling the set of keys I need when it comes to speed. I just hope the time lapse between here and there isn't one that will kill me...

CHAPTER THREE

I place my palms flat on the dresser and look at the man in the mirror. I don't recognize him. He's dead inside. Everything I've ever known has changed in an instant without my consent. The world is full of hatred. I know that now. I understand completely… but what do I do about it? "What do you fucking do about it, Cox?" I scream into the reflection in the mirror. "Huh?"

I punch my fist into the mirror, watching it crack from the center and spreading outward like a spider web. One word: pain. Physical pain hides from this. This type of pain there is no escaping from. This type of pain changes a man, making him one of two things: good or bad.

I look down at my hand: blood. The beautiful red color catches my attention. It runs down in a steady trickle. The twitch is back. Now, it's stronger than ever. A drip falls to a spot on the wood. I inhale. A high is starting to form. What does this mean? Grabbing the sides of the dresser, without thought I slam my forehead into the mirror, shattering it more.

I look at the gash that now resides in my skin. More blood. I close my eyes as it runs down my nose. My head is starting to pound. When it reaches the tip I touch my index finger to it, stopping it. I pull it back, looking at the bright red on the end of my finger. I rub my thumb and index finger together, circling the blood between them. It's a sign. I know what I have to do.

I push off the dresser and leave my old room, in search of something, but not sure what. I'll know when I find it.

Follow the mind.

Trust the heart.

Forgive.

Never forget.

Protect those that are important to you.

Never feel.

Pick a side: good or evil.

Kill or be killed.

I mentally repeat the rules over and over as I walk through the mansion he's built; the very one I grew up in.... with him.

I look around: the master bathroom, his bathroom. I open the cabinet underneath the sink and rummage through his things. There it is. What I need. I pull out the small, but slightly heavy device, and plug it into the wall. Flipping the on switch, I stare in the mirror as it vibrates in my hand.

I close my eyes. "Tell me what to do," I whisper.

Keep our worlds separate. Never be recognizable. Today we do business. Tonight we rid the world of monsters, one at a time. Be them to defeat them.

His words echo in my mind as I lift my shaggy hair and place the blade of the clippers at the base of my hairline. I glide them back in a straight line, watching as it rids me of hair with each swipe. I repeat in rows, my chocolate brown hair falling into the sink. Ten minutes start to finish. One step down.

Tossing the clippers on top of the counter, I leave the old me behind. Walking into his bedroom, I detour to his closet, opening it. Two different worlds dwell here: business to the left, and a stranger to the right. He could change them with the flip of a switch. It's my turn. I go for the right, grabbing a pair of faded jeans and pulling them on. Luckily for me we were the same size, another sign of my destiny presenting itself.

I grab a hoodie, black, also the color of death. It fits my mood perfectly. I pull it over my head, letting it fall into place. I walk to the center of his wardrobe and separate it, revealing a safe. I key in the code: my six-digit birthday, her six-digit birthday, and the year he lost her and gained me. It opens, revealing all of the major necessities for ensuring I leave nothing of myself behind. Tonight, I become a ghost. He was smart. He *always* covered his tracks.

I grab what I need and lock it back, making sure to cover it before leaving. It's nightfall. I walk into the main corridor. Jose. I flip my hood up as he turns toward me. "What do you want to do?"

"Do you have the file?"

He hands me a folder. I take it. I open it and quickly scan the contents. His photo sits on top. "This is him?"

"Yes. The informant has his location. Just tell me when. I'm ready."

I hand it back to him. "Read me the hit."

He shuffles through a few sheets of paper. "Murder. First degree. All women. He prefers blondes, middle to late twenties, all married to wealthy men. He sexually assaults them and snaps their necks upon climax, leaving them to be found. He's never been caught."

My jaw steels. Fucking sick bastard. "Who put out the hit?"

His eyes scan the sheet. "The husband of the latest kill. Her name was Melody James. Husband was well known and liked by many. He owned half of the city he was from, only a few hours from here. He witnessed it. He left her long enough to retrieve something in their hotel room and walked out as it happened. The guy disappeared as he approached the body. He went to the police, but they had no evidence to take the suspect into custody. He used a condom. There was no semen left behind. This one is local, but he's been spotted here in town. You need weapons? A new shipment arrived yesterday."

"Not for this one I don't. It seems he has a preference." I look at Jose to make sure he understands. He was important to Dad. "Tonight you drive, nothing more, nothing less. Do you understand?"

He starts to shake his head. "Do you understand, Jose? This isn't up for discussion."

He tucks the folder under his arm and turns for the door. I follow. It's showtime.

Jose pulls the black SUV into the alley. Dad kept black cars only for business, because they blended more with the night. It's dark, the only light coming from above the back door of the hole-in-the-wall bar a few feet down, not far from the dumpster. "What's the plan?"

Propping my elbow on the door, I place my fingers over my

mouth as the words exit my mouth. "We wait."

"We could be here a while. It's still a while until close."

"This we have time for; all the fucking time in the world."

I close my eyes, trying to mentally prepare myself for what I'm about to do. Hesitating in the moment can get you killed. I still can't figure out why he did it, or why he failed. He never changed the plan, no matter what the reason. Why this time? I listen to the silence, allowing my mind to roam. In the depths of nothingness in my mind, a creaking door opening makes itself known.

I open my eyes to the sick fucker stumbling out drunk. It's funny, really, how predictable evildoers are. Of course he's going to use the back door, probably shopping for his next victim; the innocent people that think the dark is fun. He might have gotten a few more arousals had he not pissed off the wrong person. He dropped a bomb...and now it's war.

"Watch my back," I say, while pulling the black, latex gloves on my hands. I open the door, stepping out. I stalk toward the end of the alley without making a single sound, watching him. He stumbles into the dumpster and props himself up on it, pulling a flask from his suit pocket before pressing it to his lips. Not only is he a sick bastard, but he's also a fraud, disguising himself as a normal human being.

My mouth twitches as he tilts his head back, letting the liquid fire run down his throat. I close my eyes and envision the scene from three days ago, letting the anger and hatred devour every cell in my body. I stop in front of him and turn my body, now standing face to face with my arms by my side.

His heavy eyes scan me. "You look like shit. Did a bar fight get the best of you? I'm guessing you were on the losing end." He laughs sadistically.

I tilt my head, a smirk playing out on the lower half of my face. Looking him in the eyes is like lighting a trail of gasoline. "I never fucking lose."

He glances at my covered hands and his eyes slightly widen. "Who the fuck are you?"

"You took something that was mine, something that I can never get back. For all intents and purposes you can call me a grim reaper. I'm only here to collect what's due. Hell's gates are open for you."

He pushes off the dumpster and stumbles forward, trying to push past me. "Fucking psycho. I don't have time for this shit."

I grab him by the neck and squeeze, hard. "Awe.... Trying to leave so soon?" I tick my tongue to the roof of my mouth. "I don't think so." He grabs my hand, trying to pry it from his neck, but I'm stronger than him. I walk forward, toward the back wall of the alley, before slamming him against the brick wall.

"What do you want from me? How the hell could I take something from you? I don't even know you."

My teeth steel together. "You may not know me, but you knew someone important to me. In fact, you were the last person to see him alive, so look into my eyes and see if you can remember," I growl out. He looks away from me. I pull him back and slam him into the wall, harder this time. "Fucking look at me!"

He does as I say, studying my eyes as if he's trying to focus. The alcohol is inhibiting his memory. As if a light switch just got flipped, his eyes widen further. "I guess your itinerary from three days ago just came back to you?"

"He tried to kill me. It was self-defense. What else was I supposed to do? Who the hell was he to you?"

That's the thing about a fucking pathological liar. They lie so much they actually believe their own lies. Sadly for him, I'm not a dumbass. I close in on him, bringing my lips just outside of his ear as I dig my fingers into the sides of his throat, wanting like hell to rip it out. He coughs. "He was my fucking father. He may have tried and failed...*this time*, but I'm going to finish what he started. I'm cleaning up the trash on the streets. Your days of raping and killing innocent women are over. Since I just had to lay his body in the ground, you're next. Blood for blood."

"He-" I cut off his words by pressing into his vocal chords.

I pull back and turn him around, his back against my front. "On your knees."

He tries to beg as he follows instructions, but all that comes out is a gargled sound. "It doesn't feel good when you're on the opposite side of the line, does it? If you scream, I'll have my partner shove something so far up your ass you'll feel it in your throat, so you can feel what the women you raped felt. If you stay quiet, I'll make this as painless as possible."

His breathing becomes uneven, quickening by the second. I cup one hand around the back of his head and the other on his chin. Adrenaline starts to spread through my body. "You have about five seconds to say your prayers and hope to God that he forgives the shit you've done, because if not you're about to bust Hell wide open. Five...Four..." He whimpers. "Three...Two...One." I swiftly twist his neck to the right, snapping his spine in two, just like he does to the women that have fallen victim to him. His body goes limp as I release him, letting him fall face first onto the concrete.

Something breaks free inside. I don't truly understand it, but I feel completely high right now. Maybe it's knowing that there is one less woman to be hurt in the world, but I feel like I'm on top of the world; untouchable.

I turn to the SUV and wave Jose toward me. He nods and steps out of the vehicle, grabbing something from the back before making his way toward me with a gas can in his hand, setting it down beside us. Flipping the lid to the dumpster open, we both grab one end of the body, tossing it inside. Jose grabs the can full of gasoline and starts pouring it in the dumpster, drenching everything inside.

I pull the small matchbook from my pocket with Dad's company logo on the front. He used to carry them around everywhere, stating they were great for business marketing with all of the smokers out there. The best business is always done over scotch and a cigar he would say. Opening it, I tear off a matchstick and swipe the red end against the starter strip. It lights instantly, quickly burning down the wooden stick.

Throwing the match inside the dumpster, I turn and walk away as the accelerant causes a combustion and heightens the fire, consuming the entire inner contents of the dumpster. I hear Jose's footsteps behind me as we make our way back to the SUV. "Rest in peace, Dad," I whisper. "It's been done."

I grab the door handle and get in the vehicle at the same time Jose does. "Do you need me to take you to the airport, boss?"

"No, Jose, you can take me home. I think I'll stay awhile. There are things that need to be sorted before I return to the states. Drive. I can't talk right now."

He quickly backs out and drives at a rapid speed, us both freeing the world from one bad soul. Now, it's time to find out what's next...

CHAPTER FOUR

Lux

I throw the strap of my gym bag on my shoulder and close the door to my beautiful, silver Porsche. I smile as I look at the black Lamborghini parked beside me that cost an ungodly amount of money. I love that car. I guess someone wants to play.

Locking the doors, I walk toward the entry of my apartment building. Two seconds up the sidewalk and already the whistles and catcalls start from the balconies around me. A little bare midriff and cleavage and they're ready to stroke themselves off in front of you shamelessly. "Come on, sweetheart. 2A. If you want a workout come see me. I'm sure I can make you sweat more than the gym ever could."

With my phone in hand, I raise it into the air and flip them off in passing. Fucking college guys are all the same. I don't have time for that shit. They're moochers, lazy, and do nothing but drink and throw around any lame line they can find to try and get a little pussy. I don't need an immature boy, I need a man, and one that can actually give me something in return, because call me crazy but dick just isn't worth a five-star review.

"Not a chance, *sweetheart.* It looks like you're stuck with your hand again tonight. You better grip it extra tight if you're going to be picturing me when you blow. You might as well get the feel right. Just a little food for thought." I wink and continue on my way, disappearing into the building.

I make my way to the stairs instead of taking the elevator. I don't workout seven days a week to keep this body to start taking the elevator now. I reserve those rare rides for when I'm avoiding sweat like a dick that has something Ajax won't wash off.

Crossing my bag over my chest, I start climbing the stairs in a run, breathing through the burn. It's only five flights. I got this. My phone starts vibrating in my hand at the beginning of the third flight. I glance down and cringe. *Fuck. What the hell does she want?*

Leaning my back against the wall, I answer the call while trying to catch my breath. "You know not to call me. Stick to the plan. You never know who I'm with. Damn, what do you want?"

"Don't be a bitch to me, Lux. I'm your mother. I fucking raised you instead of taking the easy way out and dealing with that little problem when it arose. You may not have been sprinkled with money and designer things, but you had food and a place to lay your head. Don't you dare fucking bitch at me."

"Oh, I'm sorry. I must have gotten the rotting trailer in the rundown trailer park confused with an actual real place to live. You know, if you're going to spread your legs for cash you could at least be picky like me and go after the ones that could make your life better instead of the nasty fucks you make come for a McDonald's meal and a sliver of the power bill. You embarrass me. The bad thing is you don't have to live this way. Move the fuck on and do better for yourself. Men will do anything for pussy and a pretty face to look at while they come. Scream their name and you're locked in. You're a beautiful woman. Use what God gave you. I'm not smarter than you, I just used my brain to get to where I am."

I take a deep breath. "I have to go, Mom. What do you want?"

"They shut the power off again. I need you to fix it." My head falls against the wall. I swing the backside of my fist into the wall. This shit gets old. Same shit, different day.

"It's a little late to fix it tonight and I have plans. It's Delta's birthday. I have to work tomorrow. Go to *The watering hole* and tell Ella I'll pay your tab tomorrow. Stay with her unless you meet someone that is worth a damn and not managing the local Piggly Wiggly, someone that will get a hotel for you to sleep in instead of fucking you in the alley out back. If he is not wearing a suit and tie - Leave. Him. The. Fuck. Alone. That is the only way to ensure you won't fuck up."

She breathes out, defeated. Am I a bitch to my mom? Yes. Sometimes a person needs tough love. If I don't give it to her straight then I don't love her. There is more hard evidence in a person's actions than words. Do I love her? Absofuckinglutely. She's my mom. She raised me, she fed me, and she did immoral things to scrape enough together for us to survive. I don't use that word lightly either. Survival to me means something entirely different than the Cleaver wannabes a few blocks across the tracks. After twenty-five years though, it's time to move on, no matter what haunts you everyday. I have.

"Okay. I'll go now. Bye, Lux."

"Mom."

"Yes?"

A tiny spec of hope fills her voice. That's fucking sad.

"I know I don't say it a lot, because it just makes me feel like I'm covered in flesh-eating bugs, but I love you. Get your shit together, Katherine, because unlike most things I need you in my life. See you tomorrow."

I disconnect the call and remain leaning against the wall as I stare down at my phone. I need a damn shot after that. I can't deal with feely, lovey dovey shit. For a girl I must have missed out on that gene.... or.... never mind. Soft and sweet emotions give me the damn creeps. I scratch my fingertips up and down quickly on the back of my neck, as if something is crawling on my skin and causing me to itch. "Fuck, I can't deal with this. I hope Delta is ready to do some celebrating."

Needing to burn some adrenaline, I push off the wall and take off up the remaining flights of stairs, taking them two at a time. Fifth floor - my floor. 5D - my door. I fumble with my keys until I slide the right one in the lock, turning it. I push open the door to a specially tailored suit jacket staring me in the face.

"You're late," he says as he picks up the glass of whiskey and takes a sip.

I narrow my eyes as I speak to the back of his head. "You never said you were going to be in town."

He turns around as I place my bag on the floor and shut the door, draining the last of the liquid in his glass as he takes me in heatedly. He sets the glass down on the marble countertop, the crystal making a dinging sound as it connects with the stone. He remains silent. I blink my eyes calmly. His power trips don't faze me.

We stand here in a stare off; each waiting for the other to cave and get on with what we both know is coming. He wants me to submit to his dominant nature and I will say *fuck you* every time. He knows it. Perhaps it's what keeps him coming back for more, bringing a new present each time he does.

"It's Thursday. I always come on Thursday. You know we have limited time with each other, Lux. Where have you been?"

I roll my eyes. Men. No matter how much fucking money they have, they still get paranoid and suspicious about every damn thing. "Oh, you know.... You weren't here and I was horny so I made do with someone else. What can I say? One time a week just isn't enough for a girl my age."

His jaw steels. He's pissed. Good. He fucks better when he's aggravated. He hates when I make age comments, even though we're only ten years difference in age. I wouldn't really classify thirty-five as old, but when you're going after rich, usually you have to sacrifice the hot, young ones for the sexy of the older generation, the ones that's had time to *marinate* in their careers for a while. This one is a catch though. He's sexy, has a nice body, and fucks like he's my age. I choose to think of my men like a fine wine. They taste better and become more appealing with a little age on them.

I met Callum at work. I work for a high end catering company, meeting the needs of the rich and famous. When I'm on the prowl for a new *friend with benefits,* I slip into a dress and mingle with the crowd...for research purposes of course; at least that's what I tell my boss. I'm about one hundred percent certain my version of benefits and yours are completely different.

Callum met all of the requirements on my initial checklist: Armani suit, Rolex watch, shiny black shoes, five o'clock shadow, and that natural asshole, *I can have any pussy I want,* mentality.

It makes it that much better when they find out they don't have that much control after all. I don't want to pine after a sexy, single, and wealthy bachelor so that he can leave me on the verge of emotional suicide when he's had his fill. I'm after his wallet, nothing more and nothing less. If he ends up being a good fuck, then that's just a plus, because I prefer a monogamous relationship.

We flirted shamelessly and ended up in a hotel that night. That was about six months ago. We have established a schedule since then that works for us since he's not from around here. We have a mutual understanding of what each other needs. We haven't had any problems to date.

"Don't fuck with me, Lux."

"Or what?"

He never takes his eyes off of me. Pulling his jacket over his shoulders, he lets it slide down his arms, catching it in his hand. He walks forward, laying it on the back of the barstool on the way. He stops in front of me and starts removing his cuff links, before pulling the shirttail from his pants.

He runs the tip of his index finger up the front of my neck, pushing upward as it comes to a stop on the underside of my chin. "Why can't you just answer the fucking question?"

"Why can't you ask intelligent ones and then maybe I will. I'm wearing fucking gym clothes. Where else would I wear this? Prostitution really isn't my thing."

He growls and tangles his large hands in my hair as he slams his lips against mine, now in frenzy to get my clothes off, but he waits. Pressing his body against mine, I fall into the door, my only support. My breathing becomes heightened as he slides his tongue inside my mouth. I moan as I start to become needy for his touch.

He kisses the corner of my mouth and runs the tip of his tongue along my jawbone. I tilt my head back, elongating my neck for better access. "Damn, I've fucking missed you, and this body."

I close my eyes, enjoying the feel of his lips against my skin. "Shut up and use that mouth for something other than talking. We can talk after you've given me a beautiful orgasm. You've got me horny as hell. This once a week thing really sucks."

He smiles against my skin and grabs my sports bra on each side of my body, pulling it over my head, baring me from the waist up. "You know I'd come more if I could, on both counts. I may just have to volunteer for more shit at work. I love you, angel," he mumbles between kisses down my neck and shoulder, working his way to my breast. My eyes shoot open at those three small words. *What the fuck?*

I tense up until he closes his mouth over my hardened nipple, but doesn't do anything further as if he's waiting for a response. What the fuck am I supposed to say to that? "I love you putting your dick in warm, wet places that send me over the edge. You're wasting precious time with that mouth."

As if that sufficed, he forms a hard suction over my nipple, pulling it into his mouth. I grab his wavy, blonde hair, only long enough to show its natural body. If he let it grow it'd be curly. He cups the other breast in his hand, switching from one to give it attention, flicking his tongue over the rock hard center. "You have the most beautiful fucking tits I've ever seen."

"That's because they're fake. If they weren't I'd want a refund."

He places his hands on the bottom half of my ass cheeks, the tips of his fingers running between my legs. I love that he has big hands. He picks me up and I wrap my legs around his waist instantly, my sensitive nipples rubbing against his crisp, white, button-down shirt.

My hands threaded through his hair, I look down and kiss him. He's a good kisser; makes the sex that much better. He turns and walks a few steps toward the dining table, laying me on top of it. He stands upright, looking down at me from between my legs. "I'm about to fuck you until you can't walk without feeling a soreness between your legs. When I'm gone back to the city I want your cunt to be thinking about me from now till next Thursday."

I bite my bottom lip. His dirty talking makes up from what size he lacks below the belt. Don't get me wrong, he's not small, but he's not big either. He's an average hitter, swinging with a medium length bat. Of course, it doesn't really matter all that much if a man knows how to use it. He was good at first, but he only gets better with time. That's his strong point. He's a good listener. He's yet to give me one of those mind-blowing G-spot orgasms I hear my co-workers bragging about all the time, but I'll settle for clit. "That's what I'm hoping for."

Grabbing the waistband of my shorts, he pulls them down in one swift movement, discarding them with my sneakers, not wasting any time getting me naked. He doesn't have to worry about underwear, because ninety percent of the time I go commando. Tossing them behind him, he starts to lean forward as he runs his hands up my legs, starting at my feet. "Do you want me to shower first?"

"No. For some reason you never smell of sweat. I love the way you smell and taste, even after you work out. It's why I get so paranoid about where you've been."

My mouth drops slightly. Well okay then. He stops as his palms reach the inside of my knees and he pushes outward, spreading my legs open for him. He presses his lips on the inside of my thigh, inching upward. All thoughts halt as he reaches the outer edge of my pussy lips. He hovers over my pussy and shoves his tongue inside, before he begins thrusting in and out, tongue fucking me. I moan and spread my legs as far as they will go, the outside of my knees almost resting against the tabletop.

Pressing down firmly, he runs his tongue up my center until he finds my clit, that magical button that leads to so much pleasure. He moves one hand to the top skin and pulls up, uncovering it completely to give him better access. I know exactly what he's about to do. I welcome it. Closing his mouth over my clit, he sucks it into his mouth, causing me to scream out and buck my hips upward.

As if that's what he's been waiting for, he shoves two fingers from his free hand into my pussy, thrusting as deep as he can go, submerging his fingers completely. "Harder," I scream out through clenched teeth. It feels so good I can't breathe.

He does as I ask and finger fucks me as fast and hard as he can, rubbing my clit in suction back and forth between his tongue and the roof of his mouth. I grab his hair in my hand, pulling from the overwhelming amount of blood flow. "That feels so good. Don't stop. I'm almost there."

My orgasm starts to build, and at the exact moment I start to fall over the edge he sucks me so hard that it hurts, but also feels so fucking good. I slam his head against me and close my eyes, as I get lost in my orgasm, allowing it to consume my mind. When my clit becomes sensitive, signaling the end, he pulls his hands from my pussy and stands upright with a shit-eating grin on his face.

"Fuck. You came all over my fingers. Next time it's going to be my tongue."

He kicks off his shoes as he starts to unbutton his shirt, while he stares down at me, working the buttons through the slits quickly until it's in a heap on the floor. Next comes his belt, jingling as he pulls the leather through the buckle. His black pants fall to the floor where he steps out of them. His dick is fully hard, springing free as he drops his boxers. Last are his socks. He likes to be completely naked when we fuck. I sit up. "Where's the condom?"

He reaches down and pulls it from his pocket, showing the packet to me. I reach out and take it from him with a smirk on my face. Placing my palms on the table, I hop off, now standing before him. I rub my fingers through the light brushing of blonde chest hair, confirming how much of a man he really is. Surprisingly, I kind of like it.

I grab his dick in my hand and start stroking it, rubbing my thumb through the bead of cum at the head. "I want in," he says.

"Good things come to those who wait."

I squat, kneeling on my knees to become level with his cock, quickly taking the head inside my mouth. I swirl my tongue around the head, wetting it, before relaxing my throat and taking all of him. I grab his ass for leverage and begin to suck, working him up. He loves when I suck his dick, but he never makes it very long before shoving his dick ball-deep inside of me. He moans out, grabbing my hair and twisting. "Put the fucking condom on, Lux, or else you're getting it bare."

Releasing his dick from my mouth, I tear the wrapper open with my teeth. I remove the condom and roll it on his dick, before standing to my feet. "How do you want it, Callum?"

"First, I want you wearing something that is mine." He walks over to his suit jacket and removes something, bringing it back to me. "Turn around and move your hair."

I do as I'm told.

His hands come around my neck and something cold touches my chest. I look down and place my hand over the large teardrop made from a yellow diamond, surrounded by white diamonds. My mouth drops. It had to have cost a fortune. He fastens it at the back of my neck and kisses my shoulder. "I love it," I whisper.

"You said your favorite color is yellow, so now you have something to remind you of me when I'm gone." He clamps one hand on my hip and the other covering my breasts, rubbing his thumb over my nipple. "Bend forward, angel."

Hell yeah. I love when he takes me from behind. He moves his hand from my breasts around to the back of my shoulder. I grip the edge of the table and bend over it, my breasts rubbing against the polished wood. Placing the head of his dick at my entrance, he thrusts forward until there is no space between us, grunting as he does. "Fuck. You still feel as good as the first time."

He starts to pull out and thrusts back inside, not harsh enough for my liking. I need it hard. I need him to fuck me like he means business. "Callum, fuck me. Hurt me. I want to feel you in my fucking throat."

He growls out, trailing his fingers down my back until it's resting on my free hip. He squeezes them in unison. "Dammit, I love when you talk dirty." He lifts my hips until I'm standing on my tiptoes, giving him better leverage. My head bends backward as he picks up pace, slamming his hard cock into my pussy. I can feel his balls slapping against the bottom of my ass. "It's not going to take me long. Touch yourself."

Placing my palms flat on the table, I lift my upper half giving me some space, before pressing my middle finger to my clit. He knows it doesn't take me long to get myself off, but he wants me to come again. I start to massage in circles, moaning out as I let the feeling overcome me. He continues fucking me harshly, sure to leave a sore spot. His hand returns to my breast, pinching my sensitive nipple.

Since I had them done they are more sensitive compared to what they were before.

My orgasm starts to build. I get faster to match his speed. "Oh fuck. I'm going to come. Harder," I scream.

"That's right, baby. Squeeze that beautiful pussy around my dick. I want to feel you come."

My pussy muscles begin contracting as I fall into orgasm, closing my eyes to enjoy the feeling before it ends. He pinches my nipple harder, knowing it makes my orgasm more intense. "Fuck, that feels good," he groans out, breathless as he stills inside me, relieving himself inside the condom.

Never pulling out of me or removing his hand, he pulls back until my back is flat against his front. "This never gets old. I will do whatever it takes to keep you mine. Remember that."

I turn my head to look at him and he kisses me. He pulls out, leaving me standing here naked so that he can dispose of the condom, taking his clothes with him. As he disappears into the room his phone chimes six times in a row. Maybe it's an emergency. Shit, who else blows someone's phone up like that? That's annoying as hell.

I reach into his jacket pocket and grab it. The screen is already lit up from the notifications. Each message is short, so you can read the message in its entirety without unlocking the phone. My eyes widen.

Kyla: Where are you?

Kyla: You told me you wouldn't go out of town this week.

Kyla: It's our 8-year anniversary, Callum.

Kyla: Your duty as my husband is to at least spend our anniversary with me. I miss you.

Kyla: Fuck, you can take off one damn week. I had something important to tell you.

Kyla: I'm pregnant, Callum. We're having a baby. I love you. Call me.

My hands start to shake. I'm fucking a married man. Oh, God. My hard limit has just been crossed, and it wasn't even by choice. The phone goes off one last time.

Kyla: I'm trying to respect your space. I just really wanted to make tonight special. I'm just hormonal. Please don't be mad.

"What the fuck are you doing with my phone? You know I don't like that shit. I don't go through yours."

My teeth clench together as if I could shatter them any second. I look up at him, now fully dressed, and suddenly he's not the sexy as hell man that makes my life interesting and fun. Right now he's a fucking cheater. There is one thing that I hate more than anything in this world: a cheater. His head has just become a target.

Before thinking, I sling it forward as hard as I can. "What the fuck, Lux?" He darts to the side just in time for his phone to slam against the wall instead of his head.

"You're fucking married? How could you not tell me that? Did you not think that I deserved to know that vital piece of information? Let me get this straight, dumbass. You don't want me to fuck someone else, all while you're at home coming inside of another woman?"

He runs his fingers through his hair as if he's suddenly stressed. "Lux, I can explain. Let me explain." He starts to walk forward and I hold my hand up. I can't even find words right this second.

"My parents pretty much forced me into it in order for my dad to turn the company over to me. Her family is wealthy also, and essential to this company. I've never loved her. In fact I put off marrying her as long as I could. I've never cheated on her...until

63

you. You were there that night and you looked sexy as hell. You had that I don't give a shit personality and you wanted me as much as I wanted you. You made it very clear. I couldn't fucking help myself. I thought it was going to be a one-time thing, but then I wanted more. Shit, I was going to tell you. I hardly even touch her since I met you and I work extra hours so I don't have to go home. I was trying to work out the details of what would happen financially when I left her. I need you to understand. I need you to trust me. I love you, Lux. Dammit. I fucking love you. I didn't plan this, but now here we are. It's already done. Just give me time to leave."

I just found my words.

"You don't hardly touch her my ass. If you are planning to leave someone you don't fucking come inside of her. While your fucking wife was plotting a night on your *anniversary* to tell you she was pregnant with your baby, you're here...fucking *me,* you sorry son of a bitch. I may go after rich men, but I have fucking standards. Married is fucking married, in every state, country, and continent. You made a covenant. I can't even look at you right now. If you were unhappy you should have left *first.*"

"What?" He suddenly looks confused.

"What part of I just found out you're married and expecting a baby was unclear? I feel dirty and disgusting. I fucking suck your dick and let you eat my pussy, in assumption that we are monogamous. I did trust you, but I don't anymore. If I wanted your *wife* all over me, I would go fucking eat her pussy."

"A baby? That's impossible. She's on birth control. I don't want kids. That's been very clear since the beginning."

"You can read your text messages on your way back to New York. Looks like she decided she wanted a baby with or without your consent. Get out of my fucking apartment."

He walks forward and presses his lips to mine before I can stop him. I reared back and slap the shit out of him. He looks at me with sadness in his eyes I've never before seen. "I'll fix this. All of it. When I do I'm coming back for you. You need me for money and I need you. We have mind-blowing sex and great conversation. I'm not giving that up easily. For not telling you, I'm sorry, but you also never asked. It's a mutual fault."

I'm starting to feel more nauseous with every word that escapes his mouth. "I shouldn't have to ask you. You should make it known. Get. The. Fuck. Out."

He turns and walks away. "Oh, Callum. I'm keeping the car. Try to take it and I'll tell her everything, you bastard. It's the least you can do after doing me that dirty. Have a nice life."

He slams the door, leaving me alone in my apartment. I can't do this shit. I can't stay here and think of what I've been doing. I need a fucking drink. Tonight, I need to wash away the last six months, right after I shower and remove him from my body. Fucking married bastard.

CHAPTER FIVE

My apartment door opens and closes, just before I hear footsteps against the hardwood floor. My bitch is here. It's about damn time. "Lux, bring your badass out here!"

I glance at myself in the mirror one last time and comb my hands through the blonde tips of my long, brown hair that stops at the bottom of my breasts. I like to think of myself as eccentric. I'm not the average girl you would consider a trophy, hanging on the arms of the rich and famous. My tastes are very rough around the edges.

I smack my red lips in the mirror and check my teeth to ensure I don't have lipstick smeared. All clear. When I don't hear her shoes anymore I turn around. "Where have you been, bitch?"

"Obviously missing out on some drama. Damn. Is someone

on the prowl tonight? What's with the hooker heels? Don't get me wrong, they're hot and all, but you must be looking for a new man with those heels. You're breaking out the expensive shit."

"Maybe," I say with a smirk. "I think it's time for a change."

She walks over to me and pulls me into a hug. As she pulls back she presses her lips to mine in a sisterly rendition of hello. "Nice try, lovey. Spill. The easy access black dress and siren red stilettos that match your lips don't just come out to randomly have a little fun. That outfit screams vengeance. Your tits are trying to escape. Come on. Tell me. I need an epic Thursday night, not snore bore. Do you know how fucking hard it is to get off Thursday through Saturday night when you work where I do? Whoever said bartending was a fun job was an idiot. Give me the juice."

I've known Delta since elementary school. We were those two little girls on the playground that looked like we lost our puppy on a daily basis. School wasn't an escape from a shitty life for us, it was a constant fucking reminder that we would never have what most little girls had. We didn't play with Barbies and expensive dolls. We were the little girls that ended up with sock dolls handmade by our mothers, because that was all they could afford. Looking around at all the bratty girls that screamed and giggled constantly, we fit together pretty quickly and haven't parted since.

We're both similar, yet very different. Delta has long, thick, silky black hair, she's tiny, but petite, and she has an obsession with tattoos and piercings, hence the lip and nose diamond studs adding a sparkle to her tanned skin. I've never seen a hot, feminine girl partially covered in tattoos, but she is. She has these gorgeous green eyes that deepen when she gets emotional, which is rare like me. Growing up like we did, not much pushes the sadness button anymore.

I, on the other hand, have hair the color of dark chocolate, a little drier in texture, and bleached throughout the bottom half to create a golden blonde in color. The only piercings you'll find on my body are in my ears and my belly button. My eyes are the color of sapphires and my skin is more of a creamy olive instead of baked bronze. I have virgin skin when it comes to ink, at least for now. About the only physical similarity the two of us have are the Barbie tits and long, pull-it-while-you-fuck-me hair.

I walk past her and fall back dramatically on my bed. I look up at the ceiling as I try to get the words out of my mouth without tasting the vomit that is sure to come. "I've been fucking a married man."

Silence.

I stare at the ceiling fan blades making slow circles, waiting for her to say something.

More silence.

My stomach churns at the thought of him sleeping beside her at night and telling her he loved her, then coming here once a week and fucking me like a sexually starved man. I may be a lot of things, but a whore isn't one of them, at least not in my eyes. That would be my mother. I'm at least picky with who I spread my legs for, and monogamy is a biggie. From the time his dick enters my pussy I will be the only pussy. That's my one hard rule. I'll be as kinky as he wants, but that's my only rule. Obviously, I got sloppy with this one's good looks. I do not tolerate cheaters under any circumstance.

I prop myself up on my elbows to look at her. She is staring straight ahead. "Did you know?"

I grab my pillow and throw it at her. She catches it. "Are you fucking serious? What the fuck, Delta? Do you really have to ask?

Of course I didn't know."

"You are referring to Callum, right? The guy that bought you the car? The only time I've met him he seemed crazy about you, at least in that weird possessive way. Seriously? I didn't see that one coming."

"Men are pigs. That's not even half of it. She's fucking pregnant, Delta. Apparently we found out at the same time. Surprise! He's going to be a dad." I try to laugh it off, but it just makes my stomach flip worse. "I feel like I'm going to Hell."

"If you didn't know then it isn't your fault. How could you? He isn't even from here. Damn rich city men. Southern men are better."

"Um, Delta.... Technically we are city girls now. We live in Atlanta. I would hardly call this the country."

"Whatev. Southern and country are not the same thing. It's still different; like two different worlds different. It was the accent, wasn't it? Attracts them like flies to shit every time. Sometimes I think being a hot female with a southern accent is a curse. Ya know?"

I laugh. She's a damn nutcase.

"I actually thought I liked dating someone long distance, because when he left I didn't have to deal with him bugging me. I could do my own thing. I still feel like I should've seen the signs. I'm never stupid when it comes to a guy. I can smell bullshit from a mile away."

"You know what? Fuck him. There's this new tattoo shop I've wanted to check out for a while. I think it's time to pop your ink cherry. Do it for me? It is my birthday. Then, we can go drink the pain away and crash out as the sun is rising." I shake my head as she wriggles her eyebrows.

I smile. "I guess I do owe you a birthday present. You still haven't gotten the nerve to show your portfolio, have you?"

"I'll do it...one day. It's not that easy for a girl to bust through the doors of a man's world. We can't all be Kat Von D."

"Delta, you could totally be Kat Von D. The girl is like your tattoo idol. You can draw better than anyone I've ever seen and ink has a deeper meaning to you than most. It's art to you. Just take a risk, okay?"

"I'll think about it. Oh, by the way, I've decided to gauge my ears. What do you think?"

"Eh, how big? You know that's not really my style."

"Not big. Just enough to look like a miniature cork maybe. Haven't really decided on size yet."

"Well if anyone can pull it off it's you. How can I just walk in and get a tattoo without an appointment? I refuse to get something off the wall if I'm going to do this."

"You decide what you want and leave the rest to me."

She turns and walks away, leaving me in silence. I stand from my bed and follow her. "Am I overdressed for where you want to go? You're cute and casual, and I'm going for the sexy but slutty look." She's wearing denim cutoffs, an off the shoulder, torn tee shirt showing your midriff, sneakers, and a flat bill cap with graffiti on the front. We couldn't be any more opposite ends of the spectrum if we were summer and winter.

"You look sexy and you are dressed appropriately. I think after your *situation* you need to dress like that. The fastest way to forget is to find a new toy. The place we are going has no judgments in the clothing category. It has a love for all." She winks as if I haven't been to every place in Atlanta.

I grab my clutch off the bar as she reaches for the doorknob. "Are you ready?"

"Lead the way."

I follow Delta through the glass door labeled with vinyl lettering: Inked aKross the skin. That's a strange name for a tattoo shop. "Is this going to hurt?"

"Yes," she answers, almost nervous. Why is she nervous? I mean sure, the place is big enough and it looks like it has more of a corporate feel to it instead of a random hole in the wall tattoo shop, but it's still just a tattoo shop. She's done this several times.

"Hi. Welcome to *Inked aKross the skin.* Are you going to be tattooing today or are you just here for a consultation?"

My line of vision follows the squeaky voice sitting in front of a brick wall, behind the counter in the center of the room. The brick is supporting a neon sign made into the name of the shop. The room sways my attention. I look around in awe. Nice. The whole room is like an art gallery for tattoos, showing off large poster sized one-of-a-kind pieces. It looks professional, but dark. There is no white to be found. The entire place is done in navy and brick, accented with neon pink signs in different variations. "I'm taking it the owner likes neon," I mumble to myself.

"I have two appointments with Kross Brannon."

Delta's voice brings me back to the girl in the middle of the room that doesn't fit what I would think should be behind the counter of a tattoo shop. I'm not normally one to judge, but she's wearing a navy polo with the business logo in bright pink over the left breast. Her hair is long, but she has it pulled back in a low ponytail. It's more professional instead of grungy. I think Kat Von D would walk in here, turn around, and walk out, probably cursing that this is a disgrace to the tattoo industry. She doesn't even look like she has tattoos. Isn't it kind of a requirement to advertise for the type of business that you are in? Who would want a tattoo if the staff doesn't even have them?

The girl stands and holds out her hand. I stare at it. Really? A hand shake? Delta returns the gesture. "My name is Cassie. It looks like you're a little early. Mr. Brannon is finishing up his seven o'clock appointment now." She lays down two clipboards, each attached with a form on the counter, followed by a pen. "Delta, I know you filled out the paperwork ahead of time, but we need both signatures and a copy of each driver's license to keep on file. If you'll do that for me while I lock the door, then I'll lead you both to the studio when finished. You both are his last appointments for the evening."

I remove my license and lay it flat on the counter, biting my tongue to try and remain serious as I pick up the pen to sign my ink-less skin away. "What would you have done had I said no, you sneaky ass?"

She quickly signs and whispers as she digs her driver's license out of her wrist wallet. "I would have begged you shamelessly, drug you by the hair, and then strapped you to that tattoo chair. You wait forever to get an appointment with this guy. I've had our names on the list since he opened here. He has shops all over the continental US. How we got so lucky I have no idea."

Delta never begs for anything. Noting that comment for future reference. Cassie takes our licenses and disappears into a door, what I imagine is an office, returning with a sheet of copy paper and our licenses after a few short moments. She gathers up our forms and attaches them neatly, filing them away in a drawer. "Okay. I think we're ready. Follow me."

She opens the door that resides on the same brick wall the counter sits in front of, but off to the side. The building is not huge in diameter, but it's tall. You can see that just from the outside. As the door opens a staircase is revealed. We climb them one by one until we reach the top. The walls of the top floor are painted navy just like you see downstairs, again decorated with miraculous works of framed tattoo art being spotlighted from the small lights above each one, gallery style. The floor is stained concrete, also dark in color. Stations line each of the walls, each consisting of a black, leather chair that reclines, a mirror framed in black hanging above a narrow counter with drawers and cabinets, and a neon sign above each station mirror reading the name of the artist that occupies the station. The entire room is dim, except for the hanging, black, adjustable spotlights above each chair reminding me of a surgical table.

I'd love to know how much this dude spends on fucking neon.

The buzzing of the tattoo gun stops, catching my attention. All stations are empty except the last. "Is this my eight o'clock," the deep voice asks without looking up from the area of skin he's wiping.

"Yes. The girls are ready when you are. Where do you want them?"

"Put one at Wesson's table and the other at Remington's."

His voice sounds sexy, controlling, and domineering, but I have yet to look at his face. Maybe that has something to do with me staring like an idiot into the smoldering blue-gray eyes of the one getting the tattoo. Fucking hell is he one hot piece of man-candy, completely appetizing to my lady bits. He looks a little rough around the edges with his shaved head and five o'clock shadow, both dark in color.

I allow my eyes to savor his body in its entirety, completely unashamed. Hey, there is nothing wrong with enjoying a beautiful view that is already on display. His top half is completely bare, and nothing less than chiseled muscles of perfection. He is lying on the reclined chair flat on his stomach, his arms crossed and propping his head up by his chin to allow space for breathing. The buzzing of the tattoo gun starts again as if we aren't interrupting anything at all.

My eyes stop on that marvelous fucking ass, the beginning of the climb that makes up the beautiful shape peeking out of the waistband of his jeans as if he needs a belt.

My mouth is dry.

It's getting hot in here.

I swallow, visions of that body rubbing against mine haunting my thoughts.

"You want a closer look?"

That's a different voice than the first one. I finally get knocked back into the damn present.

Shit. His voice is just as tempting as his looks.

I start blinking at a rapid rate. "Excuse me?"

My eyes quickly divert back to his face. He has a cocky grin spread across the bottom half. His mouth. Fuck, his mouth. I just want to run my fingertips over his full lips, right before nibbling on them with mine.

I cross my legs at my feet, trying to be subtle, and suddenly feeling slightly uncomfortable between my legs. What the hell? He's not even my type. He's a little too jagged for me, seeming slightly jaded, and cocky...definitely cocky. I would classify him as a bad-boy all the way. He probably is in a band or something, maybe even a bartender like Delta, the furthest from my type you can get.

My eyes connect with his...again, just before his line of vision goes directly to my crossed ankles and back. Fuck subtle I guess. Oh well. The beauty to being a strong woman is owning your sensuality. So I'm attracted to him, no big deal. A woman can be attracted to a lot of men. It doesn't mean I'm going to act on it.

"The tattoo. Do you want a closer look?"

I wave him off, metaphorically speaking. "Nah. That's okay. I don't want to be in the way."

"Come here."

I glance at Delta, but she's watching the artist like a hawk, biting her bottom lip as if she's mentally fucking him. I know this, because I've known her since we were kids.

"You won't bother him. He could tattoo in the middle of a fucking hurricane and still come out with a perfect piece."

The voice of the mysterious man I would love nothing more than to see between my legs pulls my attention back to the activity at hand. Did I just think that? I need alcohol...lots and lots of alcohol.

The artist retorts to his comment with a dry laugh. Without instructing them to, my feet start to move toward them. I grab Delta's arm along the way, pulling her with me. I'm not standing next to something that fine without a wingman, or woman in our case.

I stop in front of him and look over his head. The tattoo artist is finishing up the shading of the tattoo that runs from the flat area between his shoulder blades down to the bottom of his back, his very defined back. There is no way he's done all of that in one session, and I'm guessing what they have done today started hours ago. I'm not real sure what it is. It's dark. I know that. At first glance it looks like a grim reaper, but instead of a skeletal body under the cloak it's human flesh, perfectly sculpted to resemble a fit man, everywhere except the hands. You can only see the outline of the face peeking out of the hood, because he's looking down at the claw-like skeletal hands covered in blood, forming a shape like they're holding an invisible ball. It's huge, covering most of his back.

"Damn. That must hurt. Strangely, I like it. It's different." I say nothing more, because Delta taught me long ago that you never ask what someone's tattoo means. It's the outward proof of someone's most intimate thoughts, a way to bare their soul a little at a time. If they want you to know, then you will know the exact moment to bring it up or they will tell you before you have to.

My leg starts to give, offsetting my balance, probably from locking both knees in these heels. Without even thinking my hands grab the top of his shoulders to steady myself. The instant heating of my body as it transfers from his to my hands cause me to quickly release him. "Sorry, I didn't mean to."

"What's your name?"

I look down at his head in the same position it's been in. "Lux. And yours?"

"Kaston."

"Oh. Okay. It's nice to me-"

"Lux."

"Yes?"

"I'm not complaining of this view, but if you don't get your pussy away from my face I will not be held responsible for my actions when I get up from this chair. I may be in physical pain, but I'm still a man. At some point the brain stops working and the dick takes over. Consider yourself warned."

I immediately back up, unsure of what to say, and surprised I didn't bust my ass in my attempt to step back. Oh. My. Hell. I look around. Cassie is nowhere to be found and Delta is pursing her lips as if she's trying not to laugh at me. I narrow my eyes at her. *Bitch, I will cut you.*

For the first time since we arrived I notice the artist's face as he looks up and starts cleaning the finished tattoo with what looks like soapy water on a paper towel. The beginning of a smirk takes place in the corner of his mouth. How did we end up in the den of hot guys? "It's true though. I have to agree with him, especially after getting a look at you two. I'm Kross." He circles his black latex-covered index finger in the air. "Owner and artist. I'm almost done with my boy and you're up. Who's going first?"

"Actually, Kross, I have a little spare time. I can do Lux while you do..."

He pauses.

"Delta," she fills in.

"Delta," he repeats, finishing his sentence. "It'll give you a quicker break after the hours spent on my session. It's the least I can do."

My mouth drops. No fucking way.

Kross looks into the mirror across the room as he starts rubbing ointment over the tattoo before covering it, assuming so he can see Kaston's face. "You sure, man? It's been a while, hasn't it?"

He looks at me heatedly. I suddenly feel very naked. "I'm sure."

I look between the two of them. Shouldn't I have a say so in this matter? I am the client. Before he looks away I catch Kross scanning down Delta's body. I almost missed it had I not been looking. "Yeah, okay, if it's okay with Lux I'm down. I'd like to see your work again. I know it's good. How long has it been? Shit, college?"

"Something like that," Kaston says.

"Are you guys sure?" I look at Delta. "I kind of wanted Delta to draw it out, so I was going to let her go first. I don't really know what I want. She's the one that wants to tattoo, so I was going to let her design it for me."

Her mouth is gaping and her eyes are as big as saucers. She's pissed. One thing about Delta is that she doesn't like to be called out when she isn't ready for something, but she will never brag on herself. She's been talking about tattooing since we graduated high school. I love her, but I'm sick of hearing that she's going to and it's time for her to actually do it.

"No shit," Kross says. "Do you have a portfolio with you?"

She starts to shake her head, but I interrupt. "She's wearing it."

"Lux, shut up. I'm sure he's busy and ready to leave. Let's just get started. I'm here to get a tattoo not bore him."

Kaston stands as Kross finishes covering his tattoo and goes for his shirt, but I continue looking at Delta. I hear the spritzing of a spray bottle and look over to him wiping down the chair that Kaston was just lying on. Placing the sprayer and towel aside, he disposes of the gloves and grabs her hand, pulling her toward him. Her cheeks are starting to change color. It dawns on me.

Fucking shit, she thinks he's hot. It all makes sense now. How did I not catch this?

"Sit."

She does as he says. "I'm going to look at them."

He starts with her sleeve in progress, rubbing his hands over each one as if he's touching a sculpture. "Some of the ones I drew forever ago probably aren't that great. I'm an amateur," she says with a slight stutter in her speech. He intimidates her. That never happens.

He moves to her thigh, brushing his fingertips over the vivid colors. "Lay back." As she does he raises her shirt, looking at the art further up on her ribs, halfway hidden by her shirt. His fingers trace the lines almost as if he's worshipping them. I've never seen someone study ink that way. He never looks at her face until he's done. "Where do you work, Delta? Have you ever tattooed someone's skin before?"

Are we even still in the room? I feel like we're intruding on a business meeting. She shakes her head. "I bartend a few blocks away."

"You really want to tattoo? Do you want mediocre or do you want to learn from the best?"

She sits idle. Staring. No words are exiting her mouth. I'm not even sure if oxygen is.

"It's my only dream," is all she says. "Go big or go home is the way I live. I'm not going to change it now."

Their eyes are burning into each other's. "Well I guess you stumbled in my shop at the right time, Delta. You see this station right here?"

He points to the one next to his. She nods.

"It just so happens that it's vacant. It's missing a sign above the mirror. Be here tomorrow at noon for an interview and a test. If you pass it's yours, and I will teach you everything I know. That opportunity will never come around again. Ninety-nine percent of the time my new hire artists have years of experience when they even come and apply for a job. My shop is the best, and so are my artists. This is a once in a lifetime chance. You in or out?"

She looks at me. I can tell she's trembling inside. I slightly nod to nudge her, before she returns her attention to him. "I'll be here. Thank you, Kross."

As if a switch just flipped he doesn't acknowledge her response.

"Let's tattoo."

Weird.

The air shifts around me. The hairs on the back of my neck stand up. That's when I feel it...him. "You know, I'm pretty good at reading people," he whispers into my ear, making my eyes close upon the contact between his warm breath and my ear. "I want to take your tattoo virginity. Trust me with your body."

My internal walls are quaking from his voice alone more than any other male before. I just met him. I don't understand it, but tonight...I'm going to let it ride. "What makes you think I don't have any tattoos already?"

He places his hands on my hips and rotates us in a one hundred and eighty degree turn, until we're both looking in the mirror at each other. "Like I said, I'm good at reading people. No one has secrets, Lux. All you have to do is read between the lines."

He slides both hands down my dress, stopping at the bottom hem at my thighs. Grabbing the fabric, he starts pulling it up my legs. "What are you doing?" I whisper the question. Am I really letting a guy I met two seconds ago do this?

He continues.

I don't stop him.

I guess I am.

"Digging deeper. Respecting your body. Adding to its beauty. Every tattoo should tell a story of the person inside. Each is open to interpretation to the viewer. No one has to know the real meaning if you don't want them to."

My lips part, but nothing comes out. No words. No air. Nothing. I just stand here and watch him pull my dress up my body until it's at my breasts, leaving only the necessities covered. He tucks the fabric underneath the wiring of my bra. "The perfect canvas...is a clean one. Let me paint my interpretation of the girl that lies inside. Trust me with your body," he repeats again.

"Okay."

One word. Trust. That one word holds more meaning for me than most people. It's also one part of myself that I never give anyone. The fact that I agreed to give it to this stranger is mind-boggling.

He steps forward, inching me toward the chair, before stepping around me and straddling it. The sound of the voices and the buzzing of the tattoo gun behind us takes away my thoughts reminding me that I'm nearly naked in a tattoo shop. Kaston pats the seat in front of him as he turns and starts digging in the cabinet, pulling out ink colors and all the necessities I suppose you need for tattooing. I wouldn't really know since I'm a newbie.

Thank God I wore underwear...

I grab the back of the chair for leverage and step over the bottom seat until I'm straddling it in the opposite direction of him, trying to keep my distance by scooting as close to the back of the chair as possible while closing my knees together. He pulls a rolling tray toward the side of him with a bunch of things piled on top and turns to look at me. One look and that fucking cocky grin is back. I follow his line of vision and realize my hands are crossed over my lap, trying to hide my underwear. When did I become modest?

He stands and leans toward me, bringing his face just in front of mine. My breathing becomes rampant, unsure of what he's about to do. He grabs the side of the chair in each hand. "I need you on your back," he says and reclines the chair until it's in a lying position, just as he was earlier.

"Where are you putting it," I ask.

Returning to a sitting position he grips my thighs and pulls me toward him, the middle of our legs meeting awkwardly. He runs his hands down my legs until they are cupping my calves, pulling my legs to rest on top of his thighs so that we are closer. I shiver slightly. "On your right side. Are you cold?"

"No," I respond quickly. "I'm just a little ticklish." I lie.

"Good, because this is going to take a while. I need you to turn to your left a little to give me a better angle." I do as he says, placing my left hand behind my head and my right clenching the edge of the chair to hold still. "Is that comfortable enough?"

I nod, trying my best to avoid his face by looking in the direction that he instructed me to turn. The fact is it's really hard to stare at a hot guy while I'm half naked and my pussy is lightly brushing against his dick every time I move. His hardened dick might I add. He doesn't even seem fazed by the fact that the only things separating this from being a very hot sexual situation is my thong and his jeans.

I take a deep breath to prepare myself for the pain. I can feel him watching me as the sound of latex conforming to his hands sounds in my ears. I can see him out of the corner of my eye. *Do not look. Do not look. Concentrate on anything but his dick between your legs. Easy peasy. You're a man-eater. You got this.*

His latex-covered hands grips onto my side and thigh, pulling me against his erection that is straining through his jeans. "I need you closer."

"Oh God," I whisper, unable to contain myself. It's in the perfect position to press into the center line of my folds, exerting a small amount of pressure on my clit. I should have worn granny panties. Why did I wear a fucking lace thong?

He starts wiping my skin down with a wet paper towel, cleaning the area I guess. "You okay? I haven't even gotten to the good part yet." I can hear the teasing in his voice. It pisses me off. I don't like being in this position, out of control of my hormones and emotions. It's not normal for me. My teeth clench together.

"I'm good. We can tattoo anytime you get ready. I have places still to be, celebrating, and lots of fucking alcohol."

"Celebrating, huh," his deep voice asks as he starts to draw lines on my side, leaving wet streaks behind from the marker. "What are we celebrating? I might be looking into some celebrating of my own."

The tickling of the fast-paced lines darting in various directions is making my abs tighten. I can't even guess what he could be drawing with how fast he's doing it, changing location every few seconds. I might as well make normal conversation to veer away from the thoughts of this extremely uncomfortable situation I've gotten myself into. "Delta and I going out for her birthday. It's kind of a tradition we have. We always spend our birthdays together. Just the two of us."

"Where is this special celebration taking place?"

He almost has a mocking tone in his voice. It rubs me the wrong way. Maybe I've given him the wrong impression. I'm not a child. He can't be that much older than me. "Wherever the fuck we end up. I'm hoping I wake up surprised," I say sarcastically.

"Surprises aren't always good."

The crinkling sounds of paper cause me to rise up on my elbows to see what he's doing. Opening a new needle before loading the gun. I didn't even realize he had stopped drawing already. That had to be a record time. "Says the guy giving me a super secret spectacular surprise of a tattoo? It's also a surprise to find that men actually tattoo while the client is in the artist's lap, half naked, and sizing up the artist's gun. An artist that doesn't technically work at this shop, might I add. Saying that would kind of go against the grain of this situation...don't ya think?"

He smiles as I wink dramatically, further making my point. "You didn't strike me as a girl who meets many strangers. I didn't think it would be an issue. Maybe I was in the mood to tattoo. You caught me at a good time," he says as he returns my previous gesture.

Sexy, smart-ass bastard.

I wriggle my ass, feigning discomfort, pressing myself further into him. Two can play at this game. The bad part is it feels fucking marvelous. I feel like such a whore right now, it only being a few hours outside of the last occurrence in which I spread my legs for a man, a different man. Oh, what the hell. I've been judged for less. We only live once, right?

The side of his mouth turns up in the corner. He looks down at our connected bodies as he turns the tattoo gun on, letting the buzz sound through the room, mixing with the one that's been going pretty much this whole time. Why do I get the feeling he has somehow defeated me before the game even started?

"Pain and pleasure never looked so good."

Before I can even process what that means, the outside of his right fist connects with my skin, the needle puncturing rapidly in a repeated motion as he starts on the outline. Caught off guard, I bite the inside of my cheek from the sudden jolt of pain. "Ouch, fuck that hurt. Aren't you supposed to warn me first?"

My eyes squint as I try to get used to the pain. The only thing I can think to compare it to is something sharp scraping along my skin, hard. "Didn't anyone ever tell you it's worse when you're expecting it?"

I grab ahold of his thighs, trying to find something to take the edge off. Every few seconds he stops and wipes the area with a paper towel, then starts back again. Each time the needle starts back, the initial shock hurts worse than if he were to just keep going without ever stopping.

I breathe through the pain, trying to keep my bursts of air short to avoid expanding my ribcage. Maybe talking will help. "Now I know why people do this shit drunk. Obviously they are the smart ones."

"Alcohol thins the blood. Sober is the only way you legally tattoo. If it helps, this is the worst place to get a tattoo. If you make it through this one you can get one anywhere."

"You're giving me my first tattoo in the spot that is the most painful! That figures. I should have seen it coming. Of course that would be something a man would do."

"Pleasure feels better with a little bit of pain, beautiful."

"That's the second time you have referenced the two together, yet all I feel is pain. Am I missing something?"

Without looking up from what he's doing, he thrusts his hips forward, pressing the bulge in the front of his jeans further into my folds, exerting more pressure on my clit. I moan out accidentally as the roughness of the denim brushes over it, before slapping my hand over my mouth. The adrenaline caused from the needle quickly spikes the blood flow to my genitals, making every feeling come into focus.

Without moving his upper body, he rolls his hips upward in a subtle motion, grinding the length of his hard cock in a perfect rhythm over my clit, without it even being out of his jeans. My breathing becomes wild. My manicured nails dig into his legs. I look at him, but he continues tattooing as if he's not about to make me come on a fucking tattoo chair with my best friend and a stranger in the same room.

With each bite of pain from the needle, the pleasure following is more intense. Fuck, does this even still get girls off? I feel like I'm back in junior high, dry humping during a game of seven minutes in heaven. I bite my tongue to try and remain quiet, but right now I want to scream, and I've never been a fucking vocalist in sex or hookups. It sounds too fake to me.

His denim-covered dick continues to rub against my clit just right. The way he rolls his hips like that and without hardly any effort or concentration, you would swear he was a dancer. My muscles between my legs start to contract as my body readies for orgasm. I think I just answered my own question. I want to close my legs to stop it, to save me from the embarrassment, but then I don't. His body is blocking me anyway, and he has the advantage with the needle in his hand, permanently etching my skin right now. My eyes close on instinct.

Please don't come. Please don't come. I'm about to fucking come.

As if he knows the moment I'm about to, he disconnects the needle from my skin and rams his hips forward, starting that burst of pleasure that quickly begins to consume my body, intensifying as I ride it out, before fading out again, ending as quickly as it started.

My eyes lock on him, burning into him. He slides back enough to look at the crotch of his jeans, an unreadable expression on his face. I follow his line of vision to the wet spot on the front. My eyes widen. No fucking way did I just do that. That has to be him. Did he come in his pants? "Did you?"

His eyes meet mine. That's when his lips start to spread outward, pulling up into the slightest grin, almost unnoticeable. "That's all you, baby. It's going to take more than that to make me come."

"That sounds like a challenge."

What the fuck? What am I saying?

He bites the corner of his bottom lip, still staring at me as if he's trying to refrain from tossing the tattoo gun and fucking me right here in this chair.

Do it. Please.

What? Shut the fuck up, Lux.

Fuck, now I'm having a silent conversation with myself.

As his eyes skim down my barely covered body, the tip of his tongue glides along the edges of his top teeth. "If you ever see me again after tonight it'll be far more than a challenge, but since we don't mix with the same crowd I doubt that'll ever happen, gorgeous."

Why does that thought bum me out?

Just like that he goes back to tattooing, as if this is all completely normal. I drape my right arm over my eyes to black everything out. This session suddenly got extremely awkward. I'm such a tramp right now, and I love it. Holy shit. I've never come like that. I'm on such a high right now the needle doesn't even faze me anymore. The silence between us is deafening, but then he speaks again. "For the best chemical reaction it's all about balance. Two things you would never imagine to be are usually the most complimentary."

I like that. Who is this guy? Where the fuck did he come from? Whoever he is, he just invaded my life like an army at full speed in a surprise attack. I wasn't prepared for him, but no one will ever fucking top that first tattoo. Un-fucking-forgettable.

CHAPTER SIX

She triggers something unfamiliar. *Lux*. It rolls through my mind with ease. I have a feeling she has many layers. She spikes a curiosity I've never had with a female, a need to learn...about her. I could. I could find out everything I want to know with no effort at all. It's who I am. I've already decided I want her body. I had to have a taste. She was responding to me in a way I've never seen. There was a shift in the air. I wanted one glance at how she looked as I pleasured her. She certainly didn't disappoint. The problem I'm finding now is that I want more.

I could take her right here in this chair or I could take her to the back. She already invited me in. *A challenge.* If she could make me come, she could have anything she wanted at her fingertips. Many have tried and failed. She's given me permission to take more of her body for myself. That was her first mistake. No one should ever invite me in. I'm going to decline, for now at least...but I can't guarantee my decision won't change, because right now that constant itch only scratched with two things is silent. Interesting.

I've been back for a week now. It just felt right to stay in Spain for a while. There were things I needed to learn, to take care of. There were lots of things to get in order. The man I was died when I showed up and was faced with my new reality. That Monday I called headquarters and told them I had an emergency leave and I wouldn't be returning; then disappeared like a ghost. No one has seen me since...until now. Dad and I have known Kross for several years now. It was time I returned, and he was the first stop I made since he'll be dealing with me now, for certain...*needs*.

I'm now alone, just like I was twenty years ago. Jose has taught me everything I didn't already know. He will head up the PI firm there and I will expand here, just as Dad and I discussed before the universe decided to alter the plans. It just looks like I'll be traveling between the two more frequently than I anticipated.

The weird fucking thing was that Dad already had everything laid out for the moment he took his last breath, as if he knew it was coming. It was a matter of entrusting the right person to give me what I needed when the time came, and doing the paperwork. Seeing him, reading his words, and hearing his voice on that video when I couldn't face him like a man was the hardest thing I've ever had to do, but I understand now his need to rid the world of monsters, one at a time. I owe him everything. He started something. He wanted to try to right every wrong, and he busted his ass trying until he made one deadly mistake. The only way he'll live on is if I continue what he started, so that's exactly what I'll do. I've learned when to take and when to pass. It's all about reading the soul.

I wipe that last spot of excess ink before shutting off the gun and setting it down on the tray beside me. A couple of hours and it's finished. Her beautiful body has been inked for the first time and I was the one to do it. Taking a clean paper towel I wet it and rub it over the freshly inked skin, clearing the ink smudges. I look up at her for the first time since I had to look away. If I didn't I would have touched her, really touched her. "You ready to see it? Then I'll bandage it and you can be on your way. It looks like Kross and Delta have already finished. They must be outside."

Moving her legs off my thighs, I stand and step over the chair, holding out my hand for hers. She looks at me, clearly debating, when she pulls her bottom lip between her teeth and takes it. Tempting. I must refrain. "I might as well. My curiosity is getting the best of me."

She throws her leg over the chair and stands, facing me. I look at her new artwork. It fits her. I walk around her so that she can see in the mirror, positioning myself behind her. I want to see her reaction. She stares at me in the mirror. "Look."

Her eyes veer down, widening a little as she takes it in. "It's beautiful, but what does it mean to you? You said it was going to be your interpretation of me."

"It is. Like I said I'm pretty good at reading people, but the thing about an *interpretation* is that it can vary between viewers. There is no right or wrong answer. First I chose a Lotus flower blossoming in its natural state. They are known for their ability to grow in muddy water. Most plants wouldn't survive in that environment, but the Lotus blossoms above the murk, opening into a beautiful bloom that is admired by many. Our kind are all born into less than ideal places, places that some wouldn't survive in, but to reach for something better is an admirable trait. I left it in half bloom, because I get the vibe that you haven't reached your full potential of self-growth yet."

She looks up at me. "Why red?"

"I chose red, because even though you come off as a smartass unfazed by anyone, I think you're hiding a compassion that you don't want anyone to see out of fear."

She swallows. "And the sinking anchor?"

Our eyes locked together, I brush my fingertips along her midsection, tracing my index finger along the anchor that is wrapped around the stem of the flower, trying to pull it down. Her skin jumps as I touch the sensitive skin. "An anchor is a symbol of strength. There will always be things in life that try to pull us down, but we also define our own strength. You are as strong as you want to be. Never let anything pull you back to the place you started. Keep rising above the mud."

Her mouth parts, falling slightly. I've struck a nerve. I can read it all over her face. In an instant her expression clears and she clears her throat. "That's an interesting take on myself I've never heard. Thanks for that tattoo. You're really talented. I really need to be going."

I grab the ointment and start rubbing it over the tattoo, before covering it and shedding the latex gloves, tossing them on the tray. Opening the drawer, I dig around until I find what I'm looking for, pulling it out, and giving her a sample packet of ointment. "Here. Rub this on it until it's gone and then use lotion. Don't scrub in the shower. The key is to avoid it drying out. You want to keep as much ink as possible."

She takes it and starts grabbing for her dress underneath the under-wiring of her bra. I grab her hand. "Let me."

"Who are you, Kaston?"

I grab the fabric, pulling it out from under her bra, and then start unrolling it down her body, slowly and meticulously, wanting to remember how she looks right now. It'll make a good addition to the spank bank at the very least.

"Someone you don't want to know," I say as I release the bottom hem of her dress at her thighs. "Someone cut me at the roots before I got the chance to reach the surface. I'm lost in the murk, Lux. The tattoo is on me."

She kisses the side of my mouth, mumbling against my skin. "What if I do?"

My eyes briefly close at the softness of her full lips. "You have no fucking idea what you're saying. You don't even know me."

"Just like you don't know me…"

Something snaps. Fisting my hands in her hair, I roughly kiss her, pulling and kneading at her fucking lip with my own as I walk her backward until she's standing against the wall. She kisses back just as harsh, placing her hands on my hips. Her taste has me in frenzy, barely able to think. My cock wants her, wants to feel her. Grabbing the back of her thigh, I pull it up and wrap it around my waist, before pressing my pelvis into the spread of her legs. It's not enough.

The back of her head falls against the dark wall, separating our lips and elongating her neck. Her jugular vein is protruding, making me crazier. I swipe my tongue down the vertical line that is blue in color. It's pulsing from the rapid beat of her heart, making blood flow faster. "Damn. I want to fuck you so bad right now."

She moans. "Do it. I want you to. Then, I'll walk away and you'll never see me again. We both get something we want, we both leave satisfied, and we both win."

I growl. It's sexy as hell that she knows what she wants and isn't scared to verbalize it. My hand creeps up her leg, going for the center. My fingers find the edge of her panties, inching underneath them, and pushing them to the side. I can already feel the heat between her legs, confirming what she's already voiced she wants. My core tightens as I come in contact with her bare skin. Every feeling becomes my focus, heightening my senses.

Wet.

Hot.

Smooth.

Fucking her becomes my only thought, my primary instinct.

The pace of her breathing and controlling it becomes a necessity.

Making her orgasm and watching as she comes becomes my single-most want.

Marking her becomes my need.

My middle finger slips inside until I can feel the lips of her pussy on my knuckles. She's tighter than I anticipated. I pull out, then shove two back inside: my middle and ring finger. "Fuck," she whispers. "That feels so good."

As I pull out, I swipe the pad of my thumb up the center line, rubbing it over her clit, before coming back down as I thrust back inside. "You like that?"

"Yes."

"You want more?"

"Please."

I reach down to unbutton my pants when a reminder of what I have to do tonight occurs to me at the worst fucking time, reminding me that I'm not what she needs. My dick is most likely going to go on strike later, but I can't do this. Her soul is pure. It's strong. Souls are loud if you learn to listen. Hers is just shaded in places. Those lost in darkness are banned from taking of the light. It's one rule my conscience doesn't question.

I remove my fingers and reposition her panties into place. "Maybe some other time. Kross will be back up here any minute now. We have some things to discuss."

She drops her leg and adjusts her clothes, both of us silent. I push off the wall, giving her room to walk around me. She does, trailing her hand over my stomach as she does. "Have a good night, Kaston. Thanks for...earlier."

Her heels tap against the floor as she walks away. They stop. "Oh, and Kaston..."

"Yeah," I say to the wall, not bothering to look in her direction.

"Where I'm from, we swim in creeks and drive through mud. Some people prefer murky over crystal clear oceans. Something like that is just a personal preference."

Her heels start up again, not stopping until the door downstairs closes. My teeth clench together. I pull my arm back, preparing to swing my fist into the wall, but control the movement to only tap the sheetrock instead of slamming into it. My heart is pounding, I'm starting to sweat, and the itch is back. It's time for a monster's medicine. "You ready to see your shipment?"

I turn to Kross standing in the center of the room. Like me, the motherfucker is quiet. We have to be. "Yeah. I have places to be."

Looks like tonight is going to be messier...

CHAPTER SEVEN

"Lux, this is supposed to be my birthday shindig. Why are you pouting? What the hell happened in that tattoo chair?"

I grab ahold of the drink straw and twirl it around the interior of the glass, stirring my fruity concoction, barely hearing what Delta is saying on the stool beside me. *Our kind,* he said. Intriguing.

I've been sitting at this bar barely touching my drink since we got here an hour ago. My mind is consumed by him - the sexy stranger that obviously thrives on mystery. I can still feel him in the places he touched me. It's almost a cold tingle or burn, sort of like menthol.

I close my eyes and go back to being against that wall, pretending that he never stopped. Instead, he removes my clothes completely, picking up right where he left off.

"Hello! Earth to Lux."

I immediately open my eyes to Delta waving her hand in front of my face. What the fuck am I doing? I'm sitting here daydreaming about a sexy guy that I met a few short hours ago. What the hell has gotten into me? He's not even the type I need to be dreaming about. I have a checklist for a reason. It's imperative that I stick to it. Sexy bad-boys with alpha demeanors aren't on that list. They are considered bad for a reason. They are trouble makers. They are addictive. Easy on the eyes, fun in the sack, but hard on the heart. I'm not here to become the next knocked up girl in a trailer park working two jobs, one being in the closest diner. I have dreams, goals, and wants. I will stop at nothing to get them.

"Sorry, I was distracted by my thoughts. It was nothing. Just a way to let go of the shit that happened earlier today."

"Is that what you're calling it these days," she asks in a half laugh. "I'm going to say it's safe to assume you didn't have any problems in that department by that sex god of a man. Good lord he was hot."

"Says the one that was drooling over the sinfully sexy tattoo artist. Your ass better show up tomorrow for that interview or I will personally kill you and then bring you back to haunt your dreams and make your life miserable."

Her eyes widen. "I was not drooling. He may be hot, but he's a control freak. I can tell. I'm not into him." Her voice breaks, as the word *not* comes out of her mouth.

I take a sip of my drink as I look at her over the rim.

It's weak. No one makes drinks like Delta. Most bars are overcharged and under mixed in ratio; too much juice and not enough of the good stuff.

"Save your lies for someone that doesn't know you very intimately, as in better than anyone. You forget we have shared everything at one time or another. I know you better than you know yourself."

Her nose bunches and she bites her bottom lip. "That was back in high school. Everyone does wild things on their senior trip. I didn't work for two years saving to go to Cancun to act like a nun when I got there. We were drunk and sharing a room. Shit happens. If I recall it was you or Brody in my drunken horny state. Brody is sexy, but he can't kiss worth a shit. He had lizard tongue and fingered like he was stabbing someone. It was not sexy."

I throw my hand over my mouth to keep from spewing a mouthful of Amaretto, cranberry, and Crown. In my quick attempt to swallow before the fit of laughter exited, I forgot to do it properly and the liquid drink went down my windpipe, causing me to cough. I suck in air trying to breathe.

"Well, I was happy to oblige. It's what friends are for," I say as I get ahold of myself. "We're young, single, and know each other's likes and dislikes. I'm sure it would happen more frequently if we weren't so stuck in our ways and different in terms of living conditions that we shared an apartment. We both like the D...a lot. Actually, like is probably putting it mildly. We love the D, but sometimes a girl just needs to get an O without dealing with a man's bullshit."

She sucks down the rest of her drink as she stares at me in thought. Setting the empty glass of ice down, she says something that catches me off guard. "I totally agree with you there, but sometimes it's just not the same to get yourself off as it is from someone else. Even though the end result is the same, your own body parts don't give you the same feeling along the way."

She pauses.

"It was kind of hot, wasn't it? Well, it is my twenty-fifth birthday.

I'm game for a drunken night of fun if you are."

Something is off. It's been what...seven years since that happened. It's never been mentioned since we left Cancun. Honestly, I'm surprised I even vaguely swayed in that direction of conversation in my attempt to give her a hard time about Kross.

"Delta."

She bites the side of her lip. "Yeah?"

"When is the last time you hooked up with someone?"

"Not too long ago."

She's dodging.

"Delta. How long?"

She looks at her glass, pushing it toward the other side of the bar for the bartender to pick up. "Two years," she says in a mumble.

Two years? What the fuck?

"Uh...why? When have you ever gone that long without sexual activity since you lost your virginity freshman year? Why haven't you mentioned that little tidbit of information? You are against relationships more than anyone I know, so what the hell are you waiting for? You're fucking hot and guys try to talk to you all the time. I've even seen you leave with guys from the bar before. What did y'all go do? Watch movies and cuddle? That's just not you, either of us for that matter. We don't roll that way; never have. Explain. Now."

She looks around as if she's making sure no one is listening. "I know, but it was the same old shit over and over. Different guy here and there, making me all hot and bothered. I would get into it when we were making out and hooking up, but when it got to the sex part it was always stale. Hell I don't know. Is it possible for sex to get old? I stopped getting off about three years ago unless I gave myself a clit orgasm after he was gone. I just wasn't into it and then maybe started overthinking everything, creating a blockage during the act. For a year I tried everything. I tried wild sex, threesomes, and even some BDSM shit with this one guy. Fuck, Lux, nothing worked. After a year I figured if I could only get myself off then what's the point in someone else? My G-spot has gone kaput. It doesn't work. I can only get off by clitoral stimulation. Something is wrong with me."

"What about those guys I've seen you with. Like that one about a month ago."

"Every few months I think maybe it's just stress and try again. You were telling me hot stories about you and Callum and this little affair you two had created...no pun intended. A girl can only listen to that shit so much without wanting to try. After countless flirting endeavors I would think I was into him, but when we went back to his place it was like a switch turning off, so I would usually just come up with some bullshit excuse or get him off, fake a period, and leave. Lame huh?"

She tells me all that shit and one emotion overcomes me: guilt. I feel like such a bad friend right now. How did I not notice? Delta is like a limb that stuck to me and grew into my body after a while. She started out as a drifter and has become one of my life vessels. She's my sister, my best friend. I would be devastated and my life would be significantly altered if something ever happened to her. As horrible as it sounds, I'd be more affected if something happened to her than my own mother.

I down the rest of my drink and wave the bartender over. He comes fairly quickly for a busy night. "Want another?"

"Close out our tab. Here." I throw down a wad of cash to tip him.

"Give me a second." He takes the cash and disappears, bringing back my card and a slip for me to sign. I scribble my signature down after recording the total, minus the tip, and he takes it and leaves, heading to serve someone else.

Delta looks at me. "Where are you going? It's still early?"

I grab her hand and pull her to her feet. Pulling her into a hug, I press my lips to the side of her ear. "We're taking the party to your place, birthday girl. Wine and girl talk, then with a buzz we're going to play. After today being hot, cold, hot, and then cold again, I'm a little wound tight, and this place blows anyway. I'm down for exchanging the big O. I'm getting you off so you can sleep like a baby and dream of hot things, like a certain sexy tattoo artist that will be expecting you tomorrow. I can't send you to an interview that could quite possibly change your life if you're sexually frustrated. Then what kind of friend would I be?"

A certain pair of gray eyes flash in my mind as I start making my way to the door, Delta keeping pace beside me. *Our kind are all born into less than ideal places, places that some wouldn't survive in.* I'm not sure why that particular part from earlier keeps standing out, but for some reason I want to find out. The way he said, *our,* is sparking an interest that I don't need. I wonder if I'll bump into those deep eyes and that unfiltered mouth again...

Kayton

I walk in and instantly see her sitting at the bar, waiting for me. We don't like each other. We never have. In her eyes I took something that is hers and the feeling is mutual. She got the first eight years plus all time prior, and I got the last twenty, sharing him with her when he scheduled a meeting. They didn't have a fucking marriage, both of them just refused to see it for what it was. I guess when you invest that much time in someone the option to walk away dissipates.

I might have some sympathy for the bitch had she not kept me from knowing a father when I thought I didn't have one. My conception was my mother and her husband's fault, not mine. Kids don't deserve that shit. If she couldn't stand the thought of me in the mix then she should have walked out the day she found out he stepped outside of their marriage.

I walk forward until I reach the bar, placing my palms down on the bar top as I lean forward and look to the left, the direction in which she is sitting. "How was your flight?" My voice seethes with sarcasm, but she wasn't exactly someone I wanted to lay my eyes on after having to deny my dick something it was practically salivating over.

"It was fine. Like you really care."

"Not really. That was me being tolerant."

She huffs. I look at her, sitting perfectly pressed in her designer wardrobe, one that he provided.

"I see your settlement is treating you well."

She slaps me across the face, leaving a tingle where her hand was. I hold up my hand when I hear the bartender's footsteps heading in our direction. From the corner of my eye I notice him turn around and go back to his original location, to check on the other customers in the hotel bar. My jaw steels.

"I've put up with a lot of shit over the years...from you, from him, and from her. If I was only with him for money I would have walked the day I found out he was sleeping with that money-hungry tramp at work that seduced him and got pregnant as a life insurance policy. You don't think I could have taken him to the cleaners for adultery? Well, think again. You seem to forget that I was the one that married him when he had nothing, not a dime to his name. I also stayed with him when he left me for you and to start over in a new place, leaving behind a good job, a life we'd built, and friends we'd made. I was the one that was left alone after she died, so give me a fucking break. I'm exhausted. He's gone and everything has been sorted. I'm only here to give you something I thought you might want, and then I'm on the first flight back to New York where I can attempt at actually living a life in peace."

It stings at the mention of my mother. I haven't spoken to her or seen her since the day I walked out with my dad. I pull out the stool next to her and sit as she grabs the stem of her glass and takes a sip of her white wine. I don't deny anything she says. My mother was a vicious woman. She didn't care about anyone but herself. Even at eight I could see that. She didn't make any attempts to hide it. "What do you need to give me that's so important, Marilyn?"

She waves the bartender over. "Order a drink. We have things to discuss."

"Jim Beam, Black label, on the rocks."

The bartender sets the tumbler in front of me, leaving us alone. I immediately take a sip, savoring the taste before letting the smooth liquid run down my throat, taking the edge off. She slides a large, yellow envelope toward me. "What's this?"

"Things you never knew. Things you should know. Things you have a right to know. It may not matter now, but everyone deserves to know the truth, because if I had to bet on it, I would guess he never told you."

He...

I take another sip and set my glass down on the bar as I pick up the folder and flip it over. I pinch the metal clasps and open the flap, revealing a stack of papers inside in all shapes and sizes. I reach inside and pull out what I can grasp, inspecting each thing. The first one is a photo of him holding a baby, my sister I guess, in what looks like a hospital room. "Is this her?"

"No, that's you, Kaston. I was mad that day. Even after six months of knowing she was carrying his child I still hated your mother. We tried for years after your sister for a little boy, but due to complications when she was born I couldn't get pregnant again. That's why we were fighting so much. I blamed myself and became distant, becoming emotionally closed off from him. He threw himself into work and I let him. I knew he was seeing someone. One thing about your father was that he was honest. He didn't lie well. He wore his discomfort all over his face. I was so distraught at the time that I reasoned with myself that it was a way for him to cope with everything and pretended not to notice."

She takes another sip of her wine. I don't know why the fuck I'm sitting here listening to all this shit. I didn't know I looked like a fucking Psychologist, but because of Dad I guess I'll see what she has to say. Discretely I look at my watch, hoping she is going to be done soon so I can prepare for tonight's job.

"But then he came home and confessed he had been seeing someone, that it just happened late at night. I just wanted to go back to imagining it, to pretending I didn't know, because when he told me she was pregnant I was slapped with a reality. That reality was that he got what we both wanted...with someone else. I didn't speak to him for weeks. I couldn't. He wanted to be there for her and I couldn't stomach to stop him. Instead I sunk into a depression until the day he told me that it was a boy. I snapped. I threatened to leave and never let him see his daughter again if he didn't stop seeing her. It was too much to handle. I was angry."

"Well it looks like you got your wish. Congrat-"

"But then she called when she went into labor. I hated her. She had everything I wanted. She had you. By that time I had time to think things over. I loved your father and you were a part of him. I couldn't deny him of that."

My brows dip in confusion, my eyes squinting. "What?"

She looks at me. "I went with him to the hospital. I accepted you to be a part of our family. When we got there I took that photo at the nursery. I saw you and I fell in love with you as if you were my own."

"I'm not following you."

She takes a deep breath. "Your mother found out I was there. I obviously wasn't part of her plans. I put a dent in the wallet that she was already claiming as hers. It's why she got pregnant. She thought your father was going to leave me and marry her. When he explained that we were there to be a part of your life she made him choose. It was your sister and I or her and you. Since you weren't old enough to know the difference and he knew a judge would never take you away from your mother, he chose us and started making deposits into her bank account regularly to make sure you were taken care of, hoping over time she would come to her senses. About once a year he would try to talk to her with no avail."

She reaches over and shuffles through some of the items, mostly photos at different stages of my life up to age seven. "Here. This is where he went and got the paperwork to try and have your last name changed to ours, but she refused to cooperate. She wouldn't even have the birth certificate amended to list him as your biological father. She would act like she was cooperating so he wouldn't try to fight it in court, but then never follow through. She kept baiting him for more money and told him that if he gave it to her that she would start letting him see you, but each time he increased child support she came up with a different excuse, like meeting him would confuse you, she wasn't sure you were his, a child needs his parents together or not a all, the list goes on. We all knew you were his. You looked just like him. Even I could see that regardless of how much it hurt."

"Why are you telling me all of this? Why didn't he just tell me it was my mother instead of blaming it on himself and on you? Don't you realize how long I've hated you?"

She stands and grabs her purse, placing it on her shoulder as she looks at me. "Because, Kaston, it wasn't my place to tell you. That was your father's call to make, but he's gone, and unless your feelings about me change I doubt I'll be seeing you around. I just thought you shouldn't go through life thinking he didn't try in the beginning even though he made everything right in the end. After your sister died he realized it was better to fight and lose than to stand by and do nothing at all. If you want to know why your mother hasn't attempted to contact you, it's because your father has still been giving her money to leave you alone. He's been supporting her all of these years because he never wanted her to stir up trouble for you. He wanted you to have as normal of a childhood as possible. He was willing to do anything to make sure that happened. We will both miss him, but you don't have to live the life he did, Kaston. You don't want this life. I wouldn't wish it on anyone."

She lowers her tone so that no one can hear her. "The world will always have bad and good people. You can't change that. No matter how many bad people you remove, there will always be someone to replace them. Nothing you do will bring either of them back. I accepted that painful truth when I realized I lost two people instead of one. Life is short, Kaston. Make the best of it. The choice is yours, of course. Goodbye, Kaston."

She turns to walk away, but I grab her hand to stop her. "What was she like? He never talked about her."

"That's because he felt like he owed you the world to make up for what he missed. You were his primary focus after she died and he was scared you would resent him for choosing, but to answer your question...she was strong, outgoing, funny, and stubborn, but easy to love. I see a lot of her in you. She was a good kid. The two of you would have really loved each other had you been given the chance. Maybe you should pay her grave a visit one day and introduce yourself. I'm sure she's been waiting."

She reaches into her purse and tosses a few folded up bills on the bar. "I'm sorry things worked out the way they did. I really am."

"Thanks, Marilyn. I appreciate you coming here for this. If you ever need anything let me know. You know how to find me."

She turns and takes a step but stops. "I do have one request."

"What is it?"

"Will you bring him home and bury him where he belongs... beside Emily? He doesn't belong there. He belongs here. He's been gone long enough. It's time."

"You have my word. The second I can get him here he will be."

She nods, still facing away from me, her voice cracking as if she's trying not to cry. She puts one foot in front of another and starts to walk, leaving me in this hotel bar, my mind fucking blown. I'll be damned. The wicked witch wasn't wicked at all.

I pick up my glass and drain it, leaving nothing but the ice. As I set it back down I pull my phone from my pocket and scroll through my contacts for the person of interest. He picks up on the first ring. "Yeah, bro, what you got for me?"

"You ready for your first job?"

"Hit me with it. I'm itching to start, man."

"Anna Cox. Hometown: Newark, New Jersey. Fifty-two years of age. Dark hair and brown eyes. High school graduate. College drop-out. Gave birth to one child in New York at the age of twenty-four...a boy. Find her and get back to me with the details."

"You got it, boss. Standby."

I disconnect the call. Maybe it's time to pay mommy dearest a visit...

CHAPTER EIGHT

"Y ou want another glass," I ask as I stand from the couch with my now empty wine glass."

She takes the last sip and hands me the glass. "Sure, I'll turn on some music. Thanks for hanging out with me. If I would've had to work on my birthday I would have been mad enough to kick a kitten. This is coming from the animal lover. I swear if I get that job and it pays the rent I'm quitting. Everyone thinks that bartending is a job with perks until you see that you're working when everyone else is out for a night of play. No one wants to do shit on weeknights."

"Yeah, well, if it makes you feel any better I requested off like three months ago. There was actually a really big party tonight. I think an engagement party of some big shot bachelor. Imagine that. The tips and man-candy would have probably been enough to make me cry thinking about, but nothing gets in the way of my only friend's birthday."

"Don't you think it's kind of weird that we don't really click with normal girls? What happens when you find a new guy that lives around here and he whisks you away and marries you? Shit, that's going to be one boring life."

She giggles, clearly buzzed after our drinks at the bar and the two glasses we've both consumed already while catching up on much needed girl talk. Sometimes we go weeks where our schedules don't line up.

I place the cork back in the bottle after pouring us both half a glass, feeling pretty tipsy myself. My entire face crinkles in disgust. "Okay, that's never going to happen. Marriage is not in my vocabulary and babies are like a disease to me. I stay far away from them. I didn't sterilize myself to back out later. Mistakes are not an option. K. Thanks."

I take another sip of my freshly poured wine and dim the lights to a low amber glow. One thing the two of us have in common is that the view of our apartments was the selling feature. We live in different buildings because of that one fact. The lights of the city become more visible through the one wall of windows at the other end of the living space, without all of the interior light.

Delta starts dancing to the music playing on her iHome dock, raising her arms above her head while swaying to the music. The colors of her tattoos are motioning like a flag in the wind. "Come dance with me."

I pick up her glass in my empty hand and walk out of the kitchen area into the open living space, my bare feet cooling a few degrees with each step across the tile floor. Setting her glass down on the mantle of the fireplace I drain the remainder of wine in my glass before setting it down to accompany hers.

Playfully skipping in her direction, I wrap her in my arms as HIM starts playing, slowing down the melody from the hip-hop tune that was previously playing on shuffle. "You know you'll be my best friend till the end right?"

She lays her head against my shoulder as we sway to the music. "Yeah, but we're getting older, Lux. I don't want this phase of our lives to end. Some people want to grow up, but not me."

"Me either, boo, me either, but I promise nothing will ever change between us. Those scared little girls from elementary school still live deep inside. We're still those socially awkward girls from middle school that snuck off in the middle of the night with our moms' liquor stash to hang out in Black's field because it was far better than being at home. We'll never change from the hell-raising teenagers in high school that didn't give a shit about anyone else... and we're still the two grown adults that need nothing more than each other and an occasional good time. Love was never on our side. It's always been the two of us against the world, Delta, so your needs will always come before anyone else's. You're my family. If a man can't accept that then fuck him."

"I love you, Lux. Every birthday with a good memory has you in it."

I rub my hand up the length of her neck and stop on her cheek, followed by the other one, and I look into her eyes. "I love you too, Delta."

Leaning in, I press my lips to hers with a different meaning for the first time in years. As if a kiss has memory to a person we fall into a rhythm, re-familiarizing our lips with each other. Our tongues collide and mingle as her hands move from my hips to my lower back, steadily falling to my ass where they stop, pulling me closer to her.

I grab the bottom of her shirt and pull it up her body, removing it completely and tossing it on the floor. She smiles. It's no secret that we're both turned on. We have a history with each other that runs deep. It's nothing more than sharing a love with someone you care about, wanting to meet a need when they have one. We can do this and tomorrow wake up as if it never happened. We've done it before.

Taking hold of the front of her shorts, I pop the button through the slit and lower the zipper, before peeling them over her ass and letting them fall to her bare feet. Lowering to match the height of her waist, I kiss each hip tattoo as I clench the band of her panties in each hand, lowering them down her legs, and trailing kisses down her thigh until they are in a heap at her feet. I run my fingers over her mound and look up at her. "You're freshly shaven. I thought you haven't been hooking up with anyone."

"I haven't, but I shave once a week, always on the weekend just in case. I can't let it go very long or it annoys me. You know that."

Her skin is smooth. I glide my fingertips up the sides of her body until I get to her bra. I unclasp it and pull it over her shoulders, letting gravity do the rest. Her nipples are hard. She grabs the bottom of my dress and removes it, following the same steps as I did with her. I have a very dominant personality for a girl. Delta is a firecracker and doesn't take shit off anyone, but she's more of a follower than a leader, a lover than a fighter. It's why we've never gotten in a fight. We balance each other.

I cup her firm breast in my hand, rubbing my thumb over the hardened center. "Do you like to be touched here?"

Her breathing picks up. "Yes."

"Do you prefer my mouth or my hand?"

"Your mouth."

I lean down and enclose my mouth over the pink center, flicking my tongue up and down, wetting it. She moans out and grabs ahold of mine in return, squeezing it. It feels good, making me suck. "Oh, fuck."

Releasing it from suction, I trail my tongue up her body to kiss her. This will be so much easier in a lateral position. I release her lips. "Is your B.O.B charged?"

She bites her bottom lip. "Always. Want to go to the bedroom?"

"Yes."

She grabs my hand and pulls me through the apartment, both of us completely nude. The scenery changes from the natural cityscape and modern feel of the apartment to her dark bedroom in colors of charcoal and dark pink, accented with girly skulls. Once inside the door I shut it, locking it out of habit. She places her hands on each of my hips and pulls me toward her until our hard nipples are brushing against each other, returning her lips to mine. The heat and neediness in her kiss amplifies. I walk her backward until her body is pressed against the side of the bed. We both need more.

I cup my hand over the smooth center between her legs, checking to see if she's wet. She is. Extremely. "Sit. Where is BOB?"

"In my closet along with my new one. Bring them both."

I walk in her closet to retrieve them both, one pink and one purple, before setting them on the bed beside her. Placing my hand on her shoulder, I slightly push her backward until she lies on her back, her ass still at the edge of the bed with her feet hanging over. She wraps her leg around my waist, pulling me toward her. I grab her ankle and trace my hand up the length of her leg, stopping at the back of her knee, before mirroring it with the other hand. I spread them. "Feet on the bed."

She does as I instruct, presenting me with her pussy. Being a woman gives you certain advantages over a man in pleasing a woman. She's swollen and dripping wet. It's visible. Pressing my right, middle, manicured finger over the center of her opening, I run it up her center in a straight line, wetting her clit as I massage in a circle. Her hips buck off the bed. "Do you want me to make you come both ways, Delta? Do you want to be able to look at Kross tomorrow without coming unglued? I need you focused. I need you to be strong in order to set you apart from every other girl."

I pick up speed. She clenches the sheets as she moans out in breathy spurts. "Yes."

"You can't do that when you're sexually deprived. It makes you fucking needy. You should have come to me earlier. If no one else can do it for you...I will."

I shove two fingers from my left hand inside her pussy, hooking upward as hard as possible until I can feel her G-spot, never letting up on her clit. "Shit, Lux. That feels so good."

I start to finger fuck her in shallow thrusts, staying close to her G-spot. "You have to teach a man what you like, Delta. They aren't fucking mind readers. They don't have the same parts as us. Voice your wants, your needs. It's the only way to be thoroughly fucked and satisfied. There is no reason to miss out on great sex because you aren't getting what you need."

I can feel her starting to clench around my fingers. I remove them, all of them. She groans. "Why did you stop? I was so close. Fuck. I haven't had that feeling in so long."

"Because when I'm done with you, you'll be in such a mind fuck, but you'll at least know your body. I know you want Kross whether you admit it or not. You don't land a man like that by being fucking weak. Guys don't want what they can have with ease. They want what they have to work for. They want the one that's different from the rest."

I place my knee on the bed. She scoots toward the head of the bed with me following behind, her legs still spread. I lean down and kiss her, sucking her tongue into my mouth as it brushes along my lips. She pushes up with her feet and starts rubbing herself against my pelvis, leaving a trail of wetness behind.

I lower myself, sucking her nipple into my mouth and rolling it between my teeth, exerting the slightest amount of pressure. "Please, Lux."

I increase suction until she moans out loudly. "Tell me what you want, Delta. If I were Kross what would you want me to do to you?"

Her breathing is erratic. "Put your mouth on me."

"Where?"

"You know where."

"Say it."

"Further down."

I bite her stomach. "Here?"

"No."

"Where? Fucking say it, Delta. Own up to what you want and demand it."

She groans in agitation. I knew she was a little more modest when it came to sex than me, even though she doesn't look it, but I never knew she was this much worse. I'm probably extreme in the opposite direction. I just don't give a shit. A man will please me or I'll move on to the next one.

"I want your mouth on my clit while you fuck me with the dildo. There, I said it. Fuck, I don't know how a guy handles you."

I stand on my knees, now towering over her. A smile spreads across my face as her cheeks become flushed with a red hue. I rub my index finger down the center line of her torso until I reach her pussy again, thrusting inside. "The rougher the better. I'm a fighter," I say as I wink. I reach behind me with the opposite hand and grab the dildo. "Put that pillow under your ass."

She follows instructions. I lean down and kiss the inside of her thigh. "Wait."

"What?"

"Give me the other one and turn around. You're having all the fun."

And she's back...

This is why we are best friends: selfless, fair, and gives as much as she receives. I reach back and grab it, then look back at her. I spread her lips and extend my tongue, pressing it flat against her clit, before running it up the length of her body, stopping at her mouth. I kiss her, mumbling against her lips. "Don't stop until we both come...hard. Got it?"

"Fuck yes. Let's do it."

She grabs one dildo out of my hand and places it beside her for quick grab.

I straddle my legs to each side of her and turn around. She places her hands on the front of my thighs, inching me backward until I'm where she wants me. I rub my middle finger over her clit in circles to get her to spread wider. She gets the hint. I spread her lips open with my index and middle finger, giving my tongue better access.

She moves her hand to the back of my thigh and rubs upward toward my ass. Her hand disappears and then connects again in a slap, stinging my skin. She didn't hold back. "Fuck yeah. Again."

She repeats, but harder this time, then rubs her finger back and forth over my clit. I'm so wet right now. She inserts two fingers into my pussy as I start flicking my tongue over her clit, making me want to continue faster from the feel of her fingering me. She bites my leg beside my pussy as she fingers me, sending my hormones over the edge.

"Shit."

I suck her clit into my mouth so hard she screams out. Before I can react her fingers disappear and she rams the dildo into my pussy, filling me. A throaty moan sounds in my throat but I don't stop. She pulls out and does it again, making me arch my back, then the tip of her tongue touches my clit.

Damn. It's hard to concentrate.

Holding my weight on my forearms I free my other hand. Aligning the tip of the dildo at her entrance I push in slowly, the opposite of her. Her rhythm falters for a moment until I'm inside her fully. As if we had the same thoughts both vibrations begin at the same time. My legs tense.

She pulls out and pushes up at an angle as she shoves it back inside, hard, pushing me forward a little, but continuing to flick the point of her tongue back and forth over my clit. Each time I thrust the dildo inside her she matches me harder in the pussy and faster on the clit. It feels so good I can barely breathe. She's telling me what she wants. She wants me to mirror her...so I do.

She instantly bucks her hips upward, just as I release her clit from my mouth and narrow my tongue into a point and match her rhythm.

We both moan out together and speed up.

I can't think.

I can't breathe.

I can't stop.

I want to come.

I need to feel her come.

She places her free hand back on the front of my thigh and pulls me into her face. I increase pressure on her clit as well. Our legs are starting to shake. I can see her starting to clench around the dildo as do I. We're about to come at the same time. We clamp down on each other's clits at the same time, each massaging it between our tongue and the pallet of our mouth; so hard that I didn't even feel the build of my orgasm before it starts to consume me, making it hard to keep going, but I do anyway. I moan against her, the vibrations adding to the sensitivity of my clit. She doesn't let up. It's becoming hard to endure.

Without thinking I pull out the dildo and stop, riding out my orgasm. I need her to stop, but I can't find the will to make her. I've already come twice today. She slightly alters the angle of the dildo and presses in further. "Fuck. I'm so full."

All of my muscles tighten as she begins the short bursts with the vibrating head against my G-spot, a different feeling starting to build. It's not the first time I've ever gotten a G-spot orgasm and it won't be the last, but it's been a while. I cannot move. My toes curl as I start to come on the dildo. I can feel it. Everything is in slow motion.

"Stop."

She pulls it out. I do the same and quickly turn around to finish her off. She looks at me, unsure. I kiss her lips. "Thanks, doll, but it's your turn. This time...I'm letting you come. Scooting back down I spread her legs as far as they will go, opening the lips of her pussy, and revealing her clit.

"It's not going to take me long. I was almost there when you stopped."

I place the edge of my tongue on her clit and quickly massage it at a steady rhythm, not too hard and not too soft. She tries to close her legs but I hold them down, making her take more of the sensations. "Shit. Lux, I'm about to come. Keep going."

I insert two fingers into her pussy...for now, to feel her, to make sure she comes. Her muscles tighten and she grabs ahold of my hair, pulling it. I have one thing that is like a fucking NOS button. Pull my hair and I turn into a crazed sex addict. I never let up, slowly rubbing my tongue until I can feel her. She presses on the back of my head as she starts to orgasm. When I feel her clenching around me and my fingers become wetter I suck her into my mouth as hard as I can. She instantly arches her back, giving me my angle.

In the middle of her orgasm I remove my fingers and slam the dildo inside against her G-spot. "Oh, fuck."

I do it again.

"Shit."

Repeat.

"Fucking yes. I'm going to come."

I will not stop until she comes. I'm dedicated.

I'm back to flicking my tongue over her sensitive clit, keeping her mind in a haze, free from thought. Everyone that studies a woman knows that if she has things on her mind she can't come. Things are rarely as cut and dry as you read in fantasy romance novels.

I thrust harder, but don't alter the angle.

"Oh hell. Fuuuuuck. Now."

She pulls my hair harder then lets go and replaces them on her breasts. I look at her beneath my lashes. She is kneading them and pinching her nipples. "Dammit, yes. Oh, fuck. I'm coming."

She thrusts her hips up. My tongue is getting tired, but I will make it till the end. She becomes still, the octave in her moan getting higher.

She's coming.

I watch her, feeling a sense of pride overcome me. After two years...that's fucking talent.

Her body goes limp.

I stand to my knees and lick my lips in an attempt to rid them of excess moisture. She has a lazy smile on her face. "That was fucking awesome."

I slide off the bed. "You're welcome."

I go to her dresser and start digging through the drawers for some clothes. There is no way in hell I'm wearing what I wore earlier through Atlanta this late at night. I pull out a long sleeve cotton jersey, tunic length, and a pair of yoga leggings. I turn to her as I pull them on. She rolls over on her side to face me. "Where are you going? You know you can stay here if you want."

"I know, but you know I can't sleep if I'm not in my own bed. It's a curse, but I haven't figured out a way around it yet, and I have to work tomorrow night. Did you have a good birthday?"

"Yes. Thanks. I'll clean BOB and BOB's friend when you leave. I just need a minute."

I pull on a pair of flats and walk toward her. She pulls the covers down and gets underneath them, pulling them up to cover her chest. I lean down and pull her into a loose hug as I kiss her cheek. "Good. Get some sleep. You have a big day tomorrow. Now your mind should be clear. I'll get my clothes later, okay?"

"Okay. Whatever you want."

I walk to the door and stop. "Delta."

"Yeah?"

"Just be yourself tomorrow, okay? This is what you're meant to do. If it weren't, tonight would have never happened. You know I'm a firm believer that things always happen for a reason, whether bad or good. At some point everything will fall into place just as it was predetermined to be. If Kross is interested, give him hell but give in. Occasionally you have to go against the grain. Happy birthday, babe."

I unlock and open the door before walking through the apartment in search of my purse. It's sitting on the bar next to Delta's decorative glass bowl, etched with a black skull wearing a pink bow that she uses to hold gum and cigarettes. I shake my head. I'll never understand her taste. Gum and cigarettes: with Delta you'll never see one without the other. If you don't know her personally you would never even know she smoked.

Those cigarettes are tempting and I don't even smoke. My hand traces over the brand name across the front. *What the hell? Why not... I've already done all kinds of fucked up shit today. What's one more? All the way or none at all...isn't that an old saying? Fuck it.*

The pack is already packed and open. I grab two cigarettes from the pack and confiscate the lighter, along with a piece of gum. I know she always has extra anyway. They are lying all over the place, most of them with skulls to match the bowl. "Thank you, Delta," I mumble as I grab my purse. I suppose I should get a move on it if I ever want to get home. Catching a cab is going to be a bitch at this time.

I walk outside the building. The cool breeze of the night air hits my face. It's oddly quiet for a busy city. I prefer the fast pace over abandoned small towns any day. It's why we moved here after graduation, that and to leave Hell behind. This may not be Heaven, but purgatory is still an upgrade.

I place my purse under my arm and slip the filter end of the cigarette between my lips. Placing one hand in front of the tip to block the breeze, I light the cigarette and suck, letting the vapor enter my mouth.

I inhale, allowing the calming mixture to invade my lungs.

"Shit, that's good."

A nicotine high begins to occur since I don't smoke on a regular basis. It's actually been years since I've touched a cigarette.

I'm suddenly not in a hurry to go home. Looking from side to side, I decide to take a walk. Most of the alcohol has worn off, but I still have a slight buzz. It's probably not the safest idea, but I've done worse.

I exhale and take another drag before my feet start to move down the sidewalk. There is no excitement. It seems most have become silent.

"Please. I didn't mean to. It was an accident. Let me go." The plea of a male's voice flows through the air only feet away. The hair on the back of my neck stands up. My feet don't stop. Feet shuffling on the pavement sounds through my ears. It's getting closer.

One building ends and another begins, leaving a narrow alley between the two. Why am I still walking toward it? "An accident is once. Four times is fucking murder. There may be nothing to link you, but someone is always watching. Shadows are everywhere."

Something about that low raspy voice strikes a familiar nerve.

The cry of the man takes over once again, voicing a string of curses; one including what most would consider the absolute worst of them all. When referring to damnation, most stray from including God's name, while others obviously love that word, even him.

"You better make sure when you use his name it's sacred and holy, because you're going to need him on your side after what you've done. Say your prayers."

I turn into the edge of the alley just as the bullet penetrates his heart, causing the man trapped at the dead end of the alley to fall to his knees as the blood drains from the vital organ. His eyes are wide and he becomes silent. I should run. I should be scared. I should be in shock.... but instead, I find my head falling to the side, intrigued as I watch him take his last breath, still smoking the cigarette.

Then the killer turns around.

Everything in my world suddenly stops.

My heart starts to pound.

It's him...

"Kaston," I whisper.

His eyes lock with mine and I can no longer breathe. Every conscious thought becomes muted. The world around us fades away. The hand holding the gun immediately goes into the front pocket of his hoodie. "Come."

My feet start to inch forward. I don't hesitate. I don't ask questions. It's as if he has control over my body, my mind, and my soul, controlling me like a puppet. Where fear should be present, desire takes its place.

I stop approximately three feet in front of him.

He raises his head, showing more of himself. He's beautiful...

"Lux."

My head falls to the side again. "Who are you?"

"A monster."

"Why am I having a problem believing that's true?"

His brow raises and he looks back at the lifeless body on the ground before turning back to me. "Because I kill people. It's a high that I need. Normal people would feel remorse. I don't."

My heart pounds harder with the finality in his tone. A monster is what he calls himself, but I've never known a monster to be beautiful. He scares me, but he also makes me feel alive.

He walks forward as I take another drag of my cigarette. It's a few short from being done. I blow out into the air, never veering from his eyes. He's so close I can feel his breath on my lips. I bring the small cigarette toward my mouth but he grabs my wrist and takes it from me. "Is that supposed to scare me?"

"It should."

"Why?"

He places the filter between his lips and finishes it off in one suck, before grabbing the back of my head and pressing his lips to mine, blowing it into my mouth. If it were possible to orgasm without someone even touching your genitals I'm pretty sure I could in this exact moment. Holy fucking hell, where has he been? He may not be dating material, but a little fun never killed anyone. After all, it is officially the beginning of summer. It's always best to be single for the summer.

I inhale, taking all that he has to offer. My head falls back slightly, opening my throat even more. He hesitates before closing his lips as he drags them up my mouth, pulling my top lip out before completely releasing it.

I open my eyes. He puts the butt out on the brick wall and shoves the filter in the pocket of his jeans instead of throwing it on the pavement. "Because you're a liability. You know too much. I have no choice. You've just been marked."

I loosen the arm hold on my clutch and let it fall into my palm, gripping the bottom as I quickly open it with the other hand. Without a second's thought I pull my handheld pistol from my purse and aim it at his temple the exact moment he mirrors me. Barrel to skin we both stand here, ready to pull the trigger. He looks slightly taken by surprise with the narrowing of his eyes. I press my gun into his temple further, tilting my head for emphasis. "Awe, did you really think a girl like me wasn't packing? Let me tell you a little something about me, baby. I may look like a spoiled princess, but where I come from, cops are scared to enter. This can go down one of two ways: one, you back the fuck up, let me walk away, and we forget each other exists, or two, we become a modern day Romeo and Juliet."

I step closer, pressing my chest into his, and my barrel into his head so hard it's sure to leave an indention of the outline behind. I lower my voice. "Never underestimate my reflexes. My instincts are sharper than you can fucking wrap your head around...so what's it going to be, handsome?"

His jaw muscle twitches back and forth as he stares into my eyes so deep it makes me feel naked. Most people would be scared shitless right now, but not me. I'm no stranger to guns. I've owned one since I was big enough to pull the trigger. We didn't have much, but we had a gun, and I was alone often. If I'm going to die there is nothing I can do about it, but that doesn't mean I'm going down without a fight. The only way to live is as if the moment could possibly be your last. We are never promised another second. Fear is a weakness. It shows through more than anything else.

I'm mentally preparing for option two when a smile breaks free; a smile so big it shows in his eyes. Damn, that smile could brighten the darkest room. I remain like I am. I may be melting inside, but I have a control over my muscles that many don't, including facial ones. He lowers his gun, placing it back in his pocket. He grabs my face in his hands and kisses me again, only this time... I want to scream inside. There is a heat in his kiss that burns me from the inside out.

He releases me and I lower my gun to my side, but he moves his lips closer to my ear. A wave of dizziness takes over. I blink repeatedly, trying to gain my composure. "You just fucked up, beautiful, because one of two things is going to happen: one, I'll find you and I'll kill you because I never leave loose ends, or two, I'll find you and never let you go. Either way, I'm coming for you. Be ready. Now get out of here unless you plan on helping me get rid of this body."

He takes a step back and I turn off the wall, before I start walking backward. I press the length of my index and middle fingers to my lips, blowing him a kiss. "I'll be waiting."

After that kiss I hope it's not long...

CHAPTER NINE

After a three-hour drive I pull my silver Porsche into the parking lot of *The Watering Hole*. This place brings back bad memories, because it reminds me of the years I spent growing up in this fucked up small town. I've been back here maybe once a year since Delta and I left after graduation, usually when Mom needs something because she's a fuck up. Saying that isn't cruel, it's just the way it is.

Our only goal was to get out of this place. We made a pact freshman year that we would save every dime we could to make it happen. We didn't care about fucking college. Something like that isn't possible when you come from trash. To some people college is an expectation, a pain in the ass required by their parents, but to people like us it's like wishing on a star - useless and a waste of time, because it'll never come true.

The second we got back from our senior trip we packed everything we owned in Delta's old Volkswagen Beetle and headed north. We didn't even have a destination in mind. We just drove until we decided to stop. Atlanta just seemed to fit and we've been there ever since.

My hand starts to shake as I shift into neutral and pull the emergency brake. I clench my fist, trying to calm my nerves. I hate coming back here. I look around. The only other car in the parking lot is Mom's beat up Mercury. I'm sure Ella's car is parked out back. I close my eyes and count to ten, trying to take deep breaths in between.

My one and only fear is to be stuck back here; being her.

I kill the engine and toss my keys in my purse, before grabbing it out of the passenger seat. Placing my left hand on the door handle, I open the door. "Come on, Lux. Get this shit over with so you can go home," I mumble to myself.

I stand and look at the building before me as I lock and shut the door to my car. I walk through the front doors, knowing Ella will be working the bar until the night shift picks up. She lives at this bar, literally. This is her life. It's also the only bar for miles, making it the place to be every night of the week. For the most part it's the older crowd from open until nine and the students from the local junior college late at night. That's also usually when the high school kids sneak in. Summers here are like what I assume fucking rush week is like at universities. The fresh meat upgrades from field parties and gains their drinking panties before they get shipped off to college - their last chance to be an irresponsible kid.

Some of us never get that luxury...

Delta and I have been coming here since we were about fourteen, sneaking flasks inside to drink in the bathroom. Ella let us in because usually our moms were already here and it was safer for her to be able to keep an eye on us than the alternative. She always has been like our second mom, even though she doesn't have kids, nor has she ever been married. She claims she married the damn bar because that was the only lifelong commitment she needed. I'm with her there...

I look at the bar in the center of the room, but Ella isn't there like I assumed. Instead there is a male bartender wiping down the bar and talking to a blonde female, but she's facing away from me. She laughs, that hideous drunken flirty laugh. I clench my purse to my side and slightly hang my head. This is humiliating; that said blonde being my mother and flirting with a man half her age.

I walk forward, my wedges clunking against the aged hardwood floor. "For fuck's sake, *mother,* can't you at least wait until five p.m. to start drinking. Normal people start their day with coffee."

Her laugh stops.

The bartender looks at me. He looks familiar, but his face doesn't register with a name. Mom doesn't immediately look at me. Instead, she looks at the shelving filled with alcohol in the center behind the bar. "Lux. You came."

"Of course. You did need my help, did you not?"

"I just assumed you would take care of it over the phone."

"And give out my credit card number? I think not.... Are you ready to become a productive member of society? It's not really classy to smell like a bar before nightfall. Plus, I have to get back to the city. Some of us work for a living." She places her hand on the purse resting on the bar top. Her shoulders hang.

"Wait. Lux Larsen?"

I look at the bartender, staring between my mother and I. "Who's asking? Do I know you?"

He smiles. "Maybe not sober...or clothed for that matter, but it wouldn't take long to remind you; although, I don't have that old Ford truck anymore, so we'd have to make do with my new one at the lake house."

My eyes widen.

His smile broadens.

That feeling that you get when you see an old fuck buddy and your head is screaming at you: *what the fuck were you thinking?* That would be me at this very second.

"Paul."

He leans forward on his forearms. What the hell is he doing here? I figured he would be playing ball at some big shot college by now.

"What do you say, Lux? You game for a reunion party? I'm sure a lot of people would love to see you. What's it been...seven years?" He scans my body very slowly. "You look better now than you did in high school."

Be nice. Be nice. Be nice.

"As *tempting* as that sounds, I can't. I have to go. I only came in to take care of some business. Maybe some other time."

I walk forward and grab Mom's arm, pulling her to her feet. "Let's go."

"Suit yourself. If you change your mind you know where I'll be."

"I'm pretty sure that won't happen, but thanks. Tell Ella I stopped by. I'll call her later."

Mom stumbles and pulls her arm from my grip. "Maybe I should stay here with Paul," she slurs. "He will take care of me."

"The fuck you are, Katherine. Let's go."

I grab ahold of her arm and steady her. "I'm an adult, Lux. What's it to you anyway? I'm nothing but an embarrassment to you."

"Don't do this here."

She sways on her cheap heels. "This is the perfect place to do this. Who cares? There's no one even in here to hear, except who... some boy that you used to sleep with? I'm giving you permission to finally tell me how you *really* feel."

"Do I need to give you two a few minutes alone?"

I shoot daggers at Paul. "That would be wise."

He holds up his hands and backs out of the bar area, headed for the kitchen. When he disappears through the door I look back at the drunk that is supposed to be my mother. She stumbles again. I shove her against the wall without hurting her, giving her something to lean against. "You really want to do this? Words can't be taken back, Katherine."

"Go ahead. You barely even call me your mother anymore. It's Katherine this and Katherine that. I'm nothing but a body to you. I'm a dead limb."

I snap.

"And whose fucking fault is that? Huh? When have you ever acted like a mother? All of my life you've whored around with men that only want you for a night away from their shitty lives, or stayed in bars looking for the next temporary fix to happiness. Let's not leave out the drugs. Slinging food my way here and there or giving me a place to lay my head that is a strong wind away from collapsing isn't being a mother. I would have respected you if you had tried working a normal job, no matter how much or little money you made, but you didn't. Instead, you laid around drunk or high until you found a trick to make you feel pretty."

I dig in my purse for my compact. "Shitty situations happen to people, Katherine, but it doesn't have to ruin your entire life. That's all you've ever viewed me as, isn't it? I'm the incident that destroyed your life. Maybe you should have just aborted me, or hell, even gave me up for adoption. Then I wouldn't be the fucking reminder that made you this way. Parents should be focused on protecting their kids from bad things, but you encouraged it."

I'm shouting. I shouldn't be yelling, but she irritates the fuck out of me. I'm tired of her twenty-five year long pity fucking party. "I bet you don't even remember how old I was when I lost my virginity, do you?"

"Seventeen."

I laugh.

"Try Twelve. Twelve fucking years old. I should have been playing ring around the fucking rosie with other little girls or begging you to take us to the mall or a movie because you wouldn't let us do anything in fear we would get into trouble. Hell, I don't really know. By the grace of God I'm not a mother. What I do know is that I shouldn't have been spreading my legs in my bed for a guy thirteen years older than me, having no idea that you're supposed to use a damn condom to prevent things, because my mother never talked to me about sex. She was too busy doing it in the next room with no shame, and because you lacked parental ability I had to trade in being a kid to survive, so don't ever fucking tell me that you raised me, because I raised myself."

I adjust the strap of my purse on top of my shoulder as my shaky hands try to open the compact. "Even months later when history tried to repeat itself you didn't get the huge memo that you were being a shitty parent. I had to basically tell you what to do when someone else with a higher power was looking out for me."

A single tear falls from her tired eyes, the eyes that look like mine, our only similar physical trait. "It would have been easier if you didn't look like him," she whispers.

"And that's why even though I love you I don't like you, because after all this time you still use that as an excuse. Grow the fuck up, Katherine. If you're expecting the world to give you handouts when it doesn't sway in your favor, then you're going to be disappointed. In all these years you never stopped to ask yourself the one question that mattered, but I'll give you the answer anyway. I didn't ask to be here. None of this was my fault, but I suffered anyway, because you were too much of a fucking coward to do what needed to be done. You know, maybe I'm like him, because I sure as hell am not like you."

She slaps me across the face before her palm collides with her mouth, more tears beginning to fall. It doesn't weaken me. It only makes me stronger. "I'm so sorry."

"Don't be sorry, be angry. That's your problem. You never get angry. Get fucking angry, Katherine, then maybe you'll open your eyes and see that you could have a better life if you actually put forth an effort, instead of looking like this."

I hold the mirror in front of her, for her to look at herself. Her eyes have bags underneath them, her skin is off in color, and her mouth is lined from lack of happiness. Her hair is a dull blonde, most likely from lack in care. She's aging faster than her years. Her beauty is fading. What's sad is that it doesn't have to be. I remember what she used to look like from the few photos I've seen. She was beautiful, and she still could be, but she's the only one that can change it.

I close the mirror and grab her face in my hands, looking into her crying eyes. "Katherine, just because you have a bad past and a shitty present, doesn't mean you have to have a failing future. You can change your path anytime you get ready, but only you can take the first step. When you do, I'll be here to make sure you stay on course."

For the first time in my entire life my mother breaks down, crying so hard she can barely breathe. I wrap her in my arms and let her cry on my designer shirt, because well...she's my mom. No matter how fucked up she is, she's still my mom. I would like to think that most girls in this situation would probably cry right along with her for support, but I just stand here and become her rock, because it's the only thing I know how to do. Not once in my life have I cried, and there have been plenty of times that I've tried.

Turning toward the exit doors I pull her along beside me, still in the nook of my arms. "Come on. Tonight you can let it all go; forever, Katherine. It's time."

"Where are we." she asks in an exhausted voice, still crying all over again each time she gets ahold of herself. She's been in and out of consciousness since we left the bar.

I pull into a spot at the front entryway of the nearest extended stay hotel that doesn't look like it's infested with roaches, which is actually about an hour outside of town. Shifting into neutral I look straight ahead. "For the weekend you're staying here. I don't want you to go anywhere until I call you. There are some things I need to work out before I voice them aloud. It's on me. Get some rest, pamper yourself, and work on being a better person, because I don't know how much longer I can do this, Mom."

She intakes a wave of air as I call her Mom. I really don't do it that often. I want to, but it's a title I feel is earned. "But I don't have any clothes."

I turn to look at her and pull my right leg into the seat. "I guess it's a good thing we wear the same size then. I never leave home without a bag of clothes in the trunk. With you I just never know. I want that to change. Come on. I really do have to get to work."

I feel like the roles are reversed. It doesn't matter how fucked up of a heart I have, I still want a relationship with my mother. I don't want to be the mother, and I don't want to be the friend, I want to be the daughter...just like things are supposed to be.

CHAPTER TEN

Kaston

I stand at the wall made of windows in my office that overlooks the city as I drink my scotch; Dad's personal favorite. I remain still, people watching, as the designer and her crew continues to *put together* my office behind me. The Staton Agency, part two, is now underway. A man has to make an honest living. This was Dad's...and now mine. A hitman was only as needed and on the side. Although it pays...and well, he only took lives that needed to be taken. It was never a sport. A private investigator was something he quickly became passionate about, bringing the sins of the darkest into the light. Since I have a background in law enforcement it just fits to finish what he started. I'm the only one he had. I will keep his name alive.

The vision of that night starts playing in my head again, like a fucking record stuck on repeat. I can barely think of anything else since I watched her walk away from me. She is like no other woman I've ever laid my eyes on. Who the fuck witnesses a murder and walks away as if she saw nothing at all?

Keeping my composure when she put the barrel of that gun to my head was the single hardest thing I've ever done. My first instinct was to align her against that brick wall and fuck her until she couldn't stand. I've never had that much pent up desire for a member of the female population. I'm not sure what I should do about it.

It's been two weeks since I've seen her. I've tried to keep busy until I decide what my next course of action is going to be. It's getting harder as the days pass. I'm drinking more. Weight training is no longer taking the edge off. Work isn't even keeping my mind off of it, either job. Pussy doesn't even interest me, at least no one's but hers, and it's been a while since I've fucked a woman... The time period I was in Spain I wasn't even around women; didn't want to be. I had other priorities. The last time I let myself inside a woman was Makayla and Danyel. That's fucking ridiculous, yet I'm not running off to find the first one willing to spread her legs. I was actually content with no sex...until the night in Kross' damn shop.

I've fucking jerked off so many times in the last two weeks that even that isn't making me come anymore. What guy can't make himself come? I need to fucking blow my load, yet still I can't, and my hormones are raging at a rapid rate and steadily increasing. This is the most fucked up situation. Blue balls were a thing in male adolescence, a part of the past, until recently. My nuts are so hard they hurt, fucking constantly. I want to punch a wall until I bleed.

What to do with her?

Loose ends cannot exist.

People cannot keep secrets. It will slip out eventually; always does.

There are rules. I can't break the rules. I've heard them all of my life.

Trust no one.

Numb your heart.

Live emotionless.

Sacrifice love for the good of the innocent.

All mistakes must be fixed no matter what.

"I have some information for you, boss. I think it's something you'll want."

I turn to Chevy at the sound of his deep voice, never extending outside of monotone. Dad always believed in having a right hand man that would never betray you. That was Jose to him. Each is entitled to one, and selection is very tedious. That person is recruited to ride till you die. The search for him began the second I landed on American soil. After an extensive search here he is, my night watcher, and just as fucked up as me. There is always a way to find what you're looking for.

He stops in the center of the room as he straightens his suit jacket and overlaps one hand over the other in front of his crotch; an interrogation stance, and one he does a lot, but considering his background I overlook it. Dad always believed in looking the part. He said it took you further than those that come to work looking sloppy and casual. A uniform defines the professionalism of the company. It is uniformity, oneness. Playing the part is a requirement. He took his career seriously. It didn't matter what kind it was. All of those values were instilled in me.

"In regards to the lotus?"

He nods once. My adrenaline spikes.

"Francesca."

I turn my head to her instructing a guy on where to put a floor plant. "Yes, sir? Do you want it somewhere else?"

"You are dismissed for the day."

She looks slightly taken back. "When shall I resume?"

"Whenever the fuck you want, but it won't be today."

The guy puts the plant down where he stands. She starts to push it toward the wall. I close my eyes and shake my head. When did simple instructions become so difficult for a human to understand? "Leave the damn plant!"

"Yes, sir. Sorry, sir." She stutters.

I open my eyes to her walking as fast as her heels and tight skirt will allow, after the rest of them, closing the door behind her. I take a step toward the Oak desk, waving him toward it. Draining the rest of the glass, I set it on the edge before taking a seat in the black, leather chair. He stands on the other side, waiting for instruction. "Sit down, Chevy."

He pulls the chair back slightly and walks in front of it to sit down. He looks tense. I suppose you could say we're still learning each other. He's bigger than me so I'm not sure why, his muscles much bulkier than mine, but I guess I am the one signing his paycheck, at least one of them. I lean back, propping my elbow on the armrest, placing the lower portion of my face in my hand, before rubbing my hand against the smooth shaven skin. "I understand you just got discharged, so I'm cutting you some slack. I'm going to go out on a whim and say shit wasn't a vacation over there, or even peaceful. Things will transition for you a lot easier when you realize I'm nothing like them. I'm going to leave *them* open to your own interpretation. When you walked through my door you joined a brotherhood. A real one. This job is about trust. There is no riding the fence. It's simple. You watch my back and I watch yours. No questions asked. There is only one disclaimer. You break it, you go out in a box."

His facial expression never changes. "They required me to go through *detox* when I returned." He laughs once. "Nothing here will cleanse your mind of the filth you see over there. Nothing will make living with civilians easy. I will never be the man I was before I left. Some people don't understand loyalty. I'm not one of them. I'll take a bullet before I leave you exposed. I've only failed someone once. It won't happen again."

I nod, knowing he's said all he's going to say. "What you got for me?"

"Which one do you want first? The hottie or the older one..."

My mother is the last person of interest I want to hear about at the moment. The way I feel right now I could go on a killing spree. I really don't want to be labeled as someone that would murder his own mother, no matter what she's done. That meeting is coming, but I need to be in the right mindset. Twenty years of silence and eight years of lies becomes a lot of shit to prepare for. "Option number one. We will re-adjourn on number two later."

He grabs the edge of his jacket and pulls it out enough to reach in the pocket, removing an envelope. He extends it toward me. I lean forward and take it. "Have you seen her?"

"Yes. On several occasions. She wasn't difficult to track. She's a fairly predictable person; they usually are. Humans are creatures of habit," he says with clenched teeth.

I look up at him as I break the seal on the back, removing the group of papers in a trifold. "Which is why some need to be disposed of. Occasionally the gene pool mixes off balance. Someone has to right it before it gets out of hand."

I open the group of papers, silently studying each one: birth certificate, driver's license, social security information, credit report, and background check. Noting: *misdemeanor for public drunk, fighting, and disturbing the peace, though I shouldn't be surprised*. Followed is family information, *or lack thereof*, school records, *also noting that they end after high school, reason to be determined*, medical history, recent blood check and pelvic exam, full STD screening - *clean*, financial information, and also demographics. If only the average person knew how much of their information was available to the public with a little digging and funds at their disposal, it would blow their fucking minds.

"Does that suffice?"

I lay the stack of papers on the desk and lean on my forearms on top of them. "It does. Job well done. Where is she now?"

"Headed to a martial arts studio." He looks at his watch. "She should be arriving in approximately twenty minutes. I checked out her work schedule. She should be off tonight."

I look down and shuffle back through the papers until I locate place of employment. I tap my fingers over the black ink. "Server at a catering company?" *That doesn't make sense. She's twenty-five fucking years old and not in school. Why the hell is a girl that dresses like that still a server?*

I push my chair back as I stand, before grabbing my jacket off the back of my chair. I pull it on. "Do you need me to watch her, boss?"

"Nah. I got this one. Take the night off. We have a meeting on a new hit tomorrow. I need you ready and rested. Stake out will begin at nightfall. Lock up, will you?"

I walk away as he mumbles, "Sleep doesn't exist in my world, but sure thing."

I call out as I near the door. "Text me the details of the place. It's

Atlanta. There are several."

It's been a few years since I've set foot in a martial arts studio. A little one on one with a certain beautiful smartass sounds like an appetizing night: sweat, skin, and her marvelous rack pressed against me.... Mmm, maybe it'll do something for this raging bad mood I've been in. We'll see how much of a badass she is without a gun clenched in her hand. Whether I win or not I can already smell victory. I may even let myself have the prize this time...

I glance between the text message and the sign on the building, ensuring the names match. They do. I park towards the back and cut the engine to my truck. Reaching over the console I grab the duffel bag I always keep with me for weight training when my schedule allows. I changed back at the office to save time in having to find the locker room.

As the alarm on my truck sounds confirming it's locked, a certain license plate grabs my attention on a silver Porsche. *My Lux.* That doesn't strike me as something a girl would have put on her license plate. That thought spikes an aggression I don't need when attempting to go into a cage with a girl. When facing off with a female, a male already has to tone it down to even the score. I would never hit a woman outside of the professional art of fighting. That's mutual consent, a contact sport. Some women like to face off with a man. If they win, it's a higher level of pride and respect, because every human knows God made men stronger. I wouldn't touch her unless she chooses for me to. It's about a choice. A fine line between abuse and a sport is the option to choose.

I stop as the driver's side door opens on the car. Perfect timing. I sling my bag over my shoulder. First, out comes a leg: a long, tan, bare, and slender leg, perfect length for wrapping around...*things*... the rest of her skin disappearing into the car. Her hand grabs ahold of the roof at the doorframe, serving as a supporting device to help hoist her out of the low car. She stands, making herself visible.

Fuck, she looks even better than I remember. That body should be illegal. She knows it. She's showing it off for every fucking horny man to stare at. That thought doesn't sit well either. Those tiny black shorts look like they're painted on her body, leaving very little to the imagination. Her midriff is bare. The only thing covering the torso that I've personally marked is the red sports bra, but she's turned away from me so I can't see the ink that is being displayed on her body.

She hasn't noticed me standing here yet. She bends over and into the car as if she's looking for something. Her beautifully round and toned ass is in the perfect position for so many things. My hand is starting to twitch. I clench my fist, trying to calm the urge. It would take little to no effort at all to pull those shorts over her ass, leaving them at her thighs as I slip inside.

I close my eyes and shake my head, trying to clear the visuals already taking precedent over everything else...like control over body parts. Too late. I look down at the rather noticeable bulge in my athletic shorts. Dammit. I grab my cock and try to press it down, but it doesn't change in the slightest. It has a fucking mind of its own.

This material hides nothing. The designer had to have been a damn female. No man is going to make it so easy to have his shit on display. We are well aware sex is all we think about and our dicks are addicted to pussy. For something that doesn't have a control center for its own senses it sure as hell stands to attention when near a woman's pussy, as if it can smell it.

What the fuck ever. Might as well own it. My feet start to move forward without any thought at all, never taking my eyes off of her as her ass sways in the air.

"Where is it? Shit." Her voice carries probably more than she's aware of.

Coming to stand directly behind her, I set my bag down quietly. I press my crotch against her backside and lean forward as my hands slide across her stomach. "Right here, baby."

She stands prematurely and hits her head against the roof of the car. "Ouch! Fuck."

I break out into a smile. She does have a filthy mouth. I stand upright, but don't attempt to move any other area of my body. She presses her ass into my dick as she tries to back out of the car. As I rub my hands up the length of her body, goose bumps start to form beneath them. As if she just now noticed my erection, she jolts upright.

I press her body against mine, my mouth just outside her ear, as one hand remains flat against her stomach and the other continues upward, slipping underneath her bra, stopping in a cupped position over her breast, her firm, fake, but hot as hell breast. Call me shallow, but I love a set of beautiful tits, real or enhanced. "Easy, killer. I'm not going to hurt you...yet."

"I should be calling you that." Her nipple hardens and her breathing starts to become uneven. She lays her head against my shoulder. "What do you want? Are you switching from killer to stalker now?"

I start rubbing the pad of my thumb back and forth across her nipple. "I told you I was coming for you. I always keep my word. Does it turn you on to think about me hurting you?"

"No."

"Are you sure?"

"Yes."

My hand on her stomach veers downward, sliding beneath the waistband of her shorts. She places her hand over my wrist but doesn't stop me. I stop when my fingertips reach the smooth area above her clit. "We're in public. You shouldn't be doing this. Someone might see."

"Do you want me to stop?"

Pause.

"No."

"I'm going to ask you again. Does it turn you on to think about me hurting you?"

"No."

"Don't lie to me. I'm about to find out for myself."

"Yes. Fuck, what is wrong with me?"

"Do you want me to hurt you?"

"No. Maybe. I don't want you to kill me if that's what you're asking. What makes you think I'd let you? I can take care of myself."

She places one foot in the door jam, giving me better access between her legs. I continue over her mound until my fingertips are directly over her pussy, circling in her wetness. She's no longer able to hide that she's turned on. I remove the hand from her breast and wrap it around her hair, clenching it tight. I pull hard, revealing the length of her neck as I shove two fingers inside of her. She moans out before slapping her hand over her mouth. Fucking hell her pussy feels amazing, better than I remember from the sample I got, and this is just around my fingers. Thrusting in and out, I swipe my tongue along her neck, tasting her skin. "Oh, baby, if I wanted to bad enough I could. Never underestimate the power of someone that feels nothing."

"I'm not scared of you, you know."

"You should be."

"I'm not."

"Why is that?"

I nip her ear.

"Because you won't hurt me."

I press my thumb against her clit, hard. "Shit," she says breathless.

"You sound pretty sure of yourself."

"In the most absolute form."

"And why is that?"

Before I can register where it is, she shoves her hand down the front of my shorts and grips it around my dick, squeezing hard. I grunt. "Because if you were going to do it you would have already, just as I would have when I pointed the barrel at your head. I don't carry it around for looks. I know how to use it."

She starts to stroke her hand, driving my hormones to insane levels. I haven't felt like this without something wet and slippery since I was an adolescent discovering what it was to come. "If you're going to threaten someone, make sure it's someone that doesn't have a heart made of ice. I surprised you when I didn't run away in fear. You don't know what to make of a girl like me. I'm not afraid to die. I've seen things over the course of my life that would shock even a guy like you. A bullet is nothing to me."

She releases me long enough to turn around in my arms, twisting with me still inside her shorts, before I shove my fingers back inside while she goes back to gripping my cock in her hand once again, pulling with a tight grip. I look into those clear blue eyes. The angle is better this way. I have better control. I thrust inside her harder, pushing her up on her toes, wanting in. She smiles. We continue staring at each other, roughly pleasing the other in a face off.

"You found the ice queen. Guys like you I normally chew up and spit out, although, curiosity is getting the best of us, making us crazy. We both only want one thing from this, so why don't we just get down to business. You want to fuck me and I want you to, so do it already. Everyone needs a little adventure every once in a while. Then, you'll figure out that we're not all that different, you can move on to the next girl that turns your head, and I can work on finding the next man that can give me what I want, because I play in the majors, baby. I'll take your little secret to my grave. It wouldn't be the only one."

At the sound of the last word she clenches her pussy so tight around my fingers that I snap, pressing her against the car, not giving a damn who's watching. I press myself against her further as our lips collide in a heated need. She pushes my shorts down far enough that the waist is sitting just above the base of my dick and halfway down my ass. Two seconds from fucking her right here in this parking lot and it dawns on me. This is exactly what she wants. She's fucking playing me, baiting me.

Cold turkey I release her, removing my fingers from her pussy, before slapping my palm down on the frame of the car. I place my other hand on her neck and slightly squeeze as I place my lips next to her ear. "I'll decide when we move on from this. Sex with me isn't like sex with everyone else, beautiful. When I take you, I don't want ten minutes in a packed out parking lot. I want all night. I'm enjoying the build up, and when I blow, you're going to be the one strapped to the bomb. I think I'll stick around for a while."

She growls out in aggravation as she removes her hand from my pants. She shoves me back, or tries to anyway. Cute. "Ugh. Fuck you. You're such a damn tease. What is your problem? I'm basically giving you a free card for a night with no small print and you're seriously going to turn it down? Whatev, playa, I'm out."

She holds up a peace sign with her two fingers and tries to push off the car, but I push her back against it again, tightening my hold around her neck, but still allowing for her to breathe. "Let's get something fucking straight. My cock is going in your pussy. It's not a matter of if, but when. I'm just not giving you the satisfaction of walking away with a post-orgasmic smile on your face like you defeated the world by not getting emotionally attached like most women."

I grab her thigh with my hand resting against the car and wrap it around my waist, pressing my still hardened cock into the point between her legs. She moans out, clearly without restraint. "I'm not that forgettable, baby. Everything you know about men - forget it. I broke the mold. You may think you can just walk away, but you're wrong, and in time I'll prove it. Saddle up, Lux, because you're about to go for a ride."

"Cocky much? I could be losing interest as we speak. Dicks are a dime a dozen. They all pretty much serve the same purpose." She winks.

I take her bottom lip between mine, lightly sucking on it, before fitting my mouth perfectly with hers, our tongues instantly tangling. She leans the back of her head against the frame of the car. "Call it what you want. Your tongue may be good at bullshit but your body can't lie. We both want it. A fact that has nothing to do with cockiness."

I back off of her, dropping all hands from her body. I need a fucking drink. Grabbing my bag, I turn to walk away, leaving her standing behind me. Suddenly I'm a little too wound up for hitting. I'm liable to kill someone. That act is reserved for the evildoers. "Where are you going," she calls out in question.

I never look back as I begin toward my truck. "Somewhere else before I'm to the point of no return."

"You're getting good at pressing the stop button. Just remember a girl has to get hers. There is always someone else willing to do what you won't. I'm not waiting around for you, handsome. You've been warned."

"You'll be seeing me around, Larsen. I have eyes everywhere. You're now mine. I do not share with other cocks. Try me and see."

"I never told you my last name."

"You didn't have to. I have ways of finding out what I want to know."

I open the door to my truck as I look over at her. She's standing with her hands on her hips and her eyes narrowed. Fuck, I need to get out of here. I want to strip her of her clothes right there and fuck her on that expensive car. "Don't go digging in my shit, Kaston. Your nose doesn't belong there. You haven't seen pissed off yet. Try me and see," she copies from my previous statement.

I wink at her from across the lot. "Everything has a double meaning, sexy. My nose belongs in more places than you're willing to admit. Wait for me."

I get in my truck and shut the door, before quickly starting the engine and peeling out of the lot in a hurry. I have a strong gut feeling that I won't be able to stay away long. My gut feelings are never wrong. No amount of whiskey can calm the raging storm that's brewing inside. That girl is a fucking tsunami.

Together... we may very well destroy a piece of the world.

Lux

Ugh. He makes me fucking crazy. For someone I barely know he sure does know how to get under my skin. I don't have time for his shit. I have too much other stuff to deal with... like work and my mom coming into town before long. I may regret this, but sometimes we have to make decisions that we aren't that thrilled with to help someone else. My mom is moving in with me...for now. I don't think I can physically handle her for very long, because I've lived alone for the past four years, and before that it was just Delta and I. I'll probably be staying with her a lot, but if this helps my Mom clean up her act I'll figure it out. Shit, as much as I have to help her this should save me money.

I look back and forth between the martial arts studio and my car. My whole day has been thrown off course now. Does he really think I'm going to listen to his bullshit? I'm not waiting around on a man that can't decide whether he wants to get laid or not. It's a pretty simple decision. I am in no form in a commitment with him. He's a stranger to me. He must be out of his damn mind.

What to do? I never skip out on working out, but I don't know how I'm supposed to concentrate on my movements in the state he has left me in. I haven't gotten a piece of ass in two weeks. Leave it to fucking Callum to screw up everything.

I fold my arms together on the roof of the car and lay my head in the middle, resting my forehead on my forearms. The sound of my phone ringing startles me. It's Delta's ringtone. I reach into my car and grab it, touching the answer button before holding it to my ear. "Hey, you. What's up?"

Squeal - a high-pitched one.

"Holy shit, Delta. I like having the capability to hear. A little warning next time."

All I can hear in the phone is shuffling around and shortened breathing. I hold it out to look at the screen. The call timer is still counting. "Delta...hello."

"Sorry. I need you. Now. There was no one else to call. Are you working tonight?"

"Uh. No actually. Why? What's up?"

"I got the call, Lux. I finally got the fucking call I've been a nervous wreck about."

"And..."

"I got the job."

Another scream.

I jerk my ear away from the phone. "Ofuckingkay. That's great, and I love you, but if you do that in my ear one more time I'm disconnecting this call. Tell me. Are you really that surprised? You're great. It was only a matter of time until someone else thought so too."

"You don't understand, Lux. This is a once in a lifetime opportunity. Not just anyone works for Kross Brannon. Only the elite in the field. He is a legend already. He chose me to be his apprentice. This never fucking happens!"

A muffled scream.

"What are you doing? Is that a pillow?"

"Sorry. I can barely breathe. Let's go out. Come on. I need to calm the fuck down. I'll get a group. I want to dance and drink. We haven't really done that in a while. Will you come? For me?"

My head falls back and I glance at the sky. It's clear. Not a rain cloud in sight. When your best friend asks you out for a celebratory evening you always say yes, because that's just what you do for friends. "Sure. Why the hell not. I have to go home and shower though, so message me the details and I'll meet you there."

"Okay. Later, chica."

I think tonight I'll give myself a freebie. Normally, I never sleep with anyone at random. It's all precisely calculated, a job. Well, maybe aside from one particularly stubborn man that I stumbled upon, but his loss. I'm not turning all of my focus on one man that obviously doesn't know what he wants. I'm not a toy, at least not to someone that doesn't matter to me. Tonight, one guy is going to get lucky, because the next major event I'm finding someone new, Callum's replacement. Out with the old and out with the players of the world. Tonight, I'm just a naive and drunk twenty-five year old that wants attention...

CHAPTER ELEVEN

Lux

The cab pulls up curbside and I hand the cabby the cash before getting out. "Thanks."

I shut the car door and stand on the sidewalk as he pulls away, looking at that long ass line. I should have been here forty-five minutes ago, but it takes time to look like this. Now all of the summertime partiers are out, and cutting in line by the bouncer doesn't always work. It depends on who is working the door. It's easier in multiples of females and Delta is already inside.

I groan out in agitation. This is one of the hottest nightclubs in the city. It isn't cheap, so it's crawling with a mixture of people. I can already hear the hip-hop music blaring, even out here. I stand straight and push my shoulders back, aligning my boobs for display. Might as well see what they can do. I didn't have them done for them to fail on me now.

I look straight ahead to see what the suit-wearing doorman looks like: tall, beefy, clearly arrogant, but still has a certain sex appeal. Easy peasy. I walk to the rope in front of the door and stop. "Hey, gorgeous. Will you let me in? My friends are inside."

He adjusts the earphone in his ear as he studies me, his eyes raking down my body very slowly. A smile spreads across his face. "I wish I could, beautiful, and if it were up to me I would, but I can't. Boss said no cuts tonight. We have a full house, and max capacity brings outsiders in. You're going to have to stand in line like the rest of them." He makes a noise as his eyes stop on my cleavage. "And that's a damn shame."

"Oh, come on. There has to be something you can do. There is always a loophole."

He is shaking his head at me and holds up a finger for me to stop talking. "Yeah, boss?"

My brows dip. He looks around me. I discretely turn to see if anyone is behind me, but there is no one. "Alone, but we're at max and no one else has left yet."

He fiddles with his ear again. "Okay. Whatever you say. You're the boss," he says, while I'm hoping that he's actually talking to someone and not himself, and then removes the rope hook from the stand, giving me room to enter. He looks at me. "ID, beautiful. Looks like it's your lucky night."

I look at the people standing in line that is now groaning, cursing, and mumbling shit that is probably best I don't hear. What exactly just happened? I open my clutch and grab my license, showing it to him as I pass through. "Should I ask questions?"

He smiles at the same time that he winks. "I wouldn't if I were you."

I pass by him and through the door of the club. Yeah, okay,

whatever. It's dark inside, the only lights being the tube lights that basically border the entire club like crown molding in a bright blue, as well as the bar, and the dim spotlights scattered throughout the ceiling of the club to allow enough light to see, but nothing more.

I start lightly bumping to the music as I squeeze my way through the crowded bodies, basically stacked on top of each other. It's packed out, and that makes me excited, giving me the beginning of an adrenaline rush. That means there will be more man-candy to choose from. The liquor is flowing. I can smell it, the various scents filling the air. Some are stronger than others. The song changes to another hip-hop tune, a faster paced one. The energy changes in the air and the dancing becomes more sensual as I glance around me.

Grinding. Lots of grinding. I'm about to be one of them.

The bar finally comes into view. I turn and slide through the group that is littered in front of the bar, creating a barrier. I spot an open seat and quickly take it, laying my clutch on the bar in front of me. I lean to the side, trying to signal the bartender when I hear it.

"What you drinking tonight, beautiful? I'll buy."

That accent. Holy hell, that sexy accent.

I turn to the man sitting beside me sipping on a Corona. His physical appearance matches the sexy voice that accompanies it. From the dark complexion and sun-kissed blonde hair to the clear, baby blue eyes, I'm going to guess Australia. I glance at his left hand. No band or suntan line in its absence. Tonight, this one is mine. I'm going to have a little fun. "Long Island iced tea. Thanks. What's your name, handsome?"

Grabbing the neck of his bottle he turns it up at his lips as a smile breaks free, setting it back down moments later, now half empty. "Flynn. What's yours?"

"Well, Flynn, I'm Lux." I spin on the stool to face him and hold out my hand. He takes it as he noticeably stares at my rack peeking out of my dress. *Hook, line, and later sinker.* "Tell me, what brings you down south? I'm going to say based on that sexy accent that you're not from around here. Where are you from?"

He doesn't immediately answer, but his smile holds its position spread across his face. Instead, he drops his hand and turns his head toward the bartender now standing on the other side of us. "What can I get you?" He yells out over the music.

"Another beer and a Long Island for the lady. Add them to my tab." Hell.... I've never had one with an accent like that before. Shit, I want to hear that in action. There is just something about a foreign accent that will get your girly bits going in two seconds flat.

The bartender nods as he begins making our order while he rhythmically sways along with the beat, as if it's no longer due to the music but out of habit from working in a bar every night. Barely a few seconds in and our drinks are sitting in front of us, ready to make the night a little more fun.

I grab my cup and place the straw between my lips, sensually sucking on the tip as I wait for him to speak. I dramatically cross my legs and take notice as his mouth slightly falls open when his eyes land on the narrow, black straw fueling my aggressive personality for later.

He clears his throat and takes another gulp of his beer. "Australia. I'm down here working." The way that rolls off his tongue he probably wouldn't even need to touch me to get me ready. Hell, he could just talk to me. "Are you a local?"

"I guess you could say that. I've been living here for almost seven years. Before that it doesn't matter. You would have to have a magnifying glass and a road map to find where I came from. How long are you here?"

He leans over closer to me, resting his elbows on the top of the bar. "Long enough for fun, but short enough I know where the line lies. What's your story, Lux? Are you just having fun or is it something more you're looking for?"

Fucking hell. Screw the straw. Placing the rim of the glass to my lips, I take a long swig, swallowing the mixture of goodness. The main flavor in focus is tequila. I lick my lips to ensure no spare drops are remaining. "All I know is fun, baby. In my world nothing else exists. I guess we're just two healthy, young individuals with mutual interests. I'm an open book, Flynn. I'm not in here for a night to forget, but a night to remember. That is what will land me in your bed later."

He starts to bite the inside of his bottom lip, still watching me with that adorable, white, surfer boy smile as he drinks his beer. He seems fun, relaxed, and not a control freak like someone I'm getting to know. "Lux! Where have you been?"

I turn toward the drunken voice that I would recognize anywhere: Delta. She runs toward me, instantly wrapping her arms around me. "I thought you were going to stand me up, bitch! Where have you been? You have to come dance with me, but first I have your shots."

I slam back the rest of my drink, way too fast, and place the empty glass back on the bar. The stronger the better. Delta is pulling my arm toward her, but first I reach into my purse. I'm always prepared for anything. "One second, Delta."

He is looking at me as if he's curious. I hold out my hand as if to shake it again. He takes it, but I leave a small piece of paper behind. "When you get ready for that fun, find me. I'll be in here somewhere. First, I have to do my best friend duties." I wink. "Thanks for the drink, *Flynn*."

That smile I thought was broad earlier just got bigger. He wears it well. "Lux! Come on! Who is that guy?" Delta pulls harder, trying to pull me away, and I let her, distancing myself from the sexy Australian I will have for desert later. I guess it's true what they say – Australia has some sexy men.

You haven't really lived until you've lived free. To be wild is to explore your deepest desires. A one-night stand is just a part of being a strong woman, succumbing to knowing exactly what you want and not being afraid of going after it. Years ago, everything was about depending on a man, but now, the true definition of an independent woman is being able to satiate all desires and still live completely alone. I am that woman.

Delta pulls me through the bar as if she's a woman on a mission. If I weren't so used to heels I'd probably topple over. "Damn, Delta. Slow down. What's your hurry?".

We arrive at a table she's obviously reserved, speckled with drinks all over it, and occupied by people I recognize that she works with, sitting and drinking. I'm guessing when you work at a bar being at a bar is no longer anything special. I nod their way to be polite, even though I don't really hang out with any of them. "What's up?"

"You have to do this shot with me, La- Lux."

I look at her and down at the row of shots in front of us. "From the sounds of it you may not need any more."

"Stop it. You're only saying that because you haven't had enough. Drink."

She hands me a shot. I don't even ask what it is. I just shoot. Then she hands me another...and another. I take a deep breath between shots, trying to relieve the burn in the back of my throat.

It's a good thing I didn't skip dinner. I set shot glass number three down. She's already holding up another. I lightly shake my head. She nods. "It's power hour, baby. We haven't done this in a few years. Stigma or stamina? It's all or nothing. We party like rock stars or stay home like moms."

On that note...

I grab another shot glass and tap it on the table before turning it back, swallowing in one gulp, and then slamming it back down. She smiles. "Don't ever compare me to a mom again. I'm not cut out for that shit. Never have been and never will." For effect I grab another and repeat my previous notion.

Shots one and two in combination with my earlier drink are starting to do their job. My buzz is enhancing with every minute that passes. I start to dance by myself to the music when I feel a set of hands enclose around my waist from behind. "Dance with me," he says.

I smile and lean my head back against his chest. "I see you found me."

"I would have looked through this entire bar before I left without you. Some opportunities you don't pass up. Every businessman knows that."

I grab his hand and turn as I lift them both above our heads. "I like how you think, Flynn. All good things start with a dance." I wink and take a step backwards. "I'll be on the floor, Delta," I yell as I lead him off. The song change is perfect for two bodies introducing themselves. As we arrive on the dance floor I line his front to my back and grab his other hand.

Starting out with a small distance between us, I start to dance, closing in as the song plays, until we're so close that there is not a single space. I start to roll my hips against him, his movements matching mine. We are in a perfect rhythm with one another. He moves one hand on the front of my stomach, pressing me into him as he grinds his erection into my ass.

I move my hand to the back of his neck and hold on to give me more leverage against him, never letting up. The heat between the bodies on the crowded dance floor and us is making me hot, causing a slight sheen on my skin. The alcohol has now taken over my blood stream, giving me that bold edge I need, and making me want more from him. Me consuming alcohol is like putting my personality on steroids.

I spin to face him, still dancing and rolling against him to the music. He looks into my eyes and I can tell he's about to kiss me. I want him to. He leans in and I close my eyes, waiting, when a hand cups over my mouth and pulls me backward against a hard chest. "I thought I told you I don't share with other cocks," he whispers into my ear.

Now that voice I recognize...

What the fuck?

My eyes open and Flynn looks a little taken back. I imagine he probably is. I grab Kaston's hand and remove it from my mouth. "What do you want?"

"Oh I think you know what I want," he grits out. "And here you are trying to give it away."

Hell no....

"Should I leave?"

I hold up my index finger to Flynn and turn around, shoving Kaston in the chest, no doubt the alcohol inhibiting wise decisions. "Let's get one thing fucking straight. You do not own me, my body, or my ability to make decisions in regards to who I do or don't sleep with. You had your chance, Kaston. You walked away not once, but twice. At some point a woman moves on. You aren't the only man that can turn me on. I'm over it. Back the fuck off."

A mask falls over his face. He has this seriousness about him I haven't seen before. Hell, that's not abnormal. I hardly know him! I'm sure he has several expressions I've never seen. His jaw steels as if his teeth are about to break. "Flynn, is it? You won't be taking this one home. She's taken."

How does Kaston know his name? Oh right, probably the same fucking way he knows my last name. Damn sexy psycho. Well, psycho boy meet bitch girl. World War III is about to begin.

"Uh, no the fuck I'm not. Don't tell my date to leave. You leave."

"You want me to leave?"

Pause. Briefly thinking...

"Yes."

"Okay. I'll leave." He reaches down and picks me up, throwing me over his shoulder, my almost bare ass in the air. "But not with you still standing in front of someone waiting for the second you let him dip his dick in your pussy."

I am not a fucking child. I pummel my fist into the center of his spine. "Put me down, Kaston."

He slaps my ass, hard. Dammit. I clench my inner leg muscles together. "You're going to have to try a lot harder to hurt me, baby." Where is he even going? I see a blur of stairs. He's climbing stairs. Where is he taking me? He climbs them with ease as if I weigh nothing, one by one, until he reaches a level floor, confirming we're at the top.

"Where are we going? You can't just take me wherever you please. Have you lost your damn mind?"

"I lost my mind a long time ago, and yes, I can take you anywhere I damn well please. Do you really object?"

My body goes limp. Plotting. I'm starting to get a head rush from being upside down. This is not smart with all I've had to drink. People are getting sparser the farther he walks down the long hallway. Can he even be up here? I don't know anything that is upstairs and I've been to this club on numerous occasions. I look down at his ass. He walks with a swagger, noticeable even from this angle. His jeans are fitted but not tight. It gives me an idea.

I grab his shirttail and pull it up, revealing the waistband of his jeans. Running my hand palm down, underneath the band, I can feel the smooth skin of his buttocks. I continue down until my fingertips are gliding over the crack of his ass. I start to press between them, hoping for a minor freak out like most straight men so that he will drop me...but instead, nothing, and then I feel his hand mirror the actions of mine, after swiftly pulling my thong down by the small V that sits above my ass, toward the bottom to reside underneath my butt cheeks.

His finger is barely pressing between my ass cheeks just like mine on his, directly above the point of entry. "You want anal play, baby, I'm ready. Just remember you get what you ask for. I'm not gentle. If I break it in I break it in right."

I should have fucking known...

"Dammit, Kaston, put me down. For the love of all things holy will you decide what the hell you want? You're going to drive me insane. This is crazy. We don't even know each other that well. It was just supposed to be a random hookup. Here we are a couple of weeks later and haven't hooked up. I figured you had moved on by now."

I hear a door open and then watch as it closes, my drunken emotions spinning farther out of control. The lock on the doorknob sounds. The room is dark and cold. "You're about to find out what it is that I want. I've backed off as long as I can."

What does that vague shit even mean? He messes with something on the wall and spotlights turn up but he keeps them on dim. They are placed in the ceiling over a large, wooden-framed desk. It's neat and orderly, barely anything residing on top. That is obviously his destination as that is where he begins walking.

A desk, a dark room, an alpha-male psycho killer, and we're alone.... That could mean one of two things: one, it's about to be a blood battle, or two, this is about to be a fuckfest, and I'm more than ready. Don't ask me why I want him like I do, but I do. There is no reason to deny it. He's dangerous, but to what exactly I'm not sure.

He sets me down roughly on top of the desk. My head spins from going quickly from one position to another. I close my eyes and place my hand on my head, hoping it will stop. He places his hands firmly on my thighs and slides me to the edge of the desk, closer to his body. My already short dress is hiked up to my waist, the backside of my panties still beneath my ass.

I open my eyes. He is staring directly at me with a heat so fierce my body temperature increases. I can't decipher what he's thinking. "I can't fucking handle someone else touching you, kissing you, or fucking you, because I want to do those things to you."

"What's stopping you?"

My eyes divert as his hand disappears into his pocket. "Because I shouldn't touch anyone that makes me feel this way. Doing that is going against the rules. You're supposed to be dead. You know too much."

"Yet I don't know enough..."

I sit up and grab his shirt in my fist, pulling him closer to my level. "You don't strike me as someone that follows rules or formalities, hence me being here against my original will. I don't give a shit what you do in your spare time. We all have things we keep hidden from others. If you're worried I'll tell, I won't. I was taught a long time ago not to be a rat. If that makes me the same caliber of person as you then so be it."

I pull him to where his lips are just outside of mine. "As far as what happens between us.... Make me yours or cut me loose. You can't straddle the fence, sexy."

"Where the fuck have you been all of my life?" He grabs the back of my head with his free hand and crushes his lips to mine, instantly sliding his tongue between my lips. It is ridiculous how turned on he makes me. I just want him to do it already. The way he tastes is like getting a dose of crack cocaine. A little isn't enough.

He halts again, releasing my lips. I growl out in aggravation. "You have got to be fucking kidding me! Come on! Would you just fuck me already? I'm about to just kill you myself. Fuck."

I'm probably being a little dramatic, but this is getting ridiculous. He smiles, his eyes on me. Smiles. Is he serious? I'm about to get up and walk away when he hooks his index finger behind the fabric of my dress, in the area between my breasts. "I'm going to, but first you will be naked. I want to see it all."

Pulling his hand from his pocket, he flips a blade up on a pocketknife and places it blade down on the fabric beside his finger, point between my breasts, before swiping it downward, ripping the fabric in a straight line from hem to hem until it parts completely. I think I may have even sucked in, but the blade never cut my skin. My mouth falls slightly. I'm trying to push aside the fact that was dangerous, but hot as fuck, and focus on the part where those were designer threads he just mutilated in less than two seconds.

He closes the knife, putting the blade away, but his eyes never stray from mine. "That was lace on satin overlay! What the hell am I supposed to wear out of here at closing?"

That smile returns. "Not my problem...yet. Next time maybe you'll look a little less appetizing in your choice of clothing. You aren't leaving at closing. This may take a while."

He nods to the right. I turn to a bed across the room. It's just now that I realize how big it is in here. It looks more like a studio apartment than an office. "Where are we? Are we supposed to be up here?"

"The only thing you should be concerned about is that I have connections all over this town. How do you think you got in tonight?"

He pushes what's left of the dress over my shoulders, letting it fall to the desk. It all suddenly and very clearly makes sense. Who exactly am I dealing with? He leans in and unhooks my bra with his lips just outside my ear. "I'm warning you, Lux. I'm a bad man. I'm capable of many things, but leaving you alone isn't one of them. I know that now. Things are about to get complicated."

His breath is tickling my ear. His touch as he removes my bra is leaving chill bumps behind. He leans back to look at me as he bares my body to him. His eyes change as he takes me in. I feel barer with him staring at me like that than I ever have naked in front of a man. "Fucking beautiful. Just as I suspected."

He grabs the waistband of my thong and pulls it down my legs in a hurry, ridding my body of the one piece of fabric that remains, before leaning forward and taking my hardened nipple in his mouth. Placing my palms down on the desk, I arch my back, wanting him to suck harder from the flicking motion he's doing with his tongue. He gets the hint and sucks hard before switching to the other side.

I look down at the sexy man at my breasts. He's still wearing way too many clothes for my liking. "Ugh uh." I grab the bottom hem of his shirt and tug it up his body until it's at his underarms. "Off."

He bites down on my nipple before standing upright and raising his arms for me to remove his shirt. I have to bite my tongue to keep from moaning out in embarrassment. "You want to see the goods?"

I toss his shirt on the floor as I stare at that beautiful, sculpted torso. I scan all of the muscles slowly until our eyes meet once again. He has that cocky grin that guys get when they know that you want them. The beauty of being a woman is that you can own it or lie. I choose to own it.

I grab the waistband of his jeans as I hook my heels on the back of his thighs and slip the button through the slit. "I've wanted the goods since you made me come without even whipping it out in that tattoo shop. That takes a special brand of talent. I want an up close look at the hardware responsible."

"Well in that case, bring it out. I wouldn't want to disappoint you now," he says without that sexy grin fading one bit. I grab ahold of his hips and rub my hands around that smooth, tight skin, until they're at his lower back. I slip my hands underneath the black, elastic band of his briefs and push them both over his ass. Grabbing the front, I pull it out and push the material down until his cock springs free, my eyes focused at his crotch as it comes into view, fully hard and ready for action.

Fuck, that's one beautiful dick...

The wetness between my legs increases to an uncomfortable level as I take it in for the first time, size and all. Not only is it longer in size than average, but it also has the girth to accompany it. Seeing it is so much better than just feeling it behind shorts. This is going to be fun.

I slide my heels against the back of his legs, pulling the back off of my foot, before letting my stilettos fall to the floor. His arms remain at his sides. He doesn't make an immediate attempt to touch me again. That is a dick I wouldn't mind sucking. Placing my hands on the edge of the desk, I hop off and squat, grabbing the waistband of his jeans once again, before pulling them down to his ankles for him to step out of. He does, just after kicking off his shoes, fully baring himself.

I enclose my hand around his cock, getting a feel for his size now that I can see it. It's as hard as a rock, the veins visible. He's completely shaven, the way I like it. I glance up at him as I lightly stroke it. "You clean?"

"Always," he responds, saying nothing more.

"Do you not want to know if I am?"

"I would if I didn't already know you are. Suck away."

I'm not even going to ask. That shit is going to be discussed later. I continue to stroke, pulling him closer to me with my other hand on his ass, as I sit back on my heels, lowering my height just a little. I'm going for the balls first. Every guy likes his balls played with as long as you handle with care. I place my mouth around the soft skin, making sure I leave my teeth out of the equation, before lightly sucking, massaging it between my tongue and the roof of my mouth.

His hands immediately grab ahold of my hair, fisting it roughly as he grunts. I continue for a few seconds before switching sides. "I'm glad to see you know what the fuck you're doing," he says in an uneven tone, clearly enjoying it.

I smile inside, knowing I haven't even really gotten started yet. Narrowing my tongue into a point, I swipe it up the line that separates the two testicles, before running it along the underside of his cock as I hold it from above, not stopping until I reach the head.

I stand to my knees as I take the head into the shape of my mouth, first swirling my tongue around it to moisten it. I lick over the tip of the head, running my tongue over the slit to check for the bead of pre-cum I want present. The salty mixture is there, but only briefly.

I close my mouth around him, relaxing the back of my throat, and changing the flow of my breathing to nasal only. I take him into my mouth completely, until the head of his dick hits the back of my throat, increasing the production of saliva. When I know I'm fully relaxed, I hold the end of his shaft with only two fingers and pull back, creating suction as I do, using my mouth as a lubricant.

When I reach the head I flick my tongue over the sensitive spot on the underside, the small triangular shape between the shaft and the head, before taking him once again, only this time quickening my pace and creating a fast rhythm of repetition. His fist tightens in my hair, pulling every few seconds. If only he knew that's like hitting the NOS button in a street race. I suck faster, grabbing ahold of his balls in my free hand, massaging as I suck.

"Fucking shit. Enough," he barks out, pulling my hair, hard, until his dick falls from my mouth, making me even wetter than I already am.

I look up at him from underneath my eyelashes. "Did you come prepared?"

He reaches around the desk and pulls open a drawer. When he closes it and raises his arm, a strip of condoms fall open from the one he's holding in his hand. "The question is, did you?"

I reach up and tear off the bottom condom, before ripping it open with my teeth. I spit out the end piece, as my eyes stay locked with his. "If you can keep up with me, baby, you'll go down in my history book."

I place the opening of the condom on the head of his dick and roll it out, down the length of his cock. He's looking down at me, watching me do what most guys usually do with ease. His jaw is twitching as if he's working it back and forth. "Kaston Cox. Get ready to write it down."

With a smile on my face I stand to my feet, watching him the entire time. I cross my left foot over my right and slowly turn until I'm facing the desk. I look to my left shoulder and reach my right arm over my head, running my fingertips down my left hairline, sweeping my hair over my right shoulder, revealing my neck, before placing both palms face down on the desk as I bend forward, waving my ass seductively. "My pussy is ready for you, Kaston. Don't hold back."

He takes a step forward and wraps one arm around my waist, lifting me slightly to alter my body weight onto my toes. Not wasting any time, he presses his head to my opening, before ramming himself inside of me as deep as he can go, without even checking to see that I'm wet. My back arches on reflex as he fills me completely. He pulls back and slams into me once again, hitting something deep inside, causing me to tense. "I don't plan on it," he says between thrusts, before moving both hands to my hips for leverage.

He continues in a repeated motion, thrusting as hard as he can, not stopping before doing it again. He's not allowing me to adjust to his size, but making me. Each time he enters me he clenches tighter on my hips, digging his fingers into my skin. I moan out and grab ahold of the edge of the desk in my hands to hold me steady as I take him, all of him. He has enough length that I can feel him close to my cervix. With each hit I get a small pain in my abdomen, but as he pulls out the pleasure quickly replaces it. I will endure it. I will not be a pussy.

When he enters me again I tighten around his cock, causing

him to grind his hips into me, lifting me enough that he can press deeper. "Fuck. Pull my hair."

I hear a throaty groan from behind me as he takes my hair in his hand, wrapping it around his fist, before pulling back hard on my head, making my body arch even more, my pussy more exposed. "Again," he says. "Squeeze my cock. Show me how much you want it."

I do as told. "Fuck," he mumbles in a hushed whisper, before pulling my hair harder, standing me mostly upright. He moves one hand to my breast and the other to my clit. He remains still inside me, focusing now on massaging my clit as he pinches my nipple between his index finger and thumb. My head automatically leans back against his shoulder, unable to move with him doing that.

He presses his lips against my ear as he rubs my clit with his finger. "You want to show me how good that pussy is? Make me come...but first, I want you to turn around and memorize the face you're going to be seeing for a while. Brand me into your memory, because I will be the only one you spread your legs for. Now I've gotten a taste and I like it. You can even call me hooked. This pussy was molded for me."

"Is that a challenge?"

"It's a request."

He says that as if it's a plea... and now more than ever I want to make him come. I want to milk him dry.

He releases my breast and replaces his hold on my chin, turning my head to look at him, still bringing me to the edge of orgasm as he speaks, as if he doesn't even have to concentrate on getting me off. His eyes remain glued to mine as he kisses my lips. His voice never reaches a shout, making him more intense. "You can be stubborn or you can face it, but you know you want me too. Don't think for a second that I won't kill for you."

Most girls would be scared, but me, I guess I have to be just as fucking crazy as he is, because that has to be the sexiest thing I've ever been promised by a man. The one thing I have to remember... if he wants me, he will pay. Desire doesn't keep you alive.

Just when I'm about to come he stops, pulls out of me, and spins me around, before lifting me back on the desk and pushes me back. The wood is cold against my back. He presses into my clit as he shoves his dick back inside of me and starts up again, rubbing against my clit with a pressure as he fucks me...hard. I pull my feet to rest on top of the desk, spreading wider for him. "This pussy is mine. Say it."

"We'll see," I respond honestly.

He leans forward and grabs my hands in his, raising them above my head as he presses in deeper. "Are you trying to piss me off?"

I raise my hips, pressing closer to him. He makes me feel full, free of void. "Why do you want me? This is just sex. After we get this out of our systems you'll move on to the next one, same as me. It's no big deal. It's who we are."

"Just alike..."

He says it so matter of fact. I can't say anything more as he pounds deep inside of me, never letting up. Something happens between us that is foreign. I can't take my eyes off of him, nor can he off me. "I don't know why I want *you,* but what I do know is that nofuckingbody else is going to touch you this way until we figure it out. This. Pussy. Is. Mine. Say it," he grits out with another thrust, hitting something vaguely familiar.

"Oh fuck. Do that again."

"You like that?"

He hits that spot again. Hell, that feels so good. My back arches off the table as an abnormal build starts to occur. "Yes. Shit. Please don't stop."

"You want more?"

That dark voice only adds to it. "Yes." My mouth falls open, the moans unstoppable. An all-consuming feeling occurs, causing me to curl my toes as my legs start to close without demand, pressing against his sides. His thrusts become rougher, needy. "Oh fuck. I'm coming. Yes. Holy shit."

My pussy clenches tight around his dick as my fingers claw into the back of his hands. My feet reflexively press into the desk, lifting my pelvis into him more, as if they are working from memory. "Fuck, you are beautiful when you come. It's like it's the first time..."

It feels like it is...

Everything is playing in slow motion. I want to keep going, but I want to stop and enjoy it all. It's a strange yet amazing feeling. His mouth goes for my nipple, sucking it into his mouth as his thrusts become more shallow and slower, as if he's about to come. I control my muscle contractions, tightening around him. "Fuck," he groans against my breast. "Again." He voice deepens and his pace slows once more, until he stills completely.

My legs wrap around his waist, my pussy throbbing and wanting more. Maybe it's the alcohol and maybe it's the fact that I want another one of those. A clit orgasm feels good, but it's a short burst. That was more like an eight second ride. It probably felt longer than it was, but it was intense the entire time.

He releases the hold on my hands. "You done?" My grin is spreading, feeling like a champion.

He looks down and I can feel his dick move inside of me, flexing like a muscle, confirming he is still hard. His grin matches mine. "Hell no. You're going to make me come again. After that I'm ready to marathon, baby. I want to see what you got. You haven't been fucked properly until you walk out of here sore."

He pulls out of me and I drop my legs from his waist. I prop up on my forearms as I watch him remove the condom, tossing it in a trashcan. He quickly grabs another and tears into it, replacing the used one. Sliding his hands behind my back he pulls me toward him. "Hold on."

He picks me up and I wrap my arms and legs around him. He walks to the bed and tosses me on top, coming to lean down over me. "You ready to say it yet?"

I study his expression. You can never read him. He has an impeccable poker face. "You're really serious? You want to keep this going after only one time? Should I be concerned?"

"That's what I said isn't it?"

"Why? What's the big catch or small print disclaimer that I'm missing?"

"If I recall you said, make me yours or cut me loose. Well I'm choosing to make you mine...for now. I'm not double dipping behind someone else. I am not sharing your pussy with another dick. From the look on your face earlier I know you aren't ready to move on yet. Say it."

"You are such an ass. Fine. If you keep making me come like that then yeah, I'll agree, but I come with a warning label for a consistent relationship of sorts. If you want me beyond tonight you will pay...financially. You can call it what you want, but if we're being honest that's it. I'm not here for love and I'm not here for forever. I'm here for give and take, nothing more and nothing less. I have requirements for the men that I date, so now that you know what you're getting into, do you still want it?"

I'm sure he's going to back out and that's fine. After tonight it's time to move on. No man like him wants a woman after his wallet. He can find a willing applicant to spread her legs without the hassle anywhere. Rich men have too much fucking money to care and that's most often what they're looking for anyway, because it's a control mechanism. It works for them and it works for me, unless they're married. Even I have limits.

He just stares at me, saying nothing. He moves off of me and sits on the bed, before scooting to the center. My brows dip as I turn to look at him. He places his hands interlocked behind his head as he leans against the headboard, completely fucking naked and hard, his cock on display and ready to be ridden. Why the hell is he so fucking hot?

"No comment?"

And that smirk returns.

"You're pretty straight forward, huh?"

I shrug. "Things usually work out in my favor that way. I'm not really fond of bullshit. See, things are just better for us to have a good time and part ways tomorrow morning. We have two very different goals in mind."

"Or the same."

"Meaning..."

"We'll figure it out. For now, I'm curious. That doesn't happen very often. If you want access to my wallet, then find lots of ways to make me come. Like you said, give and take. Equal opportunity. A win for both of us."

"You're really down for this? You're okay with us just openly using each other? Have you lost your fucking mind?"

"Call it what you want," he says sarcastically with a grin, repeating me from earlier. This is becoming a pattern between us. "Good pussy might be worth it to me. Like the perfect suit yours fits like a glove, so I'll buy it, no matter what it costs. All good things come with a price. Are we going to sit here and talk or are we going to fuck?"

I stare at him, completely fucking in awe with a shit-eating grin on my face.

Where have you been all of my life...

I barrel roll onto my hands and knees, before crawling toward him. I stand to my knees, straddled over his legs. Walking up the length, I stop directly above his dick, his still fully hard dick. How is that even fucking possible without medication? We haven't touched each other for several minutes now, post orgasm.

Our eyes lock, cocky grins mirroring one another. I grab the shaft of his cock and hold it steady as I sit down, consuming it in its entirety. "You're such an asshole," I breathe out, my voice only coming out in a whisper as the pleasure of his dick inside me takes forefront in my mind once again, making it hard to think of anything else.

He presses his thumb to my clit and starts to rub as I begin to rock my bottom half back and forth, letting his dick hit the interior walls, making me almost forget the entire conversation. "It takes one to know one," he says in a deepened tone.

I lean back and place my hands on his legs, arching my back and letting my head fall back, the tips of my hair brushing against my ass. "I know. It's perfect."

I change motions, using my bent legs to push off, sliding up and down on his dick. As I start to sit back down he pushes my pelvis back, his dick hitting that spot again. I take the hint and continue in a rocking motion once again. "Then use it to your advantage. Fuck my cock, make yourself come, and make me come. It doesn't get any more perfect than that."

That's the last thing I remember before my brain detours into oblivion, something that I can't recall it doing during sex one single time in my life. If this is what it means to be marked by him, then my body is completely and irreversibly his, though I'm not sure for how long. Some marks are permanent...and that's the part that's nerve racking.

CHAPTER TWELVE

I roll over to something on the pillow crinkling under my face. I grab the note and roll back over onto my back. I have to work at opening my eyes, but after a few seconds of rubbing they come unglued from the sleep present trying to keep them sealed shut. My head is pounding and I want to do nothing but sleep. I need food, I need water, and I need to brush my teeth. That reminds me...

I sit up in a hurry and look around the room. Heavy black curtains cover the windows, to keep the sun out I'm guessing. The room is quiet and dark, as well as cold, reminding me that I'm naked. Pulling the comforter up to cover me, I look down at the piece of paper in my hand, but it's too dark to read without a light. On the nightstand is a lamp. I reach over and turn it on. I need a few minutes to wake up before I attempt to read it with this alcohol-induced headache.

Pieces of last night start to replay in my mind; so vivid that I would think it was just a dream if my vagina didn't feel like it was recently used as a punching bag. Maybe I should think twice next time, before agreeing to basically fuck all night...

Nah.

He held up his end of the bargain though. There are many men out there that are lucky to get it up for round two so soon after round one. I think I stopped counting after round four last night... or early this morning. Honestly, I'm not even sure if I've slept more than two hours total.

I quickly glance over the side of the bed on the floor for the proof that I know is there if it really happened, but everything is spotless. There isn't a condom wrapper present. I drop the paper to jump out of bed and run to the garbage can beside the desk, and then bring it back into the light. It's empty.

What the fuck?

Sitting it back down on the floor I make my way to the nearest curtain and open it for more light, looking down over the entry to the club. Is this where he was the whole time? Sneaky bastard. I'm so confused. Where is he?

I place my hands on my hips as I look around the room. Nothing looks out of place to prove last night happened...except the unfamiliar set of clothes lying at the foot of the bed that I'm just now noticing.

I walk over to look at them, inspecting them carefully. My eyes widen as I take in the brand. No fucking way. Surely he can't afford this shit.

The note...

I crawl across the bed until I reach the center where I threw it down and grab it. I hold it in both hands as I read the messy handwriting scribbled on the front.

Lux,

I had work that couldn't be postponed. On the bed you will find a set of clothing you should find presentable for your particular taste, to replace the dress that will no longer be of use. I suspect you would rather go against the grain of most women, so on the back of this note you will find my number. Give it to <u>NO ONE</u>. Use it, tonight preferably. I'm saving you the awkward tiptoeing walk of shame when you think I'm asleep that I know you would be attempting if I had stayed. You're free to go when you please. Everything said and discussed last night still stands. If you were overly intoxicated, then I suggest you start now trying to recall that conversation. Call me. Don't make me come find you...

Kayton

Asshole. I wad it up and throw it down, then pick it back up and un-crinkle it. Sexy asshole. Where the hell is my purse? I wad the piece of paper up again and toss it in the trash. I bet he would get his fine ass briefs in a bunch if I just casually misplaced his number and make him do all the work. I walk to the set of clothes and touch them. Everything is new with tags, including the underwear. He has good taste. I'll give him a little credit.

I pull on the matching lace underwear first. Sexy asshole that gives really good orgasms....

Oh hell.

I walk in a hurry to the trashcan and grab the piece of paper, opening it once again. I flip it over to stare at the ten-digit number. Fuck my life. I've already gotten addicted to sexy-man sex. I'm screwed.

Fuck him once and he does it right, then you'll fuck him twice and keep coming back...

I want to face-palm myself. I lay the piece of paper neatly on the bed beside the clothes, staring at the phone number every few seconds as I finish dressing. "What happened to your woman balls, Larsen?"

Fully dressed, I grab the piece of crinkled paper and begin looking for my purse. "If I were Kaston where would I put you?"

The desk was the first place we went. I walk toward it. My purse is lying on top. I grab it and open it, pulling out my cell phone. I don't even look through the missed calls and texts. Instead, I open the lock screen and key in the number from the piece of paper, pressing the call button. To my surprise, the name *Kaston* appears with a photo as the call dials. Was someone worried I may forget what he looks like? All I can do at this point is roll my eyes. It's scary to think of the girls in his path before me. He's a damn lunatic. Maybe I should have a password on my phone.

I'm about to hang up when the line picks up. "I see you got my note."

"How were you sure it was even me calling? You really should stop that shit. It's only going to get you in a bind one of these days. Besides, that cocky ass shit is going to land you in bed *alone....* I almost threw your little note in the trash."

"But you didn't."

"Luckily for you, you know how to use that dick of yours beautifully. It can be quite persuasive even when absent." I place my purse underneath my arm and look around for a pair of shoes.

Of course there is a pair of flats on the floor in front of the bed. Does the man miss a single detail? My heels would have been fine.

"That's interesting. I can be persuasive with a lot of things in my grasp. I thought we established that last night."

"Yeah, yeah. You got in my pants. That's not really a big accomplishment, Cox. I wanted you, so I had you. Technically you didn't have to try real hard. Nice try though. A+ for effort." I walk toward the door, checking through the room one last time.

He laughs. I stop mid step in the middle of the room. He has a beautiful laugh. I look at the phone and press the mute button, then slap myself across the face. "Stop it."

I take a deep breath. I feel better now. I un-mute the phone and press it back to my ear. "Well, I just thought I would say good morning since you were thoughtful enough to clean up and leave a note."

I open the door to the stairwell. "Oh, thanks for the clothes. It probably would have looked a little strange with me walking home naked or in a bed sheet through Atlanta. Anyway, I guess I'll see you around..."

What the hell, Lux? See you around? You just slept with him for fuck's sake.

"I have to go."

"What are you doing later?"

"Working."

"Where?"

"I prefer to keep that personal at this time. You know, you could be a stalker or some shit. I don't really know you that well. What if you try to kill me?"

He laughs again.

My heart starts to race.

I really need to clear my head. "You know my number now. I'll talk to you later."

Before he can say anything I disconnect the call, shoving my phone into my purse. I need to get my head back in the game. I'm not that girl. My heart doesn't pitter-patter at the sound of a random guy's laugh. I don't get all nervous with his touch. I sure as hell don't develop emotions with simple flirting, or sex for that matter. Emotional attachments don't exist with me. They never have. This is a business investment. This is a temporary job; common interests. We are not friends. We are sex partners; fuck buddies. Once we're finished with each other, we will go our separate ways and never see each other again.

I run down the stairs and outside of the club before anyone can stop me to ask questions. I still have a while before work. I'm not really in the mood to sleep; yet I have no idea what I want to do.

I shove my key into my mailbox and unlock the door, opening it to retrieve my mail. Once I grab it I lock my box back and extract my keys, turning to walk through the narrow hall toward the stairwell as I shuffle through the stack of mail in my hand: bills, junk, useless invites to shit that I won't attend, *Culinary Institute of America*.

I stop suddenly, causing the person walking behind me to run into me. "Shit, I'm sorry," I say as the middle-aged man continues walking, staring at me like I have a third eye as he passes. I remain standing in place as I look back down, staring at the envelope before me, imprinted with the name of such a sacred place. I run my fingers over the name in ink as if it's a mirage. I close my eyes and open them again, thinking maybe it's just the effects of no sleep and lots of alcohol, but the words are still there accompanying my name and mailing address.

My brows dip. Why would they send me something? I've never applied. It's pointless and I know that, so there was never any reason to be let down over something I can't control. I realized a long time ago that culinary school would never happen for me. Even if I was accepted, I can't foot the bill and support myself. I'll take money from men for a lot of things, but that isn't one of them, because that would require me actually giving that piece of myself away to someone else, someone besides Delta, and opening myself up to idea of letting someone in. When you reveal your deepest wants and desires to someone, it gives him the power to hurt you. That's something I'll never do.

I don't want someone knowing that part of me, the part confirming that just like everyone else I have a humble dream that isn't shallow. I'm fine taking care of myself. When Delta and I decided to stay in Atlanta I got a job doing the next best thing, still surrounded by amazing chefs. I've been fine with it ever since.

I flip over the envelope and slide my finger beneath the flap, tearing the paper along the seal until it's open. My hands start to shake as I remove the paper, creased neatly in a trifold. I open it to company letterhead that matches the envelope, taking precedent to a typed out formal letter.

Dear Miss Larsen,

Thank you for your recent application to Le Cordon Bleu, college of Culinary Arts, Atlanta division. We are pleased to inform you that you have been accepted to attend the 2015-2016 school year, the start to your path in graduating with a degree in culinary arts or baking and pastry from the number one culinary educator in the country. Please contact the registration office for schedule and financial information. We look forward to having you as a part of our program.

Best regards,

John Thomas

Director of Admissions

My arms fall to my sides as I work to breathe. My stomach feels like it's twisted into a million knots. I've been accepted? I didn't even apply. My heart is pounding a hundred miles an hour and my head is spinning. I feel sick. Why would I get this? Is this some cruel joke?

Delta…

We've been best friends for years and still we care about each other more than ourselves. God, I love her. I have one dream and this is it. Is there a way I could swing it? I keep telling her to go after her dream of being a tattoo artist, so it would be a little hypocritical not to go after my own.

My mother coming into town surfaces in my mind. As quickly as my dream was granted it was also taken away. I blow out. Who am I fucking kidding? I can't afford to pay for this shit and everything else I have going on. She needs me. She may be a pain in my ass but she's still my mother. Secretly I long for her to be well, to be more like the mother and not the child. I'm not sure she has been mentally stable my entire life. Her whole mindset is completely fucked up.

My eyes set on the trashcan at the end of the narrow hallway. My eyes develop a gloss overlay, but I blink it away. This is real life. It isn't a fairytale or a happily ever after. Girls like me don't get wishes from a genie in a bottle. Me, I just drew the short end of the stick. Crying and whining doesn't change the outcome. Sometimes life is shitty. This is mine.

I push my shoulders back and walk forward, tossing the letter into the trashcan for mail recycling. I'd probably fail anyway. Things are better this way. Success just isn't in the stars for me. I'm the girl that likes to party, the girl that spreads her legs, the gold digger, and the mistake. I'm the pretty face and sexy body that men want to fuck on Thursday nights while their wives sit at home pregnant. I'm the temporary affair they lie in order to obtain, and I'm okay with that, because in being that I ensure that I never end up completely destroyed at the hands of someone else...like my mother.

Kayton

Don't ask me why I came here. I have no fucking idea. I have a ton of other shit I need to be doing, like starting up a business that's been ran from another country for years, or meeting with prospective clients, but after she called me I had to see her, so I came. As far as I'm concerned the woman that made me come multiple times in one night deserves the world at her feet. I'm still coming down from the high. My dick is happy and exhausted, yet still wants more.

Here I stand, staring into the entryway as she tosses a piece of mail into the garbage. It's not an abnormal act. People throw away junk mail all the time, but the pause as she read the sheet of paper and the change in her body language as she did so were the hints that she's hiding things, that there's more to her than what meets the eye.

I walk to the trashcan when she's out of sight. She never looked back at me the entire time I've been standing here. I reach inside and grab the sheet of paper on top, reading the piece of mail now available for public knowledge; an acceptance letter. Who throws that away? Usually it's something a person initiates first, like applying for it.... I have questions and I don't work well without answers. I'll just have to find the answers, but now is not the time. I think I'll be making plans for tonight...

I fold the sheet of paper in its original position and put it in my interior jacket pocket. I'm about to find out why someone accepted to a culinary program at a top end school is still a willing server at a job that will never have room for climbing the corporate ladder.

I turn and walk away. I'll just have to wait a few more hours to see her. There is work to be done. I have a new set of things to do now...

Lux

I walk into my apartment and go straight for the kitchen, laying my clutch on the bar along the way. I'm hungry and I despise takeout. I prefer to cook my own food always, but not before aspirin.

Opening the medicine cabinet, I grab the small bottle before twisting off the cap and popping two small pills in my hand, tossing them in my mouth at the same time. I grab a glass and fill it with water, then drink it in its entirety to relieve the cotton mouth I've had since I woke up.

I set the empty glass on the bar. "Where have you been?"

I jump at the sound of that deep voice and turn around. He looks tired. "What the fuck are you doing here, Callum? It's not even Thursday. I'm sure your *wife* is wondering where you are. Where is my key? Give it back and leave."

He walks toward me, his arms by his sides. "Angel. We can and we will figure this out."

"We are way past figuring things out. Give me my key."

He stops in front of me and leans in to kiss me, but I turn my head. He places his palm against my cheek. "You didn't really think I was going to give you up that easily did you? Oh no, angel. I didn't get to the top by following simple orders. Everyone has a breaking point. It's just about finding it. You were mine and you still are. You will cave."

I look at him. "You have lost your fucking mind. You are married. She's pregnant, you asshole."

"I'll leave her. It's already been done." He runs his hands down my body, but instead of turning me on it now makes me feel like a cheap whore. "I never wanted kids and she knew that, but she refuses to get rid of it, so she can raise it alone. Money talks. I can make her go away."

"Who are you?"

I push on his chest, but he presses his body against mine, holding me against the counter. He leans in again and I attempt to push him again. He grabs my wrists in his hands and presses his lips to my neck, running them up the length until he's just outside my ear. "Someone else fucked you last night, didn't they? I can smell him on you."

His voice becomes angry, mine quickly matching his. "It's none of your fucking business anymore. You lost that right when I found out you were married, as in fucking another woman when you were only supposed to be fucking me. Get out of my damn apartment, Callum. I mean it."

He cups my ass and squeezes, pissing me off further. His hands are all over me. "Stop seeing him. We'll start over. Just me and you this time. You know I can give you everything you want."

For the first time that does not sway me...

His hands disappear underneath my shirt, rubbing along my sides. He's pressing his erection into my pelvis. Bringing my knee up, I drive it into his nuts, causing him to move back in a hurled over position as he grabs them in his hands. "Now get the fuck out."

He stands slowly as he steps toward the door in a limp. "Get rid of him, Lux. I'm warning you. If I can't have you, no one will. When I return I'll have the fucking divorce papers for you to see."

He opens the door and hobbles out, slamming it shut behind him. I walk over quickly and lock the door, before turning and pressing my back against the door. I really missed the red flags with that one. Sleep suddenly sounds better than food, and nothing ever takes precedent over that. I love food. It's why I work out as hard as I do, and also why my life is mapped out around it. What kind of life would it be if all a person ever ate were lean protein and veggies? Fuck that. I'd rather eat a chocolate soufflé and then run five miles immediately following.

I push off the door and begin walking toward my bedroom. I'll just grab something at work later. I may even stay with Delta until I can get my damn locks changed so Callum's crazy ass doesn't pull a repeat of just now.

Opening my bedroom door, I immediately head toward my

underwear drawer, opening it. I dig around until I find what I'm looking for hidden beneath the various shades, styles, and colors of the material filling the drawer: my pink and black Glock G42, 380 Caliber. I'm not some dumb girl living alone in a big city. I have fucking pistols hidden all over this damn apartment, as well as the smaller one I carry in my purse, and my aim is impeccable. I don't purchase them to collect dust or to brag that I have one. I purchase them for safety, knowing there is a possibility that I may have to lay someone's ass on the ground, which is why I go to the shooting range at least twice a month. I've heard all my life that an ounce of prevention is better than a pound of cure. You don't bounce back from death.

I grip the handle in my right hand and release the magazine, verifying that it's still fully loaded. I shove the magazine back inside the handle, slamming it into place, and aim the barrel at the floor as I rack back the slide with my left hand, loading a bullet into the chamber.

I walk to the right side of my bed and lift the top mattress, laying my pistol on top of the bottom one, the handle hanging off for quick grab if I need it, before laying the top mattress back in its position. I remove all my clothes but my underwear and crawl into bed, losing myself under the covers. I don't even have to work at it before my eyelids close and my eyes roll back in my head, putting me into a state of unconsciousness.

Kaylon

I'm sitting at my desk reading through the papers before me when a knock sounds at my door. It opens. I look up to Chevy walking through the door. "What is it?"

"I have some news you may be interested in."

I drop the stack of paper on my desk and lean back in my leather chair, preparing to listen. "I'm listening."

"It's about that woman you asked me to find. You may want to bump up your trip."

"To when?"

"Tonight."

"I have something to do tonight."

"You don't really have a choice if you want to see her."

"And why is that?"

"She's in critical condition at the hospital. She was involved in an armed robbery at a grocery store in New York. She took a bullet to the head. She's still alive, but it isn't looking good, and I think they're debating on whether or not to do surgery because of where the bullet is lodged. That's all of the information I could get not being family, and it took some manipulating to get that. They have her in an induced coma until they decide on the plan of care. She has no next of kin."

Fuck.

I run my hand through my short, spiky hair; new growth from the last time I shaved it off. I have a particular desired look when I work here and when I have to take care of the genetic mishaps of the world. I try not to mix the two. Never will I carry out a hit without as much differentiation in my physical appearance as I can get.

I was planning to pay Lux a special visit tonight, but it'll have to be put on hold. This takes precedent...unfortunately. I can't confirm that woman is worth it, but regardless of the way I feel we still share the same coding of DNA, and I have things that need to be said. I wish I could generate more sorrow than I feel right now, but that's what happens when you live a selfish and shitty life. No one cares whether you live or die when all you are is a self-centered person thinking of only yourself, while your own blood suffers and sacrifices.

I gather up the loose papers scattered on my desk and shove them into my briefcase before standing. "I'll take care of it. I appreciate the heads up."

"Just doing what you pay me to do, *boss.*"

I laugh as I walk around the desk and stop beside him. "You still watching the new mark? His end is coming."

"I'm on it. He doesn't even know I exist. He won't be running off anyway. I'll make sure of it."

I nod.

"If this goes over smoothly you can stop referring to me as your boss, because we will be partners. Like I've said before it's all about trust in this business, Chevy. I'm sure with a man of your success that word is cringe-worthy. No one gets to the top to then become another *employee*. See you in a few days. Keep everything in line, will you?"

"You know it."

I head toward the door and halt as I grab the door handle. "Hey, Chevy..."

"What's up?"

"Do me a favor. Keep an eye on Miss Larsen for me. I can't put my finger on it yet, but this one seems to be different. I expect her to be in mint condition when I return. I'm leaving her safety in your hands. If anything happens, call me. I don't care what time of day it is."

He places his hands in his pants pockets as he looks at me, nodding his understanding.

A short daydream starts to occur. I remember the way she looked each time she came last night. That erotic vision is forever branded in my mind. I smile incidentally. "Oh yeah. Thanks for letting me use your studio. You have a pretty good setup. My dick is probably more appreciative than I am. I don't know what fucking happened to you over there and I may never know, but you're a damn fine wingman if you ask me. If you need anything at all, do not hesitate to ask. Consider it already done."

Without another word I leave, ready to get this over with. The sooner I get this out the sooner I can come home. There are things here that are finally piquing my interest after a stale ten years. I have a feeling the pot is only going to sweeten before it's over. For once I actually like my hand.

CHAPTER THIRTEEN

My eyes pop open in panic. It's that feeling that you're late even though you have no idea what time it is. I throw the comforter off of me and jump out of bed. "Shit. What time is it?"

The room being dark is scaring the hell out of me. I've never been late for work. I cannot be late for work. I feel around for my phone on the nightstand, but it isn't there. *The bar. Callum.*

Turning, I run out of my bedroom and locate my clutch on the bar. I quickly grab it and remove my phone, unlocking it to see what time it is. 7:30. Fuck! I have thirty minutes to be at work and ready to serve. Tonight it's an engagement party so it's going to be a late one. I'm never going to make it in time. I've never been late to work a day since I started working. It just doesn't happen. My income is a key element in me being able to live on my own. It's not something

I take lightly.

I run to my bedroom and put my almost dead phone on the charger to give it some battery while I attempt in getting ready at the speed of lightning. I don't want to call my boss unless there is no way I'm going to make it. *Atlanta traffic...*

I'm just going to have to hurry. There is always a way to beat the odds. The odds are I'm most likely going to be late. I run in my closet at full speed, sliding slightly across the hardwood floor as I attempt to stop on the right side; the side that my black slacks and white button-downs hang on. I don't even look before grabbing one of each. Most of my work clothes are all the same. It's pretty uniform, even with no logo: white and black. It's required to serve for my boss. He wants everyone to look the same.

I quickly lay the pressed shirt down on the bed long enough for me to remove the slacks from the hanger and pull them on my body, wasting not a second of time. I don't have it to waste. I pull them up my legs, hopping slightly to work them over my ass, but don't button or zip them, and then follow behind with my shirt. I button it from top to bottom and shove my shirttail in the waist of my pants to tuck it in, before finishing by fastening my pants, and slightly pulling my shirt back out enough to loosen the tuck.

"Shoes, shoes, where are my fucking shoes?" I look around the room, running like a crazy person to and from my closet and then into the bathroom, before grabbing a pair of black work socks from my drawer, and then peek under the bed in hopes my shoes are there. Somehow they got shoved under the edge, hidden behind the bed skirt. I hop on one foot as I put each sock on, before shoving my feet inside. I pull at the heels with my index fingers until my foot is wedged completely inside of each shoe.

I cannot believe I'm about to go to work without showering,

especially after a night filled with sex. Smell check always works, so I grab the collar of my shirt and stick my nose inside the opening, checking for the one thing that will drive a girl's paranoia to extreme levels: body odor. The mixture that invades my nostrils is cologne, perfume, and deodorant. Cologne is not the ideal fragrance when serving young, single men. The idea is to appear flirtatious and very much available, even if you're not. Boss' rules not mine, but it's always been my favorite rule. He obviously knows what he's talking about, because his clientele proves it. Well, it was up until this point. Again, change due to a damn sexy alpha-male that is dynamite in the bed. I was just fine until I found him lying in that tattoo shop.

I walk to my mirror and brush through my hair, preparing to braid it in a hurry. I wonder what he's doing right this second....

Oh my hell I need to be punched in the face. I glance over at my phone and quickly divert my eyes back to the mirror. "Don't even fucking think about it. You will not be a twat waffle. Own your pussy. If he liked it he will come back for more."

I stare at my reflection in the mirror. "Great, now I'm talking to you like you're a different person. I've really lost my shit now."

I section off my hair and start to braid it down the back of my head loosely, tying it off with an elastic hair wrap. My makeup is smeared from my drunken overnight stay and then the all day sleep-a-thon I decided to have instead of being a productive member of society. "Ugh, I don't have time for this shit. Looks like it's mascara and light shadow tonight. I guess it's a good thing I'm not looking for a piece of ass."

I grab a makeup towelette and wipe underneath my eyes, ridding my skin of the black smudges that currently reside there, before digging through my makeup and replacing it quickly with a light shimmer eye shadow and another coat of mascara, doubling what's already there. My eyeliner is sitting on top, so I grab it and darken the line around my eyes as fast as I can.

I look myself over. "That will have to do, but something is missing. Jason is going to kill me. I look like camouflaged shit."

Lipgloss...

"First you brush your teeth. That is one form of hygiene worth being late for."

I feel like I'm never going to get there. This is completely unlike me. I don't even have a good excuse. I can see it now - walking in, staring my boss in the eyes, and reciting some lame ass line that a college student living off her parents and only working to make the time pass would use: *Oh, sorry I'm late boss. I was out all night getting drunk and getting laid, draining all of my energy, so I felt the need to sleep all day when I should have been preparing for the several grand you're getting paid for this event to go seamlessly and without mistakes. I hope you understand...*

"I don't fucking think so, Lux." I rush to the bathroom and brush my teeth, not a thought running through my mind. I have to go. I pick up the bottle of perfume as I return my toothbrush to the holder and spritz it on my chest, hoping it'll mask the masculine goodness that is lingering on my skin. I cannot smell that all night. I need to focus.

Replacing the bottle on my bathroom sink, I run into my room and grab my phone off the charger, as well as my large purse hanging from the hook on my closet door. Finally done. Now I just need to get through traffic. That's going to be a bitch. Killing all the lights to my room, I shut my bedroom door and stop at the bar to clean out my clutch and return the items to my wallet and purse, before locking up and taking off down the stairs as fast as my legs will go.

As I open the lobby door and walk to the parking lot my heart sinks. No fucking way. "Hey! What the fuck are you doing to my car? That's private property."

I take off running toward the tow truck that is hooking up to my car, my baby. "Hey asshole," I yell again. "Don't touch my damn car!"

The guy hooking my car up isn't even that old. He's probably my age. Fucker. I shove him in the back, causing him to stumble slightly. "Put my car down or I'm going to call the cops. If you scratch it you're paying for it to be fixed."

An older guy grabs something from the tow truck and starts walking toward me with a clipboard in his hand. "Ma'am, you need to calm down. We're just doing our job. This vehicle has been ordered for pickup by the owner."

"What the hell are you talking about? I am the owner. Put my fucking Porsche down. I'm late for work." I wave the keys from my fingertips in front of his face. "See. Obviously you have some wrong information somewhere. You have the wrong vehicle."

He looks down at the clipboard as if he's reading the typed information in front of him. "The vin numbers match, sweetheart. The registered owner I'm showing according to the title is Callum Callahan. He put in an order to have us pick up his property. You may want to contact him. It sounds like a domestic dispute to me. That will have to be dealt with in civil court. My hands are tied, sweetheart, unless you can produce a title with your name on it."

"Mother fucker," I mumble. "I'm going to kill him."

I look at my beautiful, silver car that is being strapped down on the tow truck by guy one. If I were a crier I would cry in this very second. The universe is against me right now. What can I do about it at this point legally? Not a damn thing. I knew I should have gotten the title put in my name. Without another word I turn and walk off as I dig through my purse for my phone. I look through the recent call log until I scroll far enough that I find the name I'm looking for. I touch it and place it to my ear.

It rings.

The line picks up. "Angel. To what do I owe the pleasure?"

"You sorry son of a bitch, Callum. I told you not to fuck with my car. It was a gift in case you have forgotten. Who the hell takes back a gift? You're a bastard and I despise you. How the hell am I supposed to get to work now? I sold my car at your request. Now I have nothing."

"Now, angel, calm down. It's still yours, and you can have it back, as soon as you come to your senses about this relationship. I miss you, Angel. I want you back. I will stop at nothing to get it."

I hear the sound of a golf ball being tapped with a club. I know that sound well. I've had to tag along a few times. He loves golf. It was boring to me. My fury is only getting stronger by the second. "Put that fucking club down before I come to New York and knock you in the head with it. This isn't a joke, Callum. You are a married man. I'm sorry, but I just don't swing that way. I may not be looking for anything serious in my own life, but I'm not a home-wrecking whore. I believe in commitment for those that choose that life. You are the one that chose that life when you married her. Own up to your decisions and be responsible. You ruined this relationship, not me. I will never trust you again. You destroyed that. When we were together you were the only person I was sleeping with. Give me back my fucking car. Do you really want me to give *Kyla* a call? She's the only thing you have going now. I wouldn't mess up both if I were you."

"It wouldn't really matter if you did. I've got my attorney handling that matter as we speak. The second I confirmed her *condition* upon my return to New York, I told her there was someone else and then I left. I've already moved out. Come back to me, Angel, and you can have anything you want. I'll buy you a new fucking car, a better one. You can quit that low-end job if you want and move in with me as soon as the divorce is finalized. Don't throw the last six months away over someone that you mean nothing to. No one can take care of you like I can."

I want to scream. I just may. I do. It was no longer containable. I take a deep breath before trying to speak again. This is like dealing with a toddler. He's a grown ass man. "As tempting as that sounds, no thanks, and stop calling me that. I'm not your angel. Ties between us have been severed. This relationship is unfixable. Learn from your mistakes and move on to someone else if you don't want to be with her, because it won't be me in her place. I don't want you anymore. Just let me go, Callum. Give me back my car," I say with a calm tone in my voice, trying to reason with an unreasonable man.

Silence.

I stand here, waiting for him to answer. "That's not an option for me. You're only saying those things because you're upset, as you should be. I fucked up. I'll own up to that, but I'm not going out without a fight. If you want the car, then you know what the stipulations are. When I told you I loved you it wasn't because my cock was buried deep in your pussy. I meant it. I haven't reciprocated that phrase to Kyla since before I met you. I'm a man of my word. I'll be waiting for your call."

The line goes dead.

I look down at the screen, now staring at my home screen. "Your money isn't going to get you out of this one, Callum. I'm better than that. I won't be a mistress in the past, present, or future."

I glance at the time. There is no making it on time now. I guess it's time to call my boss, because I'm going to have to hail a cab. I pull up my contacts until I find Jason's number. My stomach is a ball of nerves. He's the number one catering company in this city for any event, any need. People book him months in advance even for simple parties. He has one of best wine collections I've ever seen for his pastry specialty events. All food he makes and prepares himself prior to each event, no matter what it entails. He doesn't contract out for anything. His prices are fucking insane and people gladly pay it, because he's built up a spotless reputation. For that reason he doesn't put up with bullshit from employees. I'm lucky to have this job and he compensates me well.

I touch his contact and raise my phone to my ear, waiting for someone to pick up. It rings a few times before the call connects. There is a lot of background noise. "Where the hell are you? This party is packed and you're my best server."

"Hey, Jason. I'm really sorry to do this, like really, really sorry, but I'm going to be late."

"How late?"

"As soon as I can get a cab I'll be on the way. I seem to be having car trouble."

"Car trouble? You drive a fucking Porsche, Lux, a brand new one. What's going on?"

"Long story. I'll explain later. I'm carless at the moment. Please don't fire me."

He laughs.

"What's so funny?"

"You haven't been a minute late since I hired you. I hardly think one time is cause to fire you. You've earned my trust. You're my head server. If you say you're having legit car issues, then I believe you. Just get here as soon as you can. You know I don't like dealing with my other servers when I'm busy. I don't have time for the petty issues that you can fix on the spot. That's why I pay you more than them."

A wave of relief washes over me. "Thanks, Jason. I'll be there as soon as I can."

"No worries. I got to go. See you in a bit."

"Okay, bye."

I lock my phone and toss it into my purse, which is hanging from the crook of my bent arm. When I look up there is a black SUV with tinted, blacked out windows pulling in front of me. I immediately stick my hand into my purse, feeling around discretely until I'm griping the handle of my pistol. The passenger side window starts to descend as the SUV stops a mere three feet in front of me.

On the opposite side of the window in the driver's seat is a male about five years older than me, give or take a couple of years. Most people don't look their ages anymore, so it's hard to be sure. He's kind of cute actually, at least from what I can tell. Dirty blonde hair, stubble, lighter eyes, maybe green, and well built. His arms are so big that the sleeves to his polo look tight. Still, he doesn't have anything on Kaston. Face-palm. Why do I keep comparing people to him? That has to stop. "Get in. I'll give you a ride."

"No thanks. I was taught not to get in a vehicle with strangers. I'm not really in the mood to become a missing person today. Try again tomorrow."

He laughs. It's deeper than Kaston's, but oddly similar. Shit, I did it again. The way he's leaned back against the leather seat of his Cadillac Escalade with his left wrist resting on top of the steering wheel, and leaned onto his right elbow on the center console, makes me feel like I'm in a movie scene and about to be the victim of a lame pickup line.

"I can see why he likes you. You're quite the smart-ass."

"Define he."

"Boss man."

"Which is who? Everyone has a name."

"Kaston. You're the girl from my club right?" He winks as if it's not really a question that he doesn't already know the answer to.

I feel like he's fishing...

"Well I don't know. There are a lot of clubs in Atlanta. Which one are you claiming?"

"Ride or fly."

"You own that club?"

"Yep. Don't look so surprised. Nightlife works for some people. Are you going to get in?"

"Do you just randomly show up in parking lots to pick up stranded girls?"

He smiles and leans over to open the passenger door. "I was in the area looking in on some things. Boss man wouldn't be too happy knowing you are without a ride at dark, especially when he's unavailable. It seems you've left an unforgettable impression."

Something is off...

"No fucking way. Did he tell you to keep an eye on me? Where is he? His balls will be mine."

"Jump his bones all you want when he returns. I'm sure he'd appreciate the gesture. For now, make my life easier. Get in. I don't bite...unless you're into that sort of thing." He winks again. "But, you're clearly not up for grabs at the moment, so I'll be good."

I take a step forward, followed by another. Fuck it. I get in the car and shut the door, before fastening my seatbelt. My senses are on overload from the cool air blowing through the vents, the cologne circulating through the car, and the rap music turned down low, coming through the speakers.

I turn my upper body toward him. "You don't strike me as a rap kind of guy. I would have guessed heavy metal or rock."

"I reserve that for special occasions. I like a little bit of everything; I kind of have to, to run a club. Plus, what exactly does someone look like that likes rap or rock? The worst mistake you could ever make is to judge a book by its cover. It would blow your fucking mind sometimes at what lies between the pages. The name is Chevy: partner, right-hand man, confidante, assistant, or whatever the fuck else you want to call me, to Kaston Cox. And you are Lux I assume."

I roll my eyes. "And guys think girls talk. Y'all can't even get it back in your pants before you're announcing bragging rights to each other. It's a good thing I just don't give a shit or I might be slightly offended."

He laughs again. "Ninety-nine point nine percent of the time that's probably true, but since I like you I'll tell you a little secret. If you're worthy of bragging rights you're okay, but if a man keeps most of it to himself, only revealing the essentials in fear that someone else may take interest, then you're different from the rest. That girl that becomes the point one percent, a man doesn't want to share with the world."

I'm not even going to ask which percentage he's putting me in because that is a piece of knowledge I'm fine without knowing. Being in the ninety-ninth percentile suits me perfectly.

"Noted. I'm ready. Let's ride. As much as I would love to sit here and chat boy stats with you, I really need to get to work. It's across town. Then you can report back to Mr. Cox that I'll be having a word with him upon his return. I'm always packing. He knows this. I can take care of myself. He's starting to inch himself into the creepy category...just a smidge. That's not sexy. I don't need his hired eyes on me. Please and thank you."

"I'll be sure to pass the word along, *Miss Larsen*."

He starts to pull away as he looks back at the road ahead. The funny part is...he never asked me for my place of employment or the address. At this point, I'm not sure if I should get pissed off or more curious. If I were smart I'd get pissed off and run in the opposite direction of Kaston Cox, but I have a feeling he'd find me pretty quickly...and I think I want him to.

CHAPTER FOURTEEN

I've been listening to the beeping of the machines all night, occasionally dozing off. Between waiting on a flight and the layover, once I got here the doctor had already made the call to do surgery and was finished. I guess the information Chevy got was a little outdated. I suppose it was the right decision, because he removed the bullet lodged in her head.

From what I was told I'm the only relative that's come forward, not that I'm surprised. The amount of damage done to her mentally is yet to be determined. She's been sleeping since she got out of surgery...and I've been waiting since I arrived. The only reason I'm still here is because she is blood, and I'd feel like shit if I didn't at least stay for the outcome. Even a man like me has a heart. It's just been compromised.

I lean forward in my chair and lay my forearms on my thighs, tired. My phone vibrates in my pocket. Leaning back to straighten my body, I run my hand in the pocket of my jeans and pull out my phone, checking the now lit up screen. Lux. It's been a while...or at least it seems that way since I spoke with her yesterday morning.

Lux Larsen (4:01 AM): I have a bone to pick with you when you return from wherever the hell you are.

Me: Well hello to you too...

Lux Larsen: I'm not in a pleasant mood and I'm tired. That means polite salutations get bypassed.

Me: Does that ill mood have anything to do with the absence of my cock?

I smile as I lean forward once again, my back becoming stiff from this hospital chair.

Lux Larsen: Your cock won't get you out of this one...

Lux Larsen: Okay, well, maybe it could if it were here!

Lux Larsen: All jokes aside... I'm a grown ass woman. I don't need your beef stock checking up on me. Unless you have me on my back with my legs spread, my safety and whereabouts are my business. Got it, Cox?

Me: I'm assuming by beef stock you mean Chevy?

Lux Larsen: Precisely.

Lux Larsen: What is it with you people and knowing someone's personal demographics before they tell them to you. You're really getting close to that mad stalker line. You could at least make it a little less obvious.

Me: Do you always do that?

Lux Larsen: Do what?

Me: Press the send button multiple times before you finish your thought, not giving the other person a chance to respond before you immediately come back with something else.

Lux Larsen: Maybe. No one said you had to respond, killer. I didn't even think you would respond until hours later.

Me: Eh... Well I did. I'm awake. Gives me something to do. Better than what I was doing.

Lux Larsen: Where are you?

Me: You don't hold anything back do you?

Lux Larsen: Never.

My smile broadens. Suddenly I'm not tired anymore. With her, silence and solitude are no longer desired. The normal itch and twitch has steadily dulled since the night I put my hands on her body, which is pretty strange still. I don't even have the urge to smoke or drink. Something that I've become accustomed to, thinking it would forever be present if I didn't take part in certain obligations, has suddenly taken a back seat. I'm becoming... content... to just survive on a day-to-day basis, even somewhat thriving.

Me: I'm in New York taking care of a few personal matters. Where are you?

Lux Larsen: Are you a New Yorker...because I'm not a fan.

Me: That's a little stereotypical, Miss Larsen. What if I said yes?

Lux Larsen: I would say the last one ruined me and I'm good with not going down that road again, but it was fun while it lasted...

Me: I guess it's a good thing I don't give up that easily then. To answer your question, no I'm not. I may have been born here, but I haven't lived here since I was a kid. It's a foreign place to me now. You're dodging. Where are you?

Lux Larsen: Waiting for a cab. Just got done with work.

Me: This late?

Lux Larsen: Yeah...engagement party. Let's just say bachelors and bachelorettes alike don't get tired when hyped up on alcohol from an open bar and love is in the air... There is probably lots of bodily fluid scattered throughout that place. A grope on the ass and lame one-liners to get me in the bathroom later and I'm getting a pretty big bonus on my next check. I thought I was going to have to immobilize some balls.

Me: You're not painting me a pretty picture when I'm hundreds of miles away....

Lux Larsen: That's because it never is when dealing with youngins not old enough to be at an engagement party in my opinion. Boys will be boys. You people never think with the right head.

Me: I'm pleading the fifth... Where is your car?

Lux Larsen: I'm in the market for a new one. That one was getting old...

My brows scrunch. That car was practically brand new. Bull fucking shit.

Me: I can smell a liar from a mile away. Where is your car?

Lux Larsen: You sure are bossy to be hot.

Me: I'm aware... Where is it?

Lux Larsen: What do I get in exchange for that information?

Me: Do not tempt me...

Lux Larsen: Are you getting angry, Cox? Mmmm.... I may possibly like the effects of your anger.

Me: Lux. Tell me where your damn car is. Are you waiting inside for a cab? If not is someone waiting outside with you? 'Beef stock' preferably. It's like 4:15 in the morning.

Lux Larsen: Oh fine. Obviously someone needs pussy. You're cranky, and what's with the twenty questions?

Me: My need for pussy will be taken care of upon my return. There is only one I'm servicing at the moment and it's not here.

Lux Larsen: That good, huh?

Me: Lux....

Lux Larsen: Dammit, loosen up a little. I'm just pulling your dick... The jackass that gave it to me had it picked up before work. No big and definitely not your concern.

Me: Why?

Lux Larsen: Just being a dick. I'm handling it. My cab is here. I'll let you get back to your thing. I'm probably going to crash soon. Have a good trip, sexy. ;)

Me: This conversation will resume promptly when I return. Expect my call when I land in Atlanta. I would like to see you...

Lux Larsen: Maybe, if you're lucky :O Goodnight, my killer.

Me: And your face will look exactly like that. Goodnight, beautiful.

My jaw steels. There is something extremely sensual about that: *my killer.* She's marked her claim on me, and for some fucked up reason I like it, even though I shouldn't. I'm a businessman by day and a killer at night. My rules tell me she is forbidden, but everything else proves that I don't give a fuck.

I lock my phone and slide it back into my pocket. I may even be slightly happy that she's no longer driving that fucking car. I hated it from the first sight of the license plate. Nothing about her should be linked to another man. It just pisses me off. I don't do well pissed off.

"Who are you?"

My shoulders tense as I hear the weakened voice. It's like nails on a chalkboard. It may have some age on it, but it's still pretty much the same. I didn't think I'd remember, but it's more familiar than I want it to be. I look at the woman lying in that bed that gave birth to me. The only thing I recognize is her eyes.

I stand and walk to the foot of the bed. "Hello, *Mother*. It's been a long time."

She blinks a few times, as if she's confused. "I think you have me confused with someone else. I don't have any children."

Ouch. I wait, expecting to feel some sort of sadness, betrayal, disrespect, but instead, I get nothing. Interesting...

"Maybe not now, but you did...twenty years ago, before I walked out of that apartment with the only man that's ever been a parent to me."

"I have no idea what you're talking about. I'd like you to leave."

I walk around to the side of the bed as I study her face. I stop beside her and press my index finger beneath her chin, turning it up. She whines out. "That hurts."

"Look at me. I'll leave once I've said my peace."

She does. There is clarity there. Who knows what she's forgotten or what will be permanently disabled from her accident. That's the funny thing about the mind. It's an unpredictable organ, but still a vital one. There is one thing she didn't fucking forget, and that's who I am. I can see it in her eyes. Her lips start to quiver. "What's wrong? Now that I'm not a kid under your thumb you want me to leave?"

I rub my thumb along her jawline. "Time hasn't been good to you. It's ironic how being a pathological liar and abandoning your only child the second you had the chance can do that to you. At one time you had it all, and now look at you. I know your secrets, Anna. I know all the little games you used to play for money. Karma sure is a bitch though, is it not?"

I pull my wallet from my pocket and open it, removing the small, square photograph that is worn from years of carry. I extend it toward her between my index and middle fingers. Her shaky hand stuck with an IV takes it. She studies it. Her eyes grow in size. "I was your fucking son. I may have left with him, but I still wanted a relationship with you. I was a kid, a kid that shouldn't have to comprehend the evil and fucked up of this world. I called you almost daily for six months only to get a voicemail. I left countless messages. I sent you packages to keep you updated on how I was. For half a year he watched me with a saddened expression every time I asked why I wasn't good enough for you to love me, or to want anything to do with me, yet as much as he hated you he let me continue to try for all those months."

She turns the photo over and looks away. "Then, after six months, you went from unresponsive to a mystery. Suddenly that voicemail became a disconnected number and those packages started returning as undeliverable. You became dead to me. I had just turned nine fucking years old. My own mother didn't care whether I was alive, dead, thriving, or starving. Not once did you check on me. That's termed as reckless abandonment. In case you're too stupid to understand since you obviously never comprehended the opposite of that act when he actually tried to be a part of my life, I'll simplify it for you. A child needs both parents. Not a mother, not a father, but both. If you were ever more than trash you would have understood that. You could have been my superhero, but instead you were the villain."

I lean down closer to her ear to lower my voice. "And in case you were ever wondering...I turned out just fine. Unfortunately, due to unforeseen circumstances, I still have to share your last name, but now you're going to know what it feels like to be cut below the surface. That fucking money that is still being deposited in the one account you've left open all these years will cease the second you're released from care. He could have cut you off the day I turned eighteen, but because he was decent human being he didn't. I guess he had a little more of a heart than I do. Since he's dead I'm in control of all the finances. He may have been the saint but I'm the sinner. That photograph of you and me will be the last reminder you will ever have that I existed. It was a waste that I even kept it all this time. This is what I felt like twenty years ago, only I had someone that loved me. You have no one."

I stand upright and turn to walk out of the hospital room. "Kaston," she says in a whisper.

I open the door and stop. "You got a second chance. He didn't. I suggest you don't take it for granted. Goodbye, Anna."

The word mother will never again leave my lips in reference to my own. I don't have one. I had a father, and a damn good one. That was it. I'm fine with that. It's better to have had one good parent than two shitty ones. The funny thing about a con artist is that when you take away their money source they panic. I may be an asshole, but one thing I've learned is that you don't continue to feed the rich while the poor starve. If you endorse and continue to support evil, you'll have evildoers. I will not let the scum of the earth thrive while good people die out. If you cut off their air supply, water, and food source, they'll either survive or they'll die, but at some point in between they have to learn to make it on their own. I won't kill her, because she gave me life. One sacrifice for another. Now we're even, and I don't owe her a fucking thing.

Maybe Lux was right... I need pussy, and there is only one place I'm going to get it...

CHAPTER FIFTEEN

A constant buzzing sound wakes me from the peaceful sleep I was in. I reach over and feel around until I find my phone on the nightstand, and then press the side button to mute the vibrating against the wood without even opening my eyes to see who's calling.

I roll back over on my side and pull my comforter to my neck, everything buried underneath but my head. The only way I can sleep is with it freezing cold. It's easier to nestle in cold temperatures than to try to sleep if sweating. That shit just doesn't work. My phone starts vibrating again. "Seriously? What the hell?"

I roll back onto my back and grab my phone, jerking the charger from the port before swiping my thumb across the screen and placing it to my ear, still half asleep. "Hello," I say, groggy. "I hope this is important. Some people aren't up at the ass crack of dawn."

"Are you at home?"

That sexy voice radiates through the phone. If I were awake it would faze me, but there is one thing I love more than anything else and that's my sleep. No one is too important for me to pass it up. If I work nights I sleep till at least lunch. "Did you miss the part where I basically said I'm trying to sleep? Being sexy won't help you here. Can you call me later? Give me three more hours."

I disconnect the call and toss my phone down beside my head, before turning over once more. As soon as my eyes start rolling back in my head a banging starts to occur on my apartment door, causing me to jump. "Come on! This has got to be a fucking joke."

Grabbing the edge of the comforter in my hand I sling it back, off of my body. I stand in a hurry and start walking toward my bedroom door, losing my footing on the other corner of my comforter hanging in a heap on the floor beside my bed. I break the fall with my palms, missing the footboard by a few inches. "Dammit! I'm about to have someone's ass."

The banging gets louder. "I'm coming," I yell, trying to upright myself. My left wrist feels like I slightly jarred it. Walking through my apartment I attempt to wake up by rubbing the heels of my hands over my eyes with no success. I just want to crawl back in bed and sleep. I can't even see in front of me because my eyes are heavy. I'm only navigating by memory of my apartment layout. I grab the door and jerk it open. "What? Is sleep too much for a girl to ask for? There are reasons why I live alone."

"Holy fuck. No you aren't going to be getting any more sleep for a while."

The deepness of that voice sends chills down my body. I'm suddenly very much awake. The cloudy haze has cleared. What remains in its absence is one sexy as hell man standing before me. He roughly grabs the top of the doorframe in his hands, his biceps flexed as if he's squeezing the life out it. I love the muscular structure of his arms. Finally able to speak, I ask, "What?"

"Do you always answer the door like that?"

I blink a few times to comprehend what he's asking. It dawns on me. I got out of bed to answer the door. I look down at my body. The red, oversized and worn cutoff Braves tee shirt stops just below my boobs, and my nipples are hard, therefore showing through the thin material. My navy panties only cover the front and the center of my ass, revealing half of each butt cheek, but that he can't see.

I look back up at him. "My clothes?"

"Or lack thereof."

"These are my pajamas. You woke me up, so what's the problem? You are not entitled to bitch about how I answer the door when I told you I was sleeping, whether you're fucking me or not."

He steps inside the door, eying me like I'm now his prey. His eyes are glazed over as if I'm a piece of meat dangling in front of his face and he's seconds away from devouring me. I'm no longer cold, but my nipples are so hard that each time the fabric of my shirt rubs against them they hurt. I step backwards as he basically invites himself inside, slamming the door behind him. "The problem is that I was coming over here with every intention of being...tame, and then you answer the door looking like a fucking erotic dream just before a teenage boy comes all over himself in the middle of the night.

He stalks toward me, grabbing me by the bare waist. I look him in the eyes, unsure of what the hell he expects me to say. This is how I sleep. I can't stand a lot of material getting twisted up in the middle of the night. The less clothing the better. Sometimes I go completely nude. I'm a wild sleeper, hence me tripping over half of my comforter. I shrug my shoulders. "I'm not modest. At least I wasn't completely naked. I guess you caught me on a clothing kind of day."

"Fucking hell. I came over here in hopes of pussy and sleep, and in that exact order. Give an orgasm, get an orgasm, and sleep. I'm tired, I've been up all night, I have jet lag, and I have a lot of shit that I need to be doing at work, but instead of going home to rest the second I land I end up here, unable to bypass your pussy because it consumes my fucking mind. I can't get you out of my damn head."

He roughly rubs his callused hands up my sides, pushing my shirt over my breasts. I raise my arms over my head, giving my permission for him to remove it. "You better be glad you can fuck like a porn star or I'd tell you to get the hell out of my apartment. I can't remember a time when a dick was worth bypassing sleep, but for yours I may make an exception..."

He outwardly moans his aggression, and then removes my shirt over my head, returning his hands to my messy hair after dropping it to the floor. "I've never been wound so tight over a woman. Congratufuckinglations. If I didn't know any better I would think you laced your pussy with heroine, because after one night I need another fix. You're about to get fucked. Sleep can go to Hell."

He closes in to kiss me and the back of my hand goes over my mouth, stopping him. "Hold up, killer," I mumble against it. He leans back slightly, giving me space, his eyes narrowing as if I've slapped him. I move my hand. Heaven help me I'm so turned on right now. I'm almost worried that I should have worn more covering underwear with the way I feel between my legs. This is totally a temporary mood kill, and I may not give a shit about a lot of things, but hygiene is not one of them. "I have to brush my teeth.

That's just nasty."

He smirks and releases me. "By all means go ahead, because once I start on that sexy little body I'm not stopping."

Oh my hell. On that note I turn and walk away, awkwardly walking from the wetness saturating my panties. I hear a slight growl and then his footsteps on my heels. His stride never changes from the living space to my bathroom sink. I grab my toothbrush and look at him standing behind me through the mirror. I raise my brow as I spread toothpaste on the bristles. "Are you seriously going to stand there and watch me? I can't go anywhere with you standing behind me like that. Plus, I'm pretty sure you could catch me anyway."

I turn on the water. "Hell why even try? It's not like I could hide. You'd find me I'm sure. You're crazy like that. Privacy is a non-existent thing with you. You standing in my apartment is the perfect example." I point my toothbrush at the mirror. "I've never given you my address or the name of my complex, yet here you are, just like beef boy mysteriously showed up last night. Why is that?"

I run the head of the toothbrush under the stream of water and place it in my mouth, starting with my back bottom teeth and brushing in the same way that I do twice a day, but never taking my eyes off of his. He dips his hands under the narrow waistband of my panties on each hip, before pushing them down my legs far enough for them to fall in a pile at my feet, baring me completely. He doesn't act like he's going to say anything as he stares at me in the mirror, studying my face. "I own a PI company, a very successful one, because my father was the best in private investigations. He taught me everything over the years. I'm good at what I do, Lux. Knowing details is who I am. Missing a single one can make or break a case."

I lean forward and spit, then resume brushing, interested in him revealing something useful about himself for the first time. He brushes my hair over my right shoulder, revealing my left. "Attention to detail is imperative for a man like me. I never miss one. Whether client or mark, I know everything about a person, like this," he says, placing his lips on the beauty mark that resides between my shoulder and neck. It's so light in color that most people don't even know it's there. Even if it were darker, my hair usually covers it.

He reaches around and grabs the back of my left hand, pulling it to his mouth, connecting my palm to his lips. "Or this." He kisses my scar on the palm of my hand where I burned myself in one of my genius ideas to teach myself how to cook as a kid. I obviously didn't have enough brain capacity at the time to realize the pot is hot when heated. Ingredients were scarce. It took creativity, only a kid doesn't know what things taste and don't taste well together. Don't ask what all was in the concoction, but it wasn't edible.

With his opposite hand, he places the tips of his index and middle fingers at the skeletal knot between my shoulders and draws down the length of my spine, stopping at the level of the sacrum, before splitting the two to hover over my dimples. He presses inward, exerting a slight pressure. "But these are my favorite. A woman's back is one of the most sensual body parts; because of the curves, the sensitivity when touched just right, the way it reacts to pleasure, and the way it sets the character for all other body parts proves it to be beautiful. It's also a vital part for the rest of the body to be physically attractive as well as structurally symmetrical. Those are the things that make it remarkable. These, just like dimples in the cheeks, are beauty marks. Many people want them but the gene that forms them seems to be more recessive than dominant."

Toothpaste is starting to spill over my bottom lip from brushing the same area of teeth during that whole spill. I spit and quickly rinse my mouth out, followed by my toothbrush, and then return it to the holder not saying a word. I grab the hand towel off of the ring and wipe my mouth clean. "What the hell was all that? Are you possessed by a writer?"

He runs his hand down to the top of my butt cheek, his thumb tracing along the seam of my crack as he continues downward. He squeezes and mirrors one hand with the other, pulling my ass cheeks apart. Before I can think he presses his denim covered erection into the crack of my ass. "Just stating a fact. What are you trying to say? That guys can't be deep or philosophical in nature... We probably notice more and think deeper than you realize. Before another week has time to pass this will be fucked for the first time. I've marked your pussy and this is next. I will go where no other man has gone before."

I quickly retort.

"Why do you think I've never had anal sex," I ask, swallowing. My muscles reflexively tighten at the thought of his dick going there, knowing the size. I've done many things, experimented to no end, but that is not something that has ever interested me. I wasn't against it. I just was never into it either.

He presses his body into mine, lining his front to my back, placing his lips outside of my ear. "Never underestimate my ability to pick up on details, big or small. That is a skill I was taught all of my life. It's no longer a talent but an instinct. I leave nothing messy, no loose ends, and everything is calculated ahead of time. As long as you are mine, it is my job to know every fucking detail about you and where you are at all times. Get used to it. Otherwise, I can't protect you."

I turn in his grasp and he allows me to with ease, placing his hands to each side of me on the bathroom counter, blocking me from moving as his eyes scan mine. "What if there are things about myself I don't want you to know, or anyone for that matter?" I pull on the hole-punched end of his belt, sliding it through the leather loop to unfasten it. "Everyone is entitled to their privacy, Kaston. You can't just barge in to someone's personal life and open their closet door, digging through their skeletons. They are usually skeletons for a reason, no longer alive, and things that a person wants to leave hidden in the dark behind closed doors."

Once his belt is hanging loosely from opposite sides, I grab the buckle and jerk it through his belt loops, dropping it to the floor as the end falls from the final belt loop. "If you want to know something about me, then ask. It is my fucking right to decide if I want to tell you. Follow the rules of society. I don't go plundering in your shit."

He grabs me by the waist and lifts me roughly onto the counter. On instinct I place my hands to each side of me, and then lean my head back against the mirror. I just want him to touch me. He straightens his posture and begins unfastening his jeans, starting with the button. The man radiates so much controlled power that I can't focus. "The most important thing you need to remember about me is that I don't abide by fucking rules; if you haven't already noticed. I am like no other man you've ever met before. Every person is built with a totally different makeup, individual to the person like a fingerprint. There will never be another quite like me, baby. Fuck society. I play my way."

He pushes his jeans and briefs down his legs before stepping out of them. He doesn't let more than a few seconds pass before grabbing the backside neck of his shirt and pulling it over his head. There isn't an ounce of fat on his body. His stomach ripples when he exhales, contracting to form a human sculpture. "Fuck you're hot," I say in a whisper, not meaning to verbalize it.

He steps forward, grabbing ahold of my waist. His height is perfect to align his dick between my legs with the height of the counter. "I will know every fucking detail I can know about you, because I want to. There is something about you that I can't let go of. Maybe it's the mere fact that you can tolerate my fucked up lifestyle as if it's just a normal day job. That also means there's the strong possibility that you're just as fucked up as I am, allowing us to complement one another. I don't really give a shit what the reason is. With you I don't have to hide and I like it. You are mine, Lux. I will own you emotionally and physically within a matter of time. If you don't like it tough shit. You'll get there. It's not my fault you walked into Kross' shop that night. I didn't lead you to that alley for you to witness what you did. I sure as hell didn't ask you to show up at Chevy's club, so call it what you want, but either way something led you to me time and time again. Now, you know too much. It's either kill you or keep you forever."

He pulls me to the edge of the sink so that he's pressed firmly between my legs, his rock hard dick brushing against my pussy. I wrap my legs around his waist at the same time he places one hand on my cheek, his thumb rubbing the outline of my bottom lip. "You, beautiful, are far too perfect to return to dust."

My heart starts pounding in my chest, no doubt from the hormones raging through my body, multiplying profusely. I grab his hair in my hands, pulling him closer to my face. "Don't say that fucking shit to me," I say in a breathy tone. "I can't fucking think when you say that shit to me. You're a damn lunatic. Forever my ass. That term doesn't exist in my vocabulary. Nothing lasts forever."

I press my heels into his ass, trying to hint for him to do it already. He has barely touched me and I feel like I'm about to come apart. I'm starting to think this moved faster when we had both obviously been drinking. "Are you on birth control?"

His sudden outburst catches me off guard. His hand leaves my cheek. Everything is in such a haze. I never get like this. My core body temp is rising, heating to abnormal temperatures, and my skin is flushed, turning a hue of pink. I find myself wanting to look between my legs to make sure I'm not getting the counter wet, as stupid as that seems. I've never gotten wet to those extremes before. Each time I speak my voice comes out exasperated and fucking needy. I don't do needy. "What? Yes. Would you just shove your dick in already? Damn!"

He slams into me hard, filling me completely. My arm rises above my head and my palm hits the mirror to stop me when my body begins scooting backwards from his thrust. My eyes close reflexively and a moan escapes my lips. It's like my hands have been tied back with an itch so intense that I want to scream, and after being tortured for a long period of time someone finally scratches the itch for you. It's a relief. It feels so good; too good. Wait a minute.

My eyes open. "Where is the fucking condom?"

A smirk spreads across the lower half of his face. "Don't ask for things you aren't sure that you want. You said shove it in and I did. Ask and you shall receive."

"I didn't say fuck me without protection!"

He pulls out very slowly, teasing me with his dick, making it harder to rationalize this situation. "Oh, God."

My breathing becomes uneven. He bucks forward and looks at me so hard it's as if he could cut straight through me with his stare. "What can I say? I'm an asshole. I told you I do what I want and this is what I wanted. Next time you'll think before you speak. Never question me. I know you're clean and I need you to trust that I am."

"Trust," I shout, or try to anyway. I'm not very convincing at the moment. I guess that's what happens when someone with the perfect size cock is taunting you with it. "I barely even know you. Why should I trust you? I don't know where your dick has been. People lie. I don't fuck without condoms...ever."

"I've never fucked a woman without a rubber and I've never had one break. I'm even the guy that buys the same brand so I know they aren't faulty. I get tested every six months tops. Last time was when I came back to Atlanta the week prior to meeting you. Clean bill of health according to the doctor and I haven't fucked anyone other than you since. Let me fill you in on a secret."

He's still fucking me as he speaks. "Contrary to what you may think, I don't just fuck anything that walks and has a pussy between her legs. I have standards. I told you attention to detail is a must, every fucking time. This is something I want to try, and I want to try it with you. I've said it before and I'll say it again. Trust me with your body."

A man that can sound like that while saying shit like that should be banned from being anywhere near a woman. I don't care who you are, that is not easy to say no to. He has a way with words that's dangerous.

He pulls out again, never letting the tip exit before ramming his cock into me again. It's a slow torture. "Okay," I say against my will. I'm no longer controlling my own body parts. It's weird, as if someone has taken possession of my body, and muting my soul to use my body like a host, controlling me like a puppet. I will break through. I don't care how good it feels. "If you give me some bullshit you won't have to worry about killing me, because I'll fucking slit your throat. Got it? I don't play about that shit. I take care of myself. Sex is fun until you have something you can't get rid of. Protected sex is better than no sex."

He smiles. Seriously? This is not a fucking time to be smiling. I'm serious. I'm not even sure how we're both turned on still as we have this conversation. Everything between us is backwards. When I should be creeped out I'm turned on and when he should think I'm crazy he smiles. What the hell is wrong with this picture?

He runs his hand up the length of my back, grabbing the middle of my hair in his hand, jerking it. The muscles between my legs clench as my head is pulled back roughly. "Fuck yeah," he says in a deepened voice.

His thrusts become faster and shallower than before. He presses all the way inside and stops, grinding his hips in a circular motion. "What kind of birth control are you on?"

"The permanent kind," I breathe out.

He swipes his tongue up my neck as his thumb presses against my clit. I moan out as he exerts pressure against it. "Define permanent," he says in a husky voice.

"I sterilized myself at eighteen in a doctor's office."

He quickly uprights himself. "What?"

I bang my head against the mirror lightly. "Now is not the time for this conversation. This is why I don't do this heart to heart thing. It always leads to more questions. If you are concerned with my answer then pull out when you come. You're the one that shoved your bare dick in my pussy. I'm good with being your paid trophy and fuck buddy, no questions asked. You're complicating things. What does a girl have to do to orgasm now days? Why do guys want to talk?"

I breathe out aggravated as I try to thrust my own hips up and down on his cock, since he's brought his movements to a halt. "Look,

I do not want kids. Ever. That will never change. Temporary birth control fails all the time. I will not be in that percentage of failed protection because I like sex. I will never be a soccer mom or that woman running around with mismatched clothing, no makeup, and a baby on her hip, because she has no time for herself. I also will never be the married trophy wife that has kids as a social stigma and hires a nanny to raise her kids. I sure as hell am not going to be married and miserable because I was stupid or irresponsible, so I did my partner and I a favor. I took away the ability for me to conceive a baby. I use condoms to protect myself from disease not pregnancy. Now, for the love of all needing to come, please fuck me, and hard."

He slides his hands underneath my ass and lifts me, turning for my bedroom. I grab his hair again, running it through my fingers. It's getting longer, giving him a different look. I like the bad boy with a shaved head and I like the cleaned up one too. "I don't know where the fuck you've been the entire time I've lived in Atlanta, but there has never been a more perfect and appetizing woman than you," he says as he carries me to my bed and tosses me town, quickly leaning down with me as we fall, our bodies never parting.

"Perfection is in the eye of the beholder. Everyone knows that."

"That mouth of yours is digging you deeper."

"Shut up and kiss me."

He presses his lips to mine and slides his tongue inside my mouth, matching the rhythm to his thrusts as he holds himself off of me. I moan into his mouth as his taste mixes with mine. He nibbles my bottom lip and releases it, kissing down my neck and chest, stopping with his mouth spread over my nipple. He bites down hard enough to cause pain, before lightly sucking enough to make it tingle. I verbalize how good it feels; a pleasure filled whine mixed with a moan. He knows my fucking overdrive button and he's using it. "Shit. Fuck me harder."

I tighten my legs around his waist before he grabs my thighs by the underside, gripping his hands firmly around them. He pushes toward me, his strength dominating mine. My legs break free, my knees coming toward my torso, lifting my ass off the bed slightly as he pulls his cock free, immediately creating a fucking void that's already driving me insane. "What are you doing?"

"Something I've been wanting to do to you lately. Something I've been craving. I want to taste you. I want my mouth on your clit. I want to feel you come when I shove my fucking tongue in your pussy." My breathing becomes wild. I think I just got wetter. I wasn't even sure that was possible. I'm soaking wet already.

He bends forward, pushing harder on my legs to lift my ass further, bringing it at a better angle for his mouth. It's a little uncomfortable until he places his lips on one of my thighs, slowly tormenting me by kissing in various places on my soft skin; careful to never touch me on the one spot I need it. I clench the comforter in my hands as the tickling sensation runs through my body. "What are you waiting for?"

He smiles against the crevice of my leg and torso. "Taking my time for once. Usually it's not by choice, but this time it is."

I'm not even sure what that really means and I don't really care. "Fuck. Stop teasing me. Would you suck it already?"

He digs his short nails into my skin and looks up at me, his lips just above my skin this time. "You know what that dirty fucking mouth does to me. You want me to suck your clit, then show me how much."

I close my eyes and shake my head from side to side, silently cursing inside. This is fucking ridiculous. Usually guys are dying to come and move on about their day, some not even worried if the girl orgasms. It's like a race to a lot of them, but not this one. Dammit, for once I think I want a five-minute fuck just so I can get some relief.

I open my eyes and grab a fist full of his hair, pulling his face toward my crotch. "Suck my fucking clit."

He growls and clamps his mouth over it, sucking so hard I scream out, rolling my head back into my mattress. I press my hand on the back of his head, wanting more. He grabs my hand from his head and places it in the place his hand just was, making me hold my own thigh, before raising his head to look at me and mirroring the other one, giving him access to his own arms. "Don't fucking move or let go."

"If you promise to do that again I'll hold myself here until I'm numb."

He smiles that cocky-ass smile, his lips only turning up on one side as he presses the pad of his index finger over my pussy and rubs in circles, lubricating it. "I think that can be arranged."

He places his free hand just above my clit and spreads my lips open, giving him better access to the sensitive, swollen button, then runs his finger up the line from my pussy to my clit, spreading my wetness from point A to point B. He starts massaging in circles again as he exerts pressure against my clit. It's more sensitive being open like this. My first instinct is to release my legs, accidentally letting one slip from my grasp. As I do he slaps my clit with his fingers. Ironically the sting mixed with the cold air from my apartment feels good.

"Fuck. Do that again."

"Don't let go, Lux. I'm warning you."

I already had a hold on it before he even said anything. Without another word he shoves two fingers in my pussy at the same time he places his mouth back on my clit. He starts flicking the tip of his tongue over it in a constant vibrating motion. "Holy shit you're good at that."

I can feel the throbbing sensation in my clit as he stimulates it, the blood flow quickly increasing. He thrusts his fingers in and out of me as if the two simultaneous motions aren't a problem for him at all. "Harder," I instruct, needing him to finger fuck me harder. I want fast and rough.

He sinks both fingers as far as they will go and hooks them upward, digging the tips into me, pressing against that spot that feels amazing. I bite my bottom lip, pressing my nails into my skin, trying not to drop my legs. He presses his tongue upward on the bottom side of my clit as he closes the roof of his mouth over it, lightly rubbing it against the foreign texture of his mouth, making it feel that much better. I almost can't stand it. It's becoming too much.

He backs his hand out and when he thrusts back inside it doesn't feel as full, as if it's his thumb this time. His tongue goes back to a flicking motion with the hardened point, taking my focus away from the different points of pleasure overwhelming me. Then I feel it...

His wet fingers press down over my ass hole, catching me off guard. I tense. "What the fuck?"

He sucks my clit again, turning my words into a loud moan as his fingers continue to familiarize themselves with my ass, rubbing back and forth over my asshole. It feels different, a little uncomfortable, but fuck if it doesn't feel good. I immediately start to relax. How is that possible? He returns to the fast flicking yet again and I can feel an orgasm quickly building, slightly confusing me. I don't even have time to process what's happening when I start to orgasm, my clit throbbing under his tongue. He removes his thumb from my pussy and shoves his tongue inside. The hand that is holding my lips open moves down, replacing his tongue with his thumb to keep my clit stimulated as I come with his tongue inside me. All of my muscles lock down as the feeling consumes my body, amplifying before decreasing. As I come down from the peak of my orgasm my muscles start to relax, leaving me in a sensitive and limp state. I can barely move, no longer able to hold my legs back, so I place my feet flat on the bed.

He stands upright, his cock standing at full attention. Fuck, I'm going to be a lousy lay. What the hell was that? He looks down at me with a smirk on his face. "That felt...different," I say.

He holds out his tongue for me to see, a white substance coating the top of it. My eyes enlarge but just barely, before the side of my lip pulls between my teeth. His tongue goes back into his mouth and he dramatically swallows so I can see. "Ready to let me in that ass now?"

My head begins shaking side to side before changing into a half nod half shake, forming something of a circle. His smile enlarges. "That's what I thought. On your knees."

My eyes become engorged. "I'm not prepared for that shit yet. Your dick is huge."

"Not today, sexy. I may be an asshole but I'm not trying to cause a massacre. Baby steps. I'm simply stating that I think it's safe to say you won't be riding today. I want your pussy open for me."

He presses his hand to the outside of my knee, pushing it toward the other leg as if hinting for me to turn around now. Both legs fall toward the mattress from making no effort to hold them upright. He slaps my ass, hard enough to leave a sting behind, and probably even a handprint. "Turn over."

I'm still in a post-orgasmic state, but as stupid as it sounds I can physically feel my pussy throbbing between my legs. I want his cock. As a matter of fact, I've never craved a cock between my legs like this one. My pussy is salivating for it. I want him to fuck me so hard I can't walk. I suddenly get a second wind, pushing myself up on my forearms seductively with a smirk of my own. "As you wish, handsome."

I roll over, standing before him on all fours with my pussy exposed. I arch my back to make it more visible. I think I'll toy with him. Chin to shoulder I look back at him. "You want me to believe you're a true killer, then show me what you got. Mutilate my pussy. It takes a lot to hold my attention and alcohol isn't a buffer this time. You want access to *all* of me and for a *long* period of time, then now is your chance to prove yourself worthy of the title. Men are a dime a dozen. That may make me a bitch, but take it or leave it."

His facial expression leaves me satisfied. He's going to play along. His demeanor remains serious. I turn my head. "It's ready for you, Mr. Cox. Don't disappoint me."

I can feel the mattress dip as the inside of his knee comes to rest to the outside of mine, followed by the other on the opposite side. The head of his cock is brushing against my ass. I look down at the muscular legs covered in a layer of black hair, confirming the hot as fuck man behind me. He grabs me by the hair laying flat along my back and jerks on it, pulling me upright. "Fuck," I whisper, as I lay my head against his shoulder, my breathing getting harder by the second.

He runs the tip of his nose up the length of my neck, before pressing his lips against my ear. I can feel the heat radiating with each exhale. His teeth close on the lobe and skim over the skin before releasing it. "Be careful what you wish for, Miss Larsen. You may just get more than you bargained for. Men may be a dime a dozen just as women, but the most complementary isn't. I know who you belong to whether a title is involved or not. Before this is over you won't question it either. In my business, disappointed clients are a hard limit. Reputation is everything. Now you're about to learn mine."

He presses on the center of my back, pushing me back on all fours, then thrusts forward, ramming his bare cock inside of me, shoving me forward as the tip roughly connects so hard inside of me that it feels like it's about to push through my cervix. I yell out incidentally as I clench the sheets. He stops inside of me. I work to steady my breathing as the pain shoots through my abdomen. He grabs my hips in his hands. "Scream if you need to scream. I want to hear you."

Using my hips as leverage he begins fucking me, hard. My eyes close and tighten as I take each thrust. He was obviously holding back before or the alcohol was a numbing agent. Fuck it hurts, but it is the best feeling pain I've ever experienced. I want him to stop but then I don't. With each thrust it becomes harder and faster, penetrating deeper. Not once can I hear his breathing peak. I bite my tongue trying to keep quiet, trying to avoid giving him the satisfaction of knowing how good he is with his damn cock. It's enough that his dick slides in and out with ease from how wet I am.

One hand rubs up to the center of my back, stopping between my shoulder blades. He presses down, lowering me to my elbows, my ass left in the air. The angle of entry changes, sending the head of his dick into my G-spot. "Oh fuck," I scream out.

"That's it. I want to hear how much you like it."

His hand returns to my hip, but he brings them in to rest on the top of my ass. He pulls my ass cheeks open and grinds his hips against my skin as he sinks his cock inside me as deep as it can go. I can barely hold my eyes open. My mind is slipping deeper into a state of euphoria with each hard hit against my G-spot. I can't concentrate on any normal motor skill. A sheen of sweat is now covering my body. It feels like it's ninety degrees in here.

"Touch yourself."

"What," I ask breathless.

"I want to fuck you while you get yourself off."

"Just keep going. What's the point of your dick if I have to get myself off?"

"Do it."

"No. Fuck. It feels too good."

He stops inside me. "Touch yourself or I pull out."

"You have got to be fucking kidding me. You sound like a child right now."

I start to rock back and forth on his dick, attempting to deter this conversation. Self-induced orgasms are a rare thing for me. There are too many willing volunteers that will do it for you. He slaps my ass and pulls out, leaving an agitated void that could make me kill someone. I look over my shoulder at him, scanning his body. His cock is noticeably wet from me. "You fucking asshole. I hate you right now."

He bends forward, lining his front on my back, before laying his palm on the back of my hand. "Yet you still want my fucking cock inside you. Touch yourself and you get it back."

He picks my hand up and brings it to my clit. "I cannot believe I am stooping to these levels for cock," I retort in the bitchiest tone possible.

"I can. It's good fucking cock. Now touch yourself."

I want to spit nails right now. My middle finger instinctively touches my clit and begins to rub the swollen area. "Egotistical asshole. Maybe I just need to turn you loose; then maybe some of that ego will shrink. Good fucking cock, my ass."

"Don't be mad you met someone just like you. Where there is good cock there is good pussy to motivate." He aligns the head of his dick at my entrance and pushes inside, slowly this time, kissing the side of my mouth briefly, leaving the wetness of his saliva behind. "And it takes one to know one. Don't stop until you come."

"Hell yes I love the size of your cock."

He returns to his previous position, steadily getting back to a hard and fast rhythm. I continue to rub in circles over my clit as I hold my upper body weight on my one forearm, barely able to stand how full I feel with him inside of me and the clit stimulation together. It isn't going to take long to get myself off. It never does. It doesn't matter how long a girl goes without getting herself off, when she does it's a familiar act as if it's only been hours. A girl knows her own body, her likes and dislikes, what feels good and where to touch for quick release. It's already starting to build, even faster with every thrust from behind.

He pulls my ass cheeks apart again. Something wet drips at the top of my ass crack and begins sliding down the seam of my ass. *What the hell?*

He thrusts again, taking my mind off of it. I can feel my orgasm. It's about to start. My finger gets faster. "I'm about to come."

I lose focus as my orgasm consumes my body, falling into that temporary moment of bliss. My toes curl into the bottom of my feet. I can't move. It's amplified each time he hits my G-spot. My legs and arm are starting to shake from holding my weight. As my clit starts to become sensitive he thrusts again, his thumb sliding into my asshole. "Don't tense," he says as if reading my body language.

I'm not sure how I feel about it right now. I can't really process any information at the moment. It's a foreign feeling. I'm not used to things entering there. It's more like a pressure. He holds onto my waist with one hand to keep him steady, slowing his hip movements slightly as he allows me to become used to his finger with the other hand. The more I move past the fact that he has his thumb shoved in my anal cavity the better it feels. He starts to match the rhythm of his hand and hips in unison. Both of my hands become flush with the mattress, no longer able to touch myself. The muscles between my legs contract as he thrusts inward at both locations, clamping down on his dick. The sensation of both places being filled is more than I would have imagined. "Fucking shit, Lux. You need to come."

I can't even verbalize an appropriate response as his thrusts become harder and more needy. "Fuck, Kaston."

His hand slides across my pelvis from my hip to the other side and he lifts up slightly. If there were any barrier before there isn't anymore. There is no way I'm about to come again this soon. One final thrust and I can feel it starting, but it's different this time, more dramatic than a single formed orgasm. I moan out, freeing some of the pent up release, but only a whisper of a whine escapes, unable to do anything but feel through it. An interior orgasm always feels better than a clit orgasm anyway, but this...is so much more. No thoughts, no extra movements, and no words are able to form. I'm no longer coherent to anything. Instead, I've crossed over into a foreign place, Nirvana, one I've never been in before. Even if I've come close, it's been induced by intoxication. My eyes close. "I'm about to fucking come all in your pussy unless you object."

Nothing.

Silence.

An explosion of feelings envelop me.

Breathing becomes a complex activity instead of a natural one.

I hear him speak, but nothing really registers.

He could fucking stab me right now and it'd probably feel good.

I finally begin to fall over the edge. The high decreases, making me feel like I'm coming to after a black out. I open my eyes. Everything before me looks clear. I never even noticed him still inside of me until this very second. He's quiet, still standing on his knees and still ball deep inside of me as his thumb slowly exits. All I can hear are the quickened breaths as they escape his nose. "Kaston?"

"Give me a fucking minute."

His fingertips dig into my hip and then I feel his lips touch the center of my spine. For him to be so hard he has a layer of softness that comes through on occasion. His kisses are so light that it almost tickles. His hand makes its way up my stomach and encloses over my breast just before he squeezes it. His lips slowly move up my back, stopping within a whispering distance. "I just emptied my fucking load inside of you. I've never done that with anyone. I shouldn't have, because now I'm done for. This is going to end badly for one of us, because no other man is touching this body.... Ever. That's a fucking promise that won't be broken."

Without another word he pulls free from me, our bodies no longer connected. I'm not sure whether I should bring out the bitch or remain quiet. It's an odd feeling. Confusion isn't a norm for me. One side of my brain is feeding off of his claim over me and the other side wants to throw a tantrum like a toddler at his unnecessary possessiveness.

As he stands from the bed a chill runs down my body, suddenly cold. Fatigue sets in, now wanting to go back to bed. I roll over and fall on my back, before looking up at him. He's pulling his briefs up his legs, releasing the band at his waist, making a snapping sound as the elastic hits his skin. My eyes scan his body, mesmerized by his rock hard physique. Did I really just fuck that?

What have you gotten yourself into, Lux? You're in a deep pile of shit.

I feel sticky from the sheen of sweat covering my body. My core is already starting to heat again from the way he's looking at me, now remaining quiet. I push up, suddenly aware of the increased wetness between my legs. Not all of it is mine. I feel gross. He walks forward, straddling his legs to the outside of mine. I look into his eyes from beneath my eyelashes. "What are you doing," I ask as he places his palm against my cheek.

He leans in, closing his body into mine. "Taking you to bed."

He presses his lips against mine, sliding his tongue inside as he presses me down into the mattress. His hand slips underneath my back and he lifts up, sliding me up toward the head of the bed as he walks on his knees with me. Dammit, he's doing that shit again.

I pull my face free as my head comes in contact with the pillow. "Hold up, killer. Did you not just take me bed? I may kill myself for this later, but I need a break. Energy is not unlimited in supply, especially when I'm under the spell of your cock."

He laughs. Oh my god he laughed. I feel strange, slightly faint, overheated, and definitely strange. "Did I say something funny?"

"Besides the fact that you just called fucking taking you to bed, no. That's probably the most innocent thing I'll ever hear come out of your mouth. You kind of curse like a sailor and lack the filter most girls have, but I think that's why you still have my attention. As much as I like the feel of your pussy's interior, I was actually referring to sleep. I'm staying."

He stops talking, briefly studying me. "Is there a problem with that?"

I should kick him out, shouldn't I? Sober sleepovers are not going to help this situation. His hands move to the mattress on each side of my shoulders, holding himself off of me. He remains straddling my body but leaving a significant gap of distance between us. My lip draws into my mouth, sticking within the confinement of my teeth. Grabbing the top section of my bedding I lift my butt and back on the weight of my legs, before wriggling beneath the blankets.

Turning my head to the vacant space beside me, I pat the satin sheet with my palm. "Well if you must. It didn't really sound like a question anyway."

He slides beneath the covers and turns on his side toward me. I alter my position to mirror him, resting my hands underneath my face. Neither of us speaks. It's a weird curiosity it seems. We both know realistically this thing between us is a ticking time bomb. One of us will get bored and move on. There is always a dominant alpha personality in every relationship, even just casual. Two will never make it very long, but I'm not sure what to make of him, of us, or of this situation. He makes me want to run, but he also makes me want to stay.

"You going to sleep?"

He smirks. "Are you?"

"It's a little hard when someone wakes you up. I need a shower."

He shakes his head. "I like you like this."

I scrunch my nose. "I have your semen starting to come out of me, in which I still can't believe you did. I probably smell like sex, and I'm sticky from sweating. There is no way in hell a guy likes a girl like this. I wouldn't want to cuddle with you if your balls smelled like sex. Quit with your lies."

"Addendum: I like you like this when you consist of any of the above mentioned symptoms as a result from sex with me. I wouldn't want that statement to be confused."

I roll my eyes. "Guys are so territorial."

"And girls aren't?"

"Not this one."

"So what you're saying is that you'd be fine with me leaving here and fucking someone else, then coming back tomorrow and fucking you again?"

I blink.

My mouth opens.

It closes.

I blink again.

"Yes. I don't own you. I can't control your actions. You aren't married." I pause briefly. My breathing stops. "Right? Please tell me you aren't married."

"Fuck no. I may do a lot of questionable shit, but that's not one of them. Seriously? I'm a little offended."

I can breathe again. "It's not like it would be the first time it's happened," I mumble. My voice goes back to normal. "What you do when you aren't around me is really none of my business…"

"That's fucked up, but I've already told you I'm not like every other douche bag, and I call bullshit. Hesitation in your answer was more of the truth than what just came out of your mouth. I'm not a fucking idiot. I fuck you, you fuck me, and we fuck each other, exclusively, until one of us severs that verbal contract that we entered into. That's just how it's going to be."

"Who died and made you the ruler of my pussy? I think the rights belong to me, which means I choose who to license it out to.

Nowhere on my birth certificate does it say I was born in the land of Kaston and his cock."

He rolls me on my back and grabs my hands in his, pinning them beside my head. "You and that mouth are going to get you in trouble. Fuck. Do you have to have a smartass comment about everything? Damn girl." He presses his brief covered erection between my legs. "I've never been so damn sexually frustrated seconds after nutting in my entire life. The surges of aggression and possession you're causing are starting to piss me off."

I wrap my legs around his waist, unable to move my hands from his weight. He's close enough that we can touch with the simple lifting of my head. I enclose my lips over his mouth, lightly brushing the tip of my tongue to trace the shape of his lips softly pressed together, before pulling at his bottom lip with my teeth and then releasing it. "Welcome to the club, baby. I guess it's a good thing it's both of us. Over time we'll fuck it out of our systems, but for now take me to bed. I need sleep. I have to work later."

He runs his hand down my body, being sure not to miss my tattoo that he inked on my skin, before stopping at my thigh, and then turns to lay flat on his back, bringing my leg to rest on top of his waist. I turn back on my side like before to get more comfortable, but prop up on my arm to look down at him. "You want to cuddle? We aren't really the cuddling kind.... I thought we were merely sharing a bed."

"Maybe. Today, we make an exception."

He lays his arm out straight beneath the bottom edge of the pillow, hinting for me to lay my head on his shoulder. I start to get that creepy bug-crawling feeling that I get when I have to draw out the emotional shit on occasion. "I don't know..."

"Lux."

His eyes are closed, as if he's already half asleep. "What? We don't have to cuddle to sleep. It's weird. We aren't that kind of couple."

He releases a loud exhale that sounds like the result of frustration. "Cut the shit, Lux. Just lay down. We both have personal shit that creates barriers. It's why we're similar. Let it go."

"Damn lunatic. Fine...but first reach in that bottom drawer and hand me a pair of underwear. It's my emergency drawer for when I don't feel like getting out of bed. I'm not sleeping without underwear if I have to deal with your cum seeping out of me. It feels gross."

On that note his eyes open at the same time his lips curve upward. He reaches over the side of the bed and pulls the drawer open, digging around until he brings back a pair of panties dangling from his index finger. "That might have been a slight turn on. Pretty fucking strange."

I grab the panties from his finger and reach below the comforter, placing each foot into them and pulling them up my legs, slightly lifting to get them over my ass. "This whole situation is *pretty fucking strange*," I retort. "Where do you want me, sir?"

He grunts. "Where I was in the process of putting you before you had to have a fabric barrier. I kind of liked the easy access. Never mind. Lay down before I decide that sleep is overrated and give you no choice in the decision to explore some more."

I lay down, dramatically placing my head on his chest, before throwing my leg over his waist. My heart starts to race when I hear his heart pounding through his chest, as if the two are talking to each other. He places one hand on my thigh and the other encloses around me, running along my shoulder blades holding me to him. "Are you happy now?"

"Sleep."

"Easier said than done when I'm dealing with a stubborn-ass psycho that won't take no for an answer. This isn't even comfortable..."

My mind is racing a million miles a minute, signaling it's nowhere close to shutting down. This is awkward.

"Lux...."

"Kaston...."

"Sleep."

"Command me one more time and I will bite you."

"Think before you act. You never know what that may result in."

His eyes are closed again and his tone is completely calm, only aggravating me further. I huff and start to wiggle into him, before draping my arm over his stomach. He lightly rubs his fingertips back and forth on my upper arm. My eyes start to become heavy. I yawn. "That feels nice."

"So does this," I hear, or think I hear, in a mumble as I drift off to sleep. In this now relaxed state I can't be sure.

CHAPTER SIXTEEN

Kaston

I roll over on my stomach and clench the pillow to my chest, just now starting to wake. The light in the room has changed from sunup to sundown; that I can tell. My arm swipes across the mattress smoothly, confirming I'm in bed alone. My eyes open the rest of the way and I look around the room. No lights are on and the bedroom door is shut.

I move to my back so I can sit up, running my hand through my hair as I try to wake up. It's about time to shave it again. I need to go into the office. I've fucked off long enough. Sleeping during the day is abnormal for me. I feel like a stupid frat boy that doesn't care about anything but partying and failing college. I never did like frat boys...

I still, trying to listen for the sound that is now occurring. It's muted with the door shut and it's obviously turned down so it isn't loud. It sounds like... hip-hop music? I throw off the blanket and stand from the bed, before walking to the door and opening it. Two steps out the door and I halt. The beautiful ass in front of me bouncing up and down through the air in a squat catches my attention, my eyes stopping directly on it. The only visual I have right now is her doing that on my cock.

My palm instinctively travels to my dick and presses down. *Down boy...*

My eyes temporarily move past that beautiful ass to the television mounted on the wall in front of her. From the group of people mirroring her movements I'm going to assume it's a home workout DVD. I'm pretty sure I've even seen that guy on infomercials before. Lux looks between her legs from an upside down position as she stretches her thighs in the standing spread eagle she's in. My feet automatically walk forward, grabbing ahold of her hips as I line my crotch to her ass. "The perfect angle for so many things..."

She swats my hand. "Go away."

"Like hell. What are you doing?"

"Insanity."

"I would agree that you are since that clearly isn't needed with a body like this, but those are your words and not mine. It would be insanity for me not to fuck you in this position."

The top portion of my fingers fold over the waistband of her skintight spandex pants, disappearing on the other side between the material and her skin. I pull the back of her pants over her ass, leaving the band sitting at the top of her legs beneath her cheeks, making her plump ass of perfection visible. The people on the television screen are now in a totally different position than her.

"Kaston, go shower or something. The program is called Insanity. I'm going to pretend that you didn't just compare me to crazy…for your sake. Go away. You're messing up my workout vibe right now. How the hell do you think I have a body like this? I'm already off routine since I met you."

She automatically goes for her pants, trying to pull them back up, and still in a bent over position. I stop her. "Let me in the man cave."

She thrusts her ass into my crotch, gaining some distance long enough for her to stand and turn around. She adjusts her pants as she cocks an eyebrow at me. "The *man cave*? Please, do explain. I think I want to hear this. I'm pretty sure it's a necessity actually."

Grabbing the front band of her pants, I pull her toward me. She's biting her lip as if she's trying not to laugh. It actually makes her cuter, giving her a little bit of innocence mixed into that hardcore personality she has, that tough exterior she hides behind. "Well, man cave by formal but summarized definition is a room or area referred to as a man's sanctuary, designed based off of the owner's activities, preferences, or hobbies. It's off limits to other men unless invited in. It's a place used for a man's enjoyment, pleasure, or gratification. It's also used primarily to house his trophies or prized possessions. In this instance I'm referring to my cock."

I scan my eyes down her body. Her nipples are hard and showing through her sports bra. When my sight returns to her face her cheeks are flushed. "Your pussy, baby, is a perfect and accurate description of a man cave; my man cave. I want in."

A smirk starts to form on her face before a laugh escapes. "I can honestly say I've heard it all now. That shit is too good to have gotten from someone else. That was funny as hell, but so original. I will never think of a man cave in the same way again. I may even let you in my pants, Cox."

I smile as I snake my hands around her body, settling them on her ass. I pick her up, grinding her against my front until she's at my waist. She wraps her legs around me as her hands connect on the back of my neck. She weighs nothing, at least to me. She looks down at me, her crystal blue eyes staring into my gray ones. The color reminds me of the beach because that's the only place you find water that clear and blue. Her smile fades as we look at each other. "I kind of like you, Cox," she whispers. "I can deal with your dark side, just don't turn into a douche. That would be a tragedy."

I never take my eyes off of her as I turn for the couch, walking blindly. I stop just before my shins hit. "I may not be the kind to sweep you off your feet, but what you see is what you get, beautiful. From the beginning to the end I'll always be the same. I hate liars."

I bend over and lay her on the couch, holding my weight on my arms beside her, before pressing my erection between her legs. "I can deal with your broken soul, just don't ever lie to me." She draws in a breath before clearing her surprised expression and laces her fingers into my hair, pulling my lips into hers. They touch, but something feels different about this kiss. Her lips move against mine slower, not rushed, as if learning me in a more intimate way. I'm not sure what it is, but what I do know is that I want more.

I'm not that guy that was raised to use women as a tool for an orgasm. I don't feel like more of a man by upping my number on the list of women I've slept with. Sure, I've had my fair share, some once and some consecutively or repetitively over time just like most people, but it was only ever sex for the enjoyment of both parties and was understood from the beginning exactly what it was. Honestly, my partner probably got more out of it than me...until her. Until the night I fucked her for the first time, sex was more of a pastime than an enjoyment. I enjoyed drinking more than sex, but usually the two came together.

I now understand the enjoyment of sober sex...and I want more.

My father was a married man, and aside from the affair with my mother he never crossed that line. People could judge him for stepping outside of his marriage for that brief period of time, they so often do, but people make mistakes. They fuck up. Human nature likes to dip its toes into the pool of temptation, especially when the ugly parts of the world are revealed.

The bottom line is my father loved his wife. He explained it to me often, as well as his mishaps, but in that conversation I was never one of them. I had a childhood full of love, at least from one parent. Luckily I only remember a few bad years with my mom, since most kids don't have any memory earlier than the age of four or five. I never did without and I was taught wrong from right. My father didn't choose a life of evil. He was thrown into it. He made the decision he did because of love. I know what love looks like and the importance of it. I know he loved my stepmom, but unforeseen circumstances kept them apart. The way he dealt with it was by numbing his emotions and living heartless over everything but her and I. That was the only way he could cope and continue on.

I'm not the guy against falling in love. I just never met a girl that sparked my interest enough to find out if she was a potential candidate worth the risk. Watching my father's lifestyle I thought there was no way to have it and still be able to do what he did. I'm still not sure. There is a part of me that is so submerged in darkness I'll never escape, but what I do know is that I like this girl. For now, and until I can figure this out, I'm not letting her get away.

Shifting the weight onto my left arm I grab her pants with the right, working them over her butt. She unwraps her legs from my waist and places her feet flat on the couch, then lifts a little to create enough space for her pants to bypass her ass and travel down her legs. I kiss down her neck as her pants reach her thighs, leaving them there for now.

"I'm sweaty. I ran earlier."

Her words are uneven in tone, changing with the increase of her breathing.

"I don't care. Makes no difference to me."

I push the bottom of her sports bra above her breasts, before placing my mouth on one of her nipples. Her back arches, pressing her chest harder against my mouth. My hand makes its way back down her stomach as I suck, searching for the pot of gold at the end of the rainbow. It doesn't take long to get there. I press my middle finger between her lips, and then rub down to the wet spot below. Fuck I love how wet she gets. She moans as I dip two of my fingers into her pussy, lubricating them before inserting them all the way in. I pull out and push back in, harder this time.

A knock sounds at the door. I release her nipple from my mouth and look up at her, but continue fingering her. "Get rid of them," I command. Her eyes are heavy, closing more with every thrust of my fingers.

She clears her throat. "Who is it?"

Another knock sounds. It's just one knock but hard, as if not wanting to draw attention from the neighbors. It's a masculine knock, one that comes from a man. "Who is it? I'm busy," she yells as I shove my fingers deep inside her, hard, creating an offset in her voice as she speaks. "Don't stop," she whispers, grabbing my hair and trying to press my head back down.

I flick my tongue over her taut nipple, looking up at her from underneath my lashes. "Get rid of them and you can have my cock instead."

"Fuck, I love when you talk dirty."

"Angel, let me in."

My jaw steels at the sound of his voice. Every muscle in my body becomes tense. My central nervous system goes into a defense mode. *I'm sorry,* she mouths. Forget mouthing bullshit.

"Who the fuck is that?"

"Someone that is no longer important, but obviously doesn't get the memo. Fuck! Why does he have to ruin everything?" I'm not sure if she's talking to herself or me at this point. What I do know is that my blood is boiling. I have no idea why. My alter ego is starting to emerge and I'm getting the sudden urge to kill someone, literally, which would break every rule my father had and everything he stood for over the course of his life. I don't like this feeling.

I add a finger and speed up the rhythm of my thrusts, taking out my frustration on her pussy. She arches into my hand and closes her eyes. "Hell yes. Oh damn, please don't stop."

"Let me in, Angel. You've already confirmed you're in there."

I hook my fingers up as I enter again, shoving the tips into her G-spot.

"Are you still fucking him?"

She opens her eyes to look at me. "No."

"Have you since me?"

"No."

"Then what the fuck is he doing here?"

"Trying to get me back.... again."

That's not something I want to hear. "Do you want him?"

"If I did I wouldn't be with you."

"Prove it."

"Go away, Callum. My stance with you hasn't changed. I'm seeing someone else."

Motherfucker. I feel like I'm going through withdrawals. My

breathing starts to become erratic with every passing second that I look at her. It slowly feels like someone else is taking possession of my body. I need a fucking shot.

"We need to talk, Lux. I still have my key. I'll use it if I have to."

I pull my fingers from her body. "I'm going to fucking kill him."

I straighten myself in an upright position before changing the weight to my knee between her legs. She shoots up, grabbing my hand. "Wait."

I look down at her. "What?" My tone is a little angrier than I meant for it to be.

"Are you jealous?"

Another knock sounds at the door, this time more than once. He's getting needy and I'm getting madder by the minute. "Open the door, Lux."

"I fucking told you that no one else is touching your body. I'm not going to pretend that I like knowing the last person that did is standing right outside the door and has a key to where you sleep alone."

Her face softens, but only slightly. She places her hands on her outer thighs beneath the waistband of her pants and pushes them down her legs, removing them completely, before going for my briefs. I feel like I need a drink, anything to dilute this feeling. I would imagine this is how a platoon of soldiers feels when their territory is about to be invaded.

She peels my black briefs down my legs, never taking her eyes off of mine. "I had the locks changed, Kaston. He can't get in anymore. If you're upset take it out on me. Someone may need him...it just isn't me. Don't do anything stupid. He isn't worth it. Trust me."

I stand, letting my underwear fall to the floor. "You want me to fuck you with him outside the door?"

She grabs my hips, pulling me closer to her. "Callum, unless you want to listen to me fucking someone else then I suggest you leave," she yells out, her eyes still locked with mine.

He starts banging on the door, causing it to shake. "Bullshit, Lux. Open the damn door."

She lowers her voice as she pulls down on me, pulling me back on my knee. "He's been warned. If he wants to stay then let him listen. I'll put on a show. I guess I really am just as fucked up as you are. You wanted to mark me... well there's never been a better chance than now."

My pulse is going crazy. I feel like I just got done working out. The only thing missing is sweat, but as hot as I feel right now I wouldn't be surprised if it were next to come. I flex my hand trying to stop it from shaking. I fucking hate feeling like a junkie looking for his next fix, but it also piques my curiosity.

I grab her sports bra and pull it over her head, before grabbing the holder wrapped around her hair and sliding it until her hair falls free from the mess she had it in on top of her head. I'm not even going to evaluate why my cock is still hard as a rock. This should be a boner killer for sure. The doorknob starts wiggling as if he's trying to get it open. He smacks the door. "I'll give you your car back, Angel. Just open the door. Come on. Don't do this. I warned you."

I lean in, hinting for her to lay back, before placing my mouth in various places on her body, starting with her breasts. The inside of her foot touches my hip, flexed to a point like a dancer to confirm she likes my mouth on her body. My hand wraps around her ankle, before slowly sliding up the length of her leg. Little by little my vision clears, nothing else drawing my attention but her. "This time I'll behave because what you're offering is so much more enticing, but I'm teaching that bastard a lesson. He will know his place when I'm done."

She grabs my shaft and aligns the head at her pussy. "It is yours. Claim it."

I thrust inside, not stopping until my dick is buried completely inside her. Instantly I relax and my body starts climbing a high, just like when you snort that first line after being without for too long. The anger falls away and the craving diminishes. I have formed an addiction to Lux Larsen. That should be reason enough to do something about it, but I think I'm at the point of no return already. The only thing that will break it...is going out in a wooden box.

CHAPTER SEVENTEEN

Lux

Kaston pulls his truck into my place of employment and stops, shifting into park. We haven't said much the entire drive. After earlier things are a little awkward. It's that feeling like when two people meet in Vegas and form an instant attraction, leading to the act of drinking to the point of conscious blackout, getting married by Elvis, and then wake up the next morning and think, what the hell have I done, when you see the ring on your left hand and the stranger at your side...

We experienced that weird moment that crossed the line from just another fun fuck to I'm not sure, but it's different. That point changed what we are. A casual relationship is fun, but bring in jealousy and possession and you're fucked. It only leads to places you don't want to go, making you do things you never thought you would. There is no going back to before, but I'm not sure I want to continue forward either.

There is one thing that money won't control and that's my freedom. The direction we're headed is creating a noose around my neck and the longer I let him hold the rope, the tighter it's going to get. At some point it cuts off your air. That I can't handle. My mom will be here soon and I have to deal with that shit, I have a job to keep, and I can't love someone else. Hell, I don't even love myself most days. It just isn't in me. Love works for some people and others it doesn't. Maybe I'm a rare breed of female, but I don't want it. It doesn't interest me in the slightest.

I control my feelings like I control everything else in my life. It's easy. When you think there are any possibilities of attachment you cut it off at the root before it has the chance to grow. What happened on that couch I've never experienced. Sparking jealousy in a man is usually bragging rights for a girl, but this time I actually felt...guilty? For the first time in my life I wanted to give him more than my body. Maybe I should step back from this...

I grab the door handle and look over at him. "You really didn't have to drive me to work, but thanks. It beats a cab." I pause. "Look, maybe—"

"I'll pick you up at two," he says, still looking over the steering wheel.

"Kaston, my mom is going through some shit and she's going to be with me for a while. I just don't think this is going to work. My available time is going to become very narrow. Most guys demand more. I get that. I've given you all that I have to give. I'm not being a bitch. It's just easier this way. I did have fun though."

The muscle in his jaw starts to tick. He suddenly opens the door and exits the truck, slamming the door shut behind him. "Okay.... What just happened?"

My head begins to turn, following him as he rounds the truck. He reaches my door and yanks it open, almost pulling me out since my hand is still holding the handle. I catch myself by gripping onto his shoulder. "What the fuck is your problem, Kaston?"

Without a word he grabs ahold of my waist, sliding me out of the lifted truck until my feet reach the ground. I can see his chest rising and falling under the clingy fabric of his shirt hugged against his chest. "What did I fucking tell you about that mouth?"

"Excuse me? Well why don't you remind me? Obviously I must have forgotten."

He places his arms against the seat to each side of me, blocking me in front of him. "What the fuck is it with you? Just when I think it's a breath of fresh air that you aren't like normal girls, you try that hit and run shit and I want to revoke it. If I hadn't been ball deep inside the pussy between your legs I would swear you were a guy. It's driving me fucking insane. I'm not standing here pledging my undying love to you, I'm not presenting you with a big-ass diamond, and I'm not propositioning you to have my children, so for the love of mankind will you stop that shit before an innocent bystander loses a limb. You know you want to continue this just as much as I do. Stop lying to yourself. Call it curiosity or just good sex, frankly I don't give a fuck, but either way I'm picking you up at 2AM and you're staying with me. If you have to work later then I'll be sitting in this damn parking lot waiting for you to finish. We are both adults. Scheduling can be worked out."

Like it's possessed my hand swings through the air and connects with his cheek, causing a loud clap. My eyes widen as it returns to its original position. We stare at each other, both breathing harshly and not saying a word. His cheek starts to redden. Our eyes scan each other as if waiting for a bomb to detonate. "Do you feel better?

I'm going to assume that was us moving past this."

"Fucking bastard," I grit out and grab the back of his head, pulling him toward me and crushing his lips to mine. He grabs the back of my thighs and picks me up, sliding me up his front. I suck the tip of his tongue, causing him to rub my middle against his denim-covered erection. He groans into my mouth just before I pull on his hair, breaking the kiss. I wipe my mouth, ridding it of any proof that he was just there, before snaking my hand between us and grabbing his hard shaft in my hand. "No.... the pair of blue balls that you will wear until 2AM was us moving on. Sorry, not sorry. I just couldn't leave with you having the upper hand. I suppose I'm just different than most girls," I say, winking as I wiggle out of his grasp. As soon as my feet hit the pavement I release him and duck under his arm, grabbing my purse out of the seat on my way. "Have a good night, Kaston."

I walk away, listening to the string of curses behind me, inwardly smiling to myself. He may be right about a few things, but that doesn't mean I have to admit to them. Admitting defeat is a failure in itself. Boys will be boys and Lux will be Lux, but they will never quite figure out my next move, no matter how much they think they know me.

Kaston

Fucking hell...

I grab the edge of the door and sling it forward until it slams shut. My hands automatically lace on top of my head as I turn around, watching her disappear inside. "The fucking irony," I yell out into midair, not caring if anyone overhears. "Why the fuck, the first girl that has me in shambles is exactly like me only worse has got to be karma biting me in the ass."

My phone starts vibrating in my pocket. I pull it out and raise it to my ear after connecting the call. "What?"

"Good evening to you too…. You okay?"

I walk to the bed of my truck, gripping my free hand over the edge. I bend over, spitting on the pavement before responding. "Fuck no. If I get out of this shit remind me to never cross another female that has me looking first."

He laughs. "That sounds perfect for you."

"Nah, bro, I'm in Hell. This has to be it: Hell on earth. No guy wants to work this hard to keep a pussy in his grasp. I'm a good catch. I've never had to do this shit before. I'm starting to feel like I'm in a twilight zone. There is no end."

"Have you gotten the goods?"

"I wouldn't be much of a man if I started bragging and spilling information best kept to myself. I'll leave it open to interpretation."

"Well it isn't hard to guess, so I'm going to say yes. I don't see her as the type of girl that's saving herself and I highly doubt you'd waste your time on a good girl. It doesn't really seem like your style. If you're hitting it then why are you bitching like a little girl?"

"Because I'm still trying to wrap my head around it, and I consider myself an intelligent man. I've honestly never seen a girl so ready to run every time she's done fucking. Everything I knew about women is completely useless with her. I feel like the roles are reversed here. It has me uneasy."

"So drop her…. She can't be that good if she has your head all fucked up. You know what kind of shit that leads to…mistakes."

No words.

I narrow my eyes as I look across the parking lot. What the...

"That's not going to work for me."

"Why not? There are plenty more to replace her."

"Plenty more maybe, but plenty more like her, no."

"I see..."

"Don't take that tone with me, asshole. I'm not pussy whipped."

He laughs again. "That never came out of my mouth, but since you brought it up..."

Movement: two o'clock.

Suspect: male.

Ride: expensive. More expensive than anything else in this parking lot.

"Son of a fucking bitch."

Scattering sounds occur through the phone. "What is it?"

"Standby. I need you to do some digging soon. I have to go."

"We need to talk about the mark. Our window is getting narrow."

The door to the black sports car opens. An expensive shoe hits the pavement: Italian leather. I'd recognize them from a further distance than this. I knew someone that wore them all my life.

"Keep an eye on him for a little longer. It'll get done. It always does. The evil never sleeps. Chevy, I need to go. Keep your phone on you."

I disconnect the call and return my phone to my pocket. The male in the suit stands, shutting the door to his expensive car. He sticks out like a sore thumb and this is Atlanta, so that says a lot. The ones from here belong. He doesn't. Every alarm inside is going off. He is a huge target on my internal radar and it's never wrong.

My feet start to move without me instructing them. I open the door to my truck and grab my handgun from the glove compartment, shoving it behind the front waistband of my jeans, but hidden by my shirt. This one is perfectly legal and registered to none other than me. I may have two lives, but Kaston plays by the rules.... usually. I have a permit to conceal my weapons. He starts to walk toward the building and I start to walk toward him, shutting my truck door without even locking it.

I watch him fasten the button on his jacket as he gets closer to the door. I pick up pace to reach him before he enters. I'm pretty sure he's who I think he is, and something tells me he's going to be a problem for me. Even if I wasn't a pretty good judge of character, the fact that he pounded on the door while I fucked his ex-girlfriend and made her come is a pretty good hint. No real man is going to listen to that shit. Once another man dips his dick in the place yours used to be it's no longer sacred. It loses its appeal. Real men move on. For the bad seeds of the world it's a trigger to a bigger obsession, one that usually ends up in a file on my desk.

He places his hand on the door handle, getting ready to open it, when I halt beside him and shove my palm hard against the door to keep it shut, exerting a good portion of my bodyweight into it. "I don't believe you're an employee here," I grit out. "Unless you can show me a title of ownership to this building and company, then I suggest you hop back on a plane and return to wherever you came from."

He turns to look at me as he releases the door. "Under whose orders?"

Yep. Definitely New York. I would know that accent anywhere. I grew up with it for twenty years. Since my mother was actually from Jersey hers was slightly different, but still similar.

He laughs. "Son, I wouldn't advise talking to a man of my stature that way. Money talks. I can make your life a living hell. I guess you're her latest venture, acting all heroic and shit. You may have gotten between her legs, but that doesn't make you special." He looks me over as his lips draw upward into a smirk. "You can't keep a gold digger without a little gold. The pussy is just how she hooks you. It's as easy to get as a common drug on the streets. What are you? Let me guess.... Fresh out of college looking for something higher than minimum wage?"

My left arm swings upward and nails him in the right eye, causing him to stumble backward. I crack my neck to each side, trying to calm the fuck down. I'm not prepared to dispose of a body right now. The twitch is back. It's worse than it's been in a while. "Son of a bi-"

I grab his neck with my right hand, walking him backward toward the car that he parked out of eyesight from her, between two buildings. I'm itching to kill him, I so easily could, but if I do I will violate all the rules, becoming just like the ones I exterminate. He isn't a mark. There isn't proof that he's committed a crime, much less a string of them. His hands grab onto my wrist, trying to pry me off. It won't work. I'm stronger than him. I have to train as if every mark is bigger and tougher, faster and heavier. When adrenaline is pumping through the bloodstream a person gets stronger, especially when accompanied with fear.

When he can't free up his neck from my hold he slaps me. I felt more from Lux than him. What does that fucking say? "You going to slap me like a little bitch?"

I press him down onto the hood of the car. "Why don't you let me show you how real men carry?"

I move my shirt and grab the handle of my pistol, placing the barrel to his temple. His eyes widen. For such a rich bastard I can smell the fear all over him. "For starters, motherfucker, real men don't talk smack about females. Even for a man of your *stature*," I mock, "It's trashy. It's also a bit hypocritical to judge a female that likes sex when your standards are probably a lot lower. We don't live in the forties. This is the twenty-first century. Like I said before, you're going to get back on that plane and return to wherever you came from. I think I speak for us all when I tell you you're no longer welcome here. If you don't leave I'll show you a real man when I give you the gift of a bullet to the head."

I pull him off the car and walk him to the door, just before opening it and shoving him toward the interior. He stumbles but gets inside. "She'll come back to me. You can't stop it. She just needs a little push and a reminder of what it is she wants. You may have caught me at a disadvantage, but I don't give up that easily."

I kick the door shut and bend down, crossing my arms over the rolled down window on the door, my gun still in my hand. He obviously wasn't smart enough to roll it up from his spying earlier. "I don't think that's going to be the case, *Callum*. I have a feeling when a girl like Lux says she's done, it's for good reason." I press my head further into the car, invading his personal space. "And if you think for one fucking second that I'm letting her go then think again. Not all of us have to brag about our money because it isn't our most prized possession. Maybe you should rearrange your priorities, *brotha*," I grit out in sarcasm. "But with this mistake you're a little too late."

I wink and lightly pop his cheek with the side of the gun, before standing and stepping away from the car. "Have a safe flight," I say sarcastically. He starts the engine and peels out, flipping me the bird as he drives off. I salute him with my gun just before putting it back in its place.

"I think I just came a little."

My lips turn upward at the sound of that filthy fucking mouth behind me. I may just have to steal her away from her boss for a little while. After that I need an adrenaline rush.... And I know just how to get it. I do an about face to look at her, standing beside a door to the building, most likely just a service entrance for the kitchen. She does work for a catering company...

She has her hands on her hips and her legs spread, her face serious as hell. There isn't a crack of a smile present. This is slightly similar to the night she stumbled upon me in the alley, a first when on a job. Being invisible is key. Every fucking detail is timed and measured, always within a window of opportunity. Her showing up wasn't a coincidence. She was fucking meant to find me. "You did, huh? That must be one good motherfucker if he can make you come without touching you."

I take a step forward, keeping my hands at my side. She shrugs, never giving away her serious demeanor. She is the queen of dry humor and I love it. "Maybe that heroic shit really works. It made me wet. That was fucking hot. Maybe I should be the damsel in distress more often. No wonder she was in love with Spiderman. I might even give you a quickie in an alley. What do you think?"

"I don't think so."

I continue walking forward, slowly, not in a hurry to alter this moment. This scene is working for me right now. She cocks her eyebrow. "Are you seriously turning down pussy in public? That's funny. I thought there was a dick between your legs I sucked at one point, a rather large one at that. Must have mistaken you for someone else. Bummer."

I pick up pace, gaining on her. When close enough to touch, I grab ahold of her waist, before slowly scrubbing my hands down her body, stopping on her ass. I begin walking forward again, pressing her upper back against the brick wall. The back of her head bumps the brick as she stares into my eyes. I grab her hands from her hips and press my pelvis into hers, making my fucking dick known. Before long she won't question that it's there, not even in humor.

Raising her arms above her head, I hold them to the building. Her chest is dramatically rising and falling, confirming the change in her breathing. "I don't think I could deny your pussy if it was doused with poison and I knew I would die upon entry. You want me inside you, then you're getting it, but this isn't the backdrop I had in mind. Come with me. It's getting dark."

Her lips slightly part, her oxygen expelling loud enough to hear. "I can't. I have to work. I need to get back inside. Our event is here tonight. It's going to be a full house. Jason needs me. Some of us have schedules we have to abide by. Quickies can be fun. I won't even get pissed if you come before me. Fuck me here and let me go or let the blue balls ride. The decision is yours."

I move both of her wrists to one hand, freeing up my other. My hand immediately goes for the top button on her white button-down. One by one I undo them, stopping halfway, revealing her chest and white cotton bra. "I don't do well with ultimatums, Miss Larsen."

Her leg hooks around my waist as my lips become flush with her cleavage; the perfect globe sitting nestled inside of the bra cup sustaining it. The tip of my tongue emerges, tasting her skin. Her scent invades my nose. It's sweet, but not sickly sweet. My mouth migrates south as my hand pulls the fabric of her bra toward the underwire, no longer hiding her nipple. It's hard, waiting patiently for me to suck it, so I do, hard. There is a lot going on inside of me, and being gentle is nowhere in sight.

She moans out. "Fuck, just do it already. I'll bend over."

I release her from my mouth, tracing my lips up her chest and neck, stopping just outside of her ear. "I don't want other people staring at your pussy or your fucking tits. That's for me to enjoy. I have a visual, Lux, but this isn't it. Spend the night with me."

"I can't go anywhere until I'm off. I'll get fired. I can't sleep for shit in someone else's bed anyway. This is the best option."

My hand unbuttons her pants and then inches downward, underneath them as I suck the skin just below her ear into my mouth, my fingers searching for the magic spot. The tip of my middle finger becomes wet as it passes over her pussy. I pull back slightly, allowing it to slip in, before pushing it inside all the way. When I pull out I replace it with two instead of one. My knuckles line against her skin as my fingers disappear completely, but I push up harder, causing her to flex her feet to stand on her tiptoes. "Damn. That feels good."

"We somehow always end up in parking lots or alleys, Lux. I need a change of scenery. Go in there and tell your boss you have to leave. Come with me and I'll reward you in more ways than one. When I'm done with you, you won't have a problem sleeping, no matter where it is. Besides, we have some business to attend to. Tell him."

I back my fingers out of her pussy and rock my hand, pushing the pad of my thumb against her clit, before massaging in fast-paced circles. "Do it, Lux, or I will."

"Hell yes. Don't stop."

I remove my hand from her pants, leaving her wanting more, and for good reason. A horny woman will do many things. They may not always be as easily turned on as a man, but once they are they are explosive creatures. Sometimes you have to use your cock to your advantage. This would be one time. "You fucking bas-"

I press my lips against hers to silence her. Her stubborn ass tightens her lips, trying to deny me entry. I rock my hips against her, allowing her to feel my erection between her legs. Her lips instantly soften. "Mmmmm."

My lips scrape upward, enveloping around her top one, before pulling it out and releasing it. She moans. "For the record, the superhero is always trying to impress a girl no matter what the fucking comic says. Behind every man there is a woman that caught his attention before she even knew that he saw her. Keep that in mind."

I push off of her and drop her hands, giving her space to move. She releases her leg from my waist, allowing it to fall to the ground. Her eyes narrow as if she's thinking, but she never moves them away from mine. "Go get your things, Lux. I'll be waiting out front by the time you exit. Don't make me come inside."

She takes a deep breath and stands upright as she fastens her pants and buttons her shirt, covering everything that's inappropriate. "Sometimes I wonder why I don't kick your ass to the curb. Your mood changes with the flip of some internal switch."

I smirk. "Because you like my cock."

She rolls her eyes as she fastens the last button on her shirt.

"I swear on everything sometimes I think I'd be better off going back to my B.O.B when I need to come...or Delta. The hassle and effect on my daily life are slim to none."

My smirk vanishes. She just admitted to fucking around with her best friend. Would I usually find this extremely hot? Fuck yeah. Is that hormone that should be raging present at her mention of female play? Hell no. That internal meter that elevates each time another man looks at your woman just skyrocketed to an all time high. When a girl has no problem with touching another pussy a man is in deep shit. This is not good...not good at all. Suddenly,

I want to fuck her brains out, and not for the purpose you would think, but for the sole reason to remind her that a dick is so much better; my dick.

"Go get your shit now. This mission just went from important to critical. I'll be in the truck."

I turn and walk away, not saying another word.

"Kaston... what the fuck?" The frustration in her voice shows.

Silence. That's what's best. I fear the words that would exit right now would piss a certain female off. As sexy as that hot temper is, my job as a man just got a little tougher...

At least when you're competing with another dick, it's fair game. I will break every damn rule I have and kill off someone to calm myself down before I fucking compete with a woman. Fuck. That. Shit.

CHAPTER EIGHTEEN

Lux

I'm really fucking pissed off right now. I cannot believe I just told Jason I need to leave because I threw up in the parking lot. I lied. He just stared at me like I have a third eye, and why? Maybe because I've never done that, and for what, to go get a piece of ass? What the hell is wrong with me? I've let some guy come into my life and start having a negative effect on my personal life. This is one reason why I go for the wallet up front and steer away from anything that resembles traditional dating, because guys try to change you. I warned him that was part of the deal and I haven't seen anything to benefit me besides good sex since I met him.

I shove the glass doors of the building open to Kaston's truck waiting out front just as he promised. He's staring straight ahead the entire time it takes me to get in the vehicle. I dramatically slam the door, before pulling the seatbelt over my body and securing it. Nothing. Not even a flinch from him. "What exactly is your problem? What was all that shit you spewed back there? Have you seriously lost it?"

"Maybe I have," he says, before spinning his wheels as he punches the gas pedal, my back pressing into the seat. "Do you have a change of clothes in that bag you exited with?"

"Yes, I always keep a spare bag at work. Where are we going?"

"You'll find out soon enough. There's something I want to show you."

He goes back to silence as we drive through Atlanta. He never looks over at me, never touches me, and never speaks. It is total maddening silence in this truck, making me anxious. I can't stand silence. It does nothing but make you think of shit you don't want to think about.

I reach over and press the power source to the radio. Hard rock starts playing. You can tell a lot about a person based on their music preferences. The choice isn't bad, but then again I'm a little angry right now. I study the buttons to his truck, trying to figure out what it's on: Media stream, Kaston's iPhone. That's the words showing on the digital screen.

I'm about to change to regular radio when I notice him straighten the middle of his body by lifting his butt in his seat from the corner of my eye, still holding onto the wheel with one hand. He reaches into the pocket of his jeans and pulls something out, handing it over the console for me to grab: his phone. "You're letting me look at your phone? Isn't that a little personal?"

His serious demeanor is replaced with a smirk. He looks over at me. My heart rate picks up. "I think we bypassed personal when you watched me put a bullet in the chest of someone else, let a perfect stranger make you come in a tattoo chair as he broke the seal to an untouched body with a needle, and when I left my DNA inside of your body. That is as personal as you can get. Wouldn't you agree?" He winks when I grab the phone from his grasp. I bite my bottom lip, trying not to smile. "The passcode is 1127."

I mash the home button and open the camera instead of unlocking the screen. Turning the front camera on, I lean over the console and snap a quick shot of me making a goofy face next to his, before getting back on my side of the truck to look for some music. "Now when I'm gone you'll pull this up and think, damn I miss that chick. She was crazy as hell."

He grabs my left hand, catching me off guard just as I notice the Spotify app and open it. I look at him when he laces his hand in mine. I immediately start to panic inside. My fucking hand starts to shake. "That kind of effect, huh?"

"I'm just still aggravated about work. Don't let that ego get to your head." I lie.

I loosen my hand and he tightens his. This is awkward. I stare down at it and then up at him. He is smiling as he looks ahead at the road. He knows he's making me uncomfortable. "What makes you think I'd let you go?"

For some reason now I'm not sure which he's referring to. "Uh..."

"You'll believe me at some point."

"There will come a time when this will no longer work for us. You'll see."

"Or you will."

I roll my eyes. "You will get tired of my crazy, Cox. It's inevitable. I'm not like most girls. I'm not really a forever kind of girl. Besides, I really don't know anything about you. I may not even like you when I do, or vice versa. Right now we just have good sex. We're curious of the unknown in each other, the mystery. Ya know?"

"There's always that chance, but it's a risk I'm willing to take. Persuasion is a powerful tool, but something tells me I won't need it. When you know someone's worst, then everything becomes easier learning them at their best."

No words. I may know his worst, but he doesn't know mine. No one does. I try to keep my secrets buried far below the surface. That noose is starting to tighten a little. I strongly believe that when someone learns your secrets they have the power to hurt you, because then they know enough about you to like you or despise you, the real you, and not the person you let them see. The beauty in them not knowing the real you is that you don't give a shit what people think about you.

Breathe. Just breathe.

Forget that you're holding the hand of a man for the first time in your life.

Normal people do this all the time. Just act normal.

I look back down at his phone and unlock it again, this time searching for an artist to play through the speaker system. The scenery is getting more rural. Houses are becoming sparser and now it looks like we're getting into the country. "Where are we going?"

"My house."

"You don't live in Atlanta?"

"Not anymore. I decided when I came back that I needed more privacy. Things can change very quickly. Life is shitty sometimes."

"You could talk about it, you know. I doubt I'll have any real words of wisdom, because I haven't really had the rosiest life myself, but I could offer an ear void of judgment."

He looks at me, his eyes shouting something, but what I'm not sure. I'm not really a soul reader. To me it's like someone screaming in a different language, and it's maddening because you have no idea what that person is saying.

His thumb starts rubbing back and forth over my skin, causing a tingle. It's enough to make me want to close my eyes, but I refrain. "I may take you up on that sometime, but right now I just need to get lost in a world full of adrenaline with you; the legal kind. Tonight, let's pretend we're teenagers. You in?"

I smile. "Of course. I can role-play. What did you have in mind?"

He presses a button on the visor of his truck, still not releasing my hand. I turn my head toward the windshield and notice a large metal gate in front of us. I didn't even notice he had stopped. "You'll see."

The gate opens and he drives through. The driveway is a longer one than most, but the house starts coming into view. It's fucking huge. I turn to look at him as he waits for one door of the three-car garage to open. "This is where you live? Holy shit, Kaston, it's massive."

He pulls in. "It's a little big for my taste, but I liked the location. Are you really that surprised? I did basically agree to be your sugar daddy, did I not?"

"Okay, A, I was drunk and trying to get rid of you when you were saying crazy shit, and B, not that your truck isn't nice but it's a fucking Ford. Platinum edition or not, and even with it looking brand new, people that live in houses like this are celebrities or have too much fucking money to be good for them, and always there is a vehicle to match. What am I missing?"

"I'm not really into flaunting my money. Truthfully, if I knew it would bring my dad back I'd give it all up. Let's go, beautiful."

He kills the engine and opens the door, exiting after releasing my hand. Why do I suddenly feel like shit at the mention of his dad? Fuck my life... I have foot in mouth syndrome. There is a story there. I'm not sure if it'll make things worse or better for me if I knew, but I kind of want to.

I take a deep breath and exit with my bag in tow, following him inside the house. He reaches his arm back for me to take his hand. This time I do, easier than in the truck. He lightly pulls me through the huge house, turning on lights as we navigate through each room. "Disregard the moving boxes, okay? Someone's had my attention lately, so I haven't really been here to do this shit and I choose not to pay someone. I don't like people in my shit, especially when I'm perfectly capable of doing it myself."

"Okay," I say, as we walk around the large cardboard boxes, headed for the stairs. One by one I follow him up to the second floor. "That kind of makes me like you a little more."

He turns toward me as he backs into a room. I give him a half smile. He grabs my other hand and pulls me against him. "It does, does it?"

I shrug. "Yeah, I guess it does. It's attractive when a man does shit for himself. A grown child is kind of a nuisance."

"Well, if we're being honest, it needs a lot of work before it will resemble anything of a home, but having you here is a good start."

I feel like I've just run a marathon. My breathing is becoming weird as hell and I feel jittery, as if I'm on a caffeine high. The problem is I didn't get to enjoy the coffee. I don't like this at all...

He grabs the strap of my duffel bag, pulling if off my shoulder, before dropping it to the floor and then reaches for my top button as he stares at me. "This is my room. You'll sleep in here...with me, anytime you're here."

"You probably won't get much sleep. I don't sleep well in someone else's bed. I can take the guest room if you'll show me where it is. It's not a big deal."

He leans down and places his lips to the side of my neck as he continues to unbutton my shirt. I let my head fall to the side, giving him more space. Chill bumps start to sprout all over my body at the feel of his soft lips pressed against my skin, as he scatters kisses from my collar bone to just below my ear. He pushes my shirt over my shoulders after he finishes with the last button, letting it fall down my arms, before pulling the cuff of the sleeves over my hands to remove it completely. "I guess you'll just have to make it yours then, because this is where you're sleeping. Get used to it."

"You're kind of bossy, you know."

"Yeah, but it's needed to tolerate your shit. If I wasn't you would have ran the second you woke up in Chevy's bar and I would have never seen you again, so I guess it's a good thing."

His mouth traces along my jaw toward my lips. "I guess that's true," I say, breathless.

His lips finally reach mine. His tongue slides through the crack, making its way into my mouth, searching for mine. I moan against him as I get that first taste. The hormones suddenly surge through my body, making me want him. I grab his shirttail and pull it up his body, my knuckles brushing over his muscles along the way. He allows me to remove it. "I love your body. Fuck, you're hot."

My hands go for his waist, before running up his stomach. He removes my bra, then grabs my hand and places it on the hardened section running down his inner leg: his cock. "I could say the same thing about you."

I squeeze, hinting at what I want. He cups my breast and places my nipple in his mouth, sucking lightly as he turns us around, before guiding me across the room. He kisses me again as he leans in, laying us on the bed. His fingers find the button of my black pants and he works to undo them without our lips parting. His fingers grab the fabric from each hip and he roughly works them over my ass, before pulling them down my legs and removing them along with my shoes, now standing before me.

He looks at my naked body. "This isn't where I want to do this, but I want one taste."

His voice is deeper than usual, as if he's trying really hard not to ram his cock into me this very second. That's exactly what I want him to do. He grabs my legs behind my knees and places my feet flat on the bed, before pressing my legs outward, spreading them wider. I watch as he leans forward, placing his tongue inside my pussy. It feels so good, but not as good as it could. As he pulls out he runs his tongue through my lips, stopping with the tip on my clit. I buck my hips upward as he flickers his tongue back and forth. "Shit. Right there. Don't stop."

He slides two fingers into my pussy and doesn't stop. I clench around his fingers as he thrusts inside. Oral feels so much better when your pussy isn't empty. "I'm not far. Don't fucking move."

I grab his hair and he looks up at me, not moving a single muscle from the place I need it, knowing if he does all will be lost and he'll have to start over. He increases the speed of his tongue as it hits against my clit. If I weren't so close to coming that visual would get me there. There is something extremely hot about a guy looking up at you while his face is buried in your girlie goods.

I can feel my orgasm building quickly. Without much warning it starts, causing me to close my legs with his face in between. I pull at his hair, riding it as his fingers still inside me. "Fuck."

My clit becomes sensitive, making it tickle under his touch. I pull up on his hair and open my legs. "Stop. Fuck me. Now."

He removes his fingers and shows them to me, coated in my orgasm, before placing them in his mouth and sucking them clean. My mouth slightly parts as he wipes them on his jeans to dry them off, before leaning in to kiss me again. "Taste what I taste."

He presses his lips to mine and makes me taste myself on his tongue. Somehow he makes this sexy as hell. I grab for the waist of his jeans, but he stops me by grabbing ahold of my wrist, bringing it above my head and lacing our fingers together as he continues to kiss me. I wrap my legs around his waist, pulling him toward me. He makes a throaty groan as I rub my center over his denim-covered erection, releasing me. "Not here. At least not right now. If I fuck you here we'll never leave. Get dressed and meet me downstairs. I'll give you some privacy. The bathroom is through that door."

He leans back down once more, kissing me but only briefly this time. I prop up on the bed, still in a relaxed state, but also still wanting more of him. "What's so important that we have to leave? We just got here."

He grabs his shirt on his way toward the bedroom door, never stopping. "You'll see. You'll thank me later. Don't wear panties and make it quick."

He leaves, shutting the door behind him, leaving me in this massive room alone. I fall back against the bed, covering my face with my hands. My emotions are all over the fucking place. For the first time after meeting a man I'm actually slightly worried that severing ties when it's time won't be easy. No matter what he says it's going to happen, because it has to, but for once I'm actually internally debating with myself, trying to talk myself out of it. What's worse is that it doesn't even have to do with money. That alone scares the shit out of me...

Kaylon

I sit on the couch and lean forward, resting my forearms on my thighs. What I'm about to do makes me a little nervous. I run my hand through my hair as I stare at the floor. "Someone deserves it, Dad. Something tells me it's her. I didn't ship it all the way here for nothing. Isn't it that sixth sense shit you were always talking about?"

I rub my hands over my face. "Fuck, now I'm talking to myself." I'm not used to this shit, but there's something about her that I want and can't let go of, no matter what it costs me.

I hear the bedroom door open and close, then footsteps moving in the direction of the stairs. "I'm ready," she says, and I turn to look at the top of the stairs, immediately standing.

Dear God she's beautiful. Get your shit together, Cox. You aren't a teenager about to leave for prom. You're a killer for fuck's sake.

She walks down the stairs, slowly, trying not to fall in the heels I guess, but it's making it worse for me. She has legs for days with that short, black dress on. It barely covers her ass. On top of that the neckline is low cut and connects at the back of her neck, covering only the necessities, but still easily accessible. Perfect.

I walk to the bottom of the stairs and take her hand as she steps off the last one. "Are you going to tell me what the hell you're planning now?"

I wink and smile. "Soon enough. I like this dress."

"Well, I feel overdressed, even not knowing where I'm going, but I'm usually packed for partying so this is what I had in the bag."

"I think it's perfect for the occasion."

Moving my hands to her lower back I pull her toward me, before running them over her ass to the bottom hem of her dress. Easing my hands between her thighs, I rub up her legs, checking to ensure she left the underwear behind. The tips of my fingers making contact with her wet middle confirms that she did. She places her hands on my shoulders with a huge grin on her face. A smile begins forming on mine in response. "What?"

"You are not sly at all. How the hell do you get away with the shit you do?"

Without moving my hands I pick her up. She wraps her legs around my waist, securing her hands around my neck. Her perfume is suddenly wafting through the air. She smells good. It's recently added because she wasn't wearing it earlier. That little detail makes me happy. "Just because I'm bad at being covert in my actions with you doesn't mean I am with my job. Those are two very different things."

"Mmmm Hmmm. Whatever you say, cutie." She winks, playing along, making me want to bend her over the couch.

"Let's go before I change my mind." She unhooks her legs until she slides low enough for her feet to touch the floor.

"You're the one taking your time, slow poke. After all, you won't tell me what we're doing," she says teasingly.

"Right. You're distracting me. Quit dressing so fucking hot and maybe I could think straight." I scan her body one more time, before turning to walk away, grabbing her hand in the process. "Never mind. I retract that statement. That's exactly how you should dress. You look sexy as hell."

I grab my baseball cap off the arm of the couch on the way to the garage door and slide it on my head as I stop in the laundry room, now standing in front of the door. I stare at the key holder on the wall with her standing behind me. I haven't touched them since I hung them here after it arrived. It hasn't been all that long, but at that time it went from point A to point B. It was a matter of seconds. I close my eyes, trying to come to terms with it.

This is me moving on, Dad....

I grab the distinct ring of keys and open the door, locking it once she walks through and pulling it shut behind me. My heart starts to race in my chest as I lead her to the covered car at the furthest point of the garage. I stop at the hood, trying to prepare myself before uncovering it. "Are you okay," she asks.

"Never fucking better."

Pulling from the front fender on the driver's side, I lift the black cover and inch it backward, walking toward the back of the car until the cover falls to the ground, revealing the car in its entirety. I look at her. She's got her arms loosely crossed over her body, staring at it wide eyed as if she's seen a ghost. "You have a fucking Ferrari 458 Spider?"

"I see you know your cars."

"Are there really people that don't know Ferraris? What the fuck, Kaston? How much god-"

"Don't go there."

"Sorry. I'm a little in shock. It's rude to ask what someone makes, but hell you can't be more than thirty."

"Not that."

Her brows dip. "What?"

"I wasn't referring to your question. I was referring to the terminology you were going to use along the way to the question mark at the end. Use any fucking curse word you want but that one. It's my hard limit. To vaguely answer your question, I make more than I fucking need in a lifetime, without considering what I've inherited. We'll have that discussion later. It's too complex for tonight. Besides, I may need a legally binding contract for that conversation."

"Uh…okay. I guess."

"Come here."

She walks toward me, keeping her distance from the car. I hold out my hand for hers. For some reason I like the gesture of her hand in mine, more so than I ever have with a female. Her hand is dainty. She takes my hand and I pull her in front of me, her back against my front, as we stare at the back end of the car. I grab her waist, holding her to me. "This was my father's car. When he died I inherited everything with the exception of what existed in New York. This was the only thing he allowed himself to indulge in: foreign sports cars. The rest of his money he saved. Touch it. This was his favorite of them all, so I had it brought here."

She places her fingertips on the back and runs them in a horizontal line along the canary yellow paint. "It's beautiful. This is what you wanted to show me? You're lucky to have a car like this. Only a small percentage of people throughout the world get the opportunity to have this kind of luxury. Will you take me for a ride?"

"I'll do even better than that. I'll let you drive. Can you drive a stick?"

She turns around in my arms with a smile spread across her face. "I guess you could say I'm pretty good with sticks, but in regards to this one, yes I can drive a stick. The only way to drive a sports car is a manual, baby." She grabs my cock in her hand, jeans and all, catching me off guard. My semi just turned into a full on hard-on.

"Later, I'll climb over the console and show you how I can drive this stick. We can pretend we're past curfew."

I grab the back of her head and smash my lips against hers, kissing her just long enough to get a taste, before letting go. "Let's fucking go."

I dangle the keys from my fingers and she takes them. I grab her chin before she can walk away. "Don't hold back. Freedom lies between you and the floorboard."

Those blue eyes sparkle a little under the garage lights. We both get in the car and I watch as she takes it all in. There is no sight more beautiful than a girl falling in love with a car. Her hands grab ahold of the wheel at ten and two o'clock, before twisting back and forth as if she's picturing the ride before it happens. She presses her back into the seat and her legs spread slightly, hiking her dress up even more. One hand moves to the shifter and I swear on my life she moaned. Her eyes close and then open slowly, her thick lashes touching the top of her eyes. I'm completely fucking hard right now, unable to speak.

She picks the key up from her lap and starts the engine. "Oh, God, that's a beautiful sound. I think I just fell in love." Her bottom lip succumbs beneath her top teeth. My blood is running wild. This is the best natural high in the world, and I've experienced many different kinds. Not the car, but her introducing herself. There is a mutual respect between driver and car. She's waiting for that very moment when she has the approval to drive it.

The only person that deserves this car is someone that respects it like he did. This very car can turn on you and get you killed just as it can make you feel like the king of the world. Dad would be grinning from ear to ear right now, because I've seen a more masculine form of what she's doing several times over the course of my life just like this. He always did love his cars. As I watch her, I know that there is a part of her inside that I want to uncover. Her roots run deep. She's someone I want to know, from the inside out. One layer at a time I'll bring the girl she's scared to be to the surface. What I'm about to do is undeniably the right decision.

I reach in my pocket for the garage remote and press the button for the door to open. She looks at me with an excitement I haven't seen yet. Right now her soul is completely free, and I'm about to watch it fly. "Are you ready?"

"I can't fucking breathe right now." She admits.

"Shift."

"Okay."

I watch her buckle her seatbelt and press in the clutch, before shifting to reverse. She slowly backs out of the garage and turns, then stops, before shifting into first. "Where do you want me to go?"

"When you get outside of the gate, take a right. You have about six miles of straight roadway. Put the pedal to the metal, baby. Take a left at the stop sign and I'll tell you from there."

"You're really trusting me to drive this car with no restrictions?"

"As much as I trust you with my semen."

She eases forward, getting used to the car as she drives down the driveway. "What about cops?"

"Don't worry about cops. They won't be out here. There are many reasons why I chose this house. Every one of them has to do with location. Just drive."

The gate comes into view and she slows down to look at me for directions. "Just pull to the code entry. I didn't bring the remote for that, just the garage. The code is 1127 just like my phone."

She lets down the window when it's in front of keypad. "What's so special about that number?"

"It was my dad's birthday."

She looks at me with question in her eyes. I know what she wants to ask, but she's holding herself back. "He was murdered. It's been a while, but not long enough I want to elaborate. Not yet."

"I'm so-." She clears her throat, stopping herself. She's smart. Only people that have been through shitty situations understand that sorry doesn't do a damn thing to make the situation easier to deal with. "I understand."

I place my hand under her chin, holding it up to look at me on the length of my index finger, before rubbing across her bottom lip with my thumb. "Retribution was attained. That's what matters most. I need you to understand no wrong is done without proper cause. Someday you'll understand. For now, your lack of fear is what keeps me coming back for more. Now drive before I sit you on my cock and we get nowhere."

A light sound of satisfaction escapes her before she quickly keys in the code and turns to look out the windshield, no longer paying me any attention. I smirk but continue to watch her as we wait for the gate to open. She can feel my eyes on her based on her facial expressions. She pulls through and turns right just as I instructed earlier, keeping it in first. Pulling in the center of the road she stops, staring straight ahead. Her lips part and then close again.

My left hand instinctively moves over the console and rests on her thigh, my fingers touching the inside. "It's just a car. Don't be nervous."

"A very expensive one."

"Says the girl that had a Porsche."

"In my mind that's not even a comparison."

My hand migrates north, my fingertips close to her middle.

"Drive or you do it while I finger fuck you."

"Fuck, hold on. I'll wreck if you do that."

She reaches down by the pedals fiddling with something, before tossing her heels in my lap. My middle finger grazes her pussy and she releases the clutch to pump the gas, spinning the wheels as the car jerks forward, slamming me back into the seat. My right arm braces in the window as I watch her shift through the gears, increasing speed quickly. She barely lets up each time she upshifts to the purr of the engine. Not only is she hot as hell, but also she knows how to drive.

I can't take my eyes off of her. Holy fuck, watching her power shift has me hard as a fucking rock and wanting to bust a nut right here. What the hell? What am I, fifteen and looking at a Playboy magazine? My breathing is ragged as I hold myself in place, keeping my eye on the prize instead of the road. "Stop sign coming up in five minutes. Start downshifting. Stop and switch when you get there. I'm driving the rest of the way. Suddenly, I'm in a hurry."

My finger slips inside of her pussy, sinking inside the moist mancave that belongs to me. Her legs spread instantly and then start to shake from the constant motion with the pedals as she follows instructions, slowing the car with the transmission. "Fuck, I can't think with you doing that. Stop. I don't want to wreck."

I start to thrust, completely disregarding her request. My hand is backwards and this isn't very comfortable, but I don't give a fuck. It feels good. "Driving should come second nature. You need to be able to react under sudden changes in conditions."

She scoots her ass forward, creating a better angle and giving me easier access. "I'm pretty sure that's changing roadway conditions, Kaston, not..." I shove two fingers deep and start contracting my fingers toward my palm, trying to make up for the weird angle of my hand. "Fuck!"

She suddenly pops the clutch and stomps on the brake as the red stop sign makes its appearance, becoming bright from the headlights. The car halts just past the road sign, barely peeking into the road that runs atop this one, like a capital T. Her head turns with her eyes widened. I press my lips, together trying not to laugh. Her badass image is completely shattered right now with the deer in headlights look. "Fuck, I'm sorry. I told you not to do that shit."

"If I can still capture your full attention so soon after an orgasm then my job is done, and well." A competitive, cocky grin spreads across my face.

I remove my fingers from her pussy and pull my limbs back to my side of the car, preparing to change sides. I'm horny as hell and this is mentally becoming a worse idea every second that I want to fuck her. She narrows her eyes and playfully slaps my shoulder. "You ass! Just remember...payback is a bitch and I'm pretty damn vengeful when I want to be."

My face becomes blank. At this moment I have a want that is now consuming my mind...

She shifts into neutral and pulls the e-brake, before she opens the door, stepping onto the road barefoot. I match her movements and meet her at the hood of the car, both of us facing one another. She gives me a once-over before walking around me, not saying a word as she gets in the passenger side and shuts the door. What I wouldn't give to know what she's plotting...

I get in and slightly adjust the seat. Luckily it isn't much since she's a taller girl. I waste no time, shifting and pulling out at a steady pace. "So what were you thinking...awesome road head followed by blue balls just when I'm ready to fucking blow my load in your mouth," I ask half jokingly, but expecting to catch her off guard with the correct guess.

I should have known better...

"As tempting as that sounds, no. Then you could finish yourself off as soon as I take my mouth off your cock, using my saliva as a fucking lubricant. Nice try, but I wasn't born yesterday."

I grip the steering wheel tighter and aggressively upshift, increasing speed, and fighting tooth and nail not to look at her right now. My dick is straining behind my jeans, at the beginning stages of pain. I've gotten hard and soft so many times without coming in the last several hours that my cock would probably resemble that of a blowhole when I finally ejaculate. With every fucking word that comes out of her mouth, the craving to sink into her pussy becomes more prominent.

Instead of taking her bait I keep staring straight ahead, weaving left and right with the curves of the road, focusing on the final destination. "Fuck, I love this car."

Without thought my head turns toward her. Her tits staring me in the face almost causes me to lock it down in the middle of the road. She's unhooked her dress from behind her neck, letting the fabric fall to her belly. She isn't wearing a bra and her nipples are hard between her thumb and index fingers as she gropes them in her own hands.

I bite my tongue and turn back toward the road, acting completely unaffected. "I'm glad," I grit out against my clamped teeth.

Ten more fucking minutes...

She moans, drawing my attention once more. When I look back at her she has her feet propped against the dash, spread eagle, and her hand as well as the lower part of her arm have vanished down her front, both now hidden behind the fabric of her dress. Fucking motherfucker she's touching herself. I'm fucked.

I slow down to a coast and place my hand on her inner thigh, letting it fall toward the movement barely kept secret since her dress is sitting bunched at her hips. She slaps my hand without stopping. She's rubbing to come, not to tease. "No touching. You can only watch...and drive."

My head veers between her and the road. Her head falls back against the headrest and her eyes close, the movement of her hand confirming she's rubbing her clit. Her moans become more natural and less for show the longer she does it. It's only been a couple of minutes but that aggression and itch to kill someone are coming back. She grabs her fucking breast again and starts pinching her nipple. "Fuck, Lux, let me in."

She spreads her legs wider, her pussy now peeking out. Hell, it's swollen and wet, visible even under the moonlight coming through the windshield. I growl and try to touch her again. "Don't fucking touch me, Kaston," she shouts in a clipped tone. I turn back to the road, counting to calm the fuck down. She knows good and well a real man would never touch a woman without consent, taking full advantage of the power she has right now. If I pull too hard on the wheel it's either going to break or jerk, causing a wreck.

If I didn't want to fuck her so bad I swear on everything I'd strangle her for using that tone, not stopping before her world goes black, but giving in just fast enough her heart keeps beating. That's the way she makes me feel, constantly at war with myself between Heaven and Hell. I'm in fucking Purgatory on a near constant basis. She begins to come in the seat beside me, but not because of me, and for some reason that pisses me off royally.

I can't even watch, and I have found that watching her come is one of my favorite visuals. My chest expands and I crack my neck to each side. The car goes silent except for the sound of the engine as I turn into the final but narrow winding road. From the corner of my eye I notice when she starts wrapping her dress back around her neck, trying to redress herself. "Leave it. You're going to be bare for what you're about to get."

She grabs my hand and places it at the highest point on her inner thigh, my fingertips beside her pussy. There is so much aggression bottled up inside of me I'm afraid to move while operating a vehicle. I'm almost to the top of the small hill, located on a manmade lake for housing, but away from the houses that surround it.

She pulls my hand further, dipping the tip into the wet entry, but not pressing inward. She's showing me how wet she is. "Awe, don't be mad. You knew you had it coming, but don't you want to know what I was thinking about when I came...or who?"

My jaw muscles contract, as I remain silent, the road opening to a dead end circle overlooking the lake. "Not really."

I stop and kill the engine, as well as the headlights. The only light is the full moon lighting up the sky and reflecting off of the water in front of us.

"Hmmm. Well, your loss I guess. Where are we?"

I pull my hand out of her grasp.

"A fairly new real estate development for the wealthy. It was designed for the people that want to live outside of Atlanta without trading in any of the luxury they're use to, or prefer, like living next to other rich people. Phase II hasn't even started yet. It's probably a good place to think, or make someone scream without others hearing..."

She clears her throat.

"At least before all the houses sell and it's full. I'm sure then the residential teenagers will discover it for a make-out point."

"It's kind of cool seeing the lights to the houses lit up surrounding the lake."

She opens the door and gets out, sauntering to the front of the car. She turns to look at me as if waiting for me to accompany her. I need a minute. I need to figure out a way to expel this fucking anger. I can handle the onset, but the housing I can't. We stare at each other through the windshield, my left hand still clamped around the bottom of the steering wheel; seven o'clock.

She rolls her eyes and refastens her dress behind her neck, before turning around and crossing her arms over her chest. My eyes rake down her body, stopping at her beautiful round ass, barely covered by her dress.

Beautiful round ass...

It doesn't matter how much of a vixen your girl is, or how much you even like it, because at some point you still have to enforce a little control to show her who ultimately wears the pants in the relationship, as well as reminding her who she belongs to. No matter what a woman says, she wants to feel a sense of belonging. She wants to be desired. Occasionally she wants to submit to a man's wants; otherwise she would get bored. It is my job to give her all of me, the good as well as the bad. That is the only way to ensure you keep her forever...

Leaning far enough to reach the glove compartment, I take a condom from inside and shove it in my pocket. I grab the handle and open the door, my mind now made up. Walking up behind her, I move her hair over her shoulder, before unhooking the fabric. "What are you doing? I thought you were pouting," she says sarcastically.

"This is the part where you only use your mouth for sounds of sex. Any and all else becomes silent. I want your full attention and cooperation. Understood?"

I grab the bottom hem of her dress and pull it up her body, removing it in one swift motion and throwing it on the windshield. She tries to turn in my arms but I stop her. "I want you like this."

Her body shivers beneath my touch, her breathing becoming more verbal as it thickens. I step closer behind her, rubbing my hands up the length of her sides, grazing the sides of her breasts before I trace my fingers down her arms, grasping ahold of the backside of her hands. I turn us around to face the car like she was before I got out. Leaning into her to bend her forward, I place her palms on the yellow paint, but far enough up that her entire upper half is laying on the hood of the car. "Kaston," she says looking back at me as I upright myself.

"Cheek down on the car. We're about to role-play, but fuck high school. This is something high school kids can't even process. You agreed to play, so you're going to give up every need to have the upper hand. You're going to submit your control over yourself to me and I'm going to take it. This time you took it too far. At least when I toyed with you it was with *your* pleasure in mind and not *mine.* I haven't kept my body from you since I gave it to you. You came your way, not waiting for me, so now I'm going to do the same. I believe in equality, baby. Do you consent?"

She breathes for a moment as I unbuckle my belt, before finally whispering, "Yes."

I remove my shirt to get it out of the way, tossing it on top of her dress. Sliding the condom from my pocket, I place the corner between my teeth while I undo my jeans, pushing them with my briefs to my thighs. I rip the wrapper to the condom and remove it, quickly rolling it on my dick. My hand reaches for her pussy, rubbing upward toward her clit, sending her into a mind fuck; the place I need her. "Arch for me," I demand.

Without response she does. I grab her ass cheek in my free hand, spreading it from the other even more while I rub in circles over her clit, roughly and in a fast pace. It should still be sensitive enough to get her off fairly quickly. She starts to moan, giving me a hint she's about to come. I line my cock to her pussy and press inside as she starts to orgasm, letting her coat the condom with her cum.

She arches more dramatically as I fill her. I thrust hard a few times as I position an ass cheek in each hand, spreading them apart as far as they will go. Her skin makes a sound as it slides across the metal. "Oh, fuck, it's so deep."

Without missing a beat, I pull out and transition the head of my cock to her asshole, quickly exerting my weight against the opening before it can slide back to her pussy. It begins to open, slowly consuming my dick until she takes all of me. No sounds escape her, but her hands are gripped on the car so tensed it looks like she's trying to claw through the metal.

Without moving my cock, I bend forward and kiss the center of her back, giving her a minute to adjust. The muscle is so tight around my dick I won't last long. Her back finally starts to move as if she's been holding her breath. She clears her throat. "Just do it," she says with pain evident in her voice. "I can take it."

"This won't take long."

I stand upright and pull back slowly, allowing her cum and the lubrication on the condom to make it wet enough to continue, before thrusting in a steady rhythm. Every couple thrusts she flexes onto her tiptoes. I watch her back as she moves on the car with each thrust, curving to withstand it. Another thrust with her asshole squeezing my cock and I can feel the tug in my balls, preparing to ejaculate.

Pulling out, I grab the rim of the condom and slide it off my cock, tossing it onto the ground, before grabbing the base of my shaft and ramming my dick into her pussy, thrusting deep one time before blowing my load inside of her. My pace of breathing accelerates. Fuck that feels good. I squeeze her hips, grinding mine against her ass, letting it all out; every last drop. When my dick stops pulsing, immediately becoming sensitive and starting to soften, I pull out and replace my jeans and briefs in the proper position at my waist, but leave them undone.

She doesn't make any attempt to stand, so I grab her hip and arm, rolling her over onto her back. Her face is illuminated in the moonlight, showing the tear trail staining her cheeks. I lean toward her and touch one side with my thumb, but she turns her head away, trying to push my hand off. "I'm fine. Stop."

"Look at me."

She tries to wipe her face with her palms as she centers her head. "Kaston, I'm fine. So you fucked me in the ass. It's no big deal. No pain, no gain, right. Let me up before I put a dent in your car."

"It's not my car, and besides that you aren't heavy enough."

I grab her legs behind her thighs, lifting them and wrapping them around my waist, proving that denting this damn car is the last thing on my mind.

"I swear I'm going to fucking kill you if you tell me it's stolen."

"I already told you where it came from. I don't commit crimes; just right them. The world just doesn't understand corporal punishment."

I lay my lips against hers, before looking back into her eyes. "You're such a fucking guy. If he isn't here that makes it yours."

"No it doesn't."

"Then whose it is, Kaston? Enlighten me..."

"Yours."

She laughs awkwardly. "No the fuck it isn't."

"It was mine and I gave it to you. That means it is. What's the problem?"

Her face becomes serious. "You're serious, aren't you?"

"I didn't know it was associated with a joke so I guess I am."

"I can't accept this car."

"Sure you can."

"Kaston, I *will not* accept this car."

"You can and you will. The decision has already been made. I agreed to financially fund you not all that long ago, when you said that was the disclaimer to fuck you on a constant basis; my cock solely. Consider this number one."

Her lips part, her mouth falling open.

"I'm slightly offended. I may like nice things and go after them shamelessly, just in less orthodox ways, but I would never accept something that is sentimental to you."

"Just take the fucking car, Lux. If I honestly thought you were a fucking gold digger it wouldn't have been even a thought in passing. It'll take me a while to tell you things, because trusting people in my world never ends well, but it's a slap across the face if you decline the offer. It's one hundred percent yours. It's not a bargaining tool. I have no use for it and you don't have a car. No normal person leaves a car like this to sit up in a garage. The memories of him are all I need, not a damn car. I'll transfer the title in your name if you'll just take it."

My palms press onto the windshield, but close enough to the frame that it doesn't bust, to hold my weight above her as I lean in closer. "Just don't ever fucking tell me not to touch you again. I can't explain it, so don't ask me to, but whether it's sexual or not, I want you, and that includes touching. This time was me calming down. Next time I'll come unglued."

Her feet link behind me, tightening her hold around my waist as her eyes scan mine. "Okay."

"Every place on your body will be touched by me, fucked by me, licked by me, and belongs to me. You're becoming an obsession and a need. Don't deny me what's mine and I'll never deny you anything."

"I understand," she whispers. My hands snake under her back and I lift her off the hood. Her arms wrap around my neck and she presses her naked body to my bare torso. "What are you doing?"

I smile and turn for the water, running with her in my arms. "Something I've wanted to do since I got here. Hold on tight." I bend down to use my hand as leverage and slide down the embankment toward the water. Just before I'm close enough to walk in, I push my jeans down my legs and step out, trying to hold my balance, before wrapping my arms around her and running into the water until it envelops us at the chest.

"Oh my hell that's cold," she squeals, pressing herself against me and tightening her hold until she's glued to my front. The water is chilly, even though it's summer. She shivers, and then arches her back to lower her head into the water, drenching her hair. My hands move down her back, lowering to her ass to get a better hold on the weight transfer. I stare at her; mesmerized by the way she looks in the moonlight. The way it reflects across the water makes it brighter than at the car. The water is creating a gloss effect on her skin.

When she straightens her body I'm mentally stuck as she looks at me, slightly climbing me to reposition herself, tilting her head down toward me. Even in the dark the blue in her eyes is visible. She runs her fingers through my hair before laying her full lips on the corner of my mouth. "Tell me what you're thinking," she says.

"How beautiful you are," I respond honestly.

She disregards me completely, moving on to something else. I've noticed since I met her that she doesn't take compliments very well, almost as if they make her feel awkward.

"This is kind of a romantic gesture, Cox. Skinny-dipping in the lake under moonlight. What's next? Are you going to ask me to be your *girlfriend?*" She jokes, but to me it's a serious question. I guess that never really crossed my mind since it's never interested me in adulthood before. I thought it was an assumed role. It almost feels elementary to have to ask. Oh well, fuck it. Miscommunication can have detrimental effects.

"Will you?"

She places a palm on her mouth, dramatically feigning excitement, followed by a cheesy grin as she removes it. "You're asking me to be your girlfriend?" Her tone is high pitched.

"I think I am; although, you aren't Kate Hudson and I'm not Matthew Mcconaughey. The girlie impersonation isn't as believable on you."

She laughs. "Well damn. Never would I have thought you'd seen a chick flick. Sorry I couldn't resist."

"Are you going to answer the question?"

"That's not necessary. It was just a joke, Cox."

"Maybe so, but mine wasn't."

She reaches between us, grabbing my shaft in her hand; then I feel it positioned at the edge of her pussy, before she slides down completely, moaning out as she consumes my cock without asking. It's hot as hell I must admit. "If I can do this anytime I want," she says, placing her hand back around my neck to meet the other.

"How did you know I would be hard?" She slides up and down

on my dick, never stopping.

"The same way you always know I'm wet. We do that to each other. I'll agree to be your *girlfriend* for as long as I do this to you; because the day I stop making you hard is the day we know this is over. The ultimate ruin."

One hand moves along her back, wrapping into her hair. "I couldn't agree with you more," I say, pulling her lips against mine.

That is as romantic as Lux Larsen will probably ever get. She isn't designed to fit the mold of average girls. Something about love and intimacy, aside from sex, freaks her out. She's completely different from anything I've ever experienced, and that's the exact the reason I think I'm falling in love with her.

CHAPTER NINETEEN

My eyes pop open. I have no idea what time it is. Hell, I'm starting to constantly question what day of the week it is. They are beginning to run together since I met him. Fuck, how long ago was that even? My vision focuses as I wake up, glancing around the room, stopping directly to my left. Damn, that is one glorious sight. It makes my vagina hurt.

I prop up on my elbows, taking him in. He's lying on his stomach with his arms stretched underneath the pillow, the white sheet stopping mid ass, leaving the rest of him for my eyes to feast on. My head turns straight and falls backwards between my shoulder blades, my face now pointing at the ceiling. "Why do you do this to me," I ask in a whisper. "That is not fair game at all."

It doesn't look like fornication is falling off my list anytime soon if I'm beside something naked that looks that yummy. It's a good thing I'm not catholic or I'd stay in confession.

I look over at him again. He stirs and I stop breathing, afraid to wake him. His head lifts off the pillow and turns toward me, his eyes still closed as his upper body stretches, all of his muscles in his back flexing, before he lays it back on the pillow. His face is in the beginning stages of stubble and his hair falls just long enough in front to run your fingers through and grab.

His back tattoo catches my attention. As he flexes it looks like it's moving, which is pretty damn creepy considering what it is. It's as if it's staring straight at me. I haven't really paid it much attention since that night in the tattoo parlor on Delta's birthday. I sit up and lean over, studying it closely. It's so detailed and dimensional. I want to know what it means, or what it represents, possibly even why he chose that to cover most of his back. "Does it scare you?"

I jump at the sound of his voice, squealing a little from being caught off guard. When I gather myself I find him looking at me from his pillow, a serious demeanor present as if he's actually curious. "Kaston, things like that don't scare me. When are you going to actually believe the few things I tell you?"

"What comes to mind when you look at it?"

I place my fingers on the hood of the cloak, running them down the center all the way to the end at his lower back, taking in every line and detail instead of looking at him. "Beauty. Symbolism. Self-representation. Just because something isn't beautiful according to the world's standards, doesn't mean it's ugly or monstrous."

I straddle his ass, placing a kiss on each hand, the part that is the true representation of a grim reaper. It makes more sense now after the night in the alley. "How many have there been?"

He turns beneath me, grabbing ahold of my hips. "Enough to get me the death penalty if caught, but not enough to make the world a safe place."

My mouth runs dry, but not from fear. Instead, it's a turn-on. I grab his hands, bringing them to my breasts. "Will there be others?"

"Yes." He squeezes. "Does that change things?"

"No," I say honestly.

"You're telling me it doesn't bother you in the slightest knowing I murder human beings and still sleep at night?"

His forehead lines as if he's having a hard time wrapping his head around it. He remains silent as I think. Something that he said last night replays in my mind. *I don't commit crimes just right them. The world just doesn't understand corporal punishment.*

Then, without effort, my mind pulls from some of the visions of my childhood: a wreck of a mother because she was brutally raped by the fucking multimillionaire that she worked for, trusted, and even respected. That same man that is also known as my sperm donor, because that is all he was. He took away her life, her dignity, her choice, and left her with a constant reminder of what happened from that day forward. She went from not having a choice to becoming a fucking lowlife whore that turned to synthetic coping mechanisms, no longer able to function in everyday society.

I blink, trying to push the memories back where they belong. "No, it doesn't bother me. Will you tell me why you do it or how you choose your targets?"

"I can't. I want to trust you, but I can't. You already know too much. No one can keep secrets like that forever. No one can take deep shit to their graves unless it could potentially send them there. I can't," he whispers.

Don't ask me why I want his trust, but I do...

I guide his hands down my body, sweeping them over every inch, including my tattoo that he put there when he asked me to trust him. Trust is a two way street. "Look at me, Kaston. I'm naked. Who else will hear? You asked me to trust you a time or two."

"That was different," he says in a clipped tone. "That couldn't bring down everything you stand for, everything you promised you would uphold. That couldn't bring dishonor to someone that died for those very reasons because I let a little pussy and a beautiful face cloud my judgment."

Ouch.

It's a good thing I'm secure in my choices to enjoy the benefits of the physical attributes that were given to me as a result of something so fucked up. Comments don't sway me one bit. I turn his hand as I guide it down my flat stomach, brushing over my naval ring until it's touching the opening to my clit, before pressing his fingertip between my lips as I look at him. "You asked me to trust you with my body, then trust me with your life. Maybe then, will I trust you with mine."

He pushes me back just slightly, until his dick is lined between us, and then thrusts upwards, letting me feel how hard he is. "Show me I can trust you...forever."

I lean over the bed, letting him hold me from falling, and grab my purse to open it. When I find what I'm looking for I place it back in its position on the floor. I open the blade with my thumb until it locks in position. He looks at the knife, and then back at me. "There are reasons that I conceal, Kaston. I'm not a fucking spoiled rich girl that lives in a bubble of happiness and money, ready to conquer the world at the hands of someone else. If faced with a bad situation I can handle it alone. A monster is not defined by an act, but by a lack of morale for innocent human life. There is one contract that can't be broken: blood."

I place the point against my palm with a slight force and swipe down, allowing the blade to slice the skin open, and then close my hand to keep the blood from dripping. "In today's world you don't fuck with blood. It's dangerous. If you trust that I'm clean, then trust that I won't open my fucking mouth in regards to what you do. If I do, then you won't have to worry about killing me, because I'll let you watch me kill myself. You have something more permanent than my word. You want my secrets then give me yours. We'd be bound by blood."

I swing out the handle of the knife, offering it to him. "You in or out?"

"You didn't even fucking flinch."

"I've been in worse pain than that."

He holds out his right hand. "Then cut me, but this can't be undone. It's *forever,* Lux. Know the stipulations of the contract you're entering before you sign. Fuck a piece of paper that only gives you my name, fuck a ring that can be taken off, and fuck a prenuptial agreement that assigns control of money to one, but screws over the other. If you do this we are *life* partners. That means you have my back and I have yours...no matter what. The only way out of this is by going through what could have happened back in that alley. We pull the trigger at the same time. We're both in or both out."

The knife begins to shake in my right hand as my nerves take over. This has gone in a totally different direction than I was thinking. What the fuck am I supposed to do? Forever? What the fuck! That word makes hives appear on my body. I just don't know...

I can feel the blood pooling in my left hand. My heart rate is so erratic that I can't slow it down, even with breathing exercises. I feel like I'm about to panic. My world starts to spin around me, as if I'm in the funnel of a tornado with him. Nothing makes fucking sense anymore. What the hell do I really know about him? Nothing! He's a stranger that I fuck on a regular basis. We know nothing about each other…yet I feel like he knows me better than anyone. Why the fuck would someone want this? I don't even want it…do I? I'm so fucking confused.

He sits up and grabs the back of my head, fisting his hand in my hair. He places his forehead to mine, staring me in the eyes until I'm pulled from my thoughts. "Don't overthink it. You're still you and I'm still me. We work the details out together. You lose nothing. I will never try to change you, mold you, or control you. You have a *choice,* beautiful. If you want to back out, just say the word."

"How did you know?"

"Because we're a lot alike, which is scary. I'm just a little bolder when there is something I want."

"So, you want to be…" I swallow. "Like married, but not." I shiver as that very word exits my mouth. It makes me feel sick to my stomach. I can't do that. I can't be that. I can't go through with this. I don't even really know what that would entail. Then he says something that changes everything.

"I just want to be Kaston and Lux. Nothing more and nothing less."

He leans back, but only enough to put a small distance between us, placing his hand out palm up. "If you don't want to go through with this, just close my hand. It's that simple."

I look at his hand, then at the knife in mine, before closing my eyes and tightening my grip around the handle in hopes I'll stop shaking. I don't know who I am really, not anymore. The person I was has been slightly altered since I walked into that tattoo shop. The two of us are a fucking shitstorm waiting to happen. We're two lunatics mesmerized with each other's crazy. No matter how many times I fuck him, let him fuck me, try to shine my ass with shit he says or does, or get pissed off at his aggressive personality, trying to match it one for one with my own out of spite, he's still there, prepared to take my shit and give it right back to me. He doesn't back off no matter how much I want him to when things get awkward. He fucking gets me. No one has ever got me before, the real me.

"Fuck. Please don't regret this," I whisper, turning the knife around in my hand. I open my eyes and place the tip of the blade on his palm, before pressing it into his skin and dragging the blade toward me, cutting him open, but not deep enough it won't heal itself.

Holding my left fist at shoulder length, I open my hand in a full spread, letting the pool of blood run down my hand toward my arm. "Please don't make me hate you for this, because I'm swearing with blood."

I extend my arm from elbow to hand toward him, stopping halfway. He mirrors me, then presses his hand to mine, our hands and fingers aligning against each other, mixing his blood with mine. He grabs my waist with his free hand, before flipping us over, my back now against the mattress. His fingers move slightly to fall in between mine, lacing our hands together as he raises them above my head and presses them into the mattress. He squeezes, forming a tight grip, as he grabs his dick with the other hand and positions it to thrust inside me, hard. "I'm aiming for the opposite, Lux."

My legs wrap around his waist and my back arches off the bed to take him completely. He takes his time with each thrust, making me feel every inch as he pulls out and pushes back inside. "Just don't be disappointed if you fail, okay? It's not you. It's me."

"When I have a target I never fail. That's a fucking promise."

For some reason I believe him... and that fucking terrifies me.

I turn my head to Kaylan lying on his side looking at me, rubbing his hand up and down my inner thigh. This is that moment when things feel awkward for me. We've both come and I'm ready to move on to something other than staring at each other. I've never understood those couples that can lie in bed all day cuddling with hearts in their eyes as if it's been a year since their last reunion, or the ones having verbal *I love you* wars.

I witnessed that couple once at work. I was working a wedding reception, Hell on earth in my eyes, and caught the bride and groom by the champagne fountain, holding onto each other and rubbing noses. Obviously they just couldn't figure out who loved each other more, because they kept fucking saying it over and over, rotating the ending word between more, most, to the moon and back, and the list went on. It made my skin crawl. Are the newlyweds entitled to be a little mushy? Well, sure. If that's their favorite cup of tea then fine, but how the fuck can two people measure how much they love each other? It's a little much.

My gag reflex was working overtime. Someone needed to slap some sense into them before they were past the point of no return and had no friends. The man needed a pair of kinky balls to balance out all of that sugary shit he had on overload, before one of his groomsmen felt guilty for their friend's lack of penile function and took it upon himself to taint his perfect bride in white in the broom closet. It happens. I've seen it. I may or may not have said something highly inappropriate that resulted in free shit for the couple and a ban from weddings for Lux.

Later, my boss screamed, cursed me to high heavens, threatened to fire me, and asked me what the fuck was wrong with me. After explaining my dilemma and that I was doing all women a favor before men thought that shit was acceptable, among other things, he couldn't help but to see the humor. No woman, no matter what she says, wants that shit. There is such a thing known as a nice asshole. It's called balance.

Testosterone is a beautiful thing. Hot, manly goodness, with the ability to be an asshole at the right times will take a man far...like me getting brutally fucked in the ass on the hood of that beautiful car. It hurt like hell, was a little embarrassing, and pissed me off for a while, but it also put me in my place, spiking my desire for him to an all time high. No woman wants a pussy that she can run over. End of story.

I sit up, tossing the sheet off of me, and throw my legs over the side of the bed. "Where are you going?"

I rub my toes in the carpet before standing, and then walk to the dresser that lines one wall, pulling open each drawer until I find the one I'm looking for. I remove the first folded shirt I come to and pull it on my body. "Dude, I need food. Don't let the body fool you. I fuel it often. Stay or come, but I'm finding the kitchen. At this point I'll eat ketchup if I have to."

He stands and grabs his boxer-briefs from the floor, pulling them on. "Shit. My bad. We can just go out for food. I don't really have much here right now. I'll fix that ASAP though. You'll be here...a lot."

He walks toward me, clearly headed to touch me. I place my hand out to stop him. "Cox, I need distance, and to breathe. Give me ten minutes and we'll re-evaluate. We must walk before we run, spread our wings before we fly, or whatever other phrase the universe has to explain my need to take things slow. You, sir, may be secure enough in your…" I wave my hand up and down. "Sex-god ways, studliness, or alpha-ism capabilities to just do whatever the hell you want, but some of us have spent our entire lives staying away from this type of affection. I agreed to learn. That's all I can give."

He is standing with one arm crossed over his chest, the opposite elbow resting on top of his hand, leading upward to the hand that is covering his mouth. He stares at me, remaining silent. "What? Why are you looking at me?"

He drops his hand, a laugh clearly being muted from the pursing of his lips. I'm glad someone finds this funny. "I was only going to get you a bandage. You're bleeding."

He steps forward and grabs the hand that's been staring at his face, turning it palm up. The cut pulled open, bleeding again. With his other hand he grabs the bottom hem of the shirt, lifting it toward my line of vision. There is a line of blood stained on the front of the shirt that matches the cut. "But I'm glad you got all of that off your chest. We should always be on the same page. I wouldn't want you to just use me for sex and run off," he says sarcastically. "I'm not that kind of guy. I hope you understand."

I laugh. "Fuck you."

"Triggers, Lux. If you want food I suggest you refrain from anything that will remind me."

"You're such a hornball. You're going to wear my vagina out and then it will lose its appeal."

"I'm a man. It comes with the dick and balls between my legs just like an instruction manual. That's just a myth. There is no such thing as a worn out pussy unless you start fucking something on the sly with a bigger dick than me. I will know. The end."

"A man with a bigger dick than you would be a porn star. No thanks. I'd like to stay away from hospitals." He smirks, clearly amused. "You know, just in case you were wondering. I know all guys do..." I tap my head. "Want to know the comparison to the last. You, sir, have one worthy of trophies."

"Touché. I'm not sure if I should take that as a compliment or a cut down that you can still remember said previous dick sizes." He pauses. "Well at least you're honest," he says in a laugh as he shakes his head.

I roll my eyes as he pulls me to the bathroom and sits me on the counter. He squats and starts digging through the cabinets below as I look at the blood oozing out of the cut, remembering the shit I've done within the last twenty-four hours. "I think you've brainwashed my pussy anyway," I mumble. "The thought of promiscuity or changing dicks like wardrobes doesn't hold the same flame and attraction as it did not all that long ago."

He stands and grabs my hand, holding it over the sink as he pours the peroxide over the cut. I watch it bubble along the blade line. "I'm choosing to take that as a compliment or it might have the opposite effect. I don't really want to imagine you fucking someone else."

He looks at me. "Would you want to visualize me fucking another girl?"

My eyes zone out as he starts patting along the cut with cotton. "Well I mean, I'm not stupid enough to think you've never slept with anyone else."

"That wasn't my question. Do you want to have that thought developing in your mind like deadly bacteria now that I've been inside you?"

He places the large adhesive bandage over my cut and comes to stand between my legs, placing his hands to each side of my hips on the marble. "Lux, look at me."

I do as he says, not sure where this is going. "Do you want to imagine my cock being in another woman, making her come like I make you come?"

I search his eyes, my breathing changing pace. My face feels hot. My body temperature is elevating. I feel like I need water. "Do you want to visualize my mouth on another woman's tits like they suck on yours?"

My stomach starts churning, nausea setting in. I feel like I have a hangover minus the alcohol and good time. My fingertips take residence between my lips, my eyes turning away from him. He grabs my chin, pulling it back. "Do you want to mentally watch me come from another woman milking my cock like you do?"

"Kaston, stop. I get it. Fuck. Don't be an asshole."

"Exactly. Every time you mention fucking someone else that's the bare minimum of what goes through my mind. Men have carnal characteristics by nature. We're visual. We're jealous. We're fucking Neanderthals. You bait us and we're going to attack. You do not mess with a man's woman or his mancave."

He brings his hands to the sides of my face, his fingertips running into my hairline. "I don't care who was before me, because it's part of the past, but that doesn't mean I want to hear about it. Out of sight, out of mind kind of thing. Got me?"

"Okay," I say breathless. I feel like my emotions are in the front seat of a roller coaster. In a split second I can go from turned on to frustrated, then angry to guilty. I grab his waist and pull him closer. "I didn't know you really cared. I'll work on a filter."

"Lux...."

"Yeah."

"I'm a hitman."

"Do what? I am clearly hearing things."

"I would imagine you probably heard that accurately. You asked how I choose them. They are chosen for me."

"Like someone pays you to kill someone?"

"Yes."

I'm trying hard to wrap my head around this concept. I really thought those were more of a folktale or movie plot than anything. When I think of plotted killings I think of mafia or serial killers. I must be fucking insane. Am I really even having this kind of a conversation with someone? My tongue develops a mind of its own. "So you just kill for anyone that has enough money to request it?"

"No."

"Okay.... Will you explain?"

His face is serious and focused on mine, as if waiting for me to freak out any moment. He looks tense. "Promise you'll listen? Don't run."

"Yes. On blood." I lock my legs around his waist, silent for a moment. "I'm not sure that I could, Kaston."

His shoulders fall as if he just breathed for the first time in minutes. "There are those kinds of hitmen that are kill for hire no questions asked, but I'm not one of them. I would have had a sister, a half sister. We shared a father, but because of certain circumstances I never met her. She was older."

"Was?"

"She's dead. When she was thirteen she was raped and murdered one night when she was walking home from a friend's house. It was a safe neighborhood and just a few blocks from home, so it wasn't abnormal. This was twenty years ago. No one saw anything, or so they said, but she must have tried to scream because he slit her throat while he raped her, trying to sever her vocal chord but cut too far. The sick fuck continued to rape her as she bled out, getting off on it."

My insides start twisting into knots. He's shaking as he holds me, his eyes void, dark. His voice gets deeper and harsher with every sentence that is constructed with his tongue. "She was someone's daughter, sister, and a fucking kid. My dad wasn't a push over. To him the only option was to avenge her death. Finding the person that did it became his obsession, his every thought. He barely slept until he did, and when he did he killed them in the same way they killed her, only with an object instead of a person, for obvious reasons and to make it more brutal. When that sick fuck died he knew how it felt to be raped, but Dad didn't stop there. He realized how littered the world is with bad people, people that should have never been conceived, people that sit and wait to hurt those that don't deserve it. He couldn't move on without attempting to rid the world of monsters one at a time. He only took the souls of the evil, never those of the innocent, returning them to the place they belong."

My mind zones out.

Mom wonders in, drunk, with makeup smeared underneath her eyes. Her clothes are out of place, but she didn't care enough to fix them. Her hair is disheveled. She falls back first on the couch, placing her feet in my lap. "When did you get home," she slurs in question.

"I haven't been anywhere. I've been here the whole time."

"I need you to do something for me."

"What, Mom? Are you sick? Do you need some medicine?"

"We're behind on the rent again."

"What do you want me to do, Mom? I'm not old enough to work yet."

"I had to use the money I made selling to pay it, but now he's here to collect his cut. I don't have it."

Someone starts banging on the door. "Open the door, Katherine. I want my money."

My heart starts pounding in my chest. Mom sits up and looks at me. "Please, Lux. I need your help. I tried. He doesn't want me. The only way to protect us is to give him what he wants. He's willing to wipe my debt clean; a fresh start."

"Katherine, it's you or her. What's it going to be? Open the fucking door."

The doorknob starts turning, the door shaking as he tries to break through. "What am I supposed to do? What does he want?"

She fumbles to the side table and opens the drawer, pulling something out, before handing it to me. It's a small, square package. I take it, studying the writing on the front: Durex condom. The boys at school sometimes joke about these. I drop it and push her legs off of me. "No, Mom. I can't."

She grabs my face in her hands. "This isn't up for discussion. We have no choice. We're a team remember. I took one for the team once. I'm looking at it. We all have to sacrifice to survive, Lux. We have to play with cards we're dealt. There is a secret to getting through it. Be whoever you want to be. Just pretend you're a princess. He's your prince. Create a story in your head. By the time it ends it'll all be over. This one is actually cute, and young. I would do it if he wanted me, but he doesn't. He wants you."

The door opens by force and he walks in, grabbing me by the arm and pulling me into a standing position. He looks at my mother. "You so much as fucking mouth this to anyone else and I'll fucking kill you myself, then sell her off. Those guys won't take care of her like I will, so you better take this to your grave."

Mom nods and stands, before turning for the door. She slams it behind her, leaving me alone with him. I feel sick. What's going to happen to me? "Show me to your bed."

My breathing becomes loud as I lead him down the hallway of the trailer, turning into my bedroom. He walks in and shuts the door behind me, then starts to remove his belt. "Take off your clothes. I want to look at you."

He removes his shirt, revealing the gun tucked into the waistband of his jeans. My hands fumble for the button on my pants, trying to get them undone. After a few tries I get them open and push them to my feet, before stepping out of them, leaving my bottom half bare, and then follow through with my tee shirt as he lays the gun on my dresser and removes his pants, showing himself. His private part is hard. Kids at school talk about what adults do, but we've never witnessed it aside from what they show in movies. Those people are always in love, though. "Have you ever touched one?"

I shake my head.

He walks toward me, placing his hands on my body, before squeezing my butt. He rubs them up my sides, stopping next at my boobs. His thumb rubs over the center part, making it tingle. "Nature has been good to you. Your body makes you look twice your age. You can trust me. I'll be good to it. Touch my dick."

My hand inches forward, my fingertips touching it. "Hold it in your hand."

I do as he says. "Don't be scared of it. It'll make you feel good." He turns us around and sits on the edge of the bed. "Rub it."

My hand rubs up and down slowly. "Like that. Can I touch you, Lux?"

I remember what Mom said. I nod. He puts his hand behind my thigh and pulls it up into a bend, until my foot is resting on the mattress. He keeps it there and moves his other hand between my legs. "I'm not going to hurt you, okay, but it will hurt before it feels good. I'm not a bad guy. If you trust me I'll make your life better."

He presses his finger inside, catching me by surprise. It doesn't hurt. He told me the truth. He pulls out and presses back in, in a repeated motion. After a few times he pulls out and drags his finger higher, where he starts rubbing in circles with his fingertips. It feels strange at first, then good. Should it feel good?

"Kiss me, Lux. Show me that you want this."

I feel like I have butterflies in my stomach. What if I'm not good at it? "Okay."

I lean in and press my lips against his. As soon as I do he takes over, moving his lips with mine, showing me how. His tongue slips between my lips until his tongue finds mine. He makes a sound in his throat, before standing and turning us around, laying me back on the bed. He doesn't stop as he crawls us up to the center of my bed, on top of me.

He stops and looks at me. "Trust me, Lux. I'm not trying to hurt you. Do you understand? Don't scream."

I shakily nod my head, nervous. He kisses me again and spreads open my legs, gently rubbing them, relaxing me a little when I feel him there, between my legs... and then comes pain as he pushes himself inside of me. It takes my breath away. He continues to kiss me. I try to focus on that as he uses his hips against my body, steering himself into me, getting faster each time. It hurts. My mind drifts someplace else. I'm a princess and he's my prince. Today is our wedding day...

"Lux! Are you okay? Talk to me. You're freaking me the fuck out."

I blink, staring into Kaston's eyes. I can feel the stomach acid climbing my esophagus, looking for an exit. I cover my mouth with one hand and push him back, trying to rush for the toilet before it's too late.

I grab my hair as I reach it across the bathroom, kneeling in front of it on my knees as my face aligns with the bowl, expelling the contents of my stomach, over and over. "Please leave," I manage to say between heaves.

"No," he says as he lines himself behind me, grabbing my hair to hold.

"Please."

"I'm not leaving."

My stomach muscles continue to contract, even though I feel like I have nothing left. The noise comes, but nothing else. The dry heaves continue, unable to stop them. Silence fills the room when I'm finally able to breathe. I flush the toilet for the third time since I started and turn to sit on the floor against the wall. Kaston is squatting in front of me, staring at me with a serious demeanor. I can see the question written all over his face, even though it hasn't even been long enough for that to be possible. "Before you have any thoughts whatsoever, I swear on my fucking life I'm not pregnant. This isn't what it looks like."

"I never asked."

"If I were you I would have. I figured I would beat you to it."

"While I appreciate that, it's not necessary. Talk to me. What just happened?"

"I prefer not to. I think you'll be thankful if I don't."

My eyes start to water. He comes closer to my face, but I grab the collar of the shirt and pull it up over my nose, covering my mouth.

"Don't hide from me. I told you something about myself. It's your turn. That's how it works. I could find things out on my own, but I'm trying to give you what you want by letting you do it. Either way, I want to know."

I lean my head back against the wall, looking into his eyes as he grabs my waist and flips us over, pulling me in a straddling position on his lap as he takes my previous place. He grabs the shirt and pulls it back where it belongs around my neck. "I just want to know you, good or bad."

I work to get ahold of myself, pulling that shield back in place as he removes my now dirty tee shirt, leaving me naked. "When vulnerable you trust more easily. Let me show you the part that comes after sex."

The only other person that knows anything about me is Delta. How do you let someone in when you've spent your whole life keeping them out? It comes second nature to me. I've been fighting a battle since I was a kid. Sometimes, though, I'm exhausted. I'm tired of being forced to have my shit together all the time. Maybe one by one I can let go of the demons, but no matter how bad I want to I can never completely break, because nothing is ever as strong when put back together as the original piece.

I breathe deeply; making sure my stomach is now settled. I haven't thrown up over that shit in a long time. I don't like it emerging like that. "I guess I'll just introduce myself. It's easiest. The only reason I was conceived was because my mother was raped by the rich motherfucker that she worked for. I guess that's one way to take care of your personal assistant. The only reason I was born was because her conscience wouldn't let her get rid of me; that and by the time she was able to cope properly it was too late. That was the single event in life that entered us into Hell, and my life was shitty till the day I graduated high school, when I moved here. Some things I'll talk about and some will take time. I suppose, like you, I have triggers too."

He tangles his hands in my hair, pulling my face toward him. "You have got to be fucking kidding me. It just keeps getting more ironic. Fuck, Lux. It's starting to make a little sense. Where have you been?" He asks that question as if he's really asking himself. I close my mouth as his lips brush mine, my eyes now closed. "Let it go," he says, and presses his lips to mine, forcing his way inside until I cave.

One hand lowers to my waist, the other staying positioned at the back of my head as he lays me on the tile floor, holding his body on top of me, and rubbing his hand along my upper leg. My phone starts ringing as he shoves two fingers inside of me. "Dammit," I mumble against his lips.

I try to sit up, but he blocks me. "Let it go to voicemail. You can call them back. This is more important than a fucking phone call."

I kiss his lips and lightly shove his chest. "That may be, but I work today. It could be my boss and you can't get me out of it today. It's time for some kind of domesticated schedule like normal people. I have to work, Kaston."

He rolls off of me, propping himself on his elbows to look at me as I stand and walk to the nightstand where my phone is sitting. The bathroom door is directly across from the bed. I grab the phone off the table and look at him, as I press the answer button. "Don't look at me like that," I tease as I place the phone to my ear when he gives me puppy eyes.

"I'm not looking at you, but I just arrived at your apartment. The door is locked and you aren't answering. Where are you?"

My mouth drops, my expression becoming serious. "Mom. I wasn't expecting you until tomorrow."

"I decided to come early. Surprise! Can you come?"

Kaston stands from the floor and starts walking in my direction.

I turn around. "Uh, I have to work for a few hours, but then I can. If I tell you where the key is can you just hang out until I get off?"

"Of course. Where is it?"

"It's sitting on the top of the door frame. It's a short night for me at work. I'll be home at midnight, but there's food, hot water, a television with cable, and a couch. Make yourself at home."

"Okay, see you tonight."

The call disconnects. "Yeah...see you tonight."

My heart falls to my stomach, suddenly dreading going home. I'm starting to regret this decision, but what other choice do I have? She's my mother...

Kaston snakes his arms around my waist from behind. "Y'all aren't close I'm assuming."

I relax a little as his body aligns against mine. It's strange. "No. Not in the slightest. It may take a long time before I can really venture into that part of my life completely, but little by little I'll try. Your story may have been set in the shadows of the woods, but from the little I've heard there was still someone to protect you from the wolf. I was left to fend for myself, so just keep that in mind when you get frustrated from me becoming skittish if you really want this to work."

He turns me around and presses my front against him. "I promise to show you that your future won't be a repeat of your past. Does this mean you won't be staying tonight?"

"I can't. I have to deal with her. I promised myself I would try. She's my mother."

He tucks a strand of my brown hair behind my ear. "Okay. I have a job that I've been putting off anyway. Time is running out. Call me the second you can come and I'll be here. You know where I live."

"Can I ask you a question?"

"Sure, beautiful."

"Why you?"

He looks into my eyes before responding. Hell he may not even know what I'm even referring to anymore.

"Why do I continue to fight his battles? Probably for the same reason that I am almost positive you did for her then and still do now. Blood is thicker than water, and because I owe him my life. We've lived more similar lives than we both probably realize yet, but we'll discover everything in time. He deemed it important enough to die for, so this is how I repay him, by becoming him. He's all I had, Lux, and that is worth far more than a conscience for criminals."

He kisses me. I'm becoming an accomplice, but I don't care. I've been the victim of bad things, but I'm a survivor. There are so many that didn't have enough strength to overcome the shitty hand they were dealt. The world isn't black and white. There isn't a right or wrong answer. There is no longer a boundary between good and bad. Peace is fought for. The answer is often left open to interpretation of where it stands on the scale, by the person, the situation, and circumstance.

He makes himself pull free so he can speak. "When do you have to work?"

"In three hours."

He smirks, walking me backward until I fall back on the bed. "Good, because I'm going to starve you for a little while longer. I want to be inside you," he says with a needy tone and crawls up the bed with me in tow beneath him. I may actually miss this, and those words I thought would never develop in my mind.

CHAPTER TWENTY

Kaston

I stand at the mirror wearing a towel around my waist, rubbing my freshly shaved head. Opening the drawer, I grab the mold from the container and place them over my top teeth, pressing them into place to alter my dental records. I've already sealed the cut from earlier today on my hand to avoid any bleeding, and I've trimmed all other places covered with hair. My palms meet the bathroom counter, bringing me closer to the mirror. I whisper, reminding myself, but pausing long enough between each to lock it in.

"Be undetected."

"Know your surroundings."

"Kill quickly."

"Clean up."

"Leave nothing behind."

I push off the counter and make my way to the back of the closet, grabbing the fitted long sleeve Under Armour and pulling it on, as well as a hoodie, followed by Under Armour's man version of leggings and thick jeans that will be burned later. The average person doesn't think about how much hair the body sheds naturally, leaving evidence behind. Every part of my body is trimmed and covered.

I grab the black boots and slide my feet inside, before tying them tight. The doorbell rings, signaling his arrival. Opening the top drawer in my closet, I remove a beanie and shove it in my pocket, before shutting off all of the lights and running downstairs to the door. When I open it Chevy is standing on the other side. "You park around back?"

"Yeah."

"Anyone tail you?"

"Nope."

I back up, letting him inside. "Basement."

He heads that way with no other words. I walk out the door and scan the distance. Nothing. As it should be. I back up, shutting and locking the door when I re-enter. Chevy comes into view as I jog down the basement stairs to the back wall, lined with safes. I grab the dial of the one in the center, turning it until the code unlocks the door. "Synthetic fingerprints. Gloves. Then gun. In that exact order. Got it? Tonight you get to earn your stripes. Everyone needs a spotter."

He nods as I hand him the first of the three. "Slow and steady. It has to be natural. Always strive to be one step smarter than forensics."

I take my own, preparing for application on my fingertips. "Have you memorized the mark?"

"Yes."

"Recite it to me."

"White male. Thirty-two. Height: six-foot-two. Weight: a hundred and sixty-five pounds. Description: red hair and green eyes; fair skinned. Priors: domestic violence, attempted rape, and statutory rape. Attempted rape charge was tried and convicted as a juvenile. He served a partial sentence for statutory rape and was released early on good behavior. "

"Who put out the hit and why?"

"Father of a missing person case gone cold. Nineteen-year-old female, blonde, last seen at a club leaving with the mark. She still hasn't been found. He was questioned but nothing found to hold him. No body. No evidence. I think the father wants closure, and justice."

I pull on my gloves and secure them at the wrists for tight fit, before grabbing two handguns and a bandana, tossing one of the guns to Chevy. "Are you sure he's going to be there?"

"He is every week at this time. Even if I hadn't been watching him he's fucking predictable, his behavior down to a schedule. I'd bet my freedom her body is out there buried, probably under that rose bush that's planted in a location that is random as fuck."

"Let's go. I've heard all I need to hear. We'll find out soon enough. The vehicle is ready to go."

I shut the safe and spin the dial, locking it. These are the kind of sick fuckers I hate hearing about. I have a special place waiting for people like him. I hope he can endure the heat.

"Park right here. We walk. I can only do so much to tires. I can't completely wipe the tracks in dirt. They are specific to make and model." I open the glove compartment and take out the shoe covers, handing him a pair. "Put them on. When this is done cops will be crawling all over this place. We are partners, so listen to me and sear it in your mind. Pay attention to detail. Do not get us caught. We aren't in the fucking military in a foreign territory. This isn't lock and unload. Leave everything just as it was when you found it. Never develop a signature with marks. Every one must be custom. With this one, angle is imperative. This is a framed suicide. If he can't do it himself it doesn't happen. Do not so much as fucking spit in the grass. We don't add to the crime scene and we don't take part of it with us. Do you understand?"

"You're a cop, aren't you?"

"Not anymore. Let's roll."

I pull the black beanie on my head and flip up the hood to the black hoodie, before opening the door of the SUV and then closing it softly, locking the keys inside. I can see the destination through the trees. The light to the barn is on, lighting up the night sky. I glance around to ensure the coast is clear as we make our way through the woods, before veering off toward the back of the barn, Chevy slightly behind me. You can hear him shuffling around in the barn. I signal Chevy to take left and I go right, pulling the bandana from my pocket and stretching it between both hands, wrapping the ends around each slightly to get a better grip.

When I reach the entryway my head extends just enough to see inside. He's coming out of a small room, closing the door behind him and securing it with a padlock, before shoving the key in his pocket. Who the fuck puts a padlock on a tack room door? He lives out in the fucking boondocks.

He walks toward me. I stand against the wall of the barn, waiting for him to exit. When he gets far enough ahead of me I come up behind him and grab him in my hold, the bandana pressing into his mouth. He tries to scream and I pull tighter, cutting into the crease of his lips. "Say a word, motherfucker, and I'll pop a cap in your ass so fast you won't have time to blink. I'm watching your hands. Hold them up where I can see them."

Chevy appears before us, pointing the barrel of his gun between his eyes as I back into the barn, dragging him along. I have a bad feeling about this one. I lead him to the door he previously closed. "Open it, slowly."

Chevy moves closer to change positions, the barrel now pressed into the guy's temple. He reaches into his pocket and shoves the key into the lock, turning it. "Open the door." He removes the lock and flips the hinge back, replacing it to hang loosely. "The light."

He flips it on, revealing what's inside. "Dear God. You sick fuck."

Everything inside me snaps, wanting to do this fast. It's taking every fiber inside of me to remain calm. Emotions lead to sloppiness. I push him inside until his face is against one of the photos on the wall; the shrine he's created of girls ranging from eighteen to about twenty-four. None of the photos are taken as if he's a stranger to them. Each appears to be from a photo shoot, the subject posing. There has to be at least twenty photos here, about five marked with a red X. I instantly pick out the missing girl from my file in one of the five.

A surge of anger spurs, blasting through my bloodstream.

I pull his head back and shove it hard into the wall. "Do you know how bad I want to snap your neck right now? Where are the ones that are marked in red? Are they dead? Nod for yes, shake for no."

He nods.

I tie the bandana behind his head into a knot, keeping it in his mouth, and then grab his arms, securing them. "Where are the bodies? Are they here?"

He nods again.

"Did you rape them?"

Another nod.

"Who are the other girls on the wall? Are they in line to be next?" He looks at me, remaining silent this time. I kick the back of his knees in, knocking him down. He nods.

A lead rope and a rope used for cattle roping catches my attention in the corner. "Hoss, hold on to this one for me."

Chevy grabs him around the neck with his arm, the gun still pressed firmly to his head. I grab the lead rope and tie his hands together loosely, careful not to leave any marks, before sliding the rope on his head, circling around his neck, and pulling it to fit snugly, wrapping the long end around my hand a few times. I jerk him toward me and grab the red marker from where it hangs on the nail in the wall, shoving it in his hand. "Write a confession. Include the location that they're buried."

I hold the marker down for him to grab in both hands, unable to move them separately. I loosen the slack on the rope just enough for him to crawl to a void space on the wall. He removes the cap and starts writing on the wall. "Be remorseful. Make it fucking believable," I grit out.

Letter by letter it starts to form...

My name is Benton Barker. I am a rapist and a murderer. The photos represent my victims. They lie beneath the roses. I'm sorry for what I've done, but I cannot change who I am.

I jerk him backward, letting the marker fall to the floor. I've read enough. Fuck. Some people aren't worthy to be called humans. My head falls back, looking at the loft above. My eyes follow, revealing the stairway that leads to it. I grab him under the arm and drag him toward it. "On your fucking feet."

He makes an attempt to stand from his knees, successful just as we reach the first step. They are narrow and wooden, leaving only enough room for single file. I release him, but keep the rope in my hand as I grab my gun and hold it to his back as we ascend, Chevy behind me until we reach the top. The floor is rough cut wood and flat, the storage for feed and hay. There is no railing at the ledge, but there is a beam that runs across the ceiling.

I shove him forward, toward the edge. The beam is low enough from the height of the loft for me to reach if I stretch. I look at Chevy. He nods and grabs him by the arm, bringing him closer so I can secure the rope. Grabbing the beam in my left hand, I toss the rope over with my right, pulling it down and repeating until the rope is wrapped a few times, then form a simple knot that most would know how to make but still holds.

Gripping his red hair in my glove-covered hand, I pull his head back to look at me. His eyes are void, slightly glossy as if he's holding back tears. It's funny how much of a coward they become when being overpowered by someone else. "One scream and you get a bullet in your mouth as *you* pull the trigger. Fuck with me and see."

I loosen the knot of the bandana behind his head and remove the fabric, shoving it in the pocket of my hoodie. "Why are you doing this," he asks in a hushed tone. "Why do you care?"

"Because I care about people. Innocent people deserve to be left alone. You want to kill someone, kill someone that takes up air instead of those that mind their own business, abiding by the laws of the land. No sin must go unpunished, even when you're smart enough to get away with it. You have a daughter, Benton?"

"Yes."

"Imagine a lion like you luring her to his den to attack her, raping her viciously and then murdering her to shut her up or to get off on the power trip of dominating someone else. There are other acceptable ways to satiate your fucked up desires without harming someone else. Those girls were sisters, daughters, possibly even fucking mothers you selfish bastard, so now you can spend the rest of eternity regretting what you've done, as you burn alive with no relief, thirst with no water, and as your skin crawls with bugs eating at you from the inside out with nothing to stop them. You will feel their pain, plus so much more. Step forward."

"Who are you?"

I remove the rope from around his wrists, freeing his hands as Chevy aims his gun at ole Benton here. "Me, I'm just a shadow in the dark."

I push the barrel of my gun into his spine enough to offset his balance as he stands at the edge. He falls over, the rope tightening around his neck as gravity pulls his weight. His hands instantly go for the noose around his neck as his legs flail, fighting for his life, and resembling a fish out of water as he figures out he's in a losing battle. I stand here watching until he stills, his body hanging from the beam in dead weight, no longer alive.

I back up and turn to look at Chevy. "Let's get the fuck out of here before someone comes looking for him. This job is done."

I can hear Chevy follow behind me down the staircase, back into the tack room. I replace the lead rope in the exact position I found it, taking one last look at the photos on the wall. The way I still sleep like a baby after a sight like that is in knowing that five of those girls couldn't be saved, but fifteen at the very least will still get to age another day, by an act as simple as removing the predator...

CHAPTER TWENTY-ONE

I pull the car into my apartment complex, parking as far as I can from any other vehicles in the lot, afraid to scratch the yellow paint. In all my life I never thought I'd be driving a Ferrari. I glance at the digital clock, 12:30. I grab my purse after pulling the keys from the ignition, stepping out of the car.

The alarm sounds as I lock it from the keyless entry. My nerves have been fucked up all night, the reason I stopped and bought cigarettes from a gas station on the way home. I hate fucking dealing with her. I have no idea why I thought this would be a good idea. At the moment I just want to climb back into that dark cloud with Kaston and pretend time doesn't exist, because that's the way it feels when he holds me hostage, but instead I put my game face on at work, served drinks and appetizers like no one's business, and eventually found myself in the kitchen, watching Jason and practically drooling with stars in my eyes. Take out the flirting with countless men and my job isn't that appealing.

La Cordon Bleu...

"Fuck," I whisper, shoving it out of my mind. It's fucking me up mentally, detouring my thoughts to places they don't need to go. That isn't possible. "Just help her get a job and her own place, then you'll be done with her.

I open my purse and remove the pack as well as the lighter, before closing it and shoving it under my arm. I stare at my building from the short distance as I stand in the dark, out of range for the security light to make me visible. I hit the bottom of the box on the heel of my palm repeatedly, packing the cigarettes, before tearing the clear plastic to open the lid to remove one. Placing the filter between my lips I light it, inhaling deeply in an attempt to calm the fuck down. "It's peaceful out here this late, isn't it? Most people are sleeping or partying, leaving the rest of us in silence."

I turn toward the voice of the female I don't recognize: a blonde, sitting in a patio chair on her first floor balcony with her knees to her chest, sipping on a glass of white wine. That's about all I can make out since she is sitting in the dark. "I wouldn't know. Most of the time I'm at work or one of the two you just mentioned. I have a fucked up schedule to be honest."

"Yes, I'm a night owl myself, but work, always work. This is a rare moment for me, so I try to enjoy it when I can. Mind if I bum one? I have a seat and extra glass with your name on it if you want."

I take another puff, looking between her and my building, still not ready to face the pain in my ass that will be waiting when I get home. She's probably asleep anyway. If I don't know anything else, I do know that she most likely found my liquor cabinet and has already drank herself into a coma. If I go home now I'll end up staring at some stupid shit on television since it's still pretty early for me, and I haven't talked to Kaston since I left his house for work, hours ago. "Sure, I have nothing else to do at the moment."

I make my way up to her balcony and climb over the guardrail, which is pointless since it's on the first floor, but I guess it's just a decorative piece to make it match the rest. I sit in the empty chair and hold my hand over the small table that separates us. "Lux Larsen."

She takes my hand and shakes it, before pulling away. "Chaisley Bennett. You drink Moscato?"

"I drink anything that can alter my mental state."

"Be right back," she says and disappears inside of her apartment. I run my fingers through my hair, before setting my purse down on the table. My phone chimes. I drop the box of cigarettes on the table and pull out my phone, still lit up from the message. Seeing that name eases my mind a little.

I touch the home button, unlocking my phone as the fingerprint scanner reads my thumbprint. It immediately opens to the messaging box; since that's the last place I was when it timed out. That's a little pathetic...

Killer (12: 43): You up?

I really should change his name in my phone... as in now. I probably should have just left it under what he added it as, but it was funny at the time.

Me: Yes.

Kaston: Where are you?

Me: Visiting with a neighbor.... and avoiding my apartment like an STD.

Kaston: Neighbor?

Me: Yes. You know, those people that usually live beside you but not with you.

Kaston: I'm not in the mental state for smartass jokes at the moment.

Me: Ofuckingkay. Obviously...you need to get laid.

Kaston: That's a little difficult when you're there and I'm here. I thought you were going home to deal with your mother.

Me: Well that was before I met my neighbor.... It was more tempting.

Kaston: What neighbor?

Me: OMG! A girl in my building. Why?

Kaston: What are y'all doing?

Me: Seriously?

Kaston: It's a legit question.

Me: Read above text. It answers that question.

Kaston: What is your version of "visiting?"

Me: I didn't know there were different ones. Are you okay? What's wrong with you?

I put out the bud of the cigarette on the concrete as Chaisley walks outside, handing me the glass of wine. I grab the stem and take a gulp as I read his latest message.

Kaston: Well when you admit to fucking around with another female there is. My mind is a little fucked up right now. I may be an asshole for a few hours. Don't hold it against me...

My wine spews everywhere, but luckily my head was facing the grass and not Chaisley. I cough, trying to catch my breath from the small amount that went down my windpipe.

"Uh, does it taste bad," she asks.

I push the pack of cigarettes toward her as I shake my head, trying to gain my composure, my phone probably wet in my lap. "One." I cough. "Minute."

She shrugs her shoulders and sits back down, grabbing a cigarette and the lighter. I sit the glass down until I can tend to this conversation. Right now it's a hazard to my health.

Me: FYI, give me a warning before you say shit like that out of the blue. Someone almost got the gift of a wine shower.

Send.

Me: To answer your question, yes, I have fucked around with Delta...TWICE, both times years apart, and not for the reason that you would probably think. It was hot and all, but it's not for me. Sometimes you have to do things for friends that others don't understand. I'll leave it at that. I will not deny that I like dick, a lot, and preferably yours. If your jealousy over pussy weren't completely cute it would piss me off. I would never fuck or fuck around with someone else if I'm not one hundred percent single, male or female. If it would piss off or wrong my partner, currently you, I don't do it. Period. I may have no shame in a lot of things, but I'm not that kind of person. I believe in commitment if two people enter into any form of a relationship.

I send that long ass message. It doesn't show that he's typing, so I lay my phone back in my lap and grab my wine. "Sorry. That was kind of rude."

"Man troubles?"

"Something of that nature."

She laughs. "Usually is."

I take a sip of my wine, and then another. "Is that speaking from experience?"

"A time or two, but nothing major." She exhales, blowing smoke into the air. "Dating isn't really my thing. I like the sexual benefits of it, but not the rest."

My phone chimes again. "I didn't think it was mine either..."

I open my phone as I take a gulp of my wine.

Kaston: Just for the record... I'm not usually like this. I just need to clear my head, but I still have some shit to do. Message me when you get home. Okay?

Me: Just for the record... neither am I. We'll figure it out. I won't be long. I just needed a minute to clear mine and an opportunity presented itself.

Kaston: Be careful. Tomorrow I need you. Talk soon.

Tomorrow I need you...

I down the rest of my wine as I clench my phone in my hand. My heart feels out of rhythm. I think I'm done with wine tonight. I'm just not feeling it. I stand, grabbing my purse from the table after setting the glass down. "Thanks for the wine, Chaisley. I think I'm going to call it a night. Keep the cigarettes. I won't need them. If I do, I know where to find you."

I step over the railing and walk off the balcony. It's time to face the inevitable. "Hey, Lux...."

"Yeah," I ask, stopping when I reach the sidewalk, turning toward her.

She runs toward me and grabs my hand, pressing the tip of a

pen on my skin. "I don't usually make friends with my neighbors, because I like my privacy since I work so much, but I think I'd like to hang out. When you're down for a girl's night, text or call me. I have access to some pretty sweet parties in Atlanta," she says as she writes the number on my hand in black ink.

Now that she's in some light, this is the first time I've gotten a good look at her since she started talking. Her hair is blonder than I thought, and fine in texture, piled up on her head, but it can't be much longer than shoulder length. Her eyes are blue like mine, but lighter, much lighter, almost to the point of being colorless, especially against her tanned face, and she's probably around my age.

A drop of water hits my hand as she writes the last digit. I look up at the sky and feel another hit me in the face. "I'll keep that in mind. Thanks. I'm going to get out of here if I want to beat the rain."

"Sure."

She backs up toward her balcony, saying nothing more as I wave her off and follow the sidewalk toward my building entry. The rain is starting to come faster. I take off running, holding my purse over my head as if the small square is going to do anything to keep me dry. The bottom falls out just before I reach the shelter of my building, almost drenching me. I can already feel my hair starting to curl as I open the door and walk toward the stairs.

The elevator catches my attention in passing, causing me to stop. "Oh, what the hell."

I press the button on the wall, shaking the water off as I wait for it to open. I need a hot shower and comfy pajamas I guess. My days of walking around naked are over for now I suppose. Bummer. I like living alone. I don't know what I'm supposed to do with her in a one-bedroom apartment.

The vacant car opens and I step in, before pressing the button to my floor. I'm starting to feel like I need another cigarette with every floor I reach, dreading the inevitable. I haven't seen my mother for more than a few hours at a time since the day I graduated high school, and then it's usually to bail her out of whatever fucked up situation she's gotten herself into.

The doors open on my floor and I step out, tousling my hair as I walk to my door. I grab the doorknob and it turns, confirming that it's unlocked. I open it to a dark apartment, everything seemingly quiet. The couch is empty and my bedroom door is shut. "Great, I guess I'm taking the couch. That fucking figures."

I shut the door and lock it, then walk through the kitchen, tossing my things on the bar, before continuing toward the laundry room, unbuttoning my shirt along the way. When I flip the light on there are clothes speckled on the floor. I pull off my shirt and toss it in the hamper, followed by my wet pants. "Come the fuck on, Katherine. The hamper is right in front of your face. Do not start this shit. I'm not your maid. I may very well be crazy, because I'm obviously talking to myself."

Gathering the clothes from the floor, I pick them up and throw them in the hamper, leaving only one. I grab the strap, a piece of lingerie opening up. "Ewww. I don't even wear that shit." I toss it inside, ridding of it.

Chill bumps are starting to appear on my body from being wet, reminding me how much I need that hot shower. "Fuck it. I doubt she'll wake up." Opening the dryer, I dig around in the clean clothes until I find a long tank and a pair of yoga shorts so I can go straight to the bathroom and avoid turning on the bedroom light. With my clothes clamped inside my fist, I round the counter, headed for my door. When I reach it I quietly turn the knob, easing it open in an attempt not to wake her. My eyes have to readjust to the darkness after coming from the laundry room, but as they do the movement of Mom's back catches my eye; her bare back.

"Mom? Are you awake," I ask as I flip on the light. No fucking way. My eyes widen at the sight of my mom riding some guy's cock in my bed. My fucking bed! She just fucking got here today and she's already found someone's to fuck her. Who the hell does that? My mom, that's who. She's moaning, acting as if she doesn't even know I'm standing in the room. "Mom! What the fuck?"

The guy switches position, quickly laying her on her back, and then looks at me as he pounds into her relentlessly with his cock. My chest constricts as if someone just hit me with a baseball, knocking the wind out of me. He smiles, that cold-hearted smile, with eyes so dark it's as if he's possessed by the devil himself. I stand here and basically watch my ex-boyfriend, someone I know so well, or at least I thought, drive his dick into my mom's pussy while he watches me. "Callum," I whisper, as my eyes gloss over.

Do not fucking do this here. You've shed no tears for years. Do not fucking start now.

"Hello, Angel." He pulls out of her and stands from the bed, stalking toward me. For every step he takes toward me, I take a step back.

"Lux, you're home," she slurs, stopping me as she turns over on all fours, looking at me as if this is all completely normal. She's fucked up on something, and because she is a fuck up I have to stand here staring at my mother butt ass naked. Something snaps inside, all of the memories of my childhood coming to the forefront of my mind as if the dam just broke. I hate her. She's never going to change. No matter what I do to try and help her it will never be good enough.

Callum grabs my hands, causing me to jump. He pulls me into the room. I look at him. "Don't fucking touch me, you sick bastard."

He pins my hands against the wall, pressing himself against me. I dodge my hips, but not fast enough. His condom-covered dick, the one just inside of my mother's pussy, presses against me and I break. "Get off me!" I cry. "Just leave me alone, Callum."

My anger becomes more than I can bear internally. The tears fall so fast that I can barely see in front of me. "No, Angel. I'm not waiting anymore. I've waited long enough."

I begin to panic and shove into him, trying to back him off of me, but he uses more of his body strength as if he was holding back before, switching both of my wrists into one of his hands, and then starts rubbing his fingertips down my body, pulling my bra down along the way, exposing my breasts. He places his lips on my cleavage, before touching my tattoo. "This is new."

I start kicking my legs, but he's smarter this time, dodging me, and then Mom's hands grab my face, turning it toward her. My cries become louder, more frantic. "He wants you, baby. He promised to give us a good life, to never want for anything. Our days of suffering and sacrificing are over if we do this. We have no choice. We're a team. You have to do this...for me. It won't last long."

My body stills at the words I've heard so many times, weakening me, instinctively giving in. He slides his hand underneath my panties and cups his hand over my mound, rubbing his fingers between my lips. My eyes close, preparing to make up my own story, letting my mind be happy, even when my body isn't. Her begging, her cons, her using me, I can't do it anymore. I can't fight it alone. There will always be one more time. There will always be one more trick. She'll never love me like a mother should love her daughter. I'll always be her whore that she can pimp out to save her fuck ups, just because she gave me life. Just a pretty face and a fuckable body…because she doesn't care about the damage she's done and continues to do to the person that lives inside.

My happy story becomes Kaston and I earlier today, after everything happened. He was gentle, more gentle than he usually is, but not because he was scared to be rough. Instead, it was as if he was just trying to savor the flavor longer. I can still feel the way his lips felt against mine. Sometimes he looks at me…as if he loves me, but is just too scared to admit it.

My eyes open as his finger thrusts inside of me. Mom is still staring me in the face. "She's good," she says.

"I fucking hate you," I whisper. "The day you made me lose my virginity to a man thirteen years older than me to pay off your drug debt, I realized that I meant nothing to you. When you made me do it over and over again, I knew that I wasn't important enough to be protected, and the day that I found out I was pregnant and you turned your back on me, I knew you didn't love me. The day I gave birth to a stillborn at the age of thirteen, the same day you abandoned me to deal with something I wasn't mentally capable of dealing with, was the day that I realized you would never be a real mother. That was the day that my love for you became hate. That was the day that I wished I were dead so I could be free of you. Every day I wished you had aborted me. Even back then I felt guilty, as if there were some way I could win over your affection, because even in hate love tries to break through. Asking you here was my last try to win your love, but it was a mistake. I can't do this anymore. The damage you've done to me is irreversible. Today it's not me that I wish were dead, but you."

Callum's hands drop from my body before hers. "What the fuck?"

I never move my eyes from hers. She looks like a soulless woman, but then she always has been. "You don't mean that," she whispers.

"Oh, but I do," I grit out, as the tears slip into my mouth to make room for more. "You may have been raped physically once, but I was raped emotionally most of my life. I'm done with you."

She drops her hands from my face, stunned. I look at Callum with a soaked face from my tears, and more still coming. *When it rains it pours I guess...* I squat to get the clothes I dropped when he grabbed my hands. His hands are in his hair, pulling in different directions. "Angel.... Please don't run from me. Let me fix this. Let me explain."

I stand and back out of the room, watching his every movement until I reach my purse on the counter. He takes one step and I draw my pistol out of my purse, before shoving it under my arm, load a bullet into the chamber, and then aim it at him. He stops. "It's already been done. Do not fucking follow me," I say in a hushed tone as I bump into the door, immediately grabbing the doorknob with my clothes in my hand, struggling to open it with the fabric slipping in my way.

"It's not in me to let you go, Lux. I need you."

"You have no choice, Callum. Forget I exist."

"It's not possible," he says as I finally get the door open. I back out, closing it behind me, and then take off running down the corridor, pulling my bra back in place as I do. I shove the stairwell door open and never let up as I descend every flight faster than the previous one, finally at the bottom. I can't breathe, but I can't stop.

The tears fall faster than I can wipe them. I trample through my complex barefoot and in my underwear, not caring enough to try and pull my shirt on. I finally make it outside, immediately greeted with pouring down rain. I stop for a second; trying to catch my breath, but then that feeling as if someone is watching me takes over and I take off again. I look around the parking lot, barely able to see from the crying and the rain. My eyes are swollen, it's dark, and I'm scared.

My adrenaline has my heart beating so fast that I can't catch my breath, so I run faster, heading in the last direction I remember coming. "Car, car, where is the fucking car?"

I keep running, looking over my shoulder every few seconds. As my head turns I slam into a body and scream, a hand covering my mouth, the panicking cry starting all over. I'm going to die. I'm about to die. Oh, God. I'm sorry. I can't see anything but his hand, wet against my face. My chest is heaving up and down from fear, from lack of oxygen. "Shh. Calm down. It's me, Chevy. Calm down. I won't hurt you."

My cry becomes louder, but instead of being a cry of fear, it's relief, as I sink into his large, muscular chest. The hand across my stomach snakes around to the back as he moves to my side and bends slightly, removing his hand from my mouth and replacing it behind my thighs, picking me up. My hands go around his neck and my head falls to his soaked tee shirt clinging to his chest. I close my eyes. "Please get me the fuck out of here," I whisper as he begins walking through the rain.

A door opens and he places me on a leather seat, securing a seatbelt over me, and then closes the door behind me. I recognize it: his Escalade. I start to crash from the adrenaline spike, exhaustion taking over. Warm air begins blowing through the vents, heating my cold, wet skin. I can't shut the images out of my mind. The wall protecting my mental state came crumbling down from the wrecking ball that just smashed into it. Delirium is setting in. My head rolls toward him. He looks at me, placing a phone to his ear.

My beautiful Kaston.

I reach over, touching my fingertips to his face. "Kaston, you're here. You saved me," I whisper. "My killer." I'm slipping into a mental breakdown. I can feel it. I can't hold on any longer, only hearing a few words before everything becomes silent and my world is consumed with one shade: black.

"Kaston, we have a problem. It's Lux. Meet me at your house."

Kaston

One sentence and everything in my world turns upside down. Nothing scares me, or at least it didn't, until her. That proves that I'm not invincible. I have a fear. That organ that normally resides in my chest cavity just plummeted to my stomach, now floating around among the acid. I can almost feel the erosion as it begins to break down.

The line goes dead and I take off running through the abandoned house that belongs to me, leaving everything from earlier tonight to burn in the furnace. I'll check it in the morning and disperse the remains. I pass the plastic-covered couch, stopping just long enough to reach back for the gray sweatpants that are lying on the back of it, and temporarily setting down my phone and flashlight. I step in and feed my legs through each leg hole until I can see my feet again, almost losing my balance. When my feet are firmly on the floor, I grab the waistband and pull them up my body, working them over my briefs quickly, before snatching up my things and taking off toward the garage again.

I lock the door to the house and shine the flashlight into the locked SUV, making sure nothing odd remains inside. It's clear, just as it should be. I'm starting to panic, and with that comes the possibility of making mistakes. I close my eyes and pause, before opening them again. I walk to the back of the SUV and quickly remove the license plate, before tossing it in the bin with the others, out of sight for someone that walks in, in the rare occurrence they actually could.

I shine the light around this half of the small two-car garage: door rolled down and locked, car locked, house locked, everything burning and almost gone. Fuck, is that it? My phone lights up in my hand, signaling a text coming through. I look down at it.

Chevy: Where are you? I think she's in shock. I can't get her to talk to me. You need to get here. I don't know what the fuck happened to her and I don't have a key to your house.

Something comes over me. I can't even fucking think straight. A million different thoughts are plaguing my mind with no idea what is going on. All I know is that when Chevy says there is a problem he means it. The dude is a veteran of warfare. He's probably seen more shit than most care to think about.

I run around the front of the SUV, toward the old green Toyota Tacoma I paid cash for to come and go from less than ideal places such as this one. I roll up the garage door and get inside the truck, instantly shoving my left foot down on the clutch to crank it. It's going to take me ten minutes just to get to the main road and another fifteen to get there. Dammit!

I shift into reverse and back out until I'm far enough out that I can close the door. I bump it into neutral and pull the emergency break, before jumping out of the truck to shut the garage door and replace the pad lock, keeping everything locked inside. It feels like

I'm stuck in time, barely moving, just as it did the night I got the call about Dad. No matter how fast I move I feel like I'm walking in quick sand, using all my energy to pull free, yet getting nowhere.

Hopping into the truck, I throw it into first and pull out. I still have to open and close the gate at the end of the driveway. A ball of nerves is sitting in my stomach, firing off in all directions. I have a gut feeling shit is about to hit the fan and someone is about to get hurt. My inklings are never wrong.

The gate comes into view faster than I thought. Either my head is really fucked up right now or I'm flying, but both could be the case. Getting out, I work to quickly unlock the chain so I can open the gate, then pull the truck through and lock it back.

As I get in the truck I pick up my phone and text Chevy back, letting him know I'm on my way. There is only one thing standing between me and her, and that's this fucking distance. It's time to see what this truck can do...

Fifteen minutes and I'm pulling into my drive. I've been hauling ass the entire way, and trying my damnedest not to hydroplane. Just like going through a curtain, about five minutes after I pulled onto the main road it started pouring, heavy enough I could barely able to see out the windshield, even with the wipers on the fastest setting.

I punch the clutch and brake, stopping on demand when I see Lux standing in her underwear in the rain, staring at my front door. What the fuck? Where is Chevy? I kill the truck in first gear and he knocks on my window, as if appearing out of nowhere.

He steps back, letting me open the door. I'm angry he's letting her stand in the pouring rain, half naked, and possibly getting sick. I leave my shoes and tee shirt in the passenger seat as I exit the truck in a hurry, slamming the door behind me. "What the fuck, Chevy? She's going to get sick like that? I can't depend on you to take better care of her than that?"

He turns, grabbing me behind the neck, forcing me to look at her. "She won't let me touch her since we arrived. I thought she was bad not speaking in the truck after thinking I was you. I figured she was just emotionally spent from whatever happened, but the second she saw your house she got out and ran into the front yard. I tried to go after her and she ran. I tried to pick her up and she fought me. I've tried to talk to her and she just starts crying again. She fucking snapped, dude. She's been standing there in the pouring rain since I texted you, mumbling things to herself that I can't make out, and barely moving as she just stares at your door. I think she's waiting for you to come out or some shit. I can't force her. Do you want the fucking cops out here?"

Rainwater pours down my face and chest. I let it, occasionally catching in my eyelashes. It's not a normal rain. It's as if God is so angry he's crying and this is it. There is a sudden pain in my chest as I look at her, standing there like a wet doll and making no effort to move. There is one more thing I must know. He drops his hand from my neck. "Where did you find her?"

"At her apartment, running in only her underwear with a pair of clothes, a purse, and a gun."

"What were you doing there?"

"Checking up on someone. She was freaking the fuck out, as if someone was chasing her. Look, Kaston, I don't know what the fuck happened to her, because she won't speak, but I guess I was just in the right place at the right time."

I look at him briefly. I can tell he doesn't want to answer any more questions, and I don't really want to ask, but for whatever reason he was doing there, I'm glad he was, and that's good enough for me. I'm scared to evaluate the rage that is channeling through my veins, but she fucking needs me. "Can you check into that? I think we just accepted another job. This one is pro bono. Find the mark and you can have anything you want. You have my word."

He nods. "That's not necessary. This one is on the house. You're now my brother, and family takes care of each other. I'll leave her things in your truck."

He turns and walks toward his truck, not saying another word, then does just as he said he would. His truck door shuts moments later and he pulls out, leaving just the two of us. I start walking toward her. She still hasn't turned around. A clap of thunder sounds and she jumps as if she's been struck by lightning. My pace changes from a walk to a run until I'm standing in front of her, grabbing her face in my hands. Her lips are quivering, her blue eyes staring off with no personality, and dull, as if she's just a human shell. They don't have that sparkle to them that she normally has, something I've noticed often and have come to love about her. I've seen a lot of bad shit, but this has to be the worst, and I had to lay my own father in the ground. "Lux, baby, come back to me. It's me; Kaston."

Nothing.

I press my lips to hers, trying to warm them, then pull back to look at her.

Still nothing.

"He touched me. He wasn't supposed to touch me. Only you," she whispers, catching me off guard.

My vision is slowly turning a shade of red. "What?"

"You won't want me anymore. He.... tainted me."

I blink repeatedly, trying to clear the anger. Her eyes are still hollow, her words robotic. "Who? Who the fuck touched you?"

Her chest starts rising and falling more quickly. "He touched her...and then he touched me. I didn't want it. I didn't want him this time. She tried to make me, again. You don't want me," she repeats again.

"Lux, talk to me. Why wouldn't I want you? Who are they?" I tilt her head back, angling her face at me. "Baby, look at me. *Look at me.*"

"Because I'll always be a whore, just like her. She'll always sell my body to pay her debt. I'll always be...her whore."

"Jesus Christ." My heart stops beating. I close my eyes. "Calm me before I have more souls on my resume."

I open my eyes, still holding her face in my hands. "I will always want you, because I sort of fell in love with you," I whisper, admitting it more to myself than her.

Her pupils change and then her eyes gloss over. You can't tell it's a tear from the rain, but I know it is. "You're not supposed to love me."

"It's too late, because I already do."

"It'll change. There is too much you don't know about me. You aren't going to want me anymore, Kaston. I'm too fucked up. It's why I never get this involved with someone." She pauses, taking a breath. "You can't love me, because I can't love you back."

My hands glide down her body, stopping on her ass, before picking her up. She wraps her legs around my waist and her arms around my neck, looking down at me. I move one hand to the back of her head. "Lux, it doesn't matter what you tell me about your past, because it won't make my feelings for you go away. On the contrary, it will probably make them stronger, and besides that, I doubt most of it was even your fault. I wasn't out searching for something, searching for this, but it still found me. You found me. I haven't been able to shake it since. Nothing ever happens randomly. I'm not the guy that will tell you I love you a million times a day just because I figured out that I do, and you're the kind of girl that doesn't want that kind of guy. I may have figured it out earlier than you, but in time you will, and that will make it more believable than being forced. Nothing changes. We're still the same two fucked up people. I wasn't planning on even saying anything because you aren't ready to hear it, but I'll be damned if I let you walk away from this because of the shit someone else has put in your head."

I pull her head down and press her forehead to mine. "We will still talk about what happened tonight when you calm down. You won't leave out a single detail, no matter what you think it may change. Nothing will alter my perception of you, but I will fucking protect you. No one touches or takes something from me and gets away with it. I've already proven it before."

Thunder sounds again, reminding me that we're standing in the fucking rain. "Let's go inside," I say, turning us toward the door to carry her inside. "You shouldn't be out here like this." She straightens in my grasp, knocking my hand from the back of her head to the middle of her back.

"Wait."

I stop. "What?"

She crosses her arms between us, grabbing the sides of her bra, and then pulls it over her head, removing it and tossing it in the grass. I look down at her beautiful tits before looking back at her, my dick quickly hardening. There's something about the way she looks right now that completely stuns me: her body wet and almost completely bare in my arms, her hair curling and soaked from the rain, her makeup smudged from all the moisture, and her emotions completely laid bare when normally she fights so fucking hard to keep them at bay. Her big, blue eyes, one of the things that hooked me, makes it hard to focus when she stares at me like she's doing right now. "When we go inside I want you to take away the memories…"

"Okay."

She smiles, a real smile, and it's now that I know she's completely back, relieving me. "But first there's something I want to try, and I want to try it with you."

I smile back, remembering the almost identical phrase that I used when I first fucked her without a rubber. "Anything you want, beautiful."

She places her arms back around my neck, rubbing her fingertips where hair was until recently. "Kiss me in the rain."

Her request catches me off guard, something out of the ordinary with her. It's not sexual, it's not offensive, and it's not anything I would have expected. "You've never been kissed in the rain?"

"I've never wanted to be, until now."

That pain in my chest returns, but duller this time. She's breaking down my walls, weakening the muscle that's always been so strong. I promised myself when he died that I would stay away from this, since I didn't find it before, because I can't give up the part of my life that makes it unfair to her if I ever get caught, just as he couldn't, leaving the life he knew behind. I'm submerging her in my world of darkness; somewhere I would have never expected this to happen, when what she really needs is light, and I'm making her a part of something she doesn't deserve, but the conscience that most people have, I don't.

The thought of letting her go hurts far worse than the repercussions of playing God, even though I want him on my side. No matter what I have to do or how bad I am for her, I still find myself wanting to be everything she wants and needs. I want to be her first when she asks, I want to make her dreams come true, and

I want to be the one that is standing in front of her when she lets herself love someone. I'm selfish, but if being that makes her happy then I'll live with it.

"Okay, baby, I'll kiss you in the rain."

She lowers her head closer to mine, slowly brushing our lips together, but never kissing me completely. She wants me to come to her. I fall to my knees slowly, then lay her back on the grass and hold my weight off of her with one hand flat on the ground, the other still cupped around her neck, trying to shield her from the rain. She shivers. "Are you sure you don't want to go inside?"

She nods, pulling my hips toward her with her feet still linked behind my back. "I'm not cold."

She shivers again. I lift an eyebrow as a smirk starts to form. "Fuck, this is hard for me. Just kiss me already."

Lowering myself to my forearm, my body touches against hers. "I'm glad you're back," I say, and kiss her, just as she asked me to. Her taste is mixed with the taste of the rain, making it distinct, memorable. Her hands grip my sides and move around to the back, her palms becoming flush with my skin, pulling me closer, before descending, sliding underneath my pants and briefs, and continuing downward as far as she can reach. She then switches with her toes and moves her hands to the front as I suck the tip of her tongue, working my pants over my cock, then pushes my pants down to my thighs. I drag my lips over her chin and down her neck. Her head rolls back, giving me a better view. "You want it? Out here in the middle of my front yard? You want me to fuck you in the rain too?"

She moans as I move my hand from her neck, rubbing it down her body, and stopping between her legs, before slipping my fingers underneath her panties and then rub them through her wetness. "Yes."

My tongue slips between my lips and trails down her chest, stopping on her hard, wet nipple. I suck it into my mouth, before releasing it and looking up at her. "Why? You wouldn't rather go to my bed after the shit you've had to deal with? You deserve better than wet grass in the pouring rain."

She shakes her head. "I want you to show me that you meant everything you said earlier, without changing us. I still want to be Kaston and Lux, and Kaston and Lux would have sex on the hoods of cars, in parking lots, possibly on planes, and even under the rain. I still want to be us. Don't take that from me."

She still has her honesty in all of her vulnerability. Instead of withdrawing emotionally, she's trying to recover. The girl is a fucking fighter. Tonight she's different, yet the same. She may change tomorrow; back to the smartass girl with no filter that doesn't give a shit, but tonight she's not afraid to ask for what she wants. Tonight, she's acting like a typical girl that just wants to feel wanted, desired, sexy, and loved.

I turn my finger up to form a hook, wrapping the fabric of her underwear around it, before ripping them from her body and tossing them out like trash. Grabbing my cock, I guide it between her legs and roughly thrust inside, grab her hip, and then repeat; making sure she fucking feels me inch for inch.

She grabs my face, pulling my lips to hers, and spreads her legs wider, then squeezes her pussy around my dick. A throaty groan escapes. My thumb moves to her clit, quickly rubbing in circles to make her come before I do. Maybe it's all the events of the night, but I'm not going to last long; something I'm still getting used to.

Her back arches off the ground and she moans into my mouth, her kiss becoming needy, faster, and rougher. "Don't stop," she mumbles as her lips change position. The muscles start to contract and her hands fist the grass, her moans getting louder, and her eyes are rolling into the back of her head.

I grab her hands and lace them in mine, bringing them above her head as I roll completely on top of her, but still holding my weight off of her. She looks into my eyes as I release her lips and bite her bottom lip. She thrusts her pelvis upward, trying to take me deeper. I pull back and thrust harder, the head of my dick hitting against something hard inside. "Fuck, I can't hold it when you look at me like that."

She squeezes my cock again and I kiss her as I thrust inside one final time, stilling my movements as I empty my load inside of her. The head of my dick starts to get sensitive so I pull out, releasing her hands and lips to push myself off the ground. She grabs my hips, stopping me. I look down at her confused. "What's wrong?"

She blinks, clearly trying to decide whether to say what's on her mind. "Don't give up on me, okay?"

I straddle her on all fours, looking her in the eyes. "If I intended to I would have already." I kiss her nose. "Come shower with me."

I push myself off, standing to my feet. I grab my wet pants and work them up my legs to my waist, and then reach down for her hands. The corner of her bottom lip is between her teeth as she places her hands in mine. "Okay."

I pull her up a little too hard, purposefully, her body crashing into mine. "I'm not ready for you to be dry yet. I like you wet, but it's getting cold out here. I don't want you sick..."

Reaching down I grab her behind the waist and legs, cradling her in her arms. She squeals and kicks her legs back and forth as I start walking the short distance across the yard. "Because I'm nowhere close to being done with you yet."

CHAPTER TWENTY-TWO

"**H**ow could you do this to me? This could ruin everything for us. Do you want to piss him off? What are you going to do when he finds out? You can't hide this shit, Lux. He's going to be here any minute."

"Why? I thought he wasn't going to come by anymore. You said that was the last time."

She is pacing back and forth across the floor, pinching at her skin. "I just needed it, Okay? You will never understand. I just needed to forget for a little while. I thought I would have the money by now, but we had to eat. You want to eat, don't ya! Do you want us to starve?"

I hate when she screams. I pull my long sleeves over my hands and ball them up in my fists as I scoot back in the chair, making room for my feet. I bring my knees to my chest, but it's *not as comfortable as it used to be. "I'm sorry, Mom. What did I do wrong? I thought I was making you happy."*

"Not getting pregnant! Did you not learn anything from me? Do you not see how hard it's been for us? How are you going to take care of it, or feed it? You're on your own with this. I won't raise another kid." She rubs her face. "This is bad, really bad. He's going to kill me."

I don't understand how this happened. "Just tell me how to fix it. What did I do to make this happen?"

"What have you been doing with the damn condoms, Lux? I gave them to you for a reason. You don't fuck a drug dealer without a condom, even the somewhat decent ones. Fuck! When did you even start your period?"

I blink, staring at her as she stops ranting long enough to put her hands on her hips, her face all crinkled. Where does she think her pads and tampons have been going? "Last year on Halloween. I was at Delta's. Her mom explained it to me."

"Then why haven't you been using condoms, Lux? I've given you one every time he's come by. Every. Damn. Time."

I'm starting to panic. Is this my fault? "I put them in my jewelry box. You didn't tell me what to do with them. You just handed it to me. Isn't the boy supposed to do something with it?"

She slaps her palm to her forehead as if she's only getting madder. "What am I sending you to school for if they don't teach you things? Aren't they supposed to go over all of this in some class? I shouldn't have to pull all the weight around here."

"Talk about sex in my grade? That's gross, Mom."

She starts scratching at her skin and slapping herself. "Mom, what's wrong?"

She looks at the clock and comes toward me, grabbing my hand

and pulling me from the chair. "I feel sick, baby. I need it. Just a little. I can't do this, Lux. Please, help me," she begs. "You love me, right?"

"Of course I love you. Tell me what to do. Do you need medicine?"

"No. I just need it one more time and then I'll stop. Please do this for me."

She falls to her knees, holding on to my hands as she looks up at me. "I don't like when he does that to me. He's not my age."

"He cares about you, Lux. He does a lot for us. Don't disappoint him, or me. Maybe...this baby will actually help. This could be like our insurance policy. That's it, baby. Do this for us. Make him happy."

"Okay..."

A knock sounds at the door, causing her to stand as it opens. He walks in, coming straight for me with a smile on his face. He hands Mom a small, clear bag. "Get out of here. I don't want to see you for at least two hours."

She looks at me, pleading with her eyes as she walks out the door, leaving me alone...again. He looks down at me, brushing my hair behind my ear. "I've missed you, pretty girl. I shouldn't have waited so long, but I tried to stop. I tried not to touch you anymore, but I can't. He grabs my hand and pulls me to my bedroom, locking the door as it shuts. "I can't stand it anymore. I need you."

He grabs the bottom of my shirt, trying to pull it up, but I stop him. "What's wrong? Why are you wearing this big shirt?"

"I don't look the same."

"Let me see you."

My stomach is in a ball of nerves, but then I remember what Mom said. I don't want her mad at me, so I let him take it off. His eyes go right to my swollen stomach, and then back up to my eyes.

"Have you been with anyone else?" I shake my head. "Have you told anyone?" I shake my head again. He grabs my face in his hands. "Everything will be fine, just don't tell anyone. You wouldn't want to get me in trouble, would you?"

"No. I won't tell anyone."

"Good, then we won't have any problems."

He walks me toward the bed until my legs hit, then drops to his knees, placing his hands to my stomach. "I made this." He looks up at me. "I'll take care of both of you. You'll see."

He grabs the waistband of my shorts, pulling them down my legs until they reach the floor. I place my hands on his shoulders, stepping out of them. He stands, immediately removing his shirt, then goes for his belt. "Turn around, baby."

"Do you need a condom," I ask nervously.

He smirks. "It's a little late for that, gorgeous. I want you bare."

I turn around as he drops his pants and bend over the bed, placing my hands on the mattress, staring at the polka dots on my comforter, waiting. His hands touch the back of my legs, and then I feel something wet down below. He makes a noise and starts licking me. I grip the blanket. I hate that it feels good. It makes me feel dirty.

He rubs his finger over the spot higher than his tongue, fast. I don't understand why I like it. I don't want to like it, but no matter how much I hate it, it still feels really good, and it just started feeling better. I no longer feel anything for a few moments, before he enters me.

It doesn't hurt anymore, at least not like the first time. Maybe it's because I escape into story time during this part. I close my eyes as a tear falls from my eye, just before closing them. I'm wearing a pretty dress, my hair and makeup done, and he just picked me up to take me to prom. This time he doesn't just want to make himself feel good. He actually wants to spend time with me, asking me to be his girlfriend...

I snap up, my body wet from sweat, my stomach churning. I place my hand over my mouth and throw the blanket off, quietly standing from bed, before running in a tiptoe toward the bathroom. My stomach muscles start contracting as I get the door shut, barely making it to the toilet before what's left of dinner is expelled. I grab some toilet paper and wipe my mouth, throwing it in the bowl as I flush, my eyes watering from throwing up.

I stand, immediately discarding Kaston's tee shirt and my underwear to the floor, and then open the shower. I turn the water on, adjusting the temperature before stepping in and shutting the door behind me. The small space starts to fill with steam as I walk beneath the water stream, letting the hot water run down my body. My head falls back and my hands rake through my hair from root to tip, combing it off my face.

I step backward until my back hits the wall, and exhale, letting the water spray from my mouth. My knees weaken and give out, causing me to slide down the wall until I'm barely holding myself off the floor. My wrists prop on top of my knees like a tabletop, and my head falls back against the wall. I need structure. I've got to get back to structure. What layer I had built back up shatters, and the tears return, even though they aren't welcome. I want it to stop. I can't go back to this shit again. For years I've been unable to cry, even if I tried. This hasn't happened since I was a stupid kid. Now everything is coming back with vengeance, haunting me.

The shower door opens and I look up. Kaston is standing in his briefs with his hands braced on the frame of the door, looking down at me, still appearing half asleep. "I think it's time we had that talk."

I nod, and he sheds his underwear before stepping in and shutting us inside. He walks in front of me, and squats, blocking the water as it rains down on his back. I look forward at his chest, saying nothing. It's getting hard to breathe from the water being so hot, creating a sauna effect in here, but I can't find the willpower to go back to bed. This is why I don't stay over. When you finally figure out how to make the bad memories stop chasing you, you don't fuck it up. I always stay in my bed.... The one that is now filthy.

He grabs my hand from my bent knee and brings it to his lips; the one with the healing cut across it, no doubt to leave a scar, reminding me that we belong to each other in more ways than just words. "Nightmare?"

I nod. "Just a shitty past. That's all."

"Tell me what happened tonight, Lux. Let me bear some of it."

I take a deep breath, looking at him. None of the wounds will ever completely heal. I'll be lucky if I can just mend it with scar tissue. I've worked so hard to shut them out, to drown them inside so they won't bother me, but the second I feel like I'm totally rid of them they reappear, reminding me that they will have a hold on me forever. Maybe it's time to let someone else in. Maybe it's time to let someone help me fight the demons. My biggest fear is that he'll find out the things I've done and realize that I'm really not the sparkles and ray of sunshine he thinks I am, that I'm not always the strong girl on the inside that I appear to be on the outside. I don't always have it together. I use my body to hide the mess I am beneath the surface.

He reaches behind him and shuts the water off, then changes position to sit beside me. His arm runs behind my lower back and his hand grips onto my hip, lifting me as if I weigh nothing, and then pulling me to straddle him, his semi-hard dick pressed between my legs. I instantly relax when his hand cups the side of my face, wiping away the wetness, his eyes boring into mine. "No one can hear you but me. We can talk in here and no one will judge us. This can be our safe room."

I laugh, another tear expelling. "You're kind of becoming my best friend, Cox."

"I want to be so much more than your friend, Lux, but that's a start."

"Promise me you won't hold it against me?"

"I promise that nothing you tell me will change anything, and I never make promises that I'm not one-hundred percent sure I can keep."

"I made a mistake."

I can't see him breathe. All movement halts. He stays silent for a moment, blinking at me. "What kind of mistake?"

"Asking her to come here..." I whisper, the pain dispelling as the words expel.

His other hand takes residence on my face and both comb through my hair. "Fuck, you scared me. I somewhat just experienced a heart attack."

"I walked in on her fucking him." The words come out without effort now. I close my eyes, trying to get them all out. "In my bed. Then he held me against the wall." The tears begin all over again. "He touched me after he had been in my mother. I felt like I had been exposed to a disease...and then he *touched* me. I asked him to stop, to let me go, but he forced his hand on me, *in* me. I didn't say okay...this time, even when she asked me to."

My eyes open when his hands fall from my face, and the ones I'm staring into I don't recognize. They are dark, distant, and possessed by something else altogether. His dick is no longer hard at any degree, scaring me, as if he's now disgusted by me. I always make him hard. When a girl no longer turns on a man there is nothing left. If I know nothing else I know that. That is the most definite confirmation of a man's feelings, no matter what comes out of his mouth. Physical attraction and sexual intimacy are the doorways to any relationship.

Pressing on his shoulders I try to stand, but he grips onto my hips so hard it hurts, pulling me back against his lap. His chest is rising and falling at a rapid rate, as if he's working hard to slow his breathing and failing miserably. His mouth is parted, but his tongue is curled up and pressed against his upper teeth. "It changes things, doesn't it?" I laugh, trying to cover up the panic inside. "I told you my life is fucked up," I say sarcastically. "Whose mother fucks her ex-boyfriend?"

He's still staring at me, but not *looking* at me; a vacant stare. "Explain, *I didn't say okay this time, even when she asked me to.*"

His words are harsh, the sweet guy he's been all night gone, nowhere to be found. This is clearly more than he was wanting or expecting, exactly what I figured, and the reason I've never told anyone about parts of my life other than Delta. The way he looks right now is hurting me. "Do you want me to leave?"

"I want you to answer my fucking question...please." The last word comes out in a different tone. I might as well just get this all over with and then leave. I'll go to Delta's.

"My mom has pretty much had an addiction problem my entire life. The types of addiction changed from time to time, rotating out as she went through the variations, but none the less there was always something: drugs, alcohol, sex, male attention, whatever she could find to obsess with. We had no money because of those addictions, so she would whore herself out or smalltime deal when she could, over whatever she could get, but that wasn't enough to pay for her drugs and the few bills we had, so when I was twelve she figured out a different bargaining tool: me."

It starts to play over again, that first day. I swallow, trying to keep the nausea down. "My body developed faster than the average girl. I hit puberty at eleven and my breasts started to develop. I shot up in height making me thin like a model, and because we didn't have extra money I had longer hair like I do now, which also made me look older. Once, I was with her when she went to pick up from her dealer and I guess he noticed me. The problem started when her drug addiction got so bad that she would use more than she was selling. She began by bargaining with him, getting the drugs up front and telling him she would bring it as soon as it sold. He let her, at first, but then she got to where she couldn't pay it back. Instead of killing her or beating her...*he* bargained with *her,* and I was the prize, the payment for her to keep her addiction satiated."

His pupils get smaller than they were before. "He raped you?"

"No. I said okay...after she begged me and told me we had no choice. We would starve, or worse, so I did...for her. She was my mother. I was only twelve. I trusted her."

His fist flies back into the tile, cracking it. "That's the same fucking thing, Lux. You were a kid. Emotional rape, bullying, and bribery are still on the same fucked up level as physical rape. How many times did you have to do that?"

My lip starts to quiver. "It went on until I was fourteen...when we thought I was pregnant, again." More tears fall. I've never admitted that aloud to anyone else, not even Delta, because after the first time she would have found someone to kill my mother herself.

He is staring at me with no expression, no emotion, nothing, as if he's completely unsure of what to say or think. "I'm sorry," I say, covering my face in shame, pressing the tips of my fingers into my eyelids trying to stop the tears. I'm not proud of the things I've done, but it's easier to not deal with it than to be consumed with the guilt. Sex with no strings and a payout other than money was the only thing I found that kept the guilt away. It was the only thing that gave me *control*, something I never had before.

He grabs my wrists and pulls my hands off of my face. "Where is the baby?"

"In a cemetery."

"It died?"

"She was dead when I delivered her." My breathing starts shortening as those words come from my mouth. I haven't spoke of her since it happened. "I went into premature labor and lost all of her fluid before I even got to the hospital. We didn't have money for doctors and I didn't know about government health insurance, not that my mother would have helped in fear that what she had been doing would have been found out, so I wasn't getting prenatal care. I didn't even know there was anything wrong until the pain got so bad I had no choice but to go to the hospital. She was too young to make it on her own, because it was *spontaneous abortion* is what the doctor called it. He said it was most likely related to my age. My body was still developing and not ready for a baby at the age of thirteen. When most people were starting to play spin the bottle and seven minutes in heaven at birthday parties I had given birth and was burying my daughter. Sophie was her name. She just looked like a Sophie."

Unexpectedly he pulls me toward him, placing his hand on the back of my head and then lays it against his chest, over his heart. It's racing. "Is that the reason you had surgery to prevent more?"

The things he remembers... "Yes. After that Mom did more

drugs, stayed in bars, and had a new guy most nights of the week. When history almost repeated itself and we dodged that bullet, I begged Mom not to make me do it anymore. She changed dealers and put me on birth control. I became really wild, looking for attention in alcohol and sex since that's pretty much all I knew. I had a reputation. I was the girl you came to for a good time. I didn't give a shit. My life was already hell, so I just made a massacre of it. When I was seventeen, my senior year, I decided the only way for me to forget my childhood was to move, so I went to her tiny gravestone for the first time since she was buried there. I made a promise, to her and myself. I promised her that I would never conceive another child so she wasn't forgotten, but also that I would never forget the way she looked when I held her body, like a baby doll. Doctors advised against it, that I wasn't mentally capable of going through something hard for adults, but I just had to see her. She was the only thing worth loving, another victim of twisted things. The world is fucked up, Kaston. I had to grow up at the age of twelve. I've seen more fucked up shit in my lifetime at the age of twenty-five than most ever experience. I may be selfish to someone that wants kids, but I'm not selfish enough to bring someone else into something this bad. There are too many kids out there with a horrible life and having to suffer than to add to it. I don't want to be a mother. I didn't have a choice then, but I was never going to be faced with that again, so I conned her into signing the consent forms for me to sterilize myself or I'd tell shit she didn't want told. Even as fucked up as she is, she still has things she wants to remain secret."

I lay here with my head against his chest, listening to his heartbeat. It's strong, still beating fast. This is starting to feel like home. The silence between us is peaceful, but that's one thing I like about Kaston. Whether we're talking, bickering over our own stubbornness, or just sitting beside each other, I'm still content. No one has ever cared enough to want to get to know me, and I've never cared enough to open up, but with him it just felt right, and the storm inside has never felt as calm as it does right now, after I've let it all go. "You're probably the most unselfish person I know."

I sit up and look at him. His face is a little too calm from the raging waters it was just a few minutes ago. His mind has to be a scary place. Just looking at him, or hell even knowing how he can be with me some of the time, you would never think he's capable of the things I've seen him do. "What's on your mind?"

"Move in with me."

That wasn't really what I was expecting. Okay, I'm really not sure what I was expecting. Maybe to have to talk to him about the shit I just confessed to, or even to be an ear for whatever job he had to do earlier, where he came from, or what he had to do, but not something as simple as that. Of course, it doesn't surprise me. Typical Kaston as I've come to know him. What would probably haunt most people is just an everyday occurrence to him, and things that seem abnormal in relationships to the average couple becomes appealing to him.

"Uh, why?"

"Because I want you to. Do I really need to come up with a better reason?"

"This is still new. We've known each other for how long? A few weeks? A month? That's weird. We haven't even gone on a *date*. Shouldn't you at least go to dinner with someone before you share a house? A few sleepovers or your stalkerish meet and greets are not enough to know if we would be compatible roomies. I'm not even a good roommate. There are reasons as to why I live alone."

"Who are you trying to convince, me or yourself? You sure as hell aren't going back in that apartment alone. This is a new house. I haven't even finished unpacking. You can do whatever the fuck you want to do to it on my bill."

"Kaston..."

He grabs my face. I turn into his hand, his thumb rubbing along my bottom lip. His legs spread and lift, thrusting me upward slightly, then comes back down, setting me on the head of his dick, before sliding inside. It feels so good. Altering my knees to the floor, I start to move up and down. He pulls me toward him. "I have your blood and you have mine. A fucking house should be petty. I won't want you any less in six months time. Move in with me. Let me take care of you. I promised you that your future would not be a repeat of your past. Let me show you. It'll be no different than living with your best friend," he says, with a smirk on his face.

When he's in me completely I stop. "You're never going to give up, are you?"

"Nope. Not until your things are here."

I roll my eyes. Figures. I have an idea... "How about we bet on it?"

"If I win you move in and if you win?"

My grin grows. "You take me to Paris."

"Deal. What's the bet?"

"First one to come loses."

"Before you I would've had that one in the bag. I guess it's time to put my balls to the test; pun intended."

I place my palms on the shower wall on each side of his head, leaning my body into him. "I don't like to lose."

I push off of his dick and turn around, before grabbing his dick and placing it back inside, sitting down all the way with my back against him. "Fuck, Lux."

His hand runs halfway up my spine and around to my front, before cupping my breasts in his hands, pinching my nipples between his fingers. I place one hand on the back of his and the other behind me on the back of his head, while one of his descends and starts rubbing my clit. He puts more pressure than he normally does, making it feel even better. I pick up pace, getting a rhythm, before changing positions from my knees to a squatting position, preparing to bounce on his dick. He bites my shoulder, pressing harder on my clit as he rubs up and down dramatically. I scream out, picking up pace now that I have control over my legs in their entirety. "Fuck, you're wetting my cock. Shit."

It feels too good. I'm not going to last like this. I lean forward and grab his ankles to give me leverage, before bouncing at a slightly different angle, milking him. He pulls his hand from my breast, and then rubs his thumb around my pussy, before sliding it back to my asshole, still rubbing my clit. "No. Fuck. I can't."

His motions become circles, both matching each other, one on my clit and one on my asshole, while I continue bouncing on his cock, getting faster as the pleasure consumes my mind, body, and soul. "Shit, I can't.... Fuck! I'm about to come."

I dig my nails into his skin as I start to orgasm, every muscle contracting and swollen from increased blood flow, now sensitive to the touch. I stop and sit up to lean against him, no longer able to move. His hand rakes up my stomach, brushing over my naval ring towards my breast. "I guess you win," I say out of breath.

"Mmmmm."

He kisses my neck. "Let's go get your things."

"Kaston, it's the middle of the night. It can wait."

"No, it can't."

"Yes it can."

"Nope, because you're going to be busy planning a trip to Paris."

I get off his cock and turn around to face him. "What are you talking about? You won. You don't have to take me anywhere."

"I came when you started milking my cock like you were fucking thirsty, but I wasn't about to stop you. Technically you won, but in that wager you never stated if you won that you weren't moving in, only that I had to take you to Paris, which I will gladly. It was a win for me either way. Always pay attention to details, beautiful. It can be the difference in winning or losing."

He grabs my chin, the very one that's probably sitting on the floor, and pulls me in for a kiss. He fucking out conned me. How did I miss that? "Fine, but seriously, I'm not moving when it's still dark outside. You can kiss my ass. If you'll wait till daylight I'll even snuggle with you."

I stand and put my hands over my chest, waiting for him to stand too. It's starting to get chilly in here. "Don't temp me. I would gladly kiss your ass, but since you made me an offer I can't decline, okay. I love your bargaining skills. I think I'm getting the better deal."

"Yeah, yeah. So Paris? France? Really," I ask as I open the shower door and step out.

He slaps my ass and follows me out, before he grabs the towel off the bar, wrapping it around me from behind, then steps up behind me, pressing his body against mine as he stares at me through the mirror. "Paris, France. It's pretty cool. Going with you sounds fun. We aren't too old for public sex, even in foreign countries. Have you ever been?"

I laugh. "To France? No. That's a good joke though."

"Why is it funny?"

"Really, Kaston? Why the hell would you think I've ever been out of the country? I don't even have a passport."

"You were driving a fucking Porsche when I met you. Why would no one have ever taken you out of the country, yet buy you an expensive car?"

I shrug my shoulders. "I haven't really *dated* that many people. I was only really a whore when I decided to be and when there was something I wanted, like my tits. Again, control is the magic word. The car was actually a birthday gift. Fucking asshole. Who takes back a gift? You're the only one that's ever really caught me off guard and actually interested me. I usually get bored."

"Stop referring to yourself as a whore. It fucking pisses me off. I don't care under what form of humor. As freely as *most* humans have sex now, that term should be terminated from use and become extinct. Clearly we've both had sex in our pasts, a lot I'm assuming, but our bodies now belong to each other and that's all that matters. Secondly, that car would be gone by now anyway. I'm not dating someone on another man's dime. Period. I really haven't dated anyone in adulthood, but only because I haven't wanted to. It was high school, then work after college. No one ever caught my attention like you did. Maybe my dad's death changed my perspective, but I think it was just you, so here we are, and we'll figure it out together."

He starts drying me down with the towel. Watching him do it is turning me on again, oddly. Maybe it's the nurturing aspect, but since I've never had that before I'm not sure. "Tell me, why Paris?"

"If I tell you, you're going to think I'm a fat kid." I laugh.

"You, beautiful, could never be associated with that in my mind. Tell me."

"Well, you know how most people go to Paris thinking of the

Eiffel Tower? Not me. When I think of Paris it's for the food, all that way. Don't get me wrong. I want to see it in its entirety, but I want to taste the pastries and the cuisine. I want to have a food-gasm as the fork slides down my tongue, coating it in yumminess. My mouth starts watering just thinking about it. I want to put a pretty dress on, curl my hair, and sit in a five-star restaurant while I eat a four-course meal, that most people never imagine experiencing in a lifetime. That is what I call a vacation."

"So you're passionate about food?"

I laugh again. I can't believe I'm telling him this so freely. It makes me feel light. "Yes, I guess you can say that. I've wanted to be a Chef since I was a kid. Delta's mom dated this guy once that had money. For her birthday he took them out to this fancy restaurant and she got to bring a friend, me. It was like no food I had ever tasted. When we left there I was so full I didn't think I'd be able to eat for three days, but it was worth the pain in my stomach. From that day forward I wanted to be the person that created something so beautiful, yet tasty. I wanted to be the maker behind things that comfort souls. I wanted to be a Chef."

He turns me around to face him, backing me against the bathroom counter. "Why aren't you?"

"It's just a stupid dream, Kaston; one that I found when I was a child. Not all dreams come true. Life happens. It steps in the way. Finances control everything. Schools for culinary arts are expensive. Then, to really be good you have to travel to some of the most renowned culinary places in the world, training under people that have made a dent in that world. You have to be willing to let people mold you, to make you better. Education only takes you so far, but learning from those that have perfected it, getting that history and culture from different places, is what makes you the best. That's just not possible for me, and I've accepted it. It takes everything I make to survive, but that's okay, because no matter what I'm making it on my own. I may have taken handouts for things through the past few years, for things that don't matter like clothes and goods, but that's something that I keep for myself. You're the only one that knows aside from Delta, but she's like my sister. We've sat under the stars sharing our dreams. We've experienced the good and the bad together our entire lives."

"You're wrong about something," he says, interrupting my thought.

"What's that?"

"Dreams are dreams because they're meant to come true. You just have to want it bad enough to reach for it and work your ass off to hold it in your grasp. I have all of this because of my father's dream, no matter how twisted it is to the average person. He had a dream to change the world, to bring the good back by ridding of the bad, one legal and one not, but both created an empire for good to prevail." He touches over my heart with his index finger. "By letting someone in here, you just never know when you're making his dream come true, because for some people, it's their dream to make someone else's dream come true, and to make them happy."

My heart is racing. "What's your dream?"

"To live an extraordinary life, because mediocre just isn't fucking good enough, and in such a short amount of time it's only built up to something greater. Now, I want to live an extraordinary life with someone else, my best friend, and someone that can make all other females fade; someone that wants to be an outcast with me, because being like everyone else isn't an option."

I stare into his eyes, not knowing what to say. He's breaking down my walls one at a time, and to the point that they can't be rebuilt. I'm not sure if I'm ready to give my heart to someone else. I'm not sure if I want to give someone that kind of control over me, yet oddly, I don't think I have a choice, and I'm starting to become more and more curious. "I hope you find that person," I whisper.

He drops the towel and grabs me, sliding me up his front. I wrap my legs and arms around him, and then he starts walking toward the bedroom. "I believe I already have."

CHAPTER TWENTY-THREE

Kayson

I wake up to the ringing of Lux's phone for about the third time in the past hour. "Fuck!" I smile in my sleep at the sound of her voice, before opening my eyes as she sits up in bed and grabs her phone, clearly in a rage. "Hello," she says in an aggravated tone as she places the phone to her ear. "Yes, this is she."

Her frustrated facial expression softens as the seconds pass. I sit up, watching her as she listens to whoever is on the other end. "I'll be there as soon as possible."

The phone falls from her hand and hits the blanket, her face staring forward blankly, before her head turns toward me. "She's dead. The witch is dead."

My brows furrow. "Who?"

"My mother. She's dead."

"How? I can't say that I'm really that upset to be honest, but it's been what ten, twelve hours? What did they say? Who was that?"

"The police department. They're pretty sure she overdosed. They want me to come identify her at the Fulton county medical examiners office just to be sure it's her. They found my number in her cell under the recent call history. She's dead.... This looks really bad, doesn't it?" The last two lines come out in a breathy whisper, as if she's relieved. Then, she looks at me. "Did you do it?"

"How the fuck would I have done it? I've been with you. Not that I haven't thought about it..."

"No, Kaston. What I mean is did you order it?"

"No, Lux. Fuck. I may be a monster, but I'm not a demon. She's your mother. No matter how much I hate her or how much she's done to you, I wouldn't hurt you like that."

"To be clear, I wouldn't have been mad.... Does that make me fucked up? This is my fault, isn't it? It's what I said to her. It just came out. I was so angry and hurt. I told her I hated her and wished she were dead. This all is my fault. She went off the deep end this time."

Holy fuck. Maybe I should have just admitted to doing it. It would have been better than her thinking it's her fault. I grab her and pull her on my lap, before holding her face between my hands. "Don't you fucking dare. Dammit, don't take her sins and bear them. They're not yours to carry. Do you hear me? She made you do horrible things. We all have to pay for our sins. Every fucking one of us."

A tear falls down her cheek and drops. "It doesn't take away the guilt."

"What guilt? What the hell do you have to feel guilty about? She used you your entire life."

"Because for the first time in my life I feel free."

368

"Damn, baby, that's not a bad thing. Let it go. I got you. Do you understand? If you fall as you drop the weight then I'll catch you, but let it go. You tried harder than most would to save her. Some people can't be saved, yeah?"

"Yeah."

"Then bury her, say goodbye, and move on. That's the best you can do."

"Okay."

"Do you want me to come with you?"

"Thank you, but I think this is something I need to do alone. Will you take me to get some clothes and the car?"

"Sure. Do you want me to make the arrangements?"

"I can't ask you to do that, Kaston. I don't want you to. I'll figure it out."

"Then I'm hiring a moving company to clear out your things. Come here when you're done. Okay? All your stuff will be waiting. I won't touch any of it."

She exhales, defeated, but then like she always does sounds so strong. "Okay. It can't be any different than co-ed roommates. I don't think I could sleep there again anyway. Sell the bed or store it. I don't want it. I sure as hell am not bringing it into our home."

Our home. Fucking hell that makes me happy.

"Okay, beautiful. Let's get dressed. I'll go in to the office for a while."

I pull into her apartment complex and stop in the space beside the Ferrari, letting her out. She opens the door and I grab her hand, pulling her back for a kiss. "I'm going upstairs with you to change. Don't try to stop me after the shit that just happened."

She nods and I kill the engine to my truck, both of us exiting together. She's silent the entire walk to her apartment, me thinking of what I'm about to find when she opens that fucking door. When she does I move her aside, entering first, my 9mm ready to draw if I need it. It's only lit by the incoming sunlight, nothing really appearing out of place. I flip the light switch along the way, lighting the room even more. As I walk into her bedroom, a slight crack in the wall catches my attention. Immediately that story she told me starts to develop in my mind, images that no man ever wants to have of his girl and another man.

She walks past me and immediately goes for the closet, returning in a pair of jeans and a black top. She loads a duffel bag with a sports bra and a pair of shorts, as well as a pair of sneakers. "What's that for?"

"I need to go to the gym. I need a stress reliever and that's what working out is for me. I haven't really been much since I met you. I need to balance the things that make me happy, and one of those things is you, but not the only."

"Mind if I come? I enjoy it too, you know. It could be fun to work out together."

"Okay. I didn't really think that body came naturally." She smiles, but I can tell that she's a little anxious.

I pull her in my arms after she zips up the bag and pulls the strap over her head, carrying it across her body. "Just breathe. You'll only have to do this once. It gets easier. Trust me. I know."

She reaches up on her tiptoes and kisses me on the lips. "Thanks, Kaston. I'll call you when I'm done, okay?"

"Okay." I let her go, following her back through the apartment toward the door. She opens it and steps out. I grab her hand pulling her back for one more kiss. "Be careful. Call me if you need me and I'll be there. I'll just stay and wait on the movers."

"Are they really going to come this short of notice?"

"Money talks."

"Okay then. Here are my keys."

I let her go, watching her disappear down the hall before shutting the door. I need to talk to Chevy, but I have plenty of time to make calls while I'm here, because I'm not leaving anytime soon. I have a feeling he'll be back, and I'll be waiting...

Lux

I grip the steering wheel as I pull into the medical examiner's office and park. Being in places like this makes me fucking nervous. Hell, cops make me nervous. Just talking to one on the phone had me freaking out. "You can do this. Just breathe."

Before I can talk myself out of it I kill the engine and get out, locking up behind me. It's a reasonably short walk before I'm pulling open the door to the building. I walk up to the first person I see, a heavyset man behind the counter, and hair white as snow. "Can I help you, miss?"

"Yes, sir. I'm here because I was called about my mom, Katherine Larsen."

"Who sent you?"

"Um, the police department." I pause, trying to gather myself. This is worse now that it's sinking in. "I'm here to identify her body.

Officer Drake told me to come in."

His face softens, as if he knows what I'm about to have to do, and as if he feels sorry for me because I've lost my mother, but the sad part is she really wasn't a mother at all. I wish things had been different, but they weren't. I love my mother. I always have. I wish she had tried harder, but what's really sad is that this was always my fear, except now it feels like a blessing. She was never going to stop. She was a ticking time bomb.

"Come on, sweetheart. I'll take you to the morgue." He comes around the desk and I grip onto my purse as I follow him through the building. We come to the door and he looks at me. "Are you okay?"

"Yes, I'm fine. Just ready to get this over with."

He knocks on the door before opening it, then announces to someone on the other side why we're here. A middle-aged female comes to the door and lets me in. "I'm Dr. Hale, the medical examiner."

I follow her inside, my hands close to my body, suddenly creeped out. Everything is so...I don't know, cold. Silver, metal tables sit on the floor, and along the walls are the small, metal doors just like you see in the movies. This is really happening. I never really thought I'd be an orphan. "What's the name?"

"Katherine Larsen."

She walks to that wall of the dead and reads a few of the tags that label who the not so lucky winner behind each door is, before stopping at one and she grabs the handle, pulling it open. She slides the metal tabletop out until it's fully extended. My eyes immediately gloss over as she pulls the sheet down to her chest, revealing the female that lies on top. "Mom," I whisper in a cry as the tears begin to spill over.

"I'll give you a few minutes," she says and leaves, her shoes squeaking against the tile floor. The door opens and closes, confirming that I'm now alone in here.

Her blonde hair is splayed across the table, underneath her. Her skin looks pale, her cheekbones more prominent, sunken in as if she's lost more weight. I guess I was in too much shock last night to notice. She looks more peaceful than I've seen her in years. "You weren't supposed to die, Mom. You were supposed to get better. You were supposed to get help like I begged of you for years. You were supposed to live, because I was supposed to be enough for you to want to. You were supposed to love me, not because of why I was conceived, but because I was your daughter, your flesh and blood. Nothing is supposed to be more important than that." I pause. "I'm babbling."

My cheeks are stained and wet from the tears; the same ones that have obviously been missing until their sudden return this summer. I take her hand in mine and look down at her. It's cold, not warm like mine. "You remember that time when I was nine? You took me to the beach for a day; a toes in the water kind of day you said. That was right after you got that job at the hotel cleaning rooms. I'm surprised the car made it that far, but you were determined that I would get to see the ocean. I remember it like it was yesterday. We got there and you put that fancy hat on your head that you found at a thrift store. It was so ugly, but fuck if you weren't the most beautiful woman I'd ever seen. I remember thinking to myself that I wanted to look just like you. Anyway, you took my hand and pulled me out to the sand. It was the weirdest feeling having it squish between my toes as we walked toward the shoreline. It was too windy to swim, but it was warm out."

I laugh, remembering the expression on her face as we ran

toward the water. "You were so happy that day. It was as if no bad existed in the world. When we finally got to the water you twirled me around at the edge, letting the water splash around us as we screamed. I'll never forget what you said to me. You squatted down beside me and pulled me down onto my knees between yours so that you could hold me. I felt so warm, so wanted. Then you told me that the only way to be alive was to live free of secrets; that keeping things buried inside would torment a person's soul. After that you said the best way to rid of them was by writing it down, placing it in a bottle, and sending it away. Then we did. Just you and me, with those two glass, off-brand cola bottles that actually had a screw on cap instead of a twist off that we got from the gas station on the way. We stood there and watched those two note filled bottles float away as the sun went down. You never told me what your secret was, but I'll tell you mine. My secret was that sometimes I thought if I had never been born that you would have days like that day every day, and I was okay with that, because then you would be that beautiful free-spirited woman that I rarely got to see; the one that everyone fell in love with."

More tears fall as I attempt to let everything from the past go. Her death paid it. It's time. "That was the last time I ever saw you like that. If I could take your place to change the woman you were I would. It fucking killed me to see the memories eating you alive. It made it worse that I was the reminder keeping the memories coming back to haunt you. What you never understood was that you weren't the only one hurting. I was hurting because you were hurting. I'm going to choose to remember you by that day and not all the bad days, because that was a great day. I lied, Mom. I don't hate you. I never could, even when I wanted to. I forgive you for everything, and I love you. Goodbye, Mom. I hope you're no longer suffering, I really do, because you've been through enough."

I kiss her hand and lay it back down on the sheet, before wiping my face with the collar of my shirt, and then turn for the door. It opens before I get there, the medical examiner waiting on me. "You can get a police report and a copy of the death certificate as soon as it's complete. We'll notify you when the body is ready for release."

I nod and pass her, suddenly feeling unable to breathe. I need to get out of here. I need to hit something. I need to be mad, to be sad, and then to leave it all behind. I make it to the car and pull out my phone, immediately calling Kaston. He answers on the first ring. "Are you okay?"

"I changed my mind."

"About? Talk to me."

"You can make the arrangements. I want her cremated. No funeral. She didn't have anybody that would come. I don't want her to be a body with no one to say goodbye, in a place that she will be forgotten. I want her to rest where I remember her being happy: the beach. The one that she took me to when I was a kid."

"Okay. I'll take care of it."

"I'm about to go to the gym. You can come whenever you're ready."

"Okay. I'll be there shortly."

I remain silent for a few seconds. So does he. It's as if there are things we both want to say, but don't. "Kaston…"

"Yeah?"

"Thanks."

"Anything for you, beautiful."

"One more thing."

"What's that?"

"Will you go with me?"

"If you want me there, I will be."

"Okay. See you soon."

"See you soon," he repeats.

I disconnect the call, letting the phone slowly drop with my hand. Everything is hitting me full force like a metal pipe coming at my chest. My hands start shaking. "Breathe, just breathe."

I start the engine and back out of the parking space. I need physical relief, and I need it now. I just hope I can get there without fucking killing myself in this car.

Kayton

I sit on the couch, leaning forward with my forearms on my thighs, tossing my phone from hand to hand; thinking. Maybe I should just fucking get out of here and hunt his ass down when I'm ready instead of sitting here waiting when I could be doing better things. There is always the chance he won't show today. I've already contacted the moving company and Chevy is going to come wait on them to get all of her things. I'll deal with her lease later.

A knock sounds at the door, throwing my thoughts off. I look down at my watch. It's a little too early to be Chevy or the moving company. They may have worked fast last minute, but they aren't that quick. I look down beside me at the brass knuckles I got out of the truck earlier, along with the hand wrap. I'm not one hundred percent sure that it's him, but I'm just going with my gut on this one. There is only one way to find out: silence.

I slide my phone into my pocket and grab the brass knuckles, sliding them on my fingers into place. I clench my fist to ensure they are in the correct spot, before grabbing the wrap and pulling free the end with the velcro, letting the rest of it roll down to the floor. "Lux, let me in. I know you're probably home by now. We need to talk about last night."

My jaw steels at the sound of that asshole's voice. I want to kill him, but I'm not...yet. Someone with that kind of money will be searched for. Conditions here aren't ideal. I'm not trying for thirty to life. I sit patiently and wrap my hand, covering the metal beneath, ready to disfigure that fucking face of his. Someone needs to break his Godlike power trip. It's going to be me.

I secure the wrap and stand, as another knock sounds at the door. "Lux, please open the door. I'm sorry." I make my way across the room and place my bare hand around the doorknob, turning it slowly. I pull the door open all the way, now standing before the cocky son of a bitch that looks like shit in his suit, as if he stayed up all night nursing a bottle of whiskey and then fell asleep at the bar.

"I don't think you're going to be seeing Lux today, but you are going to deal with me, you fucking asshole." I grab his tie in my hand and wrap it, minimizing the slack, and then pull him through the door as I take a step back. He starts trying to fight me, so I knee him in the fucking nuts, bringing him to his knees with his hands on his crotch. He obviously doesn't need them in working condition, because he doesn't know how to use them with respect to others. Everything is good when respected and used the way it was intended. Sex is good until you rape someone. Alcohol is great until you fucking kill someone from driving drunk. Controlled fighting has its benefits until you abuse a woman or child. Weapons are even good until you use it to kill an innocent person for your own sick entertainment. He may not want it, but he's about to get a lesson from me.

I slam the door with my foot. He tries to stand. At least he's attempting to be a man. He's just a sorry fucking excuse for one. I swing my fist into his jaw, knocking him onto the floor. His hands go to the floor, trying to push himself back up. "What is your fucking problem? You're really going to beat another man's ass that you don't even know over a whore that's spreading her legs for you as well as everyone else? What about bro code, dude? Doesn't it mean anything to you?"

"Again with that fucking term." My fist collides with the side of his face again, this time in the eye. I squat, looking at him getting weaker on the floor with every hit. "You want me to tell you what my fucking problem is? My problem is sorry men like you that give the rest of us a bad rep. See, most normal men that get dumped moved on to other women. They get over it. You may be fucked up over it for a little while, but then someone else walks in front of you that catches your attention and all is forgotten; not men like you, though. Men like you feed off of control and power. Someone tells you no and you fucking snap, becoming obsessed with earning back that power, no matter who you hurt in the process."

He sits up and I punch him again in the mouth, this time drawing blood from the busted lip. He touches his finger to it and then looks at the red spot covering the tip of his finger. "I didn't say you could get up, asshole. I'm still talking. When I get up you can get up. This is nothing. I can go all day like this. This doesn't even have body weight behind it, so keep pissing me off and I'll show you a power punch. You're about to be my bitch for a little while, since you didn't believe me the first time I told you to get lost."

I raise my shirt, revealing the gun in the holster beneath it on my side. "Like I told you before, I'm not afraid to use it and I always carry. I don't think many people will miss you. While I'm at it let me tell you something, you little pussy. You ever call my girl a whore again I *will* fucking kill you, and then feed your body parts to sharks. Got it?"

He looks at me, the targets of my fist on his face already changing in color. "I have a wife and a kid on the way, asshole. Yeah, someone will miss me. What do you want?"

I release his tie and stand. He looks at me from the floor. "Stand up."

He pushes off the floor, straightening his jacket. "Are we done here?"

"Not even fucking close. You're about to fight me like a man. You're nothing but a cheating bastard. What men like you don't realize is that you're not only cheating on your spouse, but also on the person you're cheating with. It's an all around fucked up situation, and one I have no tolerance for. We're about to play a little game of trivia. Selfish responses get a hit. I'll even give you a freebie. Hit me."

He rotates his shoulders, loosening up. "You really want to do this."

"I said it, didn't I?"

"Are you fucking her?"

"Since you listened right outside that door, I think you know the answer to that question."

He swings into my face, hitting me low, on the side of the chin. I open my mouth, realigning my jaw. "Good, you agreed to play. Word of advice.... Only pussies run. Now it's my turn. Did you tell her when you met her that you were married?"

"No. It didn't matter. At the time she was a willing participant without asking any questions."

I reared back and hit him in the temple, putting my body weight into it. He stumbles into the wall. "Wrong fucking answer, asshole. You're married. You shouldn't be trying to fuck other women. What, is your wife not good enough for you? Do you think it's fair to her for you to be sticking your dick somewhere else and then coming home to her?"

He's acting like he's slightly out of it from the hit to the head. "Fucking answer me. I know that skull is a little thicker than that."

"She came on to me. I'm just a fucking man. Give me a break. We're all the same. We all think with our dicks before our heads. Then I got a taste and it was too late. I couldn't stop. I want her. I still do."

Rage, jealousy, and maddening mental images transpire into a mixture.

I nail him front and center: the nose. "Fuck," he says as he places his hands to it immediately, trying to stop the bleeding. He moves it, blood dripping from his nose. "How does it feel? Getting my sloppy seconds. At least when I got it that pussy was a little tighter." He laughs.

I hit him again, this time with everything I have, knocking him to the floor. He's out. I squat again and patiently wait for him to come to. People like him piss me off. It's always about themselves instead of the people that need them. Just like my mother, Lux's mother, and her sperm donor. People like them make the human race a disgrace.

His eyes finally open and he looks at me. I am no longer winded from the last hit. "You keep holding on to the last memory of her pussy, because that's all you'll have of her: a memory. It doesn't bother me like you think it does to know you got her first, because the *last* is the only one that counts. You're wrong about us. We don't all think with our dicks in the way that it will hurt someone.

You make a promise to someone you keep it. If you don't want it anymore you step away before you step out on your partner, but still keep your obligations. That, *bro,* is what separates the boys from the men. If you have a baby on the way then you're responsible for molding someone else into a productive member of society. If you can't do that, then get fucking snipped. I'm not leaving another kid without a parent, no matter how sorry you are, because there are enough out there already. Having enough respect for human life to let you go – that's *bro code.* I'm going to tell you this one more time. Next time, consequences are all on you. I've made a promise to her. I will protect her, because I love her, and *only* her. She is good enough to be someone's only, not someone's secret. If you so much as look at Lux again, I won't hesitate to kill you, family left behind or not. This is your final warning. After this I'll never look back. For once, think of your fucking family. Now go back to where you came from before I change my mind."

I watch him stand, still squatting, as he makes his way to the door and leaves without saying a word, slamming the door behind him. "Fucking losers. The world is full of them."

My phone rings and I stand, removing it from my pocket. I answer and place the phone to my ear, listening. "I'm here. Where do you want me?"

"I'll bring you the keys. Let me know when they're done. Follow them to my house and they can leave everything in the living room. We will take care of the rest. Lock up when you're done. I'll get both sets of keys later."

"Okay. See you in a minute."

I return my phone to my pocket and unwrap my hand, removing the brass knuckles. I feel a little more relieved knowing that she will be with me from here on out. Working out suddenly feels needed, and remembering the way she looked in workout clothes makes going a must.

I pull up and grab my gym bag from the back seat, killing the engine. Everything is on schedule for the move, hopefully that fucking psychotic asshole is well on his way out of here, and the direction can start to point forward for her. I need to deal with a few more things I've put off. It's a little coincidental that we are actually members of the same gym, yet I've never seen her here, and I've been coming here for years. Sometimes even in a big city it's a small world.

I open the console and grab my member entry swipe card, before locking up and heading for the door. As the card reader approves the strip, I open the door on the green light signaling it's unlocked, and then head straight for the dressing room to change into my gym shorts and tee shirt. Five minutes tops and I'm shoving my bag into a locker, before locking the padlock and removing the key, bringing it with me. Making my way through the building, I glance around for her as I do. Then it hits me; that last time I saw her ready for a workout was actually at the martial arts studio attached on the back of this building, both under the same owner. Clearly that is something she likes.

I veer off in the direction toward it, pushing my way through the entryway doors that lead to the warehouse style add on that it's inside of. They open into a corridor that connects the two buildings without having to walk outside. I pass a wall lined with snack and drink machines, heading toward the double glass doors that lead inside. That's when I see her through the glass. I stop, wanting to memorize that shot.

She's wearing the same red sports bra and black spandex shorts she was that day I saw her outside, her hands covered in black, leather, fingerless gloves. Her hands are clenched onto the cage of the fighting ring, her fingers hooked through the holes. She's sweating, her skin glossy as a result, and staring off toward me with her chest heaving up and down, but she still hasn't noticed me on the other side of this door, most likely from the window tint. Fuck, she's beautiful, whether she's covered in makeup or not wearing any at all like right now. I want her to know it too. More importantly, I want her to *believe* it.

I shove through the doors and walk toward her. Her lips automatically turn up into a smile when her eyes land on me, as if I'm just the person she needs to see. That makes me fucking happy. "Can I help you, sir?"

My expression matches hers. "Well that depends."

"On..."

"If you're my instructor."

"What if I say no?"

"Then I'll just have to convince you that you are."

"Oh yeah? How are you going to do that?"

I take off in a sprint. When I get to the ring I jump up on the edging of the platform, gripping onto the fence in front of her, our bodies mirroring each other, only separated by the fence between us. "By giving you the best kiss of your life."

"Eh...you're not really my type."

I bite into my tongue, trying to stay serious. "Why not? I'm everyone's type. I thought all women liked bad-boys, no?"

"I'm not like all other women, sir. I'm one of a kind. You can't just kiss me anytime you want. You didn't even ask if I wanted you to. That's kind of rude, you know."

"That you are, baby. That you are.... So, you want me to ask, huh? How do you want me to ask? Down on one knee? At our front door as we say goodnight? Out on a dinner date over wine? Lying on a blanket under the stars? Just name it and it's yours."

Her eyes widen. I wait for it....

Still waiting....

And nothing.

Then her eyes change. "Do I look like a sap to you? What the fuck happened to you? Have you been brainwashed by aliens?"

She pushes off the fence and walks backward toward the center. "Fucking stargazing and romantic dates, my ass. The only time I better see you on your knees, Cox, is when your face is between my thighs. Say more shit like that and you are banned from kissing. It's starting to go to your head."

I bite my bottom lip, almost breaking skin, my eyes probably still giving me away. "Okay, tell me what it is you want then, woman."

I climb up the fence using my upper body strength, before making it to the top and changing to the other side. I jump down, making a loud thud as my feet hit the platform. She's staring at me. "Fucking showoff."

I stalk toward her, before pulling my shirt off and tossing it by the fence. "You haven't seen anything yet. Tell me what I have to do to get a kiss."

"Work for it of course. What else would I have you do?"

I look around. Surprisingly the room is empty. "You're on. What'll it be, beautiful?"

"We fight for it. If you can get me down you can have it."

I look at her, my eyes going to the tattoo I marked on her body. It's moving with her breathing. "You off today?"

"Why?"

"Just curious."

"Yes. I took a short leave. I called Jason on my way here. He said to take all the time I need.... with pay. I guess that's what happens when you work your ass off for someone for years. Here lately, though, it's a wonder he hasn't fired my ass."

"How serious are you?"

"You can hit me and I'll leave it in the ring. Just because I'm a girl doesn't mean I'm fucking weak. I can take it."

"I don't have any doubt that you could, but that's not what I'm asking."

"Then what is it? Spit it out. Time is wastin'," she says and winks.

"I think it's time I took you on a date. A proper one."

"I'm not sure I like your version of dating, Cox. Before if you had asked I would have thought adrenaline rush, danger junkie, or seeing how many places we can experience public indecency without getting caught; you know...forbidden things, but now I'm liable to come home to a vase of roses, a box of chocolates, or a fucking love note. Cut that shit. I will never be that girl. Ever."

"You get me down, you take me on a date; anywhere you want to go, but if I get you down, where and what is my choice. Are you in, or are you scared?"

She takes a step toward me, just as I thought she would. "Nothing fucking scares me." She holds out her fist between us. My lips turn up and I press mine against hers, knuckles to knuckles. "When?"

"Right after this."

"You're on, Cox," she says as she places her fist inside of her other palm, bowing before me, and then standing. She takes her stance, fists up and ready to roll. It's hard not to laugh. I'm not about to hit her, but I will outsmart her. Not so long ago I would have, because that's just the sport. It's part of it. Now, though, I can't.

She comes at me and swings; a left hook to my face. I pop my jaw. She packs a pretty hard punch, harder than I gave her credit for. I'm sure it'll leave a discoloration for a few days. I take a few steps back. She follows me, swinging again. I dodge this time. "Fucking fight me back, Kaston. Don't act like a girl. I can take a hit. I have plenty of times before."

And that's exactly why I won't hit you...

I bend over and come running at her, acting as if I'm going to plow into her middle, but let up just as I get to her body, scooping her up and putting her over my shoulder. "Dammit, Kaston. Stop making me look weak! Put me down."

She maneuvers one leg over my head, squeezing her legs around my neck, trying to choke me out. I drop to my knees and throw her forward, letting her upper body fall over me, her back roughly hitting against the platform, before grabbing her arms and pinning them above her. I press my body on top of hers and lean down toward her, laying a kiss on her lips. "You don't have to prove to me that you're strong. I already know that you are. I've seen it over and over. It's not in me to hurt you anymore, not even in foul play."

I kiss her again and stand. "Where are you going?"

She holds out her hands for me to help her up, so I do. I smile. "To show you my version of a date. Fuck flowers, they die, fuck chocolate, it doesn't last beyond a few seconds, and fuck love notes when I can tell you what's on my mind. I aim for the things you won't forget."

Just before I turn and pull her away I notice a spark in her eyes.

She's a dare devil and I love that about her. What's coming will be priceless.

Lux

My stomach is in knots as we walk toward our destination. This is one of those things you talk about doing your entire life, but most don't have the guts to actually do it. As I'm one step from doing it, I've even considered backing out, and I live for stuff like this. "You ready?"

The small plane is only a few feet away, making me more anxious. I grab ahold of the harness covering my body in my fists for a distraction. "Hell yeah. I wouldn't miss out on this for anything. I just need to prep myself. We could die doing this."

"We could, but at least it'd be both of us. At this point I'm not sure the world would be interesting enough to live in without you." He looks at me and winks. I'm cheesing fucking big time right now and I don't even care. "Besides, you aren't really living till you're living on the edge." He grabs my left hand, linking them between us as we carry our helmets in the other. "How's this for your adrenaline rush, danger junkie, and since I just fucked you in the bathroom after the course, public indecency without getting caught, all rolled into one?"

"You fucking nailed it."

We get in the plane and position for takeoff, everything I've just been taught going through my mind. I can't believe I'm about to skydive. Holy fucking shit this is real. I can barely breathe from nerves. I look at him as the pilot starts the propeller. "Where are the instructors that are supposed to be with us?"

He smiles like the Grinch who stole Christmas and grabs my helmet, putting it on my head, and then fastening it. "Do you really think I would bring you up here and let another man strap himself to your ass? You really should pay more attention. If I didn't have enough training to go with you this wouldn't be an option."

I roll my eyes. Go fucking figure. "Is there anything you haven't done?"

"Very little. My childhood consisted of money and lots of spare time."

He puts on his helmet and tightens all the belts and harnesses. If he goes any tighter I won't be able to breathe. The plane starts to roll, increasing speed down the runway, before lifting off the ground, angled in the direction of the sky. I grab ahold of his hand and squeeze the life out of it as we elevate, getting higher in altitude. I can feel his eyes on me. "Don't judge me. I've never flown," I scream, to be heard.

He lets me squeeze as hard as I want, not saying a word. My hold begins to loosen as I look out the door in midair, the clouds floating by. "It's beautiful," I whisper, more to myself than to be heard, not even meaning to say it aloud. The colors of the sky blending is like nothing I've ever experienced. I can't turn away.

"It's time," he says, upon signal from the pilot. My stomach is about to be left behind. The only other person in the plane besides the pilot signals when to get in jumping position. Oh, God. Please don't let me die. I don't think my brain is even processing information right now as I look down at the bottomless bowl of blue, because Kaston is attached to me before I even knew he was hooking us up to jump.

We step to the edge. I think I've forgotten all of the instructions.

Fuck. What was I supposed to do? Breathe. Just breathe. He picks me up by the waist, just enough to lift my feet from the floor and jumps, sending us out the door of the airplane, and suddenly we're free falling through the air. Kaston grabs my hands in his, lacing them together and holding them out beside us; like a bird. I remember he's here, and that's when the panic vanishes. I start to breathe again. Adrenaline takes its place and the smile reappears on my face as I experience what it's like to fly. I feel like I'm high as we soar through the air at rapid speeds, gravity pulling us toward the ground. There is no other feeling in the world that I've ever experienced like this. He lets go of my hands, but I don't even care.

My body jerks as he releases the parachute, slowing us down as it opens and catches air, changing us into a vertical position. I lay my head against Kaston's shoulder, savoring every fucking second of this. From a bird to a hot air balloon in mere seconds, you can't get any better than this. Nothing else exists up here: no bad, no good, and no ugly. Up here, you can really be...free.

That fabulous high starts to dwindle the closer the drop zone gets; a small field. When our feet hit the ground we run together until we're able to stop. Kaston immediately unhooks the parachute from him and us from each other. He must have removed his helmet already, because I can hear him speak. "How was it?"

I turn around; helmet still on. I stand here for a moment, trying to calm my breathing, my body shaking from the rush, before removing my helmet and throwing it on the grass. I jump in his arms and he catches me, holding onto me underneath my thighs as I place my hands behind his neck. Without thinking I crush my lips to his, not able to explain what I'm feeling any other way. I can't explain how I feel, not even to myself. It's a mixture of so many different things and it confuses me, so I'll leave words out of it.

I kiss him as if I'm starved for his taste and he lets me, returning it back with the same neediness that I give. My mind starts to spin, making me dizzy. I roughly pull at his lips, our tongues gliding against each other. I don't even notice I'm lying on the ground until the grass tickles my face. He growls against my mouth as he sucks the end of my tongue, and then pushes my legs wider to press his hard dick between my legs. "Fucking jump suits," he mumbles against my lips, then breaks the kiss, both of us out of breath. "They're fucking useless when it comes to easy access. If people weren't about to pick us up I'd strip you naked right here. What the fuck was that? If I had known I'd get that reaction out of you we would have done this already."

I pull the corner of my bottom lip between my teeth. "That was fucking epic. I'll never forget that for as long as I live. You can *officially* kiss me anytime you want."

"That was fairly easy. I was prepared for plan B."

"Wait, there's more? What if I want to see plan B."

"Another day. I can't show all my cards at once. I wouldn't want you to get bored too fast."

I'm not sure I ever could with you...

"What next then?"

"Dinner. Your pick."

He pushes himself off the ground and helps me up. I watch him, thinking. "How about takeout and getting drunk by the sweet-ass pool I saw at your house, a little late night skinny dipping, and then desert." I waggle my eyebrows. "That's as close to fucking stargazing as you're going to come with me."

"Fucking perfect. What you want to drink? Wine coolers?"

My mouth drops. I scoff. "Fuck no. Do I look like I want to puke my guts up before I even get a buzz? I don't drink that shit." I walk toward him, passing him, before speaking again. "I want it hard or bitter, baby. You can even add a little salt, but I don't do sugar rushes."

I hear him grunt behind me, but I keep walking toward our ride now waiting to take us back. I form a gun with my thumb and index finger, holding the imaginary barrel end to my lips, blowing across it. *I still got it...*

CHAPTER TWENTY-FOUR

Lux

I turn over again, not able to sleep for shit. I can only lay here staring at the ceiling for so long before it's just uncomfortable. I can hear Kaston breathing evenly, confirming he's sleeping peacefully, probably in a beer coma from our private party on the patio. Food, alcohol, music, and Kaston, makes one hell of a good time. Just saying. I will never hear the word skinny-dipping without being turned on again. I didn't even know pool sex like that was possible. Holy hell, I need to get up. I'm still drunk from earlier, but not tired. My body is going full force, my mind unable to stop from everything that happened today.

I throw back the covers and slip out of bed, replacing them where they were, and then tiptoe out of the room, quietly shutting the door behind me. I walk to the kitchen and open the refrigerator, grabbing a bottle of water. Opening the top I take a sip, the box filled living room catching my attention. That's going to suck, figuring out where to put all my shit.

My legs start to move, migrating me toward the small pile in the center that I don't recognize, because it's noticeably different than all the crisp, brand new boxes in the room, clearly the work of movers. I flip on a lamp, take another sip of my water, and then replace the cap on the bottle, before setting it on the coffee table. It's one, worn, cardboard box, marked with *Katherine's personal items* in black Sharpie marker, along with one, large, black garbage bag tied closed. I stare down at it as I pull my hair into my fist on top of my head, securing it with the ponytail holder that I am wearing around my wrist until it remains in a messy bun.

I sit down on the hardwood floor in front of the box. Chill bumps sprout all over my legs from being left uncovered, only wearing a tee shirt and panties. It's cold in here from the air being turned down low, so I cross my ankles and bring my knees to my chest, before pulling Kaston's shirt over my legs to cover them. The box isn't even sealed, only the flaps crisscrossed over each other to keep it shut. I pull them free and then look inside. There isn't much in there. Mostly stuff I made in elementary school like Christmas ornaments, hand print pictures, and Mother's Day projects. All of it is homemade except for the large scrapbook at the bottom that's peeking through.

I lift the edge of the papers on top to grab the book, pulling it out from under everything. I pull my shirttail up to put my legs down, crossing them in front of me. I set the crimson red book in my lap, each cover pinstriped in gold. I'm not sure what she would have something like this for. We never really did anything that memorable.

My fingers clench the edge of the cover and pull it open, revealing the aged pages that it protects. Written on the first page is my name and birth announcement information.

Lux Karoline Larsen

Born on May 13, 1990, at 11:39 PM

7 pounds 5 ounces

20 inches long

Taped beneath the writing is a newborn photo of me. Resting in the crease, folded in a trifold, is my original birth certificate. I quickly flip through the pages. It's like flipping through time, starting from her pregnancy and going all the way through my life, ending at my high school graduation. I didn't even think she showed up at graduation. Where did she get that photo? Surely I would have seen her that close in radius. It's a candid shot, but I'm actually smiling beside Delta. That's the day we left for Atlanta with that crappy car packed. There is an important item for each stage of life. I'm confused. I've never seen any of this stuff before. I didn't think she even had sentimental stuff.

I flip the last page, staring between it and the back cover. Aligning against the seam is a sealed envelope, the addressee turned away from me. I pick the envelope up and turn it over, reading the cursive script across the recipient section.

Charles Williams III

323 Professional Blvd Suite 6A

Atlanta, GA 30312

I've never heard that name before, but that's local. Who is he? My gut is giving me a really bad vibe, making me nauseous. Moving my hand from the interior of the book, the envelope still in hand, I shut the book and place it back in the box.

I look around, listening to ensure I don't hear Kaston. The house is silent aside from the air conditioner. I stand and make my way to the patio doors and unlock it, before flipping on the light and stepping outside. I trip over our shoes we left at the door, making a loud noise as one ricochets off my foot and hits the window of the door. My knuckles scrape against the cement, trying to catch my fall with the envelope in my hand. "Fuck!"

I stand, my destination drawing my attention. "Of course my drunk ass is going fall and make noise when he's asleep," I whisper, frustrated. I walk toward the Jacuzzi and lift part of the lid. The temperature reads 102 degrees. Perfect. He has it on. Maybe this will make me tired.

I fold back half of the cover, narrowing the width to half the full size, and then place the envelope between my teeth to free up my hand. Grabbing two of the corners of the vinyl cover, I pull it off the corner of the Jacuzzi and turn it toward me, then point it down to the ground and slide it downward, using the edge of the Jacuzzi as a support to bear the weight of the cover until the end rests on top of the cement. I wrap my arms around the standing Jacuzzi cover, grabbing it in a bear hug and lifting it off the ground, before waddling it over to rest against the wall.

I grab the envelope from my mouth and walk to the steps, quickly shedding my tee shirt before climbing them and stepping inside. As I descend into the water, the warm temperature begins to relax me instantly. "Damn, that feels good."

I take stance on my knees, walking along the bench seat to the corner closest to the lighting, the corner beside the controls. Surprisingly there is a breeze out, making it feel even better as it cools my upper body while my core temperature rises from the hot water. I glance at the controls until I find the one that turns on the jets and the lights in the Jacuzzi. It's loud, but I can't seem to care right now. Surely he isn't that light of a sleeper. He's upstairs.

I lean forward, draping my arms over the side, and letting the jet spray against my front so I can open this sketchy envelope my mother obviously felt was important, without getting it wet.

I tear through the seal, pulling the piece of paper inside free. When I open it, I realize it's a letter. I'm more curious now.

Chuck,

It's been a LONG time. I haven't spoken to you in over twenty-five years, and for good reason. The thing is, that last time I spoke with you was the last time I ever saw you. I know I disappeared; leaving you with no assistant and no notice, but there was a reason I couldn't explain in person, because you never gave me the opportunity to. Not after what happened did. All those years ago, I fell in love with you. Late night work hours, overnight work trips, and dinner meetings, turned into so much more. When we started seeing each other intimately I said I wasn't going to, because you weren't mine to have, but I guess we can't always control who we fall in love with, right? There was something about you that I could never move past, so I continued what we had against what I knew was wrong, giving you all of me. That day I left at lunch and came in late, I tried to break it off, because I was in too deep and I knew it. I knew there was no going back to just being someone that answered your calls and scheduled your meetings, but you had a wife at home; one you had already admitted to me that you had no intentions on leaving. You were comfortable in your life and I was just a pastime. That's fine. I got it. I understood perfectly clear what we were, because you told me often, but then I walked into your office prepared to tell you that we had to end the madness and you wouldn't even let me speak. It was as if I had become nothing more than an object of your desire. I tried to stop you, but you wouldn't have it. My conscience was getting the best of me for what we were doing. I'm not sure what happened to you that day, but the man I saw when I walked in your office wasn't you. You were darker. Bear with me when reading this letter, because I've been attempting this for years now and couldn't find the right words. I left that day, because that was the day I found out I was pregnant with our child. I didn't mean for it to happen, but it did. I waited as long as I could to confirm it, living in denial that surely I was mistaken, but in my heart I knew we had conceived a child, our child. Maybe it was my parental instincts taking over, but I knew we couldn't continue like we were, so I went to sever everything we had...for her. That was before you took everything you could, squeezing the last bit of hope for love that I had. I told you no, Chuck, but you placed your hand over my mouth. I may have told you yes so many times, but that time I said no, and you took it anyway, because you assumed I no longer had a choice. You took everything from me, because I wasn't raped by someone I didn't know, but someone I loved, and that makes it so much worse. That day not only did you take away who I was, but the person I was supposed to be, the mother to our daughter. Her life has been nothing outside of Hell, and for that I blame you, because she grew up without not only one parent but also two. I've lived for twenty-five years trying to figure out why you did what you did, replaying it over in my mind countless times, and why I deserved it, but after alcohol abuse, drugs, whoring, and crying in a repeated cycle, I still come up with nothing. I've lived her entire life choosing you, but not anymore. From now on I'm choosing her. She could have given up on me so many times, but she never did. God knows she had every reason to. She still doesn't, even with all that I've done to her. I'm choosing sobriety. I'm finally forgiving you for what you did to me, Chuck, so I can try to repair what we've both done to our daughter. No matter what she thinks I love her, and dammit she makes me proud. I just wish I had been stronger earlier on, taking control of my own life and mind. The drugs won't consume me any longer. I'm finally telling them goodbye, and you. The hardest part of it all is that she looks just like you, but she has a strength I've never known in anyone else, not you or me. She's a fighter. She's selfless. That I've seen. She's better than both of us, but also the best of ourselves. Maybe one day you'll have the pleasure of knowing her, because she's truly a remarkable person, no matter how fucked up her life has been. She deserves for someone to love her, and only her. She deserves the world, because God and I both know I've failed her. Goodbye, Chuck. For once I wish you the best.

Katherine

The piece of paper falls from my grasp onto the cement, wavering in the air along the way. The tears I've been holding back as I read each word break free, no longer containable. My chest feels like it's about to burst from inhaling and being unable to exhale. "Oh God, Mom," I cry. "Why didn't you just explain? I would have understood. I would have fucking understood," I repeat in a whisper.

The guilt is becoming overwhelming. Every bad thing I've ever said to her and every judgment ever thrown are stacking up against me, her death feeling more and more like my fault with every second that passes. She wasn't a bad mother at all. She was just mentally ill and had let it incubate for years. She needed help. I should have tried more, tried harder. I need relief. I need to forget what I just read. I need to forget a look into a life that I'm better not knowing. I turn around to face the water, moving off the bench into the deeper center, and fold my body to sink below the surface as close as I can get to the bottom without floating back up, holding my breath. I open my eyes, allowing the blurry canvas to remain... trying to forget. My chest becomes tight from the lack of oxygen, but I can't seem to make myself come up for air. I feel dizzy from the temperature of the water I'm submerged in.

Something snakes beneath my arms. I'm jerked upward, catching me off guard. I break the water's surface, my breathing returning immediately. "What the fuck, Lux?"

I place my footing on the bottom and try to pull from his grip, but he doesn't allow me to. Instead, he climbs inside and sits down, pulling me to straddle his lap. "What the fuck are you doing out here? Are you trying to drown, kill yourself? You don't submerge yourself in extreme temperatures!"

"Fuck you. Don't you dare scream at me like a child. I've had a rough day. Anyone almost being raped, losing a parent, moving, and finding out who her biological father is and why her mother was so fucked up, all within forty-eight hours or less, would be overwhelmed. I'm not superwoman. Cut me some fucking slack."

He grabs my face and looks into my eyes, scanning them. His face softens as he exhales. "Do you know what that just felt like? You weren't moving. I've seen and done a lot of things, things that would terrify the average person, but nothing has scared me like that just did. Please don't do that to me again. I wasn't lying to you before. I love you, Lux. You are the only thing aside from my father that has ever given my life value. Don't take away my reason to live."

"I wasn't trying to," I say, letting his words sink in. I'm not sure if I should be more terrified that he just verbally told me he loved me, or that over the course of my life it's the first time that phrase didn't send me into a panic, ready to run. Instead, it changes the rhythm of my heart, my heart rate beating rapidly, causing my chest to hurt, as if my heart is enlarging physically. "I just needed to breathe...and the air wouldn't come."

He pulls my lips to his, kissing me roughly, fear showing through. I let him have his way with me, enduring the pain, allowing chaffing of my lips in the process. He releases me, rubbing his thumb along my lips. "I can't say it back, you know. Don't hold it against me. I can't feel something I don't understand."

"Doesn't matter. It doesn't hold the same meaning if you only say it to hear it in return. It's soon, but I do, Lux. I want you, all of you, the good and the bad, for a very long time. As long as you know that I do, then I don't care if you ever say it back. What triggered this? I want to understand."

"I couldn't sleep, so I got up to get some water. I noticed some things in the living room that couldn't be mine, so my curiosity got the best of me and I opened the box. It was things my mom kept of my life that I didn't even know she had, but then I found this letter. Hold on."

I get off of him to bend over the edge of the Jacuzzi, grabbing the letter from the floor, before resuming my position and giving it to him. "Just read it. I can't read it again. It's better for you to just read it yourself than for me to try to explain."

He shakes the water off of his hand and grabs along the edge that doesn't have ink, careful not to wet it and risk smearing the words. I wait, impatiently, as his eyes scan left to right. It's really hard to breathe normally right now. He finally folds it back up and reaches over the edge to toss it on the steps, before returning his hand to my face. I lean into it, allowing the roughness to brush against my skin. He doesn't say anything. He just keeps staring at me. "What's on your mind?"

I can see the muscle in his jaw contracting. I'm not sure what's about to come out of his mouth. You never really can tell with him. "That it's almost scary how similar our pasts are. I, too, was the result of an extra marital affair. My mother was also a shitty mother as a result, leaving me to fend for myself for the first eight years of my life while she drank herself into comas, went to bed with a different man often, and lived holding on to something she couldn't have. I lived those eight years with a lie, thinking my father didn't want me, until he came back for me at eight after my sister was murdered. When I left I never heard from my mother again, until I looked her up just recently and paid her a visit, when I went to New York. The only difference in our stories was that I was given a better life along the way, while yours got worse...until now. I'm going to be the one to change your story, Lux. Your mom was right about something. You do deserve for someone to love you, and only you. There is no better way to remember her than to give her the last request she ever made, possibly the only selfless one. The only thing that keeps me from hating my mother is that she let me walk out that door and never interfered, giving me something better than she could give."

I'm not sure whether to laugh or cry at the fucking irony here. You know, it's understandable why kids go off the fucking deep end, ending their lives or committing heinous crimes in an attempt to gain attention, and love. There is no one standing behind them to help them up when they fall, to discipline them when they do wrong, or to love them through it all, leaving them even more fucked up as adults. I just feel that there is something I have to do, for myself and for her. "I want to go see him," I blurt out.

"Hell no."

"Kaston, this isn't your choice."

"As my job to protect you and as your boyfriend I should have a say. No."

"I'm going. You can drive me there and sit in the car or I can go alone, but either way I'm going, whether you like it or not."

"Dammit, Lux. Why? Why do you want to put yourself in a position to get hurt, emotionally or physically? I'm asking you to just be content with the one that loves you; the one that's in front of you."

"I have nothing else to lose. What's it matter?"

"Yeah you do. Me." My mouth falls. "Do you remember that fear I explained several minutes ago? Well, that fear is very real. Don't fucking be careless with your life, and in turn my life."

I'm not sure I can make him understand, but I'm going to try, because something about that phrase leaves a physical pain in my chest. "If you ever want me, *all of me,* then I need to do this. This is the only way I can let everything go. I don't want any regrets, or anything left unanswered to kindle in my head like my mother, breaking her in the process. Don't try to control me, just let me go."

His head falls back. "You are the single most frustrating woman I have ever met in my life." He looks back at me and grabs ahold of my hips. "Fine, if you must, but I'm driving you there and back. I'll even wait in the truck for you to do your thing, but you have thirty minutes alone and if you aren't back in my fucking truck I'm coming in there to get you and all of Hell will break loose. Don't think I won't fucking time it down to the second. Try to fucking argue with me. I know how long it takes to commit a crime. You aren't about to become the victim. I will kill for you. I will rot in a fucking prison cell or take the needle before someone takes you from me. Period."

He has barely paused long enough to breathe between sentences. I know he's upset, because he just dropped the word fuck almost once in every sentence, just like me. We are so much alike it really is scary. I stand and slide my panties down my legs, removing them, and then grab the waistband of his briefs. "Holy shit, stop talking. I can't take anymore. You're hot when you're all wound up and upset; acting like a fucking caveman. Use that energy to *show* me how much you need me instead of *telling* me. I want you to."

His demeanor remains serious as he stares at me, his eyes narrowing slightly. He lifts his butt off the bench so that I can pull his briefs down. I stand on my knees straddled over him, giving me a height advantage over him. His hands go to my ass at the same time mine go behind his neck. "My turn to kiss you like I'm dying."

My lips crash against his, only a moment before desperately seeking his tongue, his taste. One of his hands drops from my ass. I start to lower myself to his lap and the head of his dick meets me halfway, pressing against my entrance. "You're hard for me," I mumble against his lips as I sit down on his dick, his hand leaving the base of his cock as I intake all of him.

"Aren't I always," he questions, as he thrusts upward, deepening himself inside of me. Our mouths part against each other, our tongues snaking together, both moaning from the way we feel. The stresses of the day start to slip away, and I let them, because he's right. He's always hard for me and I'm always wet for him, no matter how many times we've done this. Instead of me tiring of him I'm quickly realizing that I only want him more, and I hope that doesn't change.

CHAPTER TWENTY-FIVE

Lux

Kaston pulls into the first available parking spot of the parking garage. I have no idea what I'm supposed to expect or even say. I'm going with gut on this one. I have no idea if he's even here. I didn't call ahead. I didn't want to. Kaston shifts into park as I grab my purse. I place the straps of my purse on my shoulder and reach for the door handle. He grabs my hand, tugging my arm toward him. I look back as I pull the handle, about to push the door open. "I meant what I said. Thirty minutes, Lux. That's the limit. One second over and I'm coming into that fucking brokerage company with guns blazing. Do you hear me?"

I pull my bottom lip into my mouth, shaking my head. "Whatever you say, Killer."

He leans over the center console and grabs my chin between his thumb and index finger, then exerts a slight pressure to pull me closer. Our mouths are merely a centimeter apart. "You really have no fucking idea the things I'm capable of, especially over family. What you saw in the alley that night was nothing; a quick and easy kill. I can be ruthless with one trigger. I'm warning you. Do not test me by being intentionally late unless you're prepared for someone to possibly get hurt."

I close my eyes and swallow; my mouth feeling like it's been scrubbed with cotton. It should scare the hell out of me that I get turned on when he talks like that. His lips press against mine. My eyes open when they leave moments later. "Tell me you understand, beautiful, because the second you walk into that building and I can no longer see you the clock starts ticking."

"Okay."

He lets go of me and I push the door open, stepping out of the truck and shutting the door behind me. I walk as fast as my legs will move, checking the time on my phone as I pull the door open and step inside. It's a corridor of elevators lined against each wall to my side, the back a dead end. I press a button and wait for the doors to open. When it does there is a button for the main tower floor, so I press it.

I step off on the first floor, immediately hearing the sounds of people talking, phones ringing, and sounds that confirm I've stepped into a corporate world. I look around, suddenly a little intimated. There is a sign that points in the direction of the tower elevator. I pull the envelope from my purse to confirm the suite number, even though I'm almost positive it's engrained in my memory now. *Suite 6A.* Just as I thought.

A few turns and I'm standing at more elevators, pressing another button as if I'm stuck on repeat. Who in the hell would want to work at a place like this? I wonder if Kaston does. He did say he has a day job, yet I have barely heard anything about it. When I think of a PI firm I just envision a small building in a sketchy part of town, with a creeper mustache guy holding a camera out of a car window, trying to bust someone for an episode of *Cheaters*. Maybe I should ask more questions, because I would have never in a million years pictured someone that looks like him.

The doors open and I step inside, along with several other people behind me. I reach over and hit the button labeled with a 6, and move to the corner to make room. I glance around at all the suits and pencil skirts, suddenly feeling out of place in my black jumpsuit and heels. The car has to stop on every damn floor, making me wish I had just found a set of stairs. Enclosed spaces with strangers put me on edge.

I watch the lights above the doors, waiting for it to finally hit 6. When it does I maneuver through the bodies until I can finally break free, entering the sixth floor, immediately greeted by a long counter and the name of the company hung on the wall behind it. The receptionist is beautiful, Asian, maybe thirty tops, and her long black hair is pulled into a low bun, her makeup light but perfect. She's wearing just enough jewelry to accentuate her skin tone. I walk toward the counter and look over at her sitting in the chair at the computer screen. Typical receptionist: crisp white button-down shirt tucked in a black pencil skirt. She probably even has the immaculate designer shoes that make the entire outfit.

She has yet to even look up at me, wearing a Bluetooth earpiece that she keeps speaking the same greeting into, because the phone has already rang like four times since I've stepped up to this counter. "Please hold," she says and finally acknowledges that I'm standing here. "Can I help you?"

"I'm here to see Charles Williams III."

At the sound of his name she goes blank, staring at me as if she's suddenly forgotten her job. "I'm sorry. Do you have an appointment?"

"No. He's not expecting me."

She blinks a few times, still staring at me. "I apologize, but Mr. Williams requires all meetings to be scheduled." She pauses, staring at my face, before clearing her throat. "Are you a relative?"

"Something like that."

She stands, adjusting her shirt and then rubs her hands down the side of her skirt. "Of course. Excuse me. You can wait here. Let me see if he's available."

She walks down a hallway, leaving me at the counter alone. I place my hands on top, bending forward to glance in the direction she just left. She is standing in front of a closed door with her hand raised about to knock, but in a pause, as if she's afraid to. Damn, is he that big of an asshole?

She finally knocks, entering almost immediately after, the door shutting behind her. I pull my cellphone from my purse again, just enough to see the screen. I press the lock button to light up the screen, confirming the time. Fuck. It's going faster than I thought. I quickly pull it out and text Kaston.

Me: Hey, I'm at the reception desk waiting to see if he will see me obviously. Don't flip your shit, but we may need to re-evaluate this time frame.

I press send, waiting for an answer. One comes back almost immediately. "Damn, what are you doing, staring at your phone?" My voice is a whisper, feeling as if I need to be quiet.

Kaston: Thirty minutes was the agreement...

Me: I cannot control that shit.

Kaston: Better make it quick then.

Me: Asshole…

"He will see you now," she says, catching me off guard. Her face is stiffer than it was before she left. I toss my phone in my purse as it vibrates and follow her down the same hallway she did before.

She opens the door and steps out of the way, letting me enter. "Thanks," I say and walk in the large office. She closes the door behind me, leaving me in here alone. I glance around the fully furnished room, stocked with bookshelves and a game of put put golf close to the desk. The leather, executive style chair is turned toward the back wall, away from me. "Victoria said you're here to see me. What is it that I can do for you?"

The chair turns, revealing the man that the deep voice belongs to. His hair is dark but peppered with strands of gray showing his age. He has to be in his late fifties or right at sixty. I walk toward him to get a better view. "I came to deliver something to you."

"And you are?"

When I get within a close distance I get a better view of his face, catching me off guard. If I had to guess our faces are a direct reflection of each other right now, because everything Mom has ever said I now understand completely, even with him much older. I quickly recover from my surprise and hold out my hand. He looks at it and an arrogant grin spreads on his face. "Lux Larsen, Katherine's daughter."

At the mention of her name his smirk disappears and his eyes widen. He places his fists on his desk and stands, still looking at me. I drop my hand. We stand here, staring at each other. "Katherine Larsen," he whispers, as if he's just heard the name of a ghost. "How old are you?"

"Twenty-five."

His eyes zone out as if he's doing the math. "Who's your father?"

"Apparently you are, *Chuck*."

He walks over to the window and braces one hand on the frame, sliding the other in the pocket of his trousers. I look down at the picture frames on his desk, revealing a family. I notice a woman, assuming his wife, and two other kids, two boys, both fully grown. "Come here."

"Why?"

"I want to look at you."

I walk toward the window into the sunlight, standing before him. He looks at me again. "Fuck. I have a family. Did she set you up for this? This is about money, isn't it? Why after this long? Where is she?"

I slap him without thinking. "How dare you insult her? She never so much as breathed a syllable of your name to me. I didn't know your name from a stranger on the street until I found this in her things." I reach in my purse and grab the envelope with the letter, shoving it into his chest. "She just fucking died, you asshole. She obviously didn't have enough guts to give this to you, so I thought I would deliver it personally."

He grabs the letter and opens it, saying nothing more. I wait, watching him read it in its entirety. Upon finishing he clenches his hand into a fist around the letter, crinkling half of it. "Katherine wrote this?"

"No, I made that shit up. What the fuck do you think?"

"Damn...you're more like me than my sons. You really are mine, aren't you? Shit. I can't believe this, any of it. Do you realize what she's accusing me of? I've never fucking raped her. Is that what she thought?"

"You expect me to just believe you? I'm the one that lived with her for eighteen years. I just met you. She didn't get that fucked up over nothing."

He grabs ahold of my arm and leads me toward his desk. I sit in the chair as he props his body against his desk, and then lowers his voice.

"You don't go public with this shit, got it? I don't fucking owe anyone an explanation in regards to my personal affairs, but I'm not going to sit by and let someone that ran away like a coward instead of telling me I had a child on the way destroy everything I've spent years building. Something like this being leaked to the media could ruin me, especially as much as you look like me. It's scary to be honest. You want to know what happened? I remember that day, and I did nothing any different with her than I did any other day, but I had just lost out on a multimillion-dollar merger that almost cost me my job. I was stressed and she left at lunch without letting me know. I needed her. She was my assistant, and yes, my very private girlfriend. It was never supposed to get to that, but when you spend more time with someone at work than at home things happen, especially with a woman like Katherine. I cared about her. Plus, I had been drinking. She came in here and she seemed upset, mumbling things about leaving and starting over, but she had also done something similar when I refused to leave my wife to be with her publicly, and then I took her on a business trip with me for a few days and she was back to being my Katherine, even with all of the complications of our relationship. I'm a businessman, and with that comes a reputation. I can't trample around acting like a college frat boy. She said no all the time in this very office; worried someone would walk in. It never really meant no. She never raised her voice, never pushed me off, and never did anything to differentiate that time from all the previous ones. If she was serious and that affected her life, then I'm sincerely sorry, but I really had no idea. She should have come to me years ago."

I stand, suddenly more confused than when I walked in here. Maybe I shouldn't have come. It's solved nothing, pretty much just like Kaston said, and only making her look worse. No matter what she's still my mother. It's her words against his. I'll never really know what happened. It doesn't even matter. I don't know what I thought I would accomplish by getting a look at the man that helped create me; maybe to appease my anger, my guilt, or to help me hate him so that I could understand her behavior all those years. Instead, it's just frustrated me more.

Kaston was right yet again. I should just be content with what I do have instead of looking for what I don't.

"Lux. Where are you going?"

I stop halfway across the room and turn toward him. "You have a life. I shouldn't have come. It was a foolish mistake on my part. I'm grown. I just wanted to understand the woman she's been all of my life, and I thought I finally had."

The sound of the door opening interrupts me. "Dad, are you ready to go over the quarterly numbers?" I look at the man standing in the doorway, maybe a year younger tops. "I'm sorry. Am I interrupting something? I thought your schedule was clear for the afternoon." He walks over to me and holds out his hand. "I'm Dylan," he says, looking between his father and me. His eyebrows dip as if he's confused. "And you are?"

I look back at the man responsible for my birth, the single act that led to my hell for twenty-five years. I'm not giving the people that don't deserve it another day, because dammit I deserve happiness in some form too. "Not someone that matters, Dylan. I'm just visiting an old friend of my mother's." I pause. "It's ironic how two people here by the same coincidence can end up with such very different lives. I'm sorry to have intruded on your schedule. Goodbye, Mr. Williams." I turn. "Goodbye, Dylan."

I walk out with one thing on my mind, and that's getting the fuck out of here. I need a damn leave from an emergency leave. I may stay at the beach longer than I had originally planned.

The walk back to the parking garage is a blur. I never even checked my phone. I open the door and get in the truck, waiting for Kaston to take us away from here. "How'd it go?"

I look at him. "I think I'll let you take me on that date now."

He looks a little taken back at my response. "Where to?"

"Shooting range. The way I feel right now can only be released one way, and that's pulling a trigger. For that I need bullets and a gun. You in or you out?"

"I'm always in when it comes to you." He reaches over and kisses my lips, not asking any more questions about what happened, at least not for now. I'm sure it's coming, and I'll have to explain. I want to, because I actually want to tell him everything. He's now my best friend. I don't want to admit it yet, not even to myself, but I believe I'm going to lose this battle. Love is trying to recruit me. My heart is slipping away from me, no matter how tight of a grip I have on it.

Kaston

I walk up beside her and lay the pistol and full magazine down on the wood counter in front of us, my ear protection hanging around my neck. I look at her, staring off down the range at the target, as if she's calculating. There is something about a woman that knows her way around a gun that's sexy. It's one thing that hooked me with her, that night in the alley. Who would have ever thought you could get a hard-on with a gun pointed at your head?

She's still contemplating. I want so bad to ask her what happened up there, but I don't think it's time. I was seconds away from getting out of that truck and going up there to show my ass. "Do you ever wonder why some kids have it so shitty and some never have to deal with anything bad at all?"

She never looks at me, only keeps staring straight ahead. I turn my back toward the range and prop my hands on the wood, before looking over at her. "I have in the past. Why do you ask?"

"Just wondering if I'm ever going to get a fucking break; to be one of the lucky ones."

She places her ear protection over her ears and then picks up the pistol and magazine, before slamming the magazine into place. "Firing," she calls out as she racks the slide back, bringing a bullet into the chamber. I slide the muffs up the back of my neck, pulling them into place over my ears as she aims at the target, both hands gripped around the handle, and then starts to unload the magazine without a break. When it's empty she releases the magazine and lays the gun back down on its side, alongside the empty magazine, and then pulls her ear protection down to hang around her neck. "I feel a little better."

I match her motions and then grab her hand and pull her toward me. "No, beautiful. Why feel better when you can feel phenomenal?"

I turn us around, aligning her back to my front, and remain behind her, but facing my target. "Anyone can learn to shoot a gun, and you may even be good at it, but don't empty a full magazine on one person. It only takes one bullet. Aim for the kill shot."

I place my arms around her and lean closer to her ear, before grabbing the gun off the wood. "If you need to use a gun, it's probably because someone is trying to harm you; its intended purpose. Your adrenaline will be pumping and you won't be able to think properly, leaving more room to make mistakes. That's why it has to become an instinct, nothing more, nothing less. Let's pretend, because had Chevy not been there things could have turned out very different."

I slam the magazine in place, causing her to flinch, before placing it in the palm of her hand. "Grip it like you would my cock: firm, but gentle."

"Really," she asks sarcastically. "You're going to compare it to your cock? And this is supposed to relax me?"

"Well, in some ways they are both similar. If you don't know how to use it, it can be deadly. Both can go off prematurely if the user gets trigger-happy. Know what you're getting upfront to avoid permanent consequences that can't be reversed. Bottom line: respect it and it will respect you."

She turns her head to look at me, and starts laughing, hard, leaving me with a cocky grin on my face. "What the fuck is wrong with you," she asks between laughs, trying to catch her breath, her arms resting on the wood in front of her from being bent forward. "I will forever be scarred after that. Holy shit. Stop giving me mental associations of your cock with normal, everyday things. I think about it enough as it is. You're turning me into a nymphomaniac."

"But it worked, did it not? You're totally relaxed and thinking about my cock. I have you exactly where I want you."

She slams her ass against my crotch, no doubt aiming for my dick. "Men aren't the only ones with weapons of mass destruction, you know. No gun can be operated without an owner. Keep that in mind, killer."

I grab her chin in my hand, turning it toward me further. "I'm well aware that your pussy owns my cock. Would you like me to prove it in front of an audience?"

Her eyes veer to the security camera hanging from the overhang behind us. "Uh, no. I'm all for public fucking with the risk of being caught, but voyeurism is crossing the line."

"Then I suggest you keep that in mind, because my cock doesn't understand rules or morality. Your pussy comes within reaching distance and it's going in. That's just what comes with ownership." I kiss her and then release her. "Like I said before, grip it like my cock. You have one chance with one bullet to take him out. Understood?"

"Fine, bossy. You seriously act like I've never done this before."

"I'm sure that you have, but I'm about to teach you the best way. Always be open to learning better ways than you already know, because there is always someone else with better understanding and experience for the skill at hand. That's the ultimate way to become the best."

She grips the handle in one hand, aiming it toward the target, and then looks back at me. "Is this better?"

I grab her free hand and place it on the other side of the handle, mirroring her right, then align my body to the back of hers. I run my hands down the length of her arms, steadying her stance, and then down her body, before placing them on her hips. Her body slightly shivers when my lips come closer to her ear. "Holding it in both keeps it steadier. Pay attention to your surroundings like wind and distance since the bullet has to travel. When you aim, sight it in and then exhale to relax yourself before pulling the trigger. Instant kill shot is head or heart. Anything else is torment, making him bleed out. Avoid it. Make it quick and clean. You ready?"

"Only if you show me what you do to take your mind off of what you're about to do. I want to understand how you deal with it mentally."

"You sure?"

"Absofuckinglutely. I want to know you like you want to know me. I want to understand."

"Okay. Shut down everything else in your mind. Your target is a live body standing in the location you've deemed appropriate for the hit. We've been watching him for weeks now. We know his schedule, his favorite places, his hunting grounds. You've studied his file like you've studied for a final. You know everything he's done prior to taking his life, because you cannot make a mistake. He's useless to society. He's an endangerment to people. He's worth more dead than alive."

"I'm listening."

"This one is a sexual predator. He has a public record, but he's gotten smarter since he got caught. He's been marked. The client came in because her twelve-year-old son was a victim. The family didn't think to check the public database online when they hired him to privately coach their son for baseball, because most people don't think of sex offenders being normal people. He was a local, a residential neighbor, and he was at every ballgame. He also molested and committed sexual battery with her son one afternoon at practice, forever changing him. He quit baseball to avoid going back. He never opened his mouth, clearly ashamed and scared, carrying around that dirty laundry for months. One day it got to be too much and he put his father's .38 in his mouth and pulled the trigger. No one had any idea it had even happened until they read the suicide note. That family will now have to live their entire life without him: his sister without a brother, his father and mother without a son, and his grandparents without a grandchild. Now, when they want to go see him they have to make a special trip to the cemetery."

She starts to lower the gun. "Don't fucking move."

"Kaston, that's sick."

"It's also life, Lux. Ugly things happen in the world we live in. That was an actual case my dad had when I was in high school. The world is full of sick fucks. Some survive the madness, some eliminate themselves, and some have it taken from them. This is how I live with it. That was the same way my father lived with it. He taught me most, and some I've learned along the way from others, as well as from training of my own, but I've always been expected to respect human life. A hundred kids that don't have to live with an unwanted touch are more valuable than some piece of shit that deserves to burn in Hell. Before I turned to the dark side not all that long ago, I was a detective, hoping one day to work for the FBI or the CIA. No matter how, I wanted to put the bad people away. It's the one thing I've been passionate about all my life. It's the only thing that makes me feel like life is worth living...at least until I met you. I still find myself wanting to take away all of your pain. I got a second chance at having a normal childhood, but some don't. My father kept that part of his life separate until I was a senior about to graduate high school, and only then because I was moving back to the states for college. He wanted me to understand things in case something happened to him while we were miles apart. I had a good childhood, Lux. I got to be a normal kid, so now when you look at your target, knowing what he's done and what he's capable of still doing, what do you do?"

She stands silent for a moment. I place her muffs back over her ears and then quickly do the same with mine. The shot fires once and she places the gun back down. I look at the target closely to see where she shot: between the eyes, dead center. She turns around, a tear stain present on both cheeks. "A mind like that needs to be destroyed. I get it now, Kaston. I want you to promise me you'll never change who you are inside, because you really are a rare find."

I kiss her lips, slightly puckered still. "So are you. Let's go home. I have a DVD collection that needs some attention."

CHAPTER TWENTY-SIX

Lux

It's been a little over a week since I left Mom's side on that table. It's been an adjustment even though we weren't close. I guess when you're so used to being someone's crutch the freedom is a little frightening. As strange as it sounds, I miss her. I wish I didn't, but I do. No matter what she's done to me she's still my mother; someone I lived with my entire childhood. She always has been and always will be, no matter how good or bad she was at the part. At least I've never felt like an orphan before now.

I've been back to work now for a few days. It's not as exciting as it once was, but it's good to be back to some form of normalcy. Maybe I should look into a different career. I don't know. I just feel like I'm wasting my life away if I spend it being a server forever. Surely my life is worth more than this. Since I met Kaston and now that Mom has died, it's making me want to do more with myself. I don't want to wither away like my mother. She could have been so much more than she allowed herself to be. I'm just not sure what.

"You ready to do this?"

I look over at Kaston, sitting in the driver's side looking at me. He looks handsome like that, dressed out in a white button-down and a pair of khakis. If it didn't make me feel so crazy I'd take a photo. It wouldn't really matter, though, because I already feel crazy enough. I'm overwhelmed with emotions I thought I'd never feel. I really didn't think I would remember this place, but I do more so than I'd like. "I guess I have no choice. It's time to lay her to rest."

He gets out and rounds the truck, before opening my door and helping me out. "You look beautiful, but aren't we dressed in the wrong color to be doing this? I thought black was more of a death color..."

"Not when death sets someone free.... Think of a dove. She's been fighting a losing battle since I was a kid. Drugs had a grip on her that I'll never understand. They made her lie, connive, steal, and whore herself out for nothing. Chasing that high made her forget her morals, her values, and her responsibilities. It made her a horrible mom. As much as I will miss her because she was my mother, this is what broke the chains. Death is what brought her peace and turned her soul free, so white just seemed appropriate."

"Fair enough..."

As my feet hit the pavement, I remove my flip-flops and toss them in the truck, before grabbing the canister and letting him shut the door. He pulls me against him and kisses me. "People are going to think we're getting married on the beach with you wearing that white dress. I'm not going to lie since I'm getting a taste, but you'd make a beautiful bride."

He traces his finger down the braided rope that is tied behind my neck and runs over my chest, before it meets in the middle at the center of the fabric. It's the only thing keeping this dress from being a strapless. The dress is only fitted around the bust and then flows out to my ankles. I had my hair done in a low, messy side-bun with a braid that runs along my hairline toward the back. "This is the softest I've ever seen you. I like it. That's putting it mildly, when really you look stunning. I can't take my eyes off of you."

People probably wouldn't understand my need to look like this when doing what I'm about to do, but then those same people probably had a happy childhood full of Barbies and sunshine. I wasn't one of those people. This place is the happiest memory I have with my mother, so this is where I'm going to lay her to rest, and I sure as hell am not going to do it dressed in black; a depressing color. "She deserves to go out in style. She deserves to be forgiven before she goes. Today, I'm letting it all go."

I start to walk toward the boardwalk, heading for the beach. "Wait," he says, before removing his flip-flops to match me and throws them in the passenger side. He runs toward me and grabs my hand, lacing it in mine.

I look down at the two connected, the very intimate act he's creating for the public to see. He's showing the world that I'm his. The line between what I thought I wanted and what I really want is becoming blurred. He's pushing me in the direction he wants me to go, and I can't deny that I like it, even though it's nowhere close to being slow.

My eyes search for his. He's already looking at me when they find them. "I'm by your side the entire time. If you fall I will catch you. You don't always have to be strong, Lux. I'm your *best friend*. If you can't break with me, then you can't with anyone."

I instantly relax into him. He knows when to push me, and when to step back. That's one thing I've found that I love about him. He's the perfect balance. He's the best shade. He's exactly right...for me.

I tighten my hand around his, responding without words, and then walk forward, toward the drop to the sand. We descend the wooden steps, and then step into the white sand, letting the granules squish between our toes. It's hot to the touch, the result of a hot southern summer. My pace quickens when I take in the surroundings. I haven't been here since that day. I always avoided it when older so that the memory was more alive, and not replaced by new ones. We pass small mounds of sand and tall grass, blowing back and forth when the breeze breaks through.

The texture of the sand changes as we reach the shoreline. The separate dry granules become wet, more of a solid form, ready to make an impression upon stepping in it. I look out at the water, letting the image imprint into my mind. Kaston moves behind me, wrapping his arms around my waist and pulling my body against his. It comforts me, something I've never had until him. I've always pretty much been on my own, but with him I don't have to be.

"Go ahead, baby. I got you."

"I believe you."

I take a deep breath, preparing for what I have to say. It's time to let go...

I clear my throat, holding the canister out in front of me. "Hey, Mom. I know you're listening in spirit. You know I was never good at this sort of thing, so I'm probably going to suck at it. I guess I'm like you in that way. Anyway, I know I was an ass to you, probably more than I should have been. I feel like shit about that now, but I guess we both did things to each other that were so far past okay it's almost unbelievable. No matter what I've ever said, I want you to know that I loved you, and I still do, regardless of what you've done to me. You'll always be my mother."

I turn back to glance at Kaston, feeling slightly awkward about doing this in front of him. He gives me a small smile, pushing me forward. I look back at the water, trying my best to pretend he's not here. I hate feeling like an open book. I prefer to keep parts of myself for only me, but he's really good at changing my mind. "Okay, so I just wanted to let you know that I forgive you. I'm letting go every bad memory, every grudge I've been holding, and from this day forward I'll try to only remember you for the few good times. For what it's worth I wish you would have found a way to let it go, because watching the drugs and alcohol control your life was far harder than the things I had to endure hoping it would help you escape them."

I take a deep breath, trying to hold the tears back. As much as they're trying to break through, I'm fighting them, because I want this to be a good day; that and I feel like I've cried enough to last a lifetime. Sometimes I think it would be easier to go back to the emotionally numb person that I was before Kaston started breaking down my walls. I haven't felt things in so long. This is how I'm letting go... "I remember my seventh birthday like it was yesterday. You came home in a good mood because you had made a little money selling a few things. You brought me home a new dress and asked what I wanted to do for my birthday."

I laugh aloud, thinking back on it.

"It seems silly now, but I remember telling you I wanted to be a princess for a night. I wanted to dance beneath the pretty lights with a prince just like Cinderella did. You looked at me funny at first, as if you were stumped. You didn't think I noticed but I did. I started to change my request to something else, but then you lit up and said if that was what I wanted for my birthday then that was what I was going to get. After all, we did already have a new dress for the occasion…"

Oh fuck it. I'm going to let myself cry.

"My birthday rolled around that Friday. I had half forgotten about it, because I figured you would have been back your old self by that point, considering several days had passed, but I was wrong. You took me to Ella's place at *The Watering Hole,* after helping me put on my new dress and even a little makeup for the event. When we walked in the whole place was empty, with only a few people that we knew. I'm actually surprised that Ella closed down on one of the busiest nights for a few hours just for me. She had the lights dimmed with the party lights turned on. Ella's gift couldn't have been more perfect. I got my own pair of glass slippers, custom made blue frosted plastic with Cinderella on the top, most likely from Wal-Mart, but to me they were perfect."

It's getting hard to breathe, but I can't stop. I need her to know that I remember.

"You had even gotten me a cake. It was sitting at the bar. Most kids wouldn't have been anywhere close to a bar at the age of seven, but I still give you an A for effort. It was round and baby blue. I'm pretty sure it was your attempt at a box cake mix, but it was beautiful, complete with flaky sprinkles you said was fairy dust since my fairy godmother couldn't be present. She was on vacation, you said." A laugh escapes again. "The shit you would come up with to make it so real…"

My knees weaken, but the arms wrapped around me keep me from falling, just as he said he would. "You wouldn't let me have candles, because you said that if I just made my wish that it would come true; no amount of fire would change that, because my fairy godmother was listening. Looking back now, you were probably scared to set off any alarms that would attract cops or firemen, but it just fit with the theme I guess. I remember Derek walked out of the back all dressed out in a tux, the weekend bartender at the time. I don't even know how you knew I had the biggest crush on him, but somehow you did. My eyes lit up when he walked up to me and asked me to dance. I was so nervous all I could do was nod and slide off of my stool. When I took his hand and looked at you, you were over by the DJ booth looking for music. You ended up playing that song, *The way you look tonight,* but it was the remake done by Michael Buble, so it wasn't so far outside of my time. When we started dancing in the middle of the dance floor, you had the biggest shit-eating grin on your face. You knew how happy I was. I remember staring at the floor, trying my damnedest not to step on his feet. To this day that birthday still tops them all, because it was one of the few times I remember you smiling. It was also the night you told me as you tucked me in to never settle for anything less than a prince, because I deserved to be treated like a princess forever. You made me promise to never end up like you, because somewhere you got lost and couldn't find yourself. I didn't understand what you meant then, but I think I do now. I just want you to know that you don't have to worry about that. It may take me a while to let him love me, but he's a patient man. I'll make sure I always remember those times, Mom. You'll never be forgotten."

I remove the lid from the canister, and as if it was staged to hit at the perfect time, the breeze picks up, blowing the bottom of my dress in the wind. "Rest in peace, Mom. I know you'll be happy here."

I turn the canister over slowly, letting the ashes pour into the wind a little at a time until it's empty, watching them as they catch a ride with the air, traveling to wherever they're going to be taken.

When they disappear from sight I break down, no longer able to hold myself together. I can't explain it, but it's as if all the strength I've ever had has dissolved from my body. I feel like dead weight in his arms.

I start wheezing, unable to catch my breath as the tears fall freely down my face. My clothes feel like they're strangling me. My hands immediately go for the back of my neck, trying desperately to undo the straps. My chest is heaving and noises of me trying to catch my breath start sounding from my mouth. My eyesight is starting to go black and I feel dizzy.

I start to panic more when I can't get the straps undone. One of his arms disappears from around me and I fall to my knees in the sand. A cold blade touches the back of my neck, before the sound of fabric being severed sounds and the straps fall, now separated. I begin clawing at my skin. The air refuses to come.

My world starts to fade in and out. It takes a few seconds before I realize I'm cradled in Kaston's arms, being carried into the ocean. Water encompasses us, drenching our bodies. I stretch my body atop the water, trying to get air, but I feel like my airway is the size of a pinhole, only letting enough airflow through to keep me alive. Something soft touches my lips, and suddenly air enters my lungs, calming me. As if I just remembered how to breathe, I suddenly can. His mouth parts from mine, but I grab the back of his neck and pull him back to me, kissing him with everything that I am as he holds me in the water, not letting go. "Promise. You. Won't. Leave. Me." I say each word in a pause between kissing him.

I pull myself upright, wrapping my legs around him as best as I can with this dress in the way. I look into his eyes, feeling half crazy, until he speaks. "I don't think that I can."

My chest physically hurts; so much so that the idea of a heart attack crosses my mind. I still feel dizzy, probably from the lack of oxygen for a few minutes. "Don't quote me, but I think I might be falling in love with you too."

"Fuck," he says, and grabs the back of my neck, pulling me toward him. "That felt better than I thought it would," he whispers against my lips, and then crushes his lips to mine, holding my body against his as we make out like we're dying in the middle of the ocean.

Nothing else matters right now than the epiphany I just had. I may actually love someone. The truth is that it scares the hell out of me. I never wanted love because I thought it gave one person a power over the other that could destroy them if taken away, but he's slowly showing me that real love isn't like that. It's a constant commitment to the other person. It's sticking around through fears, joys, and sorrows. It's putting in time, and sacrificing your wants and needs for your partner. It's learning to love together, whether at the same time or months apart. I'm still unsure of a lot of things, but I do know that like him, I don't think I can run from this...

CHAPTER TWENTY-SEVEN

Kayton

I roll over to an empty bed. It instantly pulls me from a half sleep. When Lux wakes up before me it's usually a bad thing. Reaching over the bed I grab my boxer-briefs and throw my legs over the side of the bed, before pulling them on to stand, working them up to my waist.

I check the bathroom, but it's empty. My second thought is that damn Jacuzzi. I jog to the stairs and quickly make my way down. That's when it hits me - the smell of bacon frying and coffee brewing. I slow my pace, lightly stepping across the living room into the kitchen. Music is playing from somewhere, and turned up loud enough that I'm surprised I didn't hear it upstairs. A smile instantly forms on my face when I see her.

I lean against the doorframe and cross my arms over my chest, watching patiently for as long as she doesn't know I'm here. She has hip-hop playing, a strange option for morning. She's wearing one of my V-neck tee shirts, one side hanging off the shoulder, and a pair of panties, or at least I'm assuming. The bottom of the shirt stops just below her ass.

The beat of a new song starts to play, one she obviously likes, because her shoulders start bumping to the bass as she stirs whatever is in the bowl in front of her. As the song progresses it changes from two shoulders in unison with each other to opposite. Then comes the hips, swaying from side to side, hitting each time there is a major change in the beat. When the chorus comes on she belts out the lyrics and her movements become more pronounced, like a sober girl in a club that just started feeling the alcohol, making her braver.

My bottom lip pulls into my mouth as I watch her. She stops stirring and her palms go to her knees, before she starts pumping her ass up and down as if she's fucking the air. My hand instantly finds my dick, grabbing ahold of it through the material of my underwear. *Down boy...* It has a fucking mind of its own. That mental phrase is turning into a pattern.

She stands upright, grabs a spoon from the holder, and places it to her mouth, before singing and dancing to herself, spinning toward me in the process. She freezes when she sees me standing here watching her. She looks at the spoon in her hand and quickly hides it behind her back, then clears her throat. "I was just making breakfast. Are you hungry?"

"Starving."

"Okay, um, can you give me a few minutes? I wasn't expecting you to be up before the food was ready. I went with veggie omelets and bacon." She pauses. "You do eat that right?"

I shake my head.

"Shit. I should have asked first. Ugh, what about pancakes? Do you eat that?"

My lips purse.

"French toast? Sausage? Grits? Dammit, I wanted it to be a surprise. I have some mad cooking skills."

I make my way toward her, not saying a word. I fear if I do I'm going to say something really fucking animalistic and suddenly she's not going to want anything to do with food. Her appetite will dissipate. That is how fucking turned on I am right now. Take a healthy sex-driven man that's gone a month without sex, wakes up with morning wood, and amplify the results with a Viagra on steroids. That is the way my cock feels right now. It hurts. I can feel the veins and the pulse from the blood pumping throughout.

My eyes never move from hers as I round the bar. When I can reach her, I grab the spoon from her hand and toss it behind me, hearing it hit tile a few seconds later. "What I meant was, I'm starving, but not for food."

"Oh," she whispers, as I grab the bottom of her shirt and pull it up her body until it's completely removed.

I drop it on the floor. "But since you mentioned food, I think I'll combine the two." I push her panties down her legs until they fall freely, hitting the floor. My hands take residence on her waist, before lifting her and setting her on the counter.

"What are you about to do?"

"I'm going to sweeten you up a bit."

I reach behind me and open the door to the refrigerator, removing the bottle from when we made ice cream sundaes the other night. I didn't think about it then, but now it fits. Her eyes widen. "Hell no. I've already showered to go see Delta before I have to go to work." I place the cap between my teeth and remove it.

"Kaston..." I inhale through my nose and blow through my mouth, sending the cap sailing a few feet across the room.

"Phillip. Just like my father."

"Kaston Phillip Cox. Smartass. Do not fucking do that. I'm warning you."

"Do what?" I tip the bottle over, letting the chocolate syrup drizzle on her thigh, moving it up her body in a zigzag motion. "This?"

Her mouth falls open. She's watching the line of chocolate as it decorates her body. I don't stop until I get to her collarbones, and then set the bottle back down on the bar. "Seduction at its finest. This is my version of a first class dessert. My mouth is watering already."

"You are a pompous ass. That's cold. I'm going to be sticky and gross. I'm going to have to ta-"

I flatten my tongue against the top of her thigh and trace the streak of chocolate toward her inner thigh. "Ohhhhhh fuuuuuck."

I inwardly smile. I have her right where I fucking want her. Now, she is mine. I swipe back toward the top, lift, and then replace it on her stomach, next to her naval ring, before swiping in a straight line toward her breast, allowing my tongue to trace the rounded shape, stopping over her nipple. I lightly brush my tongue over the hardened center, coating it in the sweet chocolate. Then I suck, hard, tasting it, and feeding the frenzy I've started. "Hell yeah. Harder."

I bite, rolling her nipple between my teeth gently. She arches her back, leaning back on the counter as I run my tongue between her tits, toward her sternum, and down the vertical center of her body until I arrive at the destination between her legs. She moans and pulls her legs up to rest on top of the bar, spreading for me. I spread her lips apart, going straight for the sweet spot, flickering my tongue back and forth.

She screams out, her hand going for my head, but returns when there isn't enough hair to grip. I look up at her from beneath my lashes, watching the perfect curvature of her body as she arches off the counter, her hands clenched around the edge on the opposite side. I suck her into my mouth, watching her hips buck upward, but I hold her down, making her take it. When I feel her start to tense up I know she's about to come, so I replace my tongue with my thumb and thrust my tongue deep into her pussy, letting her coat me as she moans through it. She stops clenching around me and her hips start moving, trying to displace my thumb when she becomes sensitive to the touch. I pull out and swallow. "Sweet and salty, baby. You taste good."

I grab her thighs and pull her off the bar, before turning her around and bending her over it. "You're about to paint it with your tits, beautiful."

I grab the shaft of my dick in one hand and grip the lower side of her ass cheek in the other, spreading her. I align the head of my cock at her pussy and thrust forward, moving my hands to her hips for leverage to make it harder, shoving her forward. "Oh, damn. I love when you fuck me hard. Hurt me."

I run one hand up her back and cup my hand on her shoulder. "As you wish, beautiful." I pull out and thrust back in, pulling on her shoulder to hold her in place as I ram my cock inside of her, rolling my hips to push deeper. She pushes up on her tiptoes, dodging. I lift her hip a little. "Squeeze my fucking dick."

I quicken the pace, giving myself more momentum each time I pull out, leaving only the head inside, before driving my cock back inside. "I can feel you in my fucking stomach. It hurts, but it feels so good."

She pushes her ass into me, arching her back to raise her ass higher. "Right there. Oh fuck yes. Don't stop. Make me come again. I want you to come with me. I'm so close."

"You want me to unload inside of you, baby?"

"Yes. Fuck yes."

She gets wetter, clamping tighter. I feel like I'm about to explode. My nuts are so tight I can't stand it. I pull out one last time and grab both hips in my hands, before pushing inside as far as I can go and still, then grind her ass up and down against me as I bust my load deep inside of her. The head of my dick starts to tickle and I pull out.

She stands and turns around, her body smeared completely in chocolate. I grab her neck and pull her against me for a kiss, smearing myself as well. "What about breakfast? I can't finish cooking like this and the bacon is probably now burnt."

I reach behind me and turn off the eye. "Fuck breakfast. I'm full. A shower sounds better."

I slap her ass and grab her hand, pulling her behind me. Cleanup can be just as fun as getting dirty...

Lux

I fasten the towel around my wet body and sit on the edge of the bed. I comb my fingers though my wet hair, before crossing my legs. Kaston walks out of the closet fully dressed in a suit, fastening the cuffs of his sleeve. My eyes widen as they feast on the glorious sight before me. "Can you take me to work, bend me over your desk, and drop those pants just low enough to hit your thighs while you fuck me senseless. K, Thanks."

His lips remain closed, but the curve it's forming is giving him away. He's trying his damnedest not to laugh. The funny thing is I'm not joking. Holy fucking shit that is one hot cup of manliness. Why have I missed this look? Have I seriously been under a rock? Oh, that's right, stalker boy has basically taken us hostage from all normal aspects of life, one being WORK! He says nothing, just keeps fastening things like cuffs, watches, and buttons, inserting a wallet inside of a pocket. "Still not convinced? I could hide under your desk and give you a blow job while you work and meet with clients, you know, see if you can keep a straight face while I suck your dick. You up for the challenge?"

"You want to come to work with me so you can seduce me?"

I stand and walk toward him, dropping my towel along the way. He grunts as his eyes rake down my body. "I want to play your naughty little secretary. I want to fake a forbidden affair." I grab his dick through his suit pants, holding it in my hand against his leg. "And judging from how hard you are I would say you do too."

He grips my hair in his fist and pulls, tilting my head toward him. He kisses me roughly, his new growth of stubble rubbing against my upper lip. "Fucking hell, woman. You know how much I love that mouth. I will never tire of looking at that beautiful body, but I have a meeting with a potential client today. You can come with me and go shopping to buy girl things for Paris if you want before work tonight. Get dressed. You have forty-five minutes. I'll be downstairs."

He turns for the door, but stops as he places his hand around the doorknob. "Oh by the way, you had me at *can you take me to work*. I've told you before I'll never deny you anything. I meant it."

He opens the door and exits, leaving me alone in this huge room. What the fuck just happened? He barely even touched me, yet I feel like I've injected myself with caffeine. That vision I quoted earlier starts playing through my mind. I take off for the closet. There is only one thought programmed in my mind right now: easy access.

We pull into the building that looks way too familiar. I look at Kaston as he pulls into a parking space along the wall of the parking garage. "You didn't tell me your office was in the same building as my sperm donor."

"It wasn't relevant at the time," he says and kills the engine, immediately opening the door and stepping out.

I do the same, before shutting the door and rounding the back of the truck, my wedges sounding against the cement. "You didn't feel the need to warn me somewhere along the way?"

He meets me at the tailgate, immediately grabbing my face in his hands. I wrap my hands around his wrists, staring at him as he stares at me. "I got you. No one is going to mess with you unless they want to end up in a missing person case file buried on someone's desk. My job is to protect you, emotionally and physically."

He kisses me, and all of the panic and anxiety melts away. I finally came out and told him what happened when I went in there the day he brought me here, after I had time to let it all sink in. I've moved on from the man that helped conceive me, the one I look just like. I got out what I needed to say. I have no desire to see him or have anything to do with him. He was never a parent to me. It's too late now, even if he *wanted* to be. I'll never know the things that happened prior to my birth, the real story. People lie. They manipulate others to make their own shit smell like roses. I know in the country we live in it's supposed to be all people innocent until proven guilty, but in this case he's guilty until proven innocent. I have to believe in my heart that she didn't just snap and lie about what she said happened.

The part that keeps the guilt away after walking out without asking more questions was that if he loved my mother he would have went looking for her, but he didn't. He let her disappear, moving on with his life as if she never existed at all, while she disintegrated more and more with each passing day and year. Had he gave a damn I could have had a better life, but that's the problem with people. We step outside the line of morality and then turn a blind eye to the consequences that follow. No matter what I've ever done in my life, I can't deem it acceptable to find someone important enough to cheat on your spouse with and then just forget them when it turns into more than sex.

He kisses me again, pulling me out of the thoughts now racing through my mind. "I got you. Are you good?"

"Yeah. Lead the way."

He grabs my hand in his, pulling me alongside him as we migrate toward the elevators. "I'm not going to lead and you're not going to follow. We're going to go there together."

I've pretty much held my breath the entire way to his company's floor, hoping not to run into any unwanted people. Luckily, we didn't, and just like he said he's held my hand the entire time. I'm still uncomfortable with public displays of affection. I wasn't expecting it with Kaston, because he just doesn't seem like that type either, but yet he's the one grabbing my hand and holding it like his life depends on it the entire way here. People glanced along the way. I even tried to pull away, but he only tightened his grip.

Looking at us right now, we don't really look like we fit together. He's in an expensive suit and I'm a little more colorful with my ombre hair, dramatic makeup, denim skirt, and off the shoulder top. It makes me question things. With rich men I've always been the scheduled in lay or the out of town tryst that makes their lives exciting and spontaneous. Kaston wants us to be open for show. Up until this point he's always appeared normal, more on my level, but right now he's intimidating, unlike anyone before, and I've dated wealthy men. I'm more comfortable behind closed doors than in the public's eye. In those relationships we used each other, nothing more and nothing less.

We step off the elevator onto his floor. The receptionist desk gets closer with every step, a redheaded female around my age sitting behind it. She's pretty, but not what I would expect someone like Kaston to hire, though he's rarely as he seems so it shouldn't surprise me. Usually in this kind of an environment it's a typical type: the Barbie figures and Playboy bunny faces, blinding you from ever seeing past the outer appearance. She's different though. She looks...smart, independent, driven. Maybe it's the glasses.

He stops at the desk. I try to pull my hand free, but he stops me and looks at me with narrowed eyes. I feel like I'm being scolded for trying to make his life less awkward. Fuck my life. "Mary Elizabeth, do you have any messages for me?"

She opens a drawer and pulls out a stack of carbon copy telephone message slips, handing them to him. She looks between us, as if she's deciding whether to tell him in private or with me standing here. "There is one that keeps calling, but she won't leave a message. She keeps saying she'll try back later."

That organ in my chest cavity has been summoned to my stomach. I suddenly feel sick. "Next time write down the number. I'll see what I can find out."

"Um. That's the thing."

"What? You can say it with her standing here."

"Your ten o'clock is waiting in your office."

"Why not the conference room?"

"She said she wasn't here for that kind of appointment, and she wasn't on the schedule. I assumed you were expecting her and just forgot to let me know. She kept referring to you by your first name."

"You never fucking assume anything before you call me. Got it?"

"Yes, sir. I'm sorry."

That moment when you feel like you're eavesdropping on someone else's conversation and you just want to slowly slink away unnoticed... that is me at this very second. "Do you want me to wait out here? I can help her answer phones or something."

He shoots me a glare that makes me want to curl my tail between my legs if I had one. "What? It was just a suggestion. I don't want to interfere with you working."

"We'll talk about that later." He looks back at her. "I'll take care of it. Don't ever fucking let someone in my office again without checking with me or Chevy first. Where is he?"

"He came in at eight and took one of the jobs. He's been gone since."

He turns for the door on the wall, pulling me toward it. When he opens it, we enter into a long hallway full of doors. The wooden door at the end of the hall is the way he's stalking toward, making me concentrate to walk at a fast pace without twisting my ankle.

He opens the door and walks through, still towing me along behind him. A female stands immediately from the chair in front of his desk that she's occupying, and then turns toward us. "Kaston... finally." That vital organ that's been floating around in my stomach just disintegrated into liquid, leaving nothing behind. Her pencil skirt and matching jacket tells me she's the female equivalent of him, and she's beautiful. I will never be that sophisticated, career oriented, goal driven woman. I will always be the girl working the dead end job that has no other options, aside from a physical trophy and sex toy.

"Makayla, what are you doing here?"

"I've been looking for you since you left."

"If I wanted you to know where I was then I would have told you or contacted you, so why are you here?"

She looks at me for the first time since I've walked in the room. "Can I talk to you in private?"

I try to pull back toward the door, but I'm yanked forward, almost falling into him. "No. Whatever you have to say you can say now, in front of her. I haven't seen you in close to a year now. What is it that you want?"

She briefly pauses. "I just didn't want to leave things how they were. I realized after that night that I had fallen in love with you. It had started before, but that night in the club confirmed it. I was going to tell you at work that Monday. I was finally going to confess my feelings for you, but then you vanished and called in an emergency leave out of the blue. I never got a chance to tell you. We were partners, Kaston. Why couldn't you at least look me in the face and tell me goodbye. I had to use resources that could have gotten me fired to find you. If you didn't want to work alongside of me, we could have requested different partners and then seen where things went. We could have worked things out. I miss you. You don't just abandon someone you've worked alongside for multiple years. It was like you just…died."

I feel sick. My mouth is salivating, preparing to vomit everything in my stomach that no longer belongs. Not again. This can't be fucking happening again. I can't handle being with a man that is already wanted or had. One fucking time can I find a man that has no strings attached to someone, and no luggage weighing him down?

His hand loosens and I pull my hand free. I step back, but as if he just realized I'm no longer in his grasp he reaches back and slams the door shut at the same time he pulls me toward him. "Would you fucking stop trying to leave? If I wanted you to I would have already asked it of you. You aren't the one in the awkward position. It's her. You're supposed to be here. Give me a fucking second to deal with it."

My breathing is quickening, my heart rate excelling, propelling my blood through my veins faster. "Who is she?"

"Just someone I fucked once. She's an old coworker and friend. Nothing fucking more, Lux." He's yelling. "She means no more to me than Callum does to you!"

A tear falls from one eye and my shoulders fall. I look at her. Her face is soaked. My emotions are pulling me in a million different directions: jealousy, hurt, guilt, want, love, and sacrifice. I'm so confused right now. "Do you want her?"

He stares at me. "Makayla, out."

He's mad, but why I'm not sure. I can hear the footsteps closing in as her heels tap against the floor, but I can't look away from him, even if I wanted to. He knows how to hold me against my will with no effort at all. "Take care of him. He must love you, because the Kaston Cox that I know has never explained himself to anyone. He never needed to. You're one lucky girl, sweetheart. I envy you. I just couldn't move on until I tried."

The door opens and closes. He reaches over and locks it, before sliding off his jacket and hanging it on the coat rack beside the door. His belt buckle starts to jingle and then the zipper sounds as it slides down. "You know what happens to someone that's gone without the love of a parent, had it, then lost it, all within adolescence and the beginning stages of adulthood, before finding a different kind of love?"

"What?"

"You start to fucking panic when it starts slipping from your grasp. You start formulating a plan in your brain on the next move, the next course of action to hold onto it a little longer. I have to do that a lot with you, because every damn time I turn around you're trying to run. It makes me angry. You want to know why?"

He walks toward me with his pants undone, pulling his button-down shirt free from the tuck it's in. He removes my shirt in one swift motion, throwing it on the floor, before walking forward again, pushing for me to walk backward.

"Why?"

"Because you never fucking think you're good enough. You always think you're the one out of place. You always refer to yourself as the dirty little secret, the whore in the mix to satiate a man's filthy need to shove his dick within every crevice he can find. It's not totally your fault. It's hers. I've sat back and held my tongue in regards to your mother, because of her death and the mental hold she has on you, but I'm fucking fed up."

My butt runs into the desk, stopping me. He un-buttons the top four buttons and the cuffs, before he grabs the collar and pulls the shirt over his body, removing it, and baring his upper body just as me. "I'll never be what you need," I state.

"Says fucking who? Guess what, Lux? Since I fucking shoved my dick inside of you I don't want anyone else. It doesn't matter what you say or do that's not going to change. I don't care how many men you've fucked before me, how many times you've been sampled out of guilt, or how many times you've shut yourself off from me to avoid being hurt like you were growing up, because I'll still want you every damn second of every fucking day for the rest of my life. I can fuck you once a week or twenty times a day and it will never get old. I'll never want you less."

The closer he gets the faster my chest rises and falls. He reaches behind me and unhooks my bra, before scraping the straps off of my shoulders and letting it fall to the floor. "No matter how many times you run I'll chase you, how many times you hide I'll find you, or how many times you close off I'll open you back up. If you fall I'll catch you. You jump I'll jump with you. I'll never fucking give up on you, because no matter what you say I know you love me too. One day you'll realize it. One day you'll trust me. I will never leave you, forsake you, nor will I stop loving you. No one is better for me than you. I know that's what you think with her. It's written all over your face. I will spend the rest of my fucking life showing you and everyone else. I've promised in blood, I'll put a ring on your fucking finger, and I'll bind myself to you with a legal contract if that's what it takes. As I've said before the only way out of this is in a box with no heartbeat. If you think I'm bluffing, then call me on it. I have no fucking problem proving it. They say love makes people crazy and I guess they're right, because I would fucking kill for you without blinking. One question remains, because I'm so wound tight right now I can barely breathe. Do you want me?"

I blink repeatedly. I need to think, to process everything he's just said, but I can't with him staring at me like he's doing. I go with the simplest form of the truth. "Yes."

He grabs my hips and lifts me onto the desk, before running his palms across it to clear the middle, knocking things on the floor. "I'm not bending you over the desk, because I want to look into your eyes when I make you come. I want the emotional as much as the fucking physical. I'm addicted to the way you look when my dick is inside of you, pleasuring you. I'm hooked on the way your pussy feels when you come and squeeze my cock. That is my fucking mancave. Do you deny it?"

"No."

His tone is cold and angry, but at the same time packed with so much emotion it's stifling. His hands grip my thighs and rub upward, his callused hands causing chill bumps to form. My skirt rises with his hands. When he is blocked from going any further by the desk, he lifts me and continues over the curve of my ass, pushing my skirt to my midriff and leaving it, before grabbing the waistband of my panties and pulling them down my legs. I lay back. The desk is cold. "You're angry at me."

"Yes."

He lifts underneath my knees and pulls me to the edge. This is making me feel worse. He just screamed his aggravation at me, and now nothing. He's barely speaking. I feel like I'm getting whiplash from the sudden mood change. "Are you going to elaborate?"

"No. I'm talked out."

He presses his tongue to my pussy and swipes the tip between my folds, stopping on my clit. He sucks it into his mouth, before continuing up to my stomach, running his tongue over my tattoo along the way. His hands are no longer on my body. I look down. They go for the waistband of his pants, before pushing them down to his thighs. He's toying with me, not spending too much time on any one place. He's the only thing I see, the only thing that matters right now. He licks my nipple and then blows, the cool air hardening it. He then bites down as he thrusts inside of me, drawing the focus of the pain away with the addition of the pleasure. I arch off the desk; the second time today I've been on my back for him to do with me as he wants. "Always wet for me..."

"Always." His pace is slow, making me feel every inch as he pulls out and thrusts back inside. I wrap my legs around his waist, and then dig my heels into his buttocks. "You aren't going to hurt me like before?"

He kisses me, sliding his tongue inside of my mouth, and then pulls back, grabbing my lip between his teeth before releasing it. "No. Sometimes you need different things. It's my job to know what those things are and when you need them. My one fucking fear is losing you. Right now, I need to show you that you're scared to lose me too."

He reaches between us and places the pad of his thumb against my clit, rubbing up and down with pressure against it. I moan out, loud, before he smothers me with his mouth. It doesn't take long before my orgasm starts to build, and then I clench around him, but he continues to make love to me, striving to hit deeper with each thrust until he stills altogether. If I focus I can feel his dick pulsating inside of me, releasing himself. He places his palms on the desk beside me and pushes his upper body up, but doesn't pull out.

A knock sounds at the door, drawing me into the present. He's staring at me, as if he didn't even notice. "Shit. We shouldn't have done this here. This is your job, Kaston."

I place my hands on his chest, trying to push him back so I can get up. "I pay the salaries. They work for me. I'll do what I want."

"Mr. Cox. You're appointment is here."

"Just let me up. Please."

"Show them to the conference room, Mary Elizabeth. I'll be there in a minute," he yells.

"Yes, sir."

He pulls out of me, and stands, pulling his pants back in place and tucking himself in, before fastening them. "Stay here."

"I can't."

"Why not?"

"I need some air."

His eyes narrow. "You're trying to fucking run again, aren't you? Dammit, Lux, are we back to that?"

I hop off the desk and grab my underwear, quickly pulling them back on and putting my skirt back in place. I walk past him, grabbing my bra off the floor. I wrap it around me and fasten it, before turning it around and pulling it into place, then go for my shirt, pulling it over my head and aligning it in place. "I just need to think, Kaston. You take away my ability to think for myself. You consume me. It doesn't change that I'm a fucking nobody and you made something of yourself. I'm not on your level. It doesn't mean I have low self-esteem. That's just the reality, the hand that was dealt for me. I accepted it a long time ago. It made it easier. It's not a weakness. It's called being knowing my place in society. We're unequally yoked. This was just supposed to be about sex, sex for money, and for lavish things. The funny thing is that since I met you it hasn't even interested me. At least before you I knew what to expect of my life. Since I met you I'm fucking confused all the damn time, I have no idea what I'm feeling, bad memories are returning, and I'm having emotions that I've blocked out for years. You want to know why I always viewed myself as the dirty secret, because that's what I've always been."

I walk up to him and kiss him on the cheek, then point to his heart. "Your heart is like a rare diamond. It deserves to be with the person that makes it shine the brightest, not the one that makes it look dull. She's the best compliment for you, and she just admitted to loving you. That's something I'm not sure if I'll ever be able to do. I'm giving you an out. The two of you would be like Brad and Angelina, the one couple in Hollywood that's made it when the rest have failed. With me, you would probably crash and burn. I have too much baggage to be good for anyone. If you really love me, then you'll let me go, you'll choose the Emerald city instead of the farm in Kansas."

I grab my purse from where I dropped it on the floor when he slammed the door earlier. I run my fingers through my hair and look at him, memorizing that beautiful man just like he is. He's one you'll never forget. He's passionate, but hard. He loves, but he commands. I've lived my entire adult life being selfish, constantly taking from others to make up for what I couldn't provide for myself, and for what my mother couldn't ever provide for me. I used my body as a tool, because that's what I was taught. I'm done. I can't do it anymore. I laid that trade to rest when I met him, when he showed me a different life. I'm going to strive to formulate a pursuable dream and go after it. I'm going to sacrifice selfishness for him to have a better life. He deserves a wife, babies, and a white picket fence. I'll never want a white picket fence with a yard full of kids.

"Just because something is yours doesn't mean you can give it away, Lux. It doesn't work that way."

I hold up my hand for him to stop before the guilt takes over. I can already feel the blade piercing my skin, trying its damnedest to penetrate my chest. "Bye, Kaston."

I open the door and walk out, closing it behind me. I take off running through the lobby, headed for the elevator. My lungs are starting to constrict, my air supply decreasing like the day at the beach. Fuck!

I stab my thumb against the down button beside the elevator, anxiously waiting for the car before he comes running out here. It finally opens and I run in, pressing the close button. My stomach flips as the car starts to descend. I feel like I've been stabbed in the chest while having a pillow held over my mouth. I need to breathe.

When the doors open I run out, barreling into a chest. I put my palms out to stabilize myself. "I'm sorry," I say, trying to continue around him.

"Lux? Is that you?"

I look up at the recognition of my name. He, too, is wearing a suit. Fuck my life. They're everywhere now. Drunk or not, no one forgets that accent. "Flynn, right?"

"Yes, are you okay? You look flushed."

"I'm fine. Just had a rough day. It was good to see you, though. Take care."

I push past him, but he grabs my hand. "Hey, are you still dating that guy? The guy from the club."

"No," I say in a clipped tone. "Why?"

He looks at me and pulls his bottom lip into his mouth, pausing. "I don't usually do this, but I'm actually heading out for Los Angeles this weekend to take care of some things with work. My roommate backed out last minute, leaving with me an open spot and extra plane ticket. You want to tag along? We have already met, so it's not that weird, right?"

"Thanks, Flynn, but..."

"Hey, I'm not trying to sleep with you, Lux, unless that's what you want. Don't base your opinion of me by the guy you met drinking in a bar." He looks around at his surroundings. "I'm not drinking and we're no longer in a bar. Believe it or not some of us just like to make new friends. I'll be working half of the time, anyway, so you'll be on your own a good bit. You can lay on the beach or sightsee. Call it a free vacation from someone that just wants the company of a familiar face. Sometimes it can be a little awkward meeting people in a new place. I haven't been in the states all that long. I'm still adjusting."

I stare at him, thinking. What do I have to lose? I said I was going to let Kaston go. Maybe it's time to get out of Atlanta for a bit. I need a break. This could be my sign for finding a new dream. Maybe I'll go and never come back. Maybe getting out of the south is the change that I need. I'll never know if I don't try...

"Okay, if you'll take me by a friend's place to get some clothes. My stuff isn't really an option right now."

"Sure. We have time before the flight. I was going to hang around here and work, but I don't have to. It was just to kill time. It'll give us a chance to get to know each other a little better."

CHAPTER TWENTY-EIGHT

I button the last button on my shirt, leaving the top one open so that I can breathe worth a damn. Like a robot I tuck my shirt in my pants and refasten my pants and belt. I rub my hand through my short hair, trying to relax. I never thought I'd fucking be here. I feel like a pussy. I also need a drink, a stout one. If I don't get something to calm my raging blood then I'm in deep shit. I have a client. This behavior would be frowned upon.

I walk to my desk and sit down, before leaning forward in my chair and resting my forearms on my thighs, staring at the floor. It's building inside. There is nothing I can do about it. I haven't felt like this since I first moved back from my long stay in Spain. I spent six months learning everything about both businesses from the only man he trusted with his life, and taking care of Dad's death, as well as the personal shit with his lawyer like transferring ownership for pretty much everything to me. I went from a cop to a killer in a matter of days.

"Get ahold of yourself, asshole."

In a rage I yank my desk drawer open. The flask is sitting on top right where I left it. I've barely drunk anything since the night I first fucked her at the club, nothing more than a glass here or there. I don't need it like I used to. Smoking hasn't appealed to me at all either. That's what she does to me. She smothers the darkness I've always been pulled toward, she adds a burst of light to my life, and she takes away the fucking pain...of losing him. She makes living easier.

I twist off the cap and place the rim to my lips, turning it back and letting it drain. The liquid burns my throat, but it fucking feels good. I feel like I'm being gutted, bleeding slowly while my heart remains in tact, dying out as it beats slower with each passing minute of her absence.

I throw the flask across the room. "You didn't tell me it would hurt this fucking bad. You made it look easy," I say in a growl. "It's been fifteen fucking minutes since she walked out on me and it feels like an eternity. You expect me to stay on the good side like this? Huh? What reason do I have not to go on a fucking killing spree? Fuck! I wasn't ready for this. I didn't ask for this, Dad. You were supposed to wait. Everything is by the book. It was your damn rule."

I stand and walk to the wall of windows, looking out over the city. I lace my hands behind my head and rock it back and forth, thinking. "Fuck this shit. She's the one that walked away like I meant nothing. I may have only met her at the beginning of summer, but I gave her my all. She was different. She was the one I couldn't take my eyes off of. She was the one I wanted to try for. I gave her something I've never given another woman, and for what? To have it thrown in my face? *Be a fucking man. Pick up your balls and move on. You have a job, expectations, and shoes to fill."*

I walk to the door and grab my jacket, sliding it on, and then adjust it while I compose myself before opening the door. Mary Elizabeth scurries down the hall when she sees me, handing me the file. I grab it and open the cover, reviewing the first page of the new client paperwork.

I close it and open the door, before walking inside and shutting it behind me. The client is sitting on the left side closest to me. "Mrs. Smith." I drop the folder on the table at my seat and hold out my hand. "Kaston Cox. What can I do for you?"

I pull out a chair and sit to make her more comfortable, also to make this more personable. It's probably the same fucking thing, different day, usually trying to catch cheaters. They are pretty easy, because if you think your spouse is cheating then they probably are. The client just wants proof. What I really want to do is to be contracted for inside jobs by the government, but that takes a reputable name, something I'm still working towards. Marks hold my interest while this makes me a legal income, plus the business back in Spain. You can't really claim kill for hire on your tax returns. That money sits in offshore accounts, only being transferred a little at a time in deposits small enough it won't get reported to the IRS.

"I think my husband is cheating on me."

Just as I thought...

"What brings you to such a conclusion, Mrs. Smith?"

"He isn't coming home several nights a week. When he's home he barely touches me. He stays on his phone and keeps it on silent. If I get anywhere near it he gets jumpy, defensive. Money is disappearing from our account with no explanation as to what it's being used for. When he comes home he washes a load of his clothes. Until six months ago he never washed anything, not even a load of towels. When I ask him about things he jumps down my throat, accusing me of not trusting him and being paranoid because of things I watch on television like reality TV. I just get the feeling there is someone else."

Well, fuck, what do you need me for? Options one through three are dead giveaways...

"I'll do everything I can to find out what your husband has been up to, Mrs. Smith," I say like a broken record, the same thing I've said in ninety perfect of my cases since I took over this business. I'm starting to wonder if anyone believes in monogamy anymore. Fuck, why be with someone if you want to stick or spread your legs for everyone else? Just leave them and be done with it. "Did you bring all of the information requested in the packet?"

"Yes. It's all there." I'm about to get up when she touches my wrist. "I know you think I'm crazy and probably stupid for staying, but I've loved him since I was fourteen. I'm still young enough to start over, but we've been through a lot. I've been with him for half of my life and we share two kids. We've had some financial problems since he was laid off ten months ago and hasn't been able to find stable work. Sometimes the people we love hurt us and act out in distress, but that's usually the times they need us the most. A lifelong commitment doesn't burn down at the first sign of a fire; it withstands it, even if it comes out on the other side a little charred. Giving up is my last option. I don't want to stop fighting until I've been defeated and the ability to carry on is no more. This is my tool to get him in the ring."

She lays a large yellow envelope on the glass table and stands, putting the strap of her purse on her shoulder. "I came to you because I heard through the grapevine that you're the best. I'm counting on it. Thank you for meeting with me."

She walks out, closing the door behind her. I lean back in my chair and prop my elbow on the armrest. "What a mind fuck."

Please don't give up on me...

"Dammit!" I stand, shoving my rolling chair back into the door. I turn and knock it out of the way, before opening the door and jogging down the hall until I barge into the lobby. Mary Elizabeth stands as I hand her the envelope. "Put that paperwork into the open jobs file and lock my office. Hold my messages and call Chevy if anyone comes in. I have to go. Got it?"

"Yes, sir."

I halt as she starts shuffling paperwork at her desk. "Mary Elizabeth."

"Yes, sir?"

"Stop calling me fucking sir. I'm barely older than you are. Call me Kaston or you're fired." Her eyes widen and her cheeks turn red. "It was a joke, Mary Elizabeth. I'm not going to fire you, unless you let another woman into my office. After I straighten this shit out only one other woman aside from you is allowed. Are we clear?"

She smiles. I don't think I've ever seen the girl show any emotion since I hired her. This one reaches her eyes, showing the small smile lines. "You have my word."

"Good. Have a good night." I turn and start walking to the elevator.

"Tell her you need her and can't live without her." I stop again. "Girls have to feel needed. We don't want to be the girl you can live with. We want to be the girl you can't live without. It's a simple truth. Goodnight, Kaston."

"Remind me to give you a raise when I get back."

I pull my phone from my pocket as I walk to the elevator. The doors open as the call connects and I step inside. "What you need?"

Tattoo guns are buzzing in the background.

"Kross, this isn't business it's personal. I need a favor."

"What you got for me?"

"I need Delta's number."

The doors close.

Silence.

"That may cost you."

"Just name it. She's a resource I need."

"I'll text it to you. Be waiting. I'll collect in due time. I always do."

He disconnects the call and I slide my phone back into my pocket, waiting fucking impatiently for that vibration...

Lux

I'm going to look for something to drink. I'll be right back. Do you want anything?"

I look at him as he stands from his seat in the lobby of our gate, and then shake my head. "No, thanks."

He nods and walks away, my thoughts immediately going back to earlier. That speech Kaston made keeps playing in my mind on repeat as if there is something wrong with the record player. I can't shut it off. I've seemed like a zombie ever since.

I feel like I have the flu. My body aches, I feel feverish, and I feel like I could sleep for days. I have a headache from Hell and suddenly I'm not feeling sun and sand in the great west. This is the right decision. It has to be. I know I'm a fucked up person. I wish I could change it, but I can't. I don't expect others to understand. The damage started when I was too young to know any better. Kaston deserves better than what I can physically or emotionally give him. I want a happily ever after for him. You can't have that if you're constantly walking through sludge with someone else.

I look down at my phone. There is a message from Delta and a voicemail from a toll free number I don't recognize. That's weird. I never felt it vibrate during the call. Maybe my signal faded in and out.

I open the message from Delta first.

Delta: Don't do it. If you do this you're stupid. I say that with love.

Me: It's already been done. This is best. Thank you for having my back though. You always have.

A few minutes pass as I stare at the screen that says she's typing.

Delta: I don't like the sound of that damn message. Are you fucking depressed again? I'm not going through seventh grade year all over again, Lux. Fuck that. I barely pulled you out of the fire. Fuck all the haters. We are survivors. Do you hear me? We walked out of Hell with no one's help. We did it alone and we aren't going back. Smother the guilt and let yourself be happy. That's not on you, babe. We all have to pay for what we do in life. Slowly, but surely, Karma is making its rounds. Don't let them fucking win. For once in your life let someone else love you. Please. It's not your fault she didn't make it...either of them. Let someone experience the best of you, just as I have. I'm begging you."

Me: If only I knew how...

My eyes gloss over. Fuck. I won't do this here. I won't think about her. I buried her a long time ago. I lay my phone down to pull my wallet out and open it. Behind the photo of Delta and me in Cancun lies the photo that only one other person has seen: Delta. I remove the worn, folded photo and open it. I haven't looked at it since graduation. This is the main reason I only change wallets every half decade, minimum. I can rarely bring myself to touch it. It's sacred. Out of sight out of mind.

The day Sophie was born Delta was the only one that stayed by my side the entire time. Mom disappeared until she didn't have a choice when I was discharged. I was a minor. When Delta found out she didn't make it, she took every penny to her name and bought her a dress and a disposable camera. Sometimes that girl knows me better than I know myself. She finishes my sentences. I would have never made it this far without her. I don't know how she even knew to get preemie size at that age, and it still was too big. Hell, come to think of it I don't even know how she got there or who took her, but the point is that she did, because somehow she knew that even though I wasn't ready for a permanent reminder then, one day I would be. It took me a few years to even work up the nerve to have the film developed. My mind just wasn't ready then. I was so young.

I stare down at the tiny part of me that never got a chance, a part of me gone that I'll never get back. She was beautiful, even at such a tiny stage. "It feels wrong to love someone or be loved in return when you didn't get a chance to have that part of me," I whisper. A tear falls, but I quickly swipe it before anyone can take notice.

I fold it back up and put it away, remembering Flynn will be back any moment now. I return my wallet to my purse. Then I remember that voicemail. I pick my phone up and go to my voicemail app, hitting the play button before placing my phone to my ear.

The recording starts to play, a female voice...

Miss Larsen,

This is Angela with Le Cordon Bleu, office of registration, in regards to your acceptance into our culinary program beginning this fall. As you know the summer is coming to a close and fall semester is nearing. An anonymous payer has paid your tuition and all fees in full, but you have yet to come in and officially register or see someone to schedule your classes. Please call our office as soon as possible. Hope to hear from you soon. The number for callback is 888-

The phone falls from my hand into my open purse sitting in my lap. There are only two people that would even have any clue about that: Delta and Kaston. I didn't tell either one of them about the acceptance letter, and Delta can't afford to pay it if she even wanted to. How would he have known?

The trash... Was he there?

"Are you ready to go? It's time to board."

I'm pulled from my thoughts at the recognition of Flynn's return. I pull the straps of my purse on my shoulder and stand. "Yes, I'm ready."

It's time to leave the south behind. A lot of things have happened to me on Georgia soil; a lot of bad, some good, and some unfinished, but the important thing is that I'm actually putting a plan into action to change my future from the past all by myself. I haven't told Flynn yet, but this isn't a round trip for me. I just need a one-way ticket, because I'm not coming back. I haven't even told Delta, because I knew she would scream and yell, call me crazy, and then tell me this is exactly what I need. She's always been my biggest supporter, but I couldn't do the goodbye part. She's my best friend, my god-sister, and the protector of my soul until the right person comes along to release it to, but that'll never happen. The only person that would have been worthy of the title is here, holding on to my heart, because he kind of stole it and never gave it back, but he never has to know.

There, I've admitted it to myself. I love Kaston Cox. I love him with every cell that makes up who I am. He brought me back to life when I didn't even know I was dying. He brings out the best in me. He makes me a better person. Knowing his heart has been the biggest honor I've ever been given. He made me want to dream again. He made me want to fight for a better life, so that's what I'm doing. He made believe in happily ever afters again, so I'm sacrificing mine to give him a fucking great one, because that's what you do when you love someone. You do what's best for them, and sometimes that's removing yourself from the equation. In the frame of time that's passed I barely know him, yet I feel like I've known him forever. Even with everything that's happened this has still been the best fucking summer of my life, and the most memorable one.

The line moves up one body at a time. Flynn hands our plane tickets to the employee standing at the terminal. He starts walking, but I remain standing, looking back out across the lobby. I turn toward him. He's standing and waiting. "Lux, you coming?"

"Yeah…"

I catch up and we walk through the tunnel, the flight attendant getting closer with every step. Each step that I take it gets harder to breathe. I place my hand over the left side of my chest. My heart is racing…and hurting. I'm starting to sweat. I'm about to start wheezing. Just like earlier, it feels like that day at the beach all over again, just occurring slower than before.

I stop and close my eyes. Every moment since we met that night flashes through my mind like the trailer to a major motion picture. A tear slips free and runs down my cheek. "Flynn, I can't do this. I'm sorry."

My eyes open and he's staring at me with his hand on his carryon. "Is it about the guy at the club?"

"It's about the guy that owns my heart; one organ the human body can't live without. I'll never survive there, because my heart is here, with him. I'm so sorry. I thought I could, but I can't."

He walks toward me and kisses me on the forehead. "Don't be sorry, love. At least you didn't wait until it was too late...like I did. Goodbye, Lux. Maybe I'll see you soon."

He turns and walks away, disappearing when he reaches the end of the terminal. I feel so stupid. Maybe it is too late. I never thought of that. A guy like Kaston isn't really for second chances.

I walk back to the seating area and sit down in the same seat as before. I pull out my phone and open the message chat box between Kaston and I. He may not even answer, but I at least have to try.

Me: I have a bone to pick with you.

Immediately I get a response.

Kaston: Oh yeah? You miss my boners already?

I laugh.

Me: That too.
Kaston: So what'd I do?
Me: That stalker shit again...

460

Kaston: It's your fault. You kind of bring that out in me.
Me: Yeah?
Kaston: Yeah. I wear that role proudly. Although, which time are you referring to? There may have been several. If I'm pleading guilty, I'd like to know to which charge.

I laugh again, this time a little loud.

Me: I never told you I got into culinary school.
Kaston: Oh, that. So much for being fucking anonymous.
Me: I told you I didn't want anyone to pay for my dream.
Kaston: I saw talent that didn't need to go to waste, so I acted on it. You can call it a business investment for all I care. Your dreams are my reality, baby.

More tears fall.
I bite my bottom lip, blinking in an attempt to read the screen of my phone. I breathe deeply, trying to calm my nerves.

Me: You win.

I wait.
"How so?"
Oh, God. Now I'm hearing his voice. I really am going crazy.
Someone squats in front of me and I look up, a huge smile appearing. My face is making contradictory statements: crying and smiling. "You found me…"
"I'll always find you, baby. I promised you I'd never give up."
"How did you know I was here?"
"I used my stalker ways." He wipes my tears. "How did I win?"

"Because you made me fall in love with you."

The corners of his lips curve upward. "You done running yet?"

"Probably not." I laugh. "You done chasing me yet?"

He tucks my hair behind my ear, showing more of my face. "Never. I need you too much, and I can't live without you."

My heart starts beating erratically, straining against my chest cavity in an attempt to break free. "I love you, Kaston. I do. I know you could have better, but I want to try to be your Emerald City."

He slides me off the chair onto his lap. "I don't want Emerald City, Lux, if my home is in Kansas. Where you are is where I want to be. Why would I want *better* when I already have the best there is? You can't give me away, baby. When words fail me, lyrics save me. There is a song by Hinder called, *Anyone but you*, that explains it perfectly already. *I'll disappear forever, if you want me to, and I'll find somebody new, but I can't love anyone but you.*"

That is the trigger that breaks me. There is no one other man that is more perfect for me than him. He is my equilibrium, my balance. He completes me. I've lied to myself for too long already. I'll never walk away from him again. I can't. I grab his face in my hands. "I couldn't have said it any better," I whisper, and kiss him like we've been apart for an eternity, in the middle of this airport surrounded by other people, because with him I don't give a damn. He's mine; the first thing that really ever has been only mine.

We pull into his house, parking the truck in the garage. I feel like I'm really home for the first time in my entire life, even more so than before.

I exit and walk toward the door, exhausted. The house is quiet. He pulls me into the laundry room from the garage, before lifting me and setting me on top of the washer. "What do you want to do?"

"I don't really care, as long as I'm with you, but the Jacuzzi sounds nice. What do you think?"

"Whatever you want to do, I'm game." He kisses me and immediately goes for my clothes, trying to pull them off. "I just want to be inside of you. How long are you off work?"

I pull away, feeling guilty. "Um, about that."

He looks at me, confused. "What?"

"I kind of quit my job a few hours ago. I wasn't planning on coming back. I was just going to pick up and start over. California was the option that came available, a ready-made decision. Fuck, I don't know if Jason will take me back now. I left him high and dry, no notice, nothing. It was stupid, but I wasn't thinking of the consequences of hasty decisions at the time."

He smiles at me, his arms blocking me from going anywhere. I'm confused on why openly admitting irresponsibility would be a good thing. Grown adults with bills don't just up and quit their jobs. "Why are you smiling," I ask.

"Because now I really can kiss you anytime I want. Plus, I'm taking you to Paris before you start school. You don't need a job while you're in school. You need to study."

I haven't really evaluated that subject yet, but now that he mentioned it. "Uh, not a chance bossy. I'm paying you back for school if I'm really going to do this. That requires a job."

"I agree."

"See, so stop all that crazy talk about me not working."

"You aren't working for someone else. You're working for me."

"I'm confused. You want me to work at your company? Doing

what? Answering phones and being your personal assistant? I thought you already had someone doing that."

"No. You can pay me back in food that makes me have *foodgasms* as you called it not that long ago and lots of sex." He gives me a cocky grin. "I fully expect you to come see me at the office in a trench coat with nothing underneath in any spare time you have. You won't have enough time for a real job. Plus, the only bill you have is what, a cell phone? Gas? I think I'm perfectly capable of adding that bill. I would hardly consider that a burden. School is important. I went. Now it's your turn. Let me give that to you."

I grab his hand and hold it to my chest, letting him feel what's going on inside of me. My heart is pounding, working overtime to pump the blood throughout my body. My brain is still playing catch up from what my heart has known for a while now. "You're the only person that's ever done this to me. Just know that it scares me to let it go. I'll never be able to undo all the damage from growing up. I'll still make you crazy when you try to love me. It's a defense mechanism. Sometimes I may give in, sometimes I may rebel, and sometimes I may avoid doing anything at all, but no matter what remember that regardless of which I choose that day I always feel the same, because I love you. Like the scars from all the damage, that is irreversible."

"I love you too, Lux, scars and all."

He kisses my neck, his hands going for the bottom of my skirt. My hands go for his sides, getting more and more turned on as his lips move along the seam of my neck, toward my ear. Suddenly I have the desire to do this different. I want to be sexy for him. Our sex life has been sudden, passionate, occasionally a little rough or violent from our personalities, and sometimes slow and sensual, but never premeditated. I want to leave him speechless. I want him to savor me as I walk toward him. I want to feel like the only one in the room, like Cinderella did. It's not something I've ever wanted to experience before, but with him I do.

"Can you give me a minute?"

"For what?"

"I just need to go to the bathroom."

"Okay, but hurry up. Come back naked. I'll go pull the cover off for the Jacuzzi."

He moves out of the way to let me down. I rush toward the master bathroom, running pretty much the entire way. My first stop along the way is the closet, pulling open the door and running to the back of my side. I dig toward the back of all my hanging clothes where it's hidden, pulling out the designer lingerie I found a long time ago that I couldn't pass up but have yet to wear. It just never felt right.

I quickly remove my clothes, all of them, leaving them in a heap on the floor of the closet to pick up later, and then remove the band of material I had wrapped on the hanger above the sheer floor-length skirt, rehanging the hanger to temporarily free up my hands. It takes me a few minutes to figure out how the center of the band wraps from behind the neck and crosses at my collarbone, before running over my breasts and then behind my back where it ties, only covering my nipples and the center of my breasts.

I open my panty drawer and grab a pair of black thongs, pulling them on, before removing the wrap around skirt from the hanger and wrapping the sheer skirt around my waist from behind, tying the silk sash-like waistband in front to secure it. The band of black feathers lines the bottom hem like a boa. I run my fingers through my hair, tousling it, before grabbing a pair of black stilettos and pulling them on my feet.

I walk out of the closet and shut the door, continuing to my jewelry box. I grab my small diamond studs, the one real thing I've bought for myself. I saved for a year for them. They're sentimental. They're mine. I worked my ass off to get them without anyone else's help and I haven't worn them in a while. I save them for special occasions. I think this makes for a great one.

I look at myself in the mirror, taking my eyeliner and touching up my eyes from the tears, before adding a small amount of powder to my face. For the final touch I add lip-gloss and rub my lips together. "There. Much better."

The sound of something falling catches my attention. I walk to the bedroom door and open it, peeking my head outside. "Kaston," I call out. "What was that?"

Another loud bang sounds, and movement, but no words from him. "Kaston, are you down there?"

A sinking feeling occurs in my stomach when I hear something grunt, sounding more like the effects of someone becoming the victim of blunt force trauma. Something doesn't feel right. I tiptoe in my heels down the hall, turning toward the kitchen. When I reach the entry of the kitchen I stand against the wall, peeking around just enough to see. It's empty. Another loud but foreign sound occurs, causing me to jump. "Fuck," I whisper, panicked. "Where the hell are my guns?"

I step onto the tile floor and my heels make a tapping sound against it, halting me. I reach down and remove them, easing them onto the floor quietly. I'm shaking, suddenly terrified and I have no idea why. It's probably nothing and I'm being paranoid. Maybe he just stumbled. Multiple times? Kaston? No way. I quickly walk across the floor to the counter and grab a butcher knife from the block, gripping the handle in my hand by my side.

I walk toward the sounds from a few moments ago at a snail's pace. Glass shatters in the direction of the patio, causing me to take off running. The glass in the door is in a million pieces, as if someone was pushed through it. My knees weaken as shards of glass stick in the bottom of my feet, almost sending me to the floor. I catch sight of a man's back, one that I recognize, and one that isn't Kaston. The shouting voice that I've heard a million times confirms it, sending me rushing out the door, bleeding and all.

Kaston is pinned against the wall of the house with a barrel aimed between his eyes, Callum holding it in place. I can't breathe. My body starts to tremble. When you hear about those people that say they experienced their entire lives flash before their eyes, but you never really believe them because it just sounds too out there, well, now I do, because I'm experiencing it. He is my life, and if Callum pulls the trigger it will end. I barely move, trying not to be heard. I'm surprised he hasn't already as the glass crunched beneath my feet. "You're always in my way. I had her first. She's mine. As long as you're here, you're going to be a problem for me. I can't let her go. I won't. I've tried to play nice. I even killed for her, yet you're the only one left standing between me and her. Not anymore."

What did he just say? Killed for me? My eyes widen. Oh, God. It all fucking makes sense. That night I confessed things, releasing them out in the open. *Mom...*

"You think you have enough balls to pull the trigger? Do it. Blow my fucking brains out. I guaranfuckingtee she still won't want you, because she's better than you. You're the one that will have to pay for it, and without the girl. She. Doesn't. Want. You."

"Shut up. Just shut up. I gave her everything. I fucking hate you. All of this is because of you." He presses the barrel into Kaston's skin with more pressure.

"No one wears blood on their hands without paying for it. You think shoving drugs down her mother's throat is proving you love her? You're wrong. That's only crippling her. You're adding hurdles to her path. Love is just a word unless you have the actions to back it up. You want me gone to prove what I'm telling you? Are you pissed off that I beat your ass? Prove your manhood. I've had enough of you. Do it, motherfucker."

My mind has timed out. I'm trying to move and I can't. All the information is overloading my mental state. Kaston grabs the barrel in his fist and holds it to his head tighter, creating a firm hold so that the barrel doesn't waver from the lack of experience in the user. My heart becomes the control center over my body for where my brain is currently in shock, instructing my actions. What the fuck is he doing? Oh my god. A fear runs through me that I've never experienced. I can't stop shaking. I can't even spend time to evaluate what came out of Callum's mouth, or Kaston's. As if my heart was just shocked with electric paddles, my limbs form movement, operating through instinct. My fears turn into reflexes. I don't think. I do.

Rushing toward them, I bring my left arm up, my fist beside my ear, and then force my lower arm forward, driving the blade into his back until the only thing visible is the handle. "No one takes him from me," I whisper. My breathing becomes thick, heavy, and harder to control. A smothered grunt is the only sound I hear from him before his knees weaken, bringing him to the floor, his grip around the gun loosening before he drops, remaining in Kaston's hand.

I look down at my hands trembling. What the fuck did I just do? I glance at Callum, now lying face down on the floor, blood starting to pool. Tears begin to fall, realizing that I've just killed someone, driving a knife through his heart, adrenaline still pumping through my veins. Kaston squats beside him but I can't focus. I stare out but see nothing but a blur.

Hands grip my face, causing me to jump. "Shh. It's me. Kaston."

My vision clears a little. He's staring into my eyes. "I didn't mean to. I thought he was going to take you from me. I didn't know what else to do. He keeps coming back. He wouldn't stop. I've never been so scared."

"Remember what I said. Together forever. I'm not going out in a box without you. I had a plan, baby. It's going to take someone smarter than a fucking amateur to bring me down. He just caught me off guard is all. Come here," he says, and wraps his arms around me, pulling me into his chest. "You're trembling. I will fix this."

Trigger.

I push him away, suddenly angry. "Stop trying to fix everything, Kaston. That's your fucking problem. You're always trying to bear everyone else's pain and loss, never letting yourself deal with your own, yet you want to sacrifice everything to take mine away. Not once have you shown me grief over your father. Not once have you given yourself an out over what happened to your sister when your father died over the same battle you're still fighting. The world is shitty. No one but God can change that. Evil will always prevail no matter how many times you eliminate it. That's why it's evil, because it spreads at a rate that is unstoppable by mortals. It's my responsibility to bear my own sins, my own mistakes, my own demons, and the damage from things that have been done to me. All I need from you is to love me through it. It just took me a while to figure that out. I fucking did this. I knew what I was doing."

I walk closer to him and wrap my arms around his neck, before jumping in his arms. He catches me, just as I knew he would. "And I would do it again...for you. His heart was no good anyway. You think you're the only one that can give epic speeches that melt the heart? Well you're wrong. If you're a killer I'm a killer. You can never say I wouldn't kill for you, because I just proved that I will. I need you probably more than you need me. You are every bit as important to my survival as the air I breathe. My world doesn't turn without you in it. My heart doesn't beat if you aren't near. My lungs won't work without you giving me air, and I don't exist without you here. I will never fucking leave your side again unless you send me away. Die or survive, I don't care, as long as our bodies are side by side. We're two of the most fucked up people there could ever be, but that makes our love more beautiful than most. Some couples ride off into the sunset, but we own the night, because sometimes... love is born in the dark."

Something happens that I wasn't expecting. A single tear falls from the eye of the strongest man I've ever met. "I fucking love you with every portion of my soul." Then he kisses me, showing me with actions where words fall short.

Most people probably wouldn't understand loving a man that can be ruthless enough to commit murder, but that's what makes him amazing. He can submerge himself into a world so dark that most wouldn't find the light, but then he can walk right back out as if he knew the way the entire time. I don't care what he's done, or what he decides to do from here on out. I will stand by his side until the end, because no matter how many times his hands are stained with blood, with another soul, his heart is still pure, and that's how I know that every life he takes is every bit deserved. He is a grim reaper in human form, just like the tattoo that he represents. Someone has to fight for the innocent, because if not the breed will become extinct.

This is my love story...and it's a damn good one if you ask me.

EPILOGUE
Kayson

ONE MONTH LATER...

"I still cannot believe we're in Paris. This is fucking insane." I smile. The best reactions are always the honest ones. "You have got to be the best boyfriend on the planet."

I'm sort of hoping she'll be calling me something else later...

I put my arm around her, waiting for the taxi to arrive at our destination. I've been planning this since I told her I'd bring her here. Well, parts of it. There has been a recent addition to the itinerary.

She squeals and starts bouncing up and down in her seat, pulling from my hold, and then moves toward the window. "The Eiffel Tower! Look at it lit up against the dark sky. This is better than sex."

"Hey. No go, beautiful. Don't think I won't do things to remind you. With me nothing better be better than sex."

She turns to look at me and rolls her eyes. "Men are hopeless. I have never seen anything more beautiful than that."

I look at her in her strapless, pink dress, sparkling each time it hits light, her hair straight and her makeup done flawlessly, against the backdrop of the Eiffel Tower all lit up now that it's dark outside. "I have," I say honestly.

"Do not be a cheese-ball and say me, Cox. We both know that's not true."

"You have your opinion and I have mine."

"You can be so stubborn. I love that about you, you know."

"I could say the same about you."

The car stops. "Touché. So...what's the plan?"

"You'll see soon enough, beautiful."

"Really? You're killing me. We're in the middle of Paris, staring across the way from the Eiffel Tower and you're still going to try to pretend it's a surprise? Show your cards, handsome."

I smirk. "A good player never shows his cards unless he's sure he has the win in the bag."

I hand the driver money and open the door, before grabbing her hand and stepping out. She slides across the seat and follows me, adjusting her dress when she stands. I shut the door and the driver pulls out, leaving us here...at our destination. She places her hands underneath her boobs and looks down at herself, before she starts pushing them toward her, drawing my attention. "Well, you made me buy an expensive dress. It must be something good."

Each time she pushes up from underneath her boobs, her cleavage becomes more pronounced. My mouth is starting to salivate and my cock is getting hard. "Lux."

She looks up. "What?"

"Unless you want to be arrested for indecency in a foreign country I advise you to stop touching your tits."

She drops her hands and does her attempt at a curtsy. "As you wish, your highness." Her signature wink confirms she's being a smartass. If you can't beat the player, get your ass in the game and play with her. That's the only way to be with her. I take a deep breath, still looking at the woman in front of me that's mine. "What? Do I have something on me? Shit, where?"

I laugh and then grab her hand, pulling her into the crook of my arm. "No, beautiful. I was just admiring the view."

We walk side by side into the building, before a middle-aged man in a black tux, similar to mine, greets us. "Reservation pour deux. Cox."

She looks at me like I've grown a third eye when he searches for our reservation. "You can speak French? Since when?"

"There are a lot of things you still have to learn about me, beautiful. As you know I went to grade school in another country. In some things they are far more advanced than Americans," I say and wink.

"Right this way, sir," he says back in English, and steps in front of us, leading to the elevator.

She's lost focus, looking straight forward as we walk. I grab her hand. "Stop it."

"Stop what," she asks.

"Thinking you're inadequate compared to me. Stop it."

"Sometimes it's obvious, especially if you noticed."

We step into the elevator. "Nope. I just had more seasoning than you at an early age. I kind of like you raw. That only means I have a longer bucket list. We have our entire lives to catch you up."

She squeezes my hand. I pull the back of hers to my lips. The elevator stops on the top floor, and then opens to a small corridor with a door on the other side. He steps into the door, holding it open for us to exit. I place my hand on the small of her back, guiding her. "Where are we?"

I say nothing, continuing to the door until within reach to open it. She steps outside onto the rooftop, lit up with soft, cafe style lights, set up with a private table and two place settings. Music is playing low. The Eiffel Tower is the backdrop. I look at her as she takes it all in. She has her hands over her mouth, creating a line in the center that resembles a steeple. "What is this," she asks.

"Well, I remember when you told me that you wanted to come to Paris, you said you wanted to eat a four-course meal with a five-star chef, so that's what I had to do. Plus, taking you out at home is next to impossible if it doesn't involve Mission Impossible stunts. If I have to bring you to another country to take you to dinner then that's what I'm going to do."

"Your waiter will be here shortly, sir." He lightly bows when I look at him and nod my understanding, and then walks back out in the direction we entered.

I look back at Lux and she's walking toward the edge. She stops and places her hands down on the wall that rises about waist high, surrounding the entire rooftop, looking out at the Eiffel Tower and the city. I join her, placing my hands on her bare shoulders. "Tell me what you're thinking."

"That no one has ever done anything like this for me."

"Get used to it. I told you I'm here to make your dreams come true."

She lays her head against my chest. "Going to school is a dream, Kaston. This is more like a fairytale."

"Then dance with me."

"What about your dream?"

"You are my dream, Lux."

She turns around in my arms. "I haven't danced like that since I was a little girl."

I'm a little confused. "Didn't you go to things like prom?"

She gives me a half smile. "I didn't really fit in at places like prom. That involved meeting parents, taking pictures. My mom had a reputation that mothers didn't want their sons around. I was usually the girl that guys called for the after party."

Every time she says shit like that I get pissed off, wanting to beat on my chest like a caveman and then lay out every person that has ever hurt her. After Callum basically admitted to being the reason Lux's mother overdosed, it gave her some closure that she didn't have before. When it was done I made her dress and leave, giving her my credit card to go shop. She may have killed him, but there are some things you shouldn't expose the person you love to, and disposing of a body into a form to never be found would be the biggest. There are some aspects of this life she doesn't need details on.

I haven't taken a hit since before that day. I have some in files pending for acceptance, but I'm still unsure if I want them or not. I'm not saying that I'll never take another mark, because there is something deep inside of me that I believe is meant to fight for those that can't fight for themselves, but for now I'm on a break to make some decisions, and I'm content building the private investigation firm and getting to know Lux, because that girl has so many layers it'll take years to get through them all.

After I got a taste of what it felt like to almost lose her I realized exactly how much I really love her. My day starts with her and ends with her. Usually she's even present somewhere in between, and you know what? It's the best fucking thing in the world. We've become domesticated, in a routine. Over the past month I've actually realized how sorry I feel for my dad, knowing he went through a life of solitude, and living without the one person that made his life complete. He sacrificed his wife for his kids, love for honor, and because of him I cherish her. I am more grateful for this. It's made my feelings so much stronger, which brings me to tonight.

It doesn't matter what type of person you are inside or what you've become from occurrences in your life, because every color has a complement, even black and gray, and she's mine.

I wrap my arms around her and look into her bright blue eyes, picking up a glossy effect that sparkles from catching the light, and then kiss her on the tip of the nose. "Mothers are overrated. Let me start over. May I have the first dance?"

She smiles. It's one of those bright white smiles, nothing hidden. "I guess in our cases they are. You can only have the first dance if you teach me how."

I put some space between us, but not much, and place one hand at the small of her back, then grab her hand with the other, positioning it in the appropriate place. I pull her body against me, and then I start to sway. "Just like this."

She lays her head on my chest and follows my movements. "I kind of like this. Maybe we should do it more often."

"All you have to do is ask and it's yours."

"You kind of have a soft spot, Mr. Cox."

"Only for you, Miss Larsen."

"Mmmm."

"I love you."

"I love you too, handsome."

"Are you excited about starting school next week?"

"Yeah. It's still kind of surreal though. I guess it'll start to sink in when I get there. I owe you a lot, Kaston. Really, I owe you everything."

"There's only one thing that I want."

"What's that?"

"Forever."

"I'm not going anywhere."

I stop dancing so that I can look at her, placing my hand into my pocket. "Promise me."

"I promise. I already told you that…with blood to be exact."

"Then wear my ring."

"Your ri-"

I pull out the small, velvet box and open it, presenting her with a diamond. Her eyes widen as she stares down at it. "I know I told you once that I wasn't standing in front of you pledging my love to you, presenting you with a big ass diamond, or asking you to bear my children, but I've lied on two of the three. I've pledged my love to you and here I stand with a big ass diamond, yet it's still insubstantial to what I feel you deserve. Yes, it's only been one summer since I met you, yet I find myself constantly wishing for one more day. My dad once told me that when you find *the one* you just know. There is no instruction manual for love. When it's presented to you the heart gives off a signal, and that's what mine did when I met you. No amount of time will ever be enough. I want forever. I want you to be my wife. I don't need a time frame…. I just need a promise.

I drop to one knee, slightly nervous. "Lux, will you marry me?"

She bites her bottom lip, looking between the ring and me. I'm not real sure what her response is going to be, until she smiles at the same time tears fall down her face. "You bet your fucking ass I will."

"That's my girl," I whisper, as I pull the ring from the box and slide it on her left ring finger, fitting it in place perfectly. I stand and grab her in my arms, lifting her slightly above me. She places her hands on top of my shoulders and I twirl her around. "I'll never fail you."

"Yes you will, Kaston, and I'll fail you, but then we'll make up and move on, still loving each other just as hard if not harder, because that's what you do when you find the one that's worthy enough to be called your soul mate."

"Never fucking change, beautiful. Never."

I wave the waiter over, knowing he's waiting to pour the champagne, and giving him the cue that he can, because she said yes, giving us a real reason to celebrate. "Now I want to witness you while you have amazing foodgasms."

"Only if you dance with me one more time, fiancé."

I smile, mesmerized by the way that sounds coming out of her mouth.

The love of my life wants to dance, so I do, because I love her, and making her happy makes me happy. I may not have foreseen this, and probably would have laughed if I had, but now that I'm here I sure as hell am not going back.

THE END.

Up next is Kross and Delta's story in Love and War, Shadows in the dark book two. Stay tuned.

ALSO BY CHARISSE SPIERS

ACKNOWLEDGMENTS

I want to say a special thank you to not only the people that contribute to the creative process, but also you, the reader. Seriously, the average reader doesn't realize how much they matter in an author's life. You are the best motivator, the strongest support, and the part that makes all of the hours, hard work, and heartfelt emotion that goes into these stories worth it. I'm speaking for myself, but I'm sure I'm not the only one that feels this way. There is no greater feeling than writing a character's story and someone loving them just as much as me. Without your feedback I wouldn't grow like I do from book to book. From every message telling me you loved it, to participation on social media as I post things, do not ever go unnoticed. I remember those that stay with me through each book, whether you think I do or not.

I also read reviews; even the not to pleasant ones. Growth can come out of constructive criticism. It has since I toughened up with reviews after publishing my first book. I'll give you a little piece of me. As a writer, I pour my heart and soul into my books. I write the story exactly as the characters lead me. I don't write the story that I think everyone will love, but the story that is supposed to be written. I experience the emotions writing and reading it through that you will experience when you read it. Their stories play out in my head as I write them. The characters are very personal for that reason.

Some reviews put a massive smile on my face, some make me laugh, make me cry, and make me proud, and then there are some that give me another perspective from the outside looking in. Sometimes an opinion, and sometimes merely something I didn't see before, and that's when I grow. Then there are a select few that could make a grown man cry, and as much as those few hurt, I pick myself up and move on—another story, another couple—and remind myself that no two readers are the same, and not every reader will like every book from an author they generally enjoy. That's okay. The world is a diverse place and everyone is different; has different likes and dislikes. Not everyone will like Kaston and Lux, maybe even some that like my other books, or some of them. The point in this is that I'm going to try something different. Usually I ask that if you enjoyed the book to please leave a review, but that's not really fair, as nervous as writing that very phrase makes me. No author anywhere wants or likes bad reviews. It seems many readers have gotten scared of writing reviews, so I'm asking that if you have the time, even if only a few words, please leave a review. There is no requirement in how many words it has to be. Something as short as "I like it," is sufficient. The more reviews for a product, the higher it gets bumped up for someone else to see it and see if they are interested, because the pool of books is vast.

Thank you so much for giving their story a chance, whether you liked or disliked. I hope you loved their personalities as much as I did. I really had fun with this one.

I do skip around with my characters in writing, as well as my series. They choose who is next, so that will answer questions about side characters. Most side characters in each series do have a book planned, it's just a matter of me having a chance to pound out the story. Kross and Delta will come before "Forever Marked" in "Love and War" as Kaston and Lux's continuation picks up at the end of "Love and War."

To my contributors, you are a necessity I cannot live without. Jessica Grover, you know how special you are to me without me having to write two pages. Thank you for helping me eliminate as many errors as possible for a better reader experience. Words fail me here, but you are irreplaceable, as an editor and a friend.

Elizabeth Thiele, you are without a doubt the best PA a writer could ask for. Even with a busy home life, you make it easier for me to still love writing by taking some of the burden of marketing and the stress that comes with it away. You bear it with me. I'll always be thankful I found you, as a PA and a friend.

Nancy Henderson, my friend, my signing partner, and my right hand person—you help me so much in ways I cannot explain. We balance each other in all things involved in author life. You too help me edit, because we all know one person cannot possibly catch all errors, you help me format to create a beautiful paperback for the readers, and together we learn so much together. Over the years you have become one of my best friends, and here's to many more. To the characters that brought us together and the characters that keep us going. I love you my friend. Thank you.

Last but not least, my betas, people that I've become very close friends with as well. Thank you for taking the time to walk the journey with me, thank you for loving my characters, and thank you for helping me make it the best possible story I can. Susan Walker, Christina Thompson, Heidi Sturgess, Tori Herring, Tammy Huckabee, Melonie Merritt, and Morgan Pomphrey, you all are simply amazing and are very much needed in my life.

Thank you Clarise Tan with CT Cover Creations for another beautiful cover. It's always a pleasure to call you a friend and my designer. Cheers to many more covers and years to come.

ABOUT THE AUTHOR

I found books when I was going through a hard time in life. They became my means of escape when things got bad. I realized quickly how much I loved to take a backseat to someone else's life and watch the journey unfold. That began my journey with books in November of 2012. I constantly had a book open on my Kindle app. Never in a million years would I have imagined myself as a writer, because I never thought I was creative enough. I'm living proof that things will fall into place when they're meant to be. People will make their way into our lives when we don't expect it, setting the path for what we are meant to do. Never give up on people. Never stop taking a chance on others. Someone took a chance on trusting me with her work when she didn't know me from a stranger on the street and gave me the opportunity of a lifetime as our relationship progressed, which led me to editing and writing as well. This is my dream I never knew I had. As soon as I sat down and gave writing a shot, it was like the floodgates opened. Now, I am lost in a world of fiction in my head, new characters constantly screaming for their stories to be told. Continue to dream and to go for them. No one ever found happiness by sitting on the sidelines. Sometimes we have to take risks and put ourselves out there. Thank you for all of your support, and may there be many books to come. XOXO- C

Stay up to date on release info
www.charissespiers.com
charissespiersbooks@gmail.com

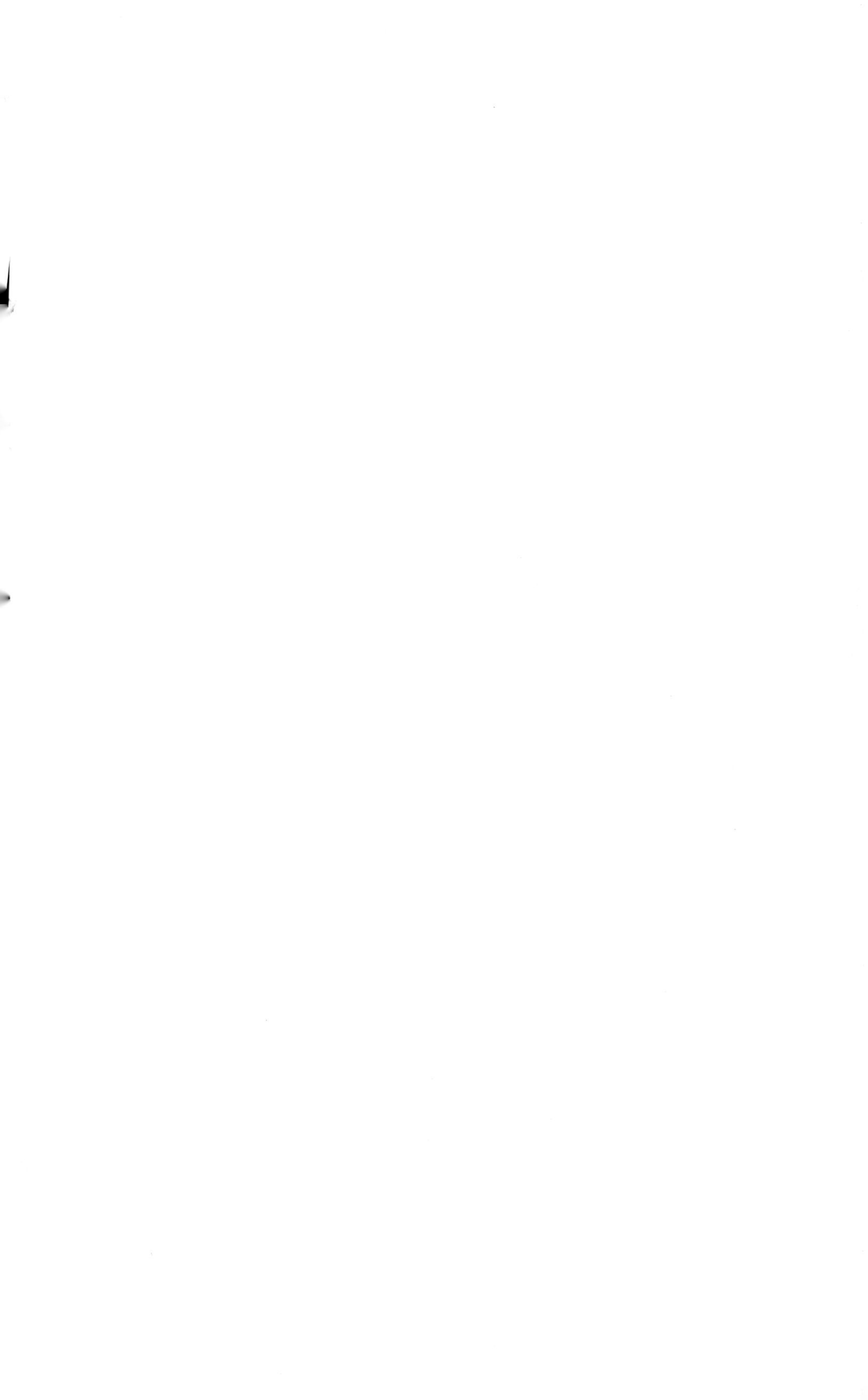

Made in the USA
Las Vegas, NV
27 May 2024

90398382R00272